TWO TESTAMENTS

Two

A NOVEL

Testaments

Elizabeth Musser

Chariot Victor
PUBLISHING
A DIVISION OF COOK COMMUNICATIONS

Victor Books is an imprint of ChariotVictor Publishing, a division
of Cook Communications, Colorado Springs, Colorado 80918
Cook Communications, Paris, Ontario
Kingsway Communications, Eastbourne, England

All Scripture is from the *Authorized (King James) Version.*

Design: Bill Gray

Editors: LoraBeth Norton, Barbara Williams

Cover Illustration: Andrea Boven, Bill Gray

Maps: George Arthur Bush

1 2 3 4 5 6 7 8 9 10 Printing/Year 01 00 99 98 97

To my husband, Paul Alan Musser

If I spend the rest of my life writing stories about
people who keep loving each other in the midst of
life's challenges, I will never be able to create a
story as beautiful as the one I have lived with you.
You are my favorite example of the Scripture verse:

*"Now to Him who is able to do exceeding
abundantly beyond all we ask or expect . . . "*

Two are better than one, and my life is filled up to
overflowing because of you. *Je t'aime.*

Acknowledgments

I think I was born with a love for God and a love for writing. Through no merit of my own, they became the central passions of my life. But often, the Lord had to gently pull me away from my stubborn ideas of how to put these "passions" into practice and redirect me into a "much better way." His way. I offer to Him all my praise for allowing me to serve Him through missions and through writing. The words in this book are mine, but the timing of so many details and ideas are His. I thank Him for anything herein which touches a heart and brings a soul closer to the One who is indeed the God of the impossible.

I especially thank the Lord for these special people:

—to my parents, Barbara and Jere Goldsmith, you are great "publicity agents." As with all you do in life, your enthusiasm and fervor for my books have made a big difference. You never cease to amaze me. Many thanks.

—to my brothers, Glenn and Jere, my sister-in-law, Mary, and my grandmom, Allene, thank you for your advice, your encouragement, your support of my work, and coming to the book signings. What would I do without family?

—to Laura McDaniel, Kim Huhman, and Margaret DeBorde, my dear friends from so far back, you read my first poems when I was a child, and you have encouraged me along throughout my life. Thank you for your prayers, your letters, your insights, and for all the times you have made me laugh. You are priceless to me.

—to Jill Briscoe, who believed in me many years ago and published my first article, thank you for your continuing support. You are an inspiration and role model to me.

—to David Purdum and Jacqueline Wachs, who taught me English and French many years ago and have offered helpful critique for my books, you inspired me as a student and I am very grateful.

—to Dave Horton, my friend and editor, you have once again walked with me through this exhilarating process of producing a book. *Merci pour tout.*

—to Greg Clouse, Barb Williams, and the other folks at ChariotVictor, thank you for all your hard work.

—to Lora Beth Norton, the editor with the expert eye, it is a blessing to work with you.

—to Maurice Delacoux, Lili Botella, Eliane Martinez, Josie Rivière, Ian Campbell, Muriel Butcher, Marc Roche, Annette Manzano, Mme Hernandez, Mme Krieger, and many others here in France who have taken the time to help me understand what life was like in Algeria during the war, I am deeply indebted to you.

—to Maryvonne and Bernard Millerand who have been my real life *boulangers* and have given me advice about bread and Senegal, *merci beaucoup.*

—to my friends in our church here in Montpellier,

8

France, this place feels like home because of you. Your stories, your fresh faith, the changes God has wrought in your lives, have inspired me to write of others whose lives have been changed. Thank you for being so very real. We have been though a lot together, and you still love me.

—to all our prayer partners around the world who have prayed me through some very difficult months of illness, God has used you mightily in my life. Thank you.

—to Trudy Owens, my dear friend, teammate, and patient proofreader, you are a godly woman who listens to the Lord. He always seems to give you just the right words to encourage me.

—to Cathy Carmeni, my talented "pre-editor," your insights have been invaluable, your friendship enriching, your faith a joy to watch as it blossoms.

—to Christine Montgomery and Cathy Carmeni, my prayer partners, you have watched the dream become a reality during those blessed Monday afternoon prayer sessions. *Je vous embrasse très fort.*

—to Andrew and Christopher, my sons, what would I do without you? Thank you for loving me just as I am, for helping me so much and for never running out of kisses for Mommy.

—to Paul, my husband and partner in everything, what more can I say? You are very patient, very giving, and very wise, and I love you very much.

Terms used in Two Testaments

Algerian War for Independence—Algerian nationals' fight for independence from France, 1954–1962

boulangerie—bread store

centre aéré—recreational child-care center

FLN *(Front de libération nationale)*—revolutionary group of Algerians who started the Algerian War for Independence in 1954 after a century of French colonization; began as a handful of revolutionaries and became an army

harki—Algerian soldier who remained loyal to the French Army, and therefore fought against his fellow Algerians

Madame—French equivalent of Mrs., abbreviated Mme

Mademoiselle—French equivalent of Miss, abbreviated Mlle

Monsieur—French equivalent of Mr., abbreviated M.

OAS *(Organisation de l'Armée secrète)* —an underground movement begun in the last years of the war, made up of Europeans *(pied-noirs)* and deserters from the French Army, who were determined to keep Algeria French

pied-noir—European living in Algeria

Paris

Geneva

Castelnau
Montpellier
Arles

Marseilles

MEDITERRANEAN SEA

Philippeville

Algiers
Constantine

Oran

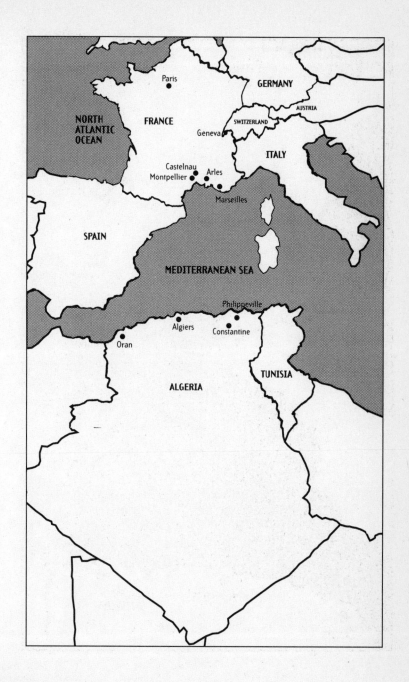

PROLOGUE

Algiers, Algeria

MARCH 21, 1962

It was mid-afternoon at the Place du Gouvernement in downtown Algiers. The great Cathedral of Saint Philippe formed an imposing barrier that separated the steep, narrow roads of the Casbah from this tree-filled square that teemed with pedestrians, shopping, sipping mint tea at a *café*, milling about in carefree jubilation. There was a feeling of peace and security among the Muslims of Algiers that bright afternoon. The cease-fire to end Algeria's seven-year war for independence from France had gone into effect two days ago.

Now was the time to breathe openly, to relax, to hope. Hussein hung out at the corner of the square, tossing marbles with two of his friends. Their smiles were imbued with confidence, pride, a victory for Algeria. The crowds in the square were almost entirely Arab. No *pied-noirs* had ventured out into the sunshine today, Hussein mused with grim satisfaction. Anyway, what did they have to celebrate? Ali promised they would leave Algeria *en masse* before official independence was declared on July 2. That was fine with Hussein. Get rid of the filthy French and their colonial ways.

He wished still that he could find the woman, Anne-Marie,

to placate Ali's fury. *Ali Boudani,* Hussein thought to himself, *was a man obsessed with revenge.* Algeria would be independent soon. Was this not enough? Ali was at one moment delirious with joy, the next moment brooding with contempt. His personal mission was not over. Maybe, just maybe, Hussein could spot this woman and her curly-haired *harki* friend, and the traitors would be silenced once and for all.

The noise from the square was merry, loud, jovial. This was the Algiers Hussein knew and loved. Seven years of war had stolen his boyhood away. At fourteen, he had seen more violence than many a soldier. He secretly longed for peace. Beyond the war, beyond the hatred.

Hussein glanced up at the sky, hearing a noise that sounded like a plane overhead, or maybe a missile being launched. Then his body tensed. He stood transfixed in the shadow of a building as above him one, then two bright flashes exploded with a terrible boom in the center of the Place du Gouvernement. Debris from the street, chairs from *cafés,* and bodies seemed to dance on the tips of the bright flames before his eyes. For a brief moment the deafening roar of the explosions silenced the screams coming from everywhere in the square. Hussein blinked, shook his head, and realized that it was his own voice crying out, a thick, anguished, guttural howl.

Clutching one another, panic on their faces, the crowds of people clamored toward the shadows of the buildings, some fleeing in the direction of the cathedral. Dead and maimed lay in the center of the square; a shrill cry of agony pierced through the din of confused voices. For a moment, no one dared move from their refuge. Hussein read the fear in their eyes. *What if there are more bombs planned?*

Then almost at once, the masses surged forward to help the wounded. Arab FLN terrorists worked alongside the French police for perhaps the first time in Algiers' bloody history. Hussein watched it all. An old woman, bloodied and disfigured, collapsed against the stones of a building. Three men lay dead. The peaceful, leafy square of five minutes earlier resembled a battleground. Hussein closed his eyes to the blood, the moans, the horror. He turned on his heels and fled, vomiting as he ran.

It was a lie! There was no peace for Algeria! None. Up the layers of tangled, dilapidated buildings of the Casbah Hussein ran, until he stumbled into the one-room office where Ali sat.

"Ali! The Place du Gouvernement! Explosion!" He choked on his words and took in gulps of air, his lungs burning.

Ali stood, nodding, his thin, muscular frame towering above the boy. Already the Casbah was ringing with cries of indignation and fury. Ali stepped into the street as young men poured forth from their whitewashed stalls.

Other members of the FLN were already holding men back, some of them forcefully.

"Not yet! Do not run to your deaths. This is what the OAS is waiting for. Hold your ground. It is their last effort to win back Algeria. It will never work. Do not lose your *sang-froid*. We must be clearheaded. We must be prepared."

Ali grabbed Hussein by the shoulders. "It is not over yet. You are not afraid of bloodshed, my boy?"

Hussein gazed at him and shook his head, knowing all the while that the fear in his eyes betrayed him.

"Go then, and tell me what you see. Go to Bab el Oued and wait. Take it all in. We must be ready."

Hussein turned and escaped through a narrow alleyway. Tears ran down his cheeks. Oh, for peace. Oh, for a moment of peace. Then he could play as he had when he was seven and war had only been a handful of plastic toy soldiers on the floor of his room.

CHAPTER ONE

Marseilles, France

MARCH 1962

David Hoffmann stood at the Bassin de Joliette in Marseilles where the ferries were coming in from Algeria. Amidst the huge ferries, *paquebots,* and steamships, he spied a comparatively small black-and-white sailboat called the *Capitaine.* It was empty now of children, and a grisly old Frenchman named Jacques waited for what he doubtlessly hoped would be one of his last trips back to Algeria.

David watched in a daze as families debarked from the boats with their trunks and suitcases. The faces of adults and children alike looked confused, sad, hopeless. David shook his head. One little orphanage in the south of France that sheltered *pied-noir* and *harki* children was a drop in the bucket. These people were French citizens, but where would they go? Did France want them? David knew it did not.

He slipped onto the boat, greeting Jacques with a handshake.

"Bonjour," the rough sailor replied solemnly. "You sure you want to go back there now? Mighty bad situation. Mighty bad. And gonna get worse. Lots worse." He stared at David as one who had already seen the atrocities of war.

"Yes, I'm sure I must go."

Jacques looked at the ground, shuffling his feet. "I can't go back no more, M. Hoffmann. Too dangerous. *Punaise!* There's nowhere for me to dock my boat. The ferries taking up all the room. Thousands of them *pied-noirs* are running away faster than the Mistral gusts down the Rhone Valley. I'm sorry for you. But if you're so sure you gotta go back, well, I advise you to take one of them ferries. I guarantee you there's nobody goin' on 'em to Algeria. The boats'll be completely empty. Take one of them back, if you want. It'll be safer than with me, M. Hoffmann. A lot safer."

David frowned, contemplating the sailor's words, then he shrugged. "I understand, Jacques. Thanks for all your help. There are a lot of kids in Castelnau who are grateful to you." The two men shook hands.

"*Bonne chance*, M. Hoffmann. You be careful now. Raving crazy, that country is now. Raving crazy."

* * *

David stood on the deck of a huge, empty ferry, his tall frame silhouetted against the night sky. Jacques had been right. No one was going to Algeria now. The wind whipped across the sea. His hair blew back, his eyes squinted against the wind, and his jacket billowed and filled with air. David gripped the railing with his good hand, his other shoulder and arm bandaged and tucked inside his leather jacket.

The whitecaps of the waves rose up to touch the sky, and a thousand stars blinked back, as if flirting with the water. The sea air smelled fresh and strong. He wished briefly that Gabriella were snuggled beside him, then pushed the thought away.

He had twenty-four hours alone before he would step into a world of chaos, and he wanted to spend this one night well. The scene before him reminded him of a night on the beach one month ago. The night of his surrender, he called it in his mind. His surrender to the God of Gabriella.

There was no doubt that something inside of him had changed. He had lived a strong, emotional moment. He had actually felt forgiven, and there had been too many coincidences lately even to deny intellectually that God seemed to be up to something in his life. The power. Gabriella talked about the power, God's power in the life of a man. He was twenty-five years old, and yet he was somehow new. A new man. A new conscience. A presence that was with him. For the first time in his life, David was not alone. And he had a suspicious feeling that he would never be able to get rid of this God now, even if he wanted to.

From the back of his mind came the words of the psalmist. He closed his eyes and saw his mother kneeling beside him, holding his small hand, his sister Greta snuggled close on her other side. Mama was reciting a psalm, whispering it in the frosty night, as David and Greta watched her with fear in their eyes.

The moans of others crammed around them in the dank, putrid dormitories in that death camp were momentarily forgotten as Mama whispered, "Whither shall I go from Thy spirit or whither shall I flee from Thy presence?... If I say, 'Surely darkness shall cover me'; even the night shall be light about me. Yea, the darkness hideth not from Thee, but the night shineth as the day. The darkness and the light are both alike to Thee...."

David silently mouthed the words as he watched the seawater lap onto the sides of the ferry. He remembered suddenly the warmth he had felt next to his mother and sister. It was a hazy picture in his mind. His mother had bent over and kissed him on the forehead, and he had fallen asleep. It was the last time she ever kissed him, for the next morning dawned to her death. But looking out at the sea, David did not relive the shooting. He held onto the kiss and the promise of the psalm.

20

"And so after all, You never have left me, have You?" He spoke out loud and was immediately silenced by the thought of the absolute omniscience of God. A God who knows the individual. Who cares. Who seeks him out wherever he goes.

"You are even bigger than I bargained for. I'm glad. I am glad that I cannot understand You. But I will try, and I will fight against what does not make sense. It is in my nature. Sometimes, God, I will wish I could get away from You and do things my way. I will try that too. I figure I might as well be honest with You from the start, if this relationship is going to last for eternity. I've been on my own for so long."

He paused, watching the endless sky. "But tonight I am asking You to please help me. I hate to admit it, but I'm afraid. Help me to know how to hear You. I've only been listening to myself for such a long time now. Amen."

The wind blew through his hair, and the salt air stung his face. He tasted it. Closing his eyes, he allowed himself to open another corner of his memory. A young family was laughing. A toddler looked up from her plate with cake smeared over her face. A towering, strong father kissed his beaming wife and laughed heartily. Then he patted his young son on his back and said, "You've got quite a little sister there, Son." The father's eyes narrowed and he spoke only to the boy. "I'm going to have to leave for a few days, but I'm not worried. You're a big boy now. You take care of your mother and sister for me, okay?" The child nodded and the scene blurred before his eyes.

In that brief memory, David had read trust and love in the eyes of his father. It had been there at one time. At one time before his father had abandoned them and placed a man's role on David's small shoulders. That burden had been too heavy to bear.

A rush of wind burst against the boat and at the same moment, David felt a power course through him. He could not explain it. He stood for a long time staring out into blackness.

"Even darkness is not dark to Thee," he whispered and turned to walk to his cabin.

* * *

A ricochet of bullets sounded in the street below as Anne-Marie Duchemin watched Moustafa Dramchini from the window. He hurried a young man into the apartment building. Anne-Marie felt a quickening in her heart. She stood quickly and limped to the mirror that hung on the flaking wall. She felt a pang of despair as her reflection stared back at her. Her black hair hung limp without sheen. Her eyes were deep-set in the hollows of their sockets, and her cheekbones protruded much too sharply. Her skin was pale and almost yellowish. There was nothing attractive about her, and she turned away quickly.

A thick gray sweater from Marcus Cirou, in whose apartment she was staying, hung impossibly over her thin frame, but she felt completely naked. David Hoffmann was about to walk back into her life, and she was not ready. She was not sure what she wanted to be ready. Her heart belonged to Moustafa. With him, she was not afraid to be sick and disheveled. She read devotion in his eyes. But David! Her lover when they were but adolescents. She had not seen him in so long.

She felt suddenly afraid. He was risking his life and wasting his time to help her. Why? Would he be angry to see what she had become? A pitiful, withered flower...

The door swung open, and David Hoffmann filled it completely. Anne-Marie swallowed hard and met his eyes. His six-foot-one inch frame had filled out so that he looked every bit the grown man he was. His black eyes were softer than she remembered, and the tenderness she saw in them scared her even more. His coarse black hair was swept back away from his face in a sophisticated style, but one wisp hung forward, tickling his forehead. A black leather jacket was swung over his shoulders. He leaned down and set a suitcase on the floor. She saw then that the other arm was bandaged. He straightened up, not moving forward, as if waiting for her invitation. His mouth whispered "Anne-Marie" without a sound.

My God, you are a beautiful man, she thought, fighting to stand her ground, willing herself against running into his arms, forcing herself to forget that last embrace seven years ago when he had kissed her good-bye even as the tiny seed of Ophélie was forming in her womb.

David cleared his throat and interrupted her thoughts.

"Anne-Marie." He said it almost reverently, and then he moved toward her, slowly, with his long strides. He reached out to her and touched her frail hand. She could not look at him. His hand brushed her face. "My dear Anne-Marie," and she detected the sorrow, the groan of pain in his voice, the hurt for her suffering.

She bit her lip and closed her eyes, but she could not keep the tears from flowing. She rested her head against his chest and let his strong arm enclose her, and she sobbed. It was a hysterical cry, like that of a terrified child who had been rescued at last and now fell into the arms of her father.

Somewhere inside Anne-Marie she watched the years of horror and death, killing and running for life, the years that had followed her happiest moments with David. If only . . . if only . . . . The questions of a lifetime swam before her in liquid reality until they ran down her cheeks. Her feeble energy was spent. And though she had not uttered a word, she had the feeling that David Hoffmann understood everything she felt perfectly well.

* * *

David was not used to dealing with the emotions that surfaced in him as he held Anne-Marie in his arms. It was as if he had been playing happily in his little university world while this young woman lived in true hell. He had not really

known. He had cared, and yet . . . Even the operation in
France, with all its dangers, could not be compared with what
he saw in Anne-Marie: true human suffering. The weight of
guilt pulled on his shoulders and bound him more tightly
than the sling in which his arm rested. There was a sick,
painful anger welling in his soul as he held this woman who
was no more than a dried twig, fallen from a branch.

God, forgive me, he prayed as she sobbed into his shirt.
God, forgive me. I had no idea. She looked more like an aging
grandmother than a twenty-four-year-old woman. An aging
grandmother or a malnourished child. She did not want pity,
David was sure, but pity overwhelmed him. A fleeting thought
crossed his mind. *If only . . . if only you had left with me for
America. Ophélie would have been born. We would have
made it, somehow. If only . . .*

And then the angry *why? Why?* Why did life twist and turn
and torture?

He stepped back from Anne-Marie and let his good arm
fall to his side. A searing pain shot through his shoulder, and
he grimaced.

"You are hurt?" Anne-Marie whispered and touched his
bandaged arm.

"It is nothing," he replied awkwardly.

Silence engulfed them.

Anne-Marie wiped her eyes with the sleeve of the sweater.
She sniffled. "I'm sorry." She ran her hand through her hair.

"Perhaps we could sit down for a minute?"

"Yes, of course." Anne-Marie shot him a weak smile. "I'm
sorry. I'm afraid I, I . . . I'm so glad to see you, David. Thank
you for coming. It is the worst time." She sighed heavily and
looked as if she might collapse right in front of him.

David grasped her arm and led her out of the room.
"Moustafa is waiting for us in the kitchen, I believe."

"Oh, yes. Moustafa." Anne-Marie blushed. "Yes, you must
be so tired after your trip. Let me fix you some mint tea. You

remember the mint tea, don't you?" As she looked at him, he saw she was reminiscing. Algeria seven years ago. Algeria a lifetime back.

The small kitchen was dark as they entered. Moustafa stood with his back toward them, already preparing the tea. He turned and greeted them with sullen eyes. David helped Anne-Marie to her seat as Moustafa set a tray with a pot of steaming tea on the table. He rested his hand on Anne-Marie's back and eyed David suspiciously.

"When do you plan to leave?"

"It's your call, Moustafa. As soon as you can arrange it."

Anne-Marie looked up suddenly. "Tell me of Ophélie. How is she?"

David relaxed and smiled. "She is fine. She is a beautiful, happy child who misses her mother very much." He reached into his pocket. "She sent this for you." He held out a drawing of a rainbow with the words "I love you, Mama" written in the cursive of a six-year-old.

Anne-Marie's eyes filled with tears. She ran her fingers lovingly over the picture and then pressed it to her breast. She closed her eyes and tears trickled down her cheeks. "Ophélie."

The men watched her in silence. Finally Anne-Marie spoke, her voice catching. "I have clung to the hope for these months. I have forced myself to believe, to be strong. But to know for sure that she is safe. To dream of holding her in my arms again soon. Now I can cry. Now I can cry, and I don't know if it is joy or fear or sorrow. Now I can believe that we are going to be okay."

David put his hand inside his leather coat and felt for a gold chain. Finding it, he handed it to Anne-Marie. "Ophélie sent this with me. She wanted me to have it, as you gave it to her. To keep me safe. Take it. She said it has kept her safe and now it will bring you back to her, safe *aussi.*"

Anne-Marie held the chain with the small Huguenot cross on it as if it were a priceless jewel. "My father's cross. I'd

forgotten how beautiful it was. Thank you." She traced its
outline with her finger and then slipped it around her neck.
"Ophélie never realized the real significance of it?"

David smiled. "I don't know if I would say that. She has
learned an awful lot about the cross and what it stands for in
the time she has been at the orphanage. But she never
understood why it was so important for us." He closed his
eyes, picturing his daughter. "She is a secretive child. Do you
know she kept your letter hidden and learned to read so she
could know what you were telling her?"

Anne-Marie smiled briefly. "And how did you find it?"

"I didn't. It was Mother Griolet, the head nun at the
orphanage. I had no idea. Ophélie suddenly appeared in my
life, but I never once thought she was someone of utmost
importance to me."

He explained how he had found her, a terrified and
wounded child, in Paris. He told of his discovery of Anne-
Marie's friend M. Gady and of his decision to bring Ophélie to
the orphanage.

"I had no idea what to do with a small child. But I knew
Gabby would."

"Gabby?" Anne-Marie questioned.

David's face reddened against his will. "Gabriella
Madison. She is a young woman on the exchange program
who helps out with the orphanage."

"The woman with the red hair," Moustafa volunteered.

"Precisely," David answered. He did not want to talk
about Gabriella now. There would be time to tell Anne-Marie
and time to understand what he was reading in the angry eyes
of Moustafa. But that time had not yet come.

* * *

Darkness blanketed the streets of Algiers as Moustafa
slipped out the kitchen door of Marcus Cirou's apartment. "I
will be back shortly," he mumbled, and his soft brown eyes,

filled with distrust, met David's.

"Good." David nodded. "Then we will discuss the plans for leaving."

"Yes, then."

David watched him go into the street and shuddered unconsciously. He was eager to get Anne-Marie to the port and out of the war-ridden city. They would cross the Mediterranean, and then life would resume. Anne-Marie would be with Ophélie. Her health would improve. And he would be back with Gabriella . . . .

The sound of a chair being dragged across the floor startled David. He turned from the window. Anne-Marie stood by the kitchen table, a thick robe now pulled around her thin frame.

"I didn't mean to surprise you. Would you like some more tea?"

He pulled out a chair, and they both sat down. "No, I'm fine." The silence was heavy. He studied her carefully. A hundred questions raced through his mind. He did not know where to begin.

Anne-Marie played with the ties on her robe, twisting them and twirling them around her hands. Her head was bent, and for a brief moment, he remembered her as a radiant, rebellious adolescent. His heart ached.

"Are you feeling strong enough to leave on the boat soon?" he asked, breaking the quiet.

She did not look up, but still twisted the ties between her fingers. "I'm sorry I never answered your letters," she began. "How could I answer? How could I write you back and keep silent about what was happening to me?"

David reached over and took her hand. "What did your parents say when they found out you were pregnant?" He spoke softly, hesitantly.

Anne-Marie looked up for the first time. "They did all the right things. They got mad. Papa ranted for a while. Then they apologized. They listened. We talked. We cried a lot. They asked me to let you know, but I couldn't. I couldn't put that on you." She frowned, and her eyes wore the saddest of expressions. "I knew you would come back. You would come back just to hurt your father. I was afraid you would come back for all the wrong reasons."

David stiffened and set his jaw. She was right. Perhaps. Perhaps he would have come back to Algeria out of rebellion and not love. Intellectually he had loved her. Physically he had loved her. But emotionally? He could not say.

"I cared deeply about you, Anne-Marie."

"I know."

Sweat was beading on his forehead. A stabbing guilt made him wince involuntarily.

"They helped me with Ophélie. Mama was a saint about it. You know, I broke their hearts and they forgave me." She laughed. "I thought they were weak. It angered me that they kept going. But somewhere inside, I admired them.

"And oh, how they loved Ophélie. Captain Duchemin, the staunch, strong military man! I wish you could have seen him cooing at his granddaughter." She smiled at the memory. "He rocked her to bed every night that he was home, and sang her the most beautiful songs. We were a happy, odd family for a while. Until Ali Boudani ripped everything apart." She slapped the table and stared at him, and her face grew hard and determined. "You know the rest."

"Perhaps not everything," he whispered. "Tell me about Moustafa."

Anne-Marie looked angry, then she smiled. "Dear Moustafa. My childhood friend, the one who helped me escape to France, then betrayed me to Ali." Her voice was barely audible. "The one who loves me."

"And do you love him?"

She closed her eyes and withdrew her hand from his. He was sorry that he had asked her so soon. Softly she answered,

"I love him, David. I love him, and every time he leaves this filthy apartment, I am terrified I will lose him. I am so afraid that he will be found in some back alley with his throat slit, like the other *harkis*. Like his father. These Arabs have remained loyal to France, fought alongside the French soldiers. But they are not French—and," she said it sadly, "they are seen as traitors by their own people. What hope is there for the *harki* families?"

She stood up and held onto the back of the chair. "I love him and I wish I didn't. What future is there for us? An ostracized Arab and a *pied-noir*. And he will stay. He will stay for his people. He won't come to France, I know. I am so afraid that in a few days he will walk out of my life forever. And it hurts so much. It hurts like . . . it hurts the way. . . . "

She let the phrase dangle, but David knew the next words. *It hurts the way it hurt when you walked out of my life seven years ago.*

Chapter 2

CASTELNAU, FRANCE

Poppies were springing up in the fields beyond Castelnau like bright red drops of blood, staining the countryside. Seeing the poppies, Gabriella took a deep breath. Lifeblood and hope eternal. A simple, uncomplicated wildflower that nonetheless drew attention to itself.

She closed her eyes and felt a stinging sensation inside her chest. Poppies reminded her of David. And poppies reminded David of her. But now he was in Algeria and no doubt in the company of Ophélie's mother, Anne-Marie. How she wished that he were standing here beside her instead.

Ophélie's laughter interrupted her thoughts. "Do you think it will be today that Papa and Mama get back? Could it be today?"

Gabriella shook her red head, and her hair glistened like sun on the river. "Not today, I think, Ophélie. But very soon." Were they laughing together, reliving old times, catching up on seven lost years? Was David explaining what had been happening here in lazy Castelnau? Had he even mentioned her name to Anne-Marie?

They had been walking, Gabriella with a whole troop of

children, toward the edge of Castelnau, where the village fanned out into farmland and vineyards. The children trailed behind their young *maîtresse* in groups of two, holding hands and chattering excitedly. Gabriella glanced back to see Sister Rosaline, red-faced and out of breath, waving from the end of the line. "They're all here," she called out happily in her singsong French. "All forty-three of them."

Gabriella waved back, smiling to the children. "Do you want to go a little farther? We're almost to the park."

A chorus of *Oui, Maîtresse* sang back to her, and so they proceeded down a narrow dirt road to where it opened into a grassy sanctuary enclosed by tall cypress trees. The field was large and sparse, an unused soccer terrain. At the far end several seesaws, a monkey bar, and an old swing set waited for the invasion of little hands, bodies, and feet.

It had become Gabriella and Sister Rosaline's daily ritual after lunch, weather permitting, to take the children on a walk outside the orphanage. Mother Griolet had hesitated at first. What if people began questioning? After all, the population of the orphanage had doubled in a few short months. But Gabriella and Sister Rosaline had insisted. The new arrivals were loud, afraid, and restless. Together, the children acted like pent-up animals, and they needed to be uncaged in a space bigger than the courtyard inside the orphanage.

In truth, Gabriella worried for Mother Griolet. With David in Algeria and all the new children here, Mother Griolet's usually predictable schedule had come tumbling down. "It's always this way at first," the old nun had reassured Gabriella. "During the Second World War we scrambled for a while, but we eventually settled into a routine."

But Gabriella was not convinced. Over fifteen years had passed since that war, and Mother Griolet was far from young. Seventy-two and still spry, yes, but she was suddenly looking quite old beneath her nun's habit. Her face, with its translucent creamy bluish hue, looked more wrinkled, and her green eyes had lost some of their sparkle.

Forty-three orphans and forty-two American college women were plenty for an energetic young woman to handle, Gabriella reasoned. She wondered if they were not, after all, a bit too much for this devoted old nun who seemed to hold the secrets of life in her heart.

* * *

Forty-five minutes passed quickly as the children played. A game of hide-and-seek brought shrill screams from several girls who had just been discovered by Sister Rosaline, who now hovered over them, clucking like a proud mother hen. A large group of boys danced around the center of the soccer field in a game that resembled a cross between tag and tackle. Presently Ophélie left her friends and joined Gabriella, who was refereeing *Un, deux, trois soleil,* the French version of Red Light, Green Light.

"Bribri," the child began, fiddling with Gabriella's long red curls. "Bribri, what will it be like when Mama, Papa, and you are all here together?" She scrunched up her nose, her brown eyes shining and sincere.

Gabriella cleared her throat, stroking the child's hair. "It will be a wonderful reunion, Ophélie. A time to rejoice. An answer to prayer."

Ophélie continued with childlike bluntness. "And who do you think Papa will choose? You or Mama? And who will I live with?"

Gabriella squinted, wrinkling her brow and bending down beside Ophélie. She hoped her voice sounded light and carefree. "Little Ophélie. Your papa will not choose your mama or me. He will choose *you!* He will pick you up and swing you around, and the whole orphanage will ring with your laughter. Don't you worry, now. Don't worry."

Take your own advice, Gabriella reminded herself as she sent Ophélie off with a soft pat on the rump. Three days ago

David Hoffmann had kissed her—really kissed her—and then he had left. Left on a humanitarian mission in a country gone mad. She did not want to dwell on it, for the possibilities were too frightening. Better to think of the children.

A fight broke out between two boys, and Gabriella dashed over, yelling, *"Eh! Ça suffit!"* She pulled the children apart, scolded them playfully, and began chasing several of the smallest boys, tagging them and calling, "You're it!" She stumbled, out of breath, to the side of the field, crushing a red poppy beneath her feet.

* * *

Two days after the cease-fire was announced, the talk among the young women at the Franco-American exchange program was not so much about the fate of Algeria, but why David Hoffmann had left his teaching post to go to that godforsaken country. It seemed to them preposterous. When Caroline Harland realized that M. Hoffmann was not coming back to teach, she fired off an angry letter to her father.

March 23, 1962

Dear Father,

In my opinion, this program is going straight downhill. The best teacher is off in Algeria doing who knows what and has missed most of the second-term classes. His replacement is an old bore who is not qualified to teach in the first place. I suggest you talk with other members of the board and try putting a little pressure on Mother Griolet. It's pointless to run an exchange program without competent staff. Her loyalties are to the Arab kids who keep finding their way to this orphanage. It is a mess . . . .

Four other girls, following Caroline's example, wrote similar letters to their parents and grandparents. Caroline made sure that a stenciled copy of hers went straight to the president of the board, Mr. Harold T. MacIlvain, Sr., who had founded the Franco-American exchange program fourteen years ago. If the girls were not to enjoy the company of David Hoffmann, well, someone should hear about it. And soon.

* * *

David woke abruptly, his body drenched with sweat. He pulled the sheets off and struggled to remember where he was. *Oh . . . Algiers. Anne-Marie.* The dream came back to him. The same dream as before. Ophélie reaching out to him and laughing. "Papa! Look who is here with us." And a woman in a white robe walking slowly to greet them, her face obstructed by the bright glare that came from the cross she wore around her neck. But then the dream had shifted and someone was screaming. When he looked toward the woman, the robe was red.

David swallowed hard and wiped his brow. He propped himself up on the mattress with his good arm and sat still, listening to the cool Algerian night. He remembered listening to the locusts chirping in the summer nights long ago. Then he would lie awake for a long time, thinking of Anne-Marie and their clandestine encounters where their passion was spent.

He closed his eyes to the memory. They had been teenagers. Rebellious kids. His first experience of love. He had not known what had happened to her when he returned to the States. His letters unanswered, he had no way of knowing. And yet he felt responsible now, housed in the same apartment. It was not lust that made him want her again. Perhaps it was pity. Or the desire to protect. For a moment he considered slipping into her room, holding her in his arms, and kissing away the pain.

Moustafa lay a few feet from him, asleep. The young Arab loved her fiercely. His eyes burned with it. But Anne-Marie was right. Their future was doomed. No *pied-noir* would marry a *harki*. It was beneath them. It would mean ostracism from society.

Why was life so complicated, he wondered angrily. Why was there an angelic redhead waiting for him on the other side of the Mediterranean with the taste of his kisses on her lips? Yet he was not afraid for Gabriella. She had the spunk and the faith to pull her through a long line of disappointments. Yes, the faith.

He groaned to himself. Anne-Marie did not need him. She had lived through hell and, though scarred, she would come out fighting. Perhaps it was for Ophélie, then. To give his daughter an intact family. He rolled over and closed his eyes, listening again to the heavy, encumbering silence. Maybe if he listened long enough, this strange new God would tell him something.

He whispered without making a sound. "Show me, God. It hurts to care too much. Show me, please."

When he finally drifted back to sleep, the first light of dawn was peeking over the horizon.

* * *

Moustafa shook David awake. "Listen! Do you hear it?" David squinted and blinked, his eyes adjusting to the morning light. The sound of gunfire peppered the air.

He turned to Moustafa, a baffled expression on his face. "What is it?"

"The OAS. You know, the secret group made up of dissenters from the French Army. They've taken over this neighborhood of Bab el Oued during the night. They will oppose the French Army. It could get very bloody."

"Here?" David was incredulous. "How do you know?"

Moustafa met David's eyes with his own somber gaze. "I know."

David quickly roused and dressed himself. "Should we tell Anne-Marie?"

Again Moustafa was sullen in his response. "She's already up."

David nodded, brushing his fingers through his hair. "What do you propose we do, Moustafa?" he asked calmly.

"There is nothing to do but wait."

Anne-Marie entered the room, a thick, oversized bathrobe pulled around her. Moustafa took her hand. "It is the OAS," he said softly. "They have set up a military fortress in Bab el Oued. They think they can oppose the French Army." He cursed. "This is not good. Trouble is coming to our doorstep. Mark my words."

*   *   *

Hussein slipped down the alleyways of the Casbah into the streets of Bab el Oued in the early morning. Hiding behind an old building on rue Christophe Colombe, he peered down the street to where a group of *pied-noir* teenagers had surrounded two Army Corps trucks. The youths held submachine guns, pointing them cockily at the soldiers. For a moment it seemed the soldiers would easily relinquish their arms. Then one of them made a move, and a *pied-noir* opened fire, spraying the two trucks with bullets. The driver of the first truck slumped forward until his forehead touched the shattered windshield.

Hussein's eyes grew wide as he watched two other soldiers, wounded, fall from the truck. The youths grabbed the guns of the dead soldiers and fled down the street. Hussein retreated into the shadows of the building, his heart thumping wildly. *More blood!* And this time the blood was spilled between Europeans. The *pied-noirs*—French citizens themselves—were firing on the French Army. The Army would no doubt fire back. This was news for Ali. He would smirk and nod. "Let them try," Hussein could imagine the raspy voice of his leader crooning. "Let the OAS try to stop us."

Hussein felt like a small boy watching a war movie as he witnessed the Battle of Bab el Oued. Indeed he tried to record it on his mind, to be replayed before Ali, detail by grisly detail. Now fidgeting in the *boulangerie* on the neighborhood's main shopping street, Avenue de la Bouzareah, he watched several tanks rumbling down the street, a steady stream of bullets emptying from their turrets. From atop a roof, a man fired a bazooka, which missed the tanks but smashed into an approaching ambulance.

Hussein glanced up as the whirring sound of a helicopter was drowned out by the sound of the grenades it dropped, exploding on the roof where the sniper had been.

War. War between the Europeans.

Hussein could feel the tension in the *quartier*, as sporadic shelling continued throughout the afternoon. He dodged in and out of the small streets of the neighborhood, adrenaline pumping through his small frame, his eyes glazed, impersonal as he observed another day of murder. He was nothing but a reporter, doing his job. He repeated it time and again in his mind. A reporter for Ali.

By late afternoon, Hussein could tell the Army was winning. Four T-6 training planes zipped through the sky, launching rockets and diving toward several snipers who were still visible on rooftops. The Army had come in by force. The OAS would not hold Bab el Oued.

No *pied-noirs* were venturing out of their apartments, as Hussein fled from the *quartier*. He had not seen Anne-Marie Duchemin or Moustafa Dramchini. But he had seen plenty else. It would have to be enough for right now.

* * *

David stared from the balcony as French Army tanks rumbled through the street, sending vibrations like a herd of wild elephants on the march. The tanks' guns shifted in a circular pattern, pointing toward the apartment buildings.

"Are you crazy!" Moustafa scolded, pulling David back into the bedroom. "Don't you understand? The Army has made its stand clear. They want order. And if anyone opposes, they'll fire, be he Arab, *pied-noir,* or American." The last word he pronounced as if it were a spoon of thick, foul-tasting medicine.

Darkness had fallen, and the whole *quartier* of Bab el Oued appeared to be in a state of shock. Marcus Cirou had rushed into the apartment and was now furiously smoking and pacing in the den, sliding his fingers through his slick gray hair. He announced the verdict to his three house guests.

"Must be over a hundred dead or wounded among us," he ranted. "And the Army's blockaded the neighborhood. No one can get in. No ambulances, no doctors. The wounded are being hidden in homes. Bloody mess. Bloody, catastrophic mess," he moaned. "The whole neighborhood, a filthy battleground." Sweat beaded on his forehead as he blew smoke in the air, his eyes fiery with anger and fear.

Without warning, the entrance door to the apartment splintered open and two *gendarmes* forced their way inside, brandishing pistols and shouting for everyone to lift their hands. While one of the French police, young and gloomy, held his pistol on the four people in the kitchen, the other, older and heavyset, tramped his way through the apartment. He threw open closets, smashed in the television, yanked clothes off their hangers, then came back to the kitchen, livid with rage. "Are you traitors too? Filthy OAS! Murdering your own countrymen. Your army! Do you want to know how we feel about that?" He jerked Marcus by the collar, the pistol butt thrust under his chin.

Anne-Marie clutched Moustafa's arm, terrified. The officer noticed, looked confused for a moment, then snickered. "What are you, anyway? Crazy swine! Hiding Arabs in Bab el Oued! The OAS is hiding Arabs. Well, if that don't beat all! Let's have a look at you, there." He moved forward, grabbing Anne-Marie and shoving her to stand alone beside the second officer. His breath reeked of liquor.

She trembled before them.

"Did you hear me," he screamed in a sort of drunken rage. "Undress! What other secrets are you hiding, woman!" She did not budge. Forcefully the heavy officer yanked at her sweater, laughing cruelly as the collar ripped, exposing her bare shoulder.

"Please!" Moustafa stepped forward, looking the officer in the eye. "You are right. I am in hiding. These good people have taken me in. My father fought with you. Lieutenant Dramchini. A *harki*. Perhaps you knew him. He was murdered by the FLN, and I am hiding. These people are not traitors. I am the traitor. The traitor to my people for *you*. Surely you won't deal with us in the same manner as the FLN."

The officer's lip twitched uncomfortably. He released Anne-Marie, who fell toward David. He caught her and held her tight as Moustafa continued.

"We are trying to escape to leave this madness. Please, do not harm her."

The officer gave a disgusted grunt and motioned to his partner. He shook his head. "You'll never get out of this hellhole, *harki* boy. Never. Passage is for *pied-noirs* first. And after tonight, I guarantee you, there'll be a whole mass of them fleeing like scared rabbits." They spun on their heels and walked out of the apartment, leaving the door standing wide open.

* * *

The next day it rained a gray, drizzly cold rain that stayed in the bones and caused one to shiver unconsciously. Seated at the kitchen table in Marcus Cirou's dingy, mold-covered kitchen, Moustafa watched the rain. The entrance door had been forced shut and bandaged, but the wounds were deep in Bab el Oued. Sipping mint tea, Moustafa brooded while David stared out the single kitchen window onto the street below.

"Quarantined? That was what Marcus said?"

Moustafa did not speak for a moment. "Yes, the whole

neighborhood is quarantined for a week. All telephone communications are cut off. The roads are barricaded. The women can leave the house one hour a day to shop for groceries. The French Army wants Bab el Oued to think long and hard before it stages another insurrection."

Moustafa slammed his fist on the table and cursed. "A week! I want Anne-Marie out of here now! As it is, our best chance is for the thirtieth."

"So we must wait." David pronounced the words resignedly.

Moustafa looked up quickly. "I don't like it any more than you do, M. Hoffmann."

"Call me David, please."

"David then. What does it change?"

"It makes things less formal."

"Less formal. Ha! And what do you want? To be my *pote?* I don't need a friend like you, David Hoffmann. I just want you to get Anne-Marie out of here safely. If I could do it, believe me, I would never have asked you." He looked away, fighting with himself to keep control.

Moustafa could not remember when he had first started loving Anne-Marie. Was it when they were schoolchildren, playing outside on her father's farm? For three generations the Dramchinis had worked for the Duchemins on the plot of land outside Algiers. They had been employees and also neighbors. Moustafa had grown up beside the Duchemins' only daughter, and their friendship had been sudden and natural. And for him, so had the love.

She was the mischievous one, always taking risks, pulling her Arab friend along. She had never seen the difference, never understood the wall that stood between her culture and his. He had first loved her for that. Her wild, beautiful naiveté.

She had not guessed for the longest time, not until her fourteenth year, when somehow it was no longer appropriate to hold hands and drag each other along through the orange groves just for fun. Their last run through the groves had ended with a kiss that Moustafa had planted squarely on Anne-Marie's lips. She had pushed him back, surprised, furrowed her brow, and asked, "Now why in the world did you do that?"

He had shrugged, turning his eyes down, hidden beneath the unkempt black curls that tumbled to his shoulders. Why indeed. He had known then, at twelve, that Anne-Marie would never understand. He had sworn, though, that he would love her and protect her as far as was in his power for the rest of his life. A boyhood dream . . .

He realized suddenly that he was smiling and remembered David's intrusive presence. The tall American's back was turned to him. Moustafa felt the smile leave his face. What right had this cocky American teenager had to take away Anne-Marie? Steal her heart and leave her with a child. David Hoffmann was the kind of man who got his way. The kind that women looked at twice, giggling and blushing amongst themselves. He had money and wits and a long list of other qualities that were sure to charm. He was the kind of man Moustafa hated. A man with no loyalties. Why be loyal when he could be free and taste the honey from many a hive?

And he was an American. A free man from a super power. What had brought him back to this tangled mass of cultures? Was it after all a desire to possess Anne-Marie again?

"I'm glad you said what you did last night, Moustafa. You saved Anne-Marie further humiliation, no doubt," David commented, his back still turned.

Moustafa winced at the sound of David's voice, calm, controlled, condescending. "For how long? I have spared her for how long?" he seethed. "That is the question. There is no telling who will crash through the door tomorrow to level us all."

"Do you support the OAS?" David asked, turning slowly to face Moustafa.

Moustafa laughed. "I support my people, plain and simple, the *harkis*. And Anne-Marie." He rose and walked over to where David stood. Both stared out the window. Moustafa watched the rain on the window sliding into little puddles on the frame. All the drops eventually ended up in a little lake of rain enclosed by the windowsill.

"I don't disapprove totally of the OAS, you must understand. You know what the *pied-noirs* say?" He continued without waiting for David's reply. "They say the OAS is like the Resistance during the other war. How can they sit idly by while their people are massacred arbitrarily? The FLN started this war seven years ago—a handful of Algerian terrorists who wanted Algeria to be free. Terrorism has always been the FLN's way. It is not war. It is not combat. It is cold-blooded murder, instilling fear. Anyone and everyone is in danger.

"But now the OAS are being called the assassins. They strike back and they are murderers. The FLN is in a sense pardoned of its years of barbaric acts, and the OAS are the assassins.

"Who can make any sense of it? It is an awful war when a son finds his father slaughtered. When an Arab maid is given a choice—either she cuts the throats of the *pied-noir* children she has helped raise, or the FLN will cut her children's throats. What do you do in a country gone mad? Where you could just as easily be blown up at a sidewalk *café* in the middle of the afternoon as shot to death in your apartment in the middle of the night. It is past understanding. . . . "

David, his forehead against the window, seemed lost in thought. In barely a whisper he asked, "And what will happen to your people once independence is declared?"

Moustafa's answer was matter-of-fact. "It will be a genocide. A complete genocide of *harkis*. And the world will never blink an eye."

It intrigued Moustafa to see the play of emotions crossing David Hoffmann's face. It looked like a pained anger, as if something from deep within him were welling up and threatening to spill over. Perhaps there was depth to this man after all.

David turned abruptly from the window. "Do you still have family here in Algeria? Who is still alive for you, Moustafa?"

"My mother, two sisters. And my older brother who is in the French Army. A real *harki*. They are all here. I ran away once to France because I was afraid. I will not do it again. I will stay with them and die. You must take Anne-Marie on the thirtieth. Take her to Ophélie. Give her daughter back to her. Then she will forget me. Then one day she can love again." Moustafa walked out of the kitchen, feeling that, with his last words, he was once again a traitor. He had betrayed his country; he had left his family. And soon, his loyalty to Anne-Marie would be but a stained memory of an unfulfilled dream.

* * *

David could not sleep. In his mind he saw the curly black hair of Moustafa shaking back and forth, resigned to a fate of certain death. He reached toward the suitcase that lay at his feet and brought out the Bible Gabriella had given him. He let the large book fall open to where a folded paper had been tucked between its pages. Taking it out, David unfolded the paper, staring at it in the moonlight.

Six different colored ponies, drawn in the uncertain hand of Ophélie, were running toward the sun. He closed his eyes and remembered Ophélie's explanation. *"I am the pink one. I am leading us to Jesus. He is in the sky, in the sun. And the red pony is Gabriella, because she has such long, pretty red hair. And then, after her comes Mother Griolet. She is the gray pony there, see? And you are the black one. You are catching up with us and running to the sun. And the beautiful white pony with the black mane and tail, that is Mama. She is far behind, but she is coming. She is coming with the brown pony.*

That is Moustafa. They are coming too. I am sure."

How I wish you were right, little Ophélie, David thought. *How I wish you were right.* But the word *genocide* throbbed like a migraine in David's mind. And he wondered if the brown pony would make it after all.

Chapter 3

The War Monument stood impressive and silent in the middle of downtown Algiers, a testimony to the bravery of Algerians, *pied-noirs,* French, and Arabs from another war. Rémi Cebrian, in his early thirties, compact and thick with pure muscle, reread the tract he had received earlier in the week urging *pied-noirs* to assemble at the monument on Rue Michelet at 1 P.M. on March 26. The tract called for a peaceful protest march on the quarantined district of Bab el Oued in the west part of Algiers.

It was past one when Rémi arrived at the Place, where hundreds of high-spirited young people already waited in happy expectation. More and more *pied-noirs* appeared, many laden with baskets of cheese and fruits and other provisions to take to their cut-off counterparts in Bab el Oued. A few teenagers began singing the "Marseillaise" and soon hundreds of voices joined them. Children held their mothers' hands. Dogs wagged their tails, straining on their leashes. The mood was bright.

Rémi was not sure why he had come. To see. To take part. To support his fellow *pied-noirs* as they desperately tried to preserve their place in an Algeria that was fast becoming hostile to them. He thought of his wife, Eliane, and their three children, back at the farm on the outskirts of Algiers. He was marching today with a prayer in his heart. A prayer that they could stay in their country, on their farm, in their house.

As the crowd grew in size, it surged forward, pushed by those in the back. People waved flags, swung their baskets of provisions, and laughed. But Rémi noticed the blockades of soldiers who stood rigid and tense, placed there to make sure another insurrection never got off the ground.

Soon the crowd of over 2,000 *pied-noirs* fanned out onto the central street of Rue d'Isly. Rémi, who was walking on the side of the pack near the front, caught his breath. Before them stood a dozen Muslim *tirailleurs,* young *harki* riflemen from the French Army, looking angry and tense beside the young French lieutenant commanding them.

Even afterward, no one could be sure what happened first. Rémi recalled that one of the *tirailleurs* nearest him was shaking violently, obviously terrified by the approaching mob. Suddenly from somewhere a series of shots burst dryly through the jubilation. At once the *tirailleurs* panicked and began firing point-blank into the crowd. A woman screamed, hit in the face. The *pied-noirs* ran in all directions, stampeding like a herd of wild buffalo. Rémi grabbed a small child who was wailing hysterically and dragged him onto the sidewalk, ducking as bullets sped and shattered above them. A shop door opened and an elderly man shouted, motioning for Rémi and the child to come inside.

His face plastered against the shop window, Rémi watched masses of terrified people running, screaming. Blood was everywhere. Men were yelling, *"Arrêt au feu! Arrêt au feu! Stop shooting!"* For a few seconds the shooting ceased, then started up again. An old woman collapsed on the sidewalk, blood seeping from her neck. Rémi dashed outside, seized the woman under the arms and dragged her into the store. Others had the same reflex, as makeshift stretchers were carried into the streets during the brief periods when the rifle fire calmed before suddenly bursting forth again.

"*Seigneur,*" Rémi sobbed. "Another massacre." The firing lasted no more than ten minutes, but the carnage was sickening. Blood formed puddles in the street as if the skies had dumped red rain. Bodies lay strewn and twisted, eyes open with complete stupefaction and agony written on dead faces. Rémi stumbled into the street and reached the bleeding form of a teenage youth who coughed up blood and died in his arms. Sirens screamed from far away. Slowly, dazed, Rémi removed the stained French flag from the dead boy's hand, revolted by the sight. Then he fled, tripping over an abandoned basket, knocking neatly wrapped parcels of cheese into the street.

He fell onto the sidewalk, his bloody hands leaving an imprint on the pavement, and vomited.

* * *

Hussein could feel the pent-up tension in the Casbah that night. He passed between the adults, listening, watching, wondering what further plans were being made. It seemed to him that the *pied-noirs* needed no further encouragement from the FLN to leave Algeria. The French Army was providing the impetus to leave.

"Hussein," Ali hissed as the boy walked through the tiny room where ten Arab men were huddled together, nodding their turbans up and down, up and down. Silently, Ali clasped Hussein's arm so tightly that the boy almost cried out. The tall officer with yellowed, crooked teeth pulled Hussein into an adjoining room, no larger than a closet, and shut the door behind them.

Hussein watched as his leader's eyes shone bright and red in the dark room. He knew Ali was exhausted, that the red tint came from fatigue and yet, looking into those eyes, Hussein recoiled within himself. The eyes looked mad, as if they belonged to a rabid dog.

"I have a plan," Ali stated simply. "And you will accomplish it for me. It is quite simple." He spoke with a self-assured, harsh tone that made Hussein tremble inside. Hussein blinked hard, twice, determined not to show his fear. He nodded, wishing that Ali would not regard him so intently.

"You are going to France. To Montpellier, France. You are going to that filthy orphanage, posing as a helpless *harki's* son, a victim of the war. You will be taken in, and then you can finish the work for me." He smiled, his lips parting so that the teeth appeared suddenly, as twisted as the mind of their master. "I have my work here. It is important." He turned his back to Hussein, his hands on his hips. Then he wheeled around and caught the boy by the collar, pulling him up to within inches of his face.

"I will have my place in the new Algeria. I am needed here. But you—" He released the boy. "You will finish the work for me in Montpellier. I will give you everything you need. Do you understand?"

Hussein swallowed hard. He knew he should simply agree, but the question tumbled out, unchecked. "But how? How will I get there?"

Ali shoved him hard against the cement brick wall. His breath reeked of cigarettes. "You will go to the docks! To the docks tomorrow, and you will wait with all the *pied-noirs.* You will wait every day until you find that Duchemin woman, and when you do, you will snivel and cry until her heart breaks for you. You will go to that place with her when she leaves. You will be the devil incarnate for them." He laughed wickedly as Hussein's eyes grew wide. "I'll have everything ready for you tomorrow night," he whispered. "Everything you need." He left Hussein standing in the dark.

Hussein felt a tightening in his stomach. It was impossible, what Ali was asking. Crazy! There was no guarantee that Anne-Marie Duchemin was leaving Algeria. But it did not matter, he realized. Ali had decided, and he had no choice. No choice but to kiss his mother quickly, as if he were simply leaving for the afternoon as he so often did. Then he would disappear somehow, on a ferry to France with a suitcase full of weapons.

He felt his childhood slipping away before him. So it was not to be. He was not to know the peace of a free Algeria. His was another role. A hired assassin for Ali. Many other boys his age prided themselves on the number of *pied-noirs* they had killed. Now he would join them. It was a role he despised. But he had no choice.

*   *   *

The news of the disastrous results on March 26 crushed the already dampened spirits of the *pied-noirs* in the quarantined district of Bab el Oued. The casualty report that swept through the neighborhood listed 80 demonstrators dead and at least 200 wounded. It seemed to many *pied-noirs* that not only had President de Gaulle betrayed them, but now the French Army was no longer neutral in this war. They too would kill *pied-noirs*, the citizens of their own country. The gruesome events of the last week had proved it to be so.

Like everyone else, David was anxious for the quarantine to be lifted. Two more days and he would take Anne-Marie to the port and escape to France. Escape was the right word, he thought. Escape by the skin of their teeth. He had almost forgotten how much he feared war. Danger, adventure, these he could handle. But war, and especially this kind of war with its terrorism, torture, and hundreds of innocent victims, left a very bad taste in his mouth. This was the war he had known and lived as a boy. Hiding, fear, then betrayal and imprisonment and death. He wanted to get out soon. Before he panicked.

His mind went back to poetry, as it so often did when he was troubled. It was his familiar friend John Donne whose words played through his mind.

I have a sin of fear, that when I have spun

My last thread, I shall perish on the shore
Swear by Thy self, that at my death Thy Son
Shall shine as he shines now and heretofore;
And having done that, Thou hast done
I fear no more.

He smiled to himself at the puns Donne had placed throughout the three verses of this otherwise quite serious poem. *Thou hast done.* Thou hast Donne! That was, of course, the reason the poet could at last be free of fear. God had gotten hold of him. And so He had now done the same thing with David. This was the answer to his fear. This Being, this God had answers. But was He talking?

And then David thought of Matthew Arnold's *Dover Beach.* It was one of Gabby's favorites, tragic, *triste.* Was it true?

Ah love, let us be true
To one another! for this world, which seems
To lie before us like a land of dreams
So various, so beautiful, so new,
Hath really neither joy, nor love, nor light,
Nor certitude, nor peace, nor help for pain;
And we are here as on a darkling plain
Swept with confused alarms of struggle and flight,
Where ignorant armies clash by night.

Perhaps that was truth! How could Gabby claim that her God made sense of the senseless! Why, why, why? Why this struggle and war? Ignorant armies clashing! Why? And death, which sought to destroy anything various or beautiful or new, as Arnold had said.

From within the deepest part of him, David was angry. Before, he had known that life was tragic and that survival meant dependence on himself alone. And he had survived. But now, by some cruel irony, he believed in Someone bigger and beyond, and he was caught in that belief. Frustrated.

Before, he would have known how to simply get Anne-Marie out of Algeria. Quickly, methodically, feelings aside. But now a heaviness engulfed him, as if he must somehow ask permission from this God to do it his way. Or did this God have another way?

L'Eternel combattra pour vous et vous gardez le silence.

It was a round the children sang at the orphanage, a verse taken straight from the Bible. He knew the context. Moses had led the Israelites out of Egypt. Now the Egyptian army was at their backs and the Red Sea before them. And what did Moses say? "The Lord will fight for you while you keep silent!"

Oh, how maddening was this God. He was always asking the strangest things of His people. And why, why right now was he remembering that verse? He laughed wryly. Maybe it was prophetic. The FLN was behind them and the Mediterranean was in front. Was this crazy God going to open up this sea too?

It is a matter of trust. That was what Gabby had said. Trust. But trust seemed so stagnant. Did trust have feet and a brain? Did trust act? Was trust always silent?

David Hoffmann did not know, and his head ached from trying. He closed his eyes and formed a silent prayer in his mind. "In two days, God. In two days we will leave. Come with us, please. Come with us."

* * *

A hollow gnawing inside of her reminded Eliane Cebrian what the day held as she awakened to a gray dawn. Today she was leaving Algeria. Today she was loading her three precious children into their car with two small suitcases and heading for Algiers. And sometime very soon she would kiss her husband, Rémi, good-bye for who knew how long and sail to France.

She hated the thought that already made her eyes sting with tears. She stared out the window, her hand against the cool pane, and saw in the distance the orange groves and farther out the olive trees soon to be laden with their fruit. Her stomach turned, and she rested her head against the window.

She was only thirty-one, a gregarious young woman with three small children. She loved for her house to be filled with people, with the smell of roasting fowl and brewing tea. Petite and plump, she delighted in bustling through the farmhouse, serving her guests, changing the baby, laughing with Madira the maid.

She gazed again out the window and saw her husband deep in conversation with the farmhands, Abdul and Amar. She buried her head in her hands and cried. Algeria, her home. Her country. All she had ever known, all she had ever wanted for her family was this little farmhouse on the outskirts of Algiers.

She closed her eyes and remembered yesterday. Madira had clung to her, the young woman's face streaked with tears. "But *Madame*, you must not leave! What will become of us? We need you! Algeria needs you."

It had been the echo throughout the village as she had bade farewell to the shopkeepers. "Don't go. Perhaps there will finally be peace. Don't go."

But Rémi was insistent. He had been there three days ago when the peaceful march had turned into a blood bath. She would never forget the expression on his face when he had returned home late that afternoon. A mixture of disgust, fatigue, and terror shone in his eyes. He was covered in blood himself. At first Eliane had thought he had been hurt. But Rémi's wounds were not physical.

That day his dream to stay in Algeria had died. "You must leave," he had said flatly. "Soon." It was not the first time either of them had witnessed the treacheries of this war, but Rémi had decided it would be the last, at least for his wife and children.

She could not shut out the memory of the massacred body of their next-door neighbor, Robert Préfet. He had fired a lazy Algerian worker against everyone's advice. "You must not do it now, in times like this," Rémi had warned. "The FLN . . ."

Two days later, Robert's body had been found behind the chicken coop, stabbed countless times. Yes, Robert had provoked them, but nonetheless Rémi wanted his family out. Safe in France. He promised to come soon after.

Eliane heard the soft padding of little feet entering her room. Four-year-old Rachel looked up with her cherubic blue eyes. "Is it time to get up, Mama?" she chirped.

Eliane wiped her eyes, knelt down, and pulled the child to her breast. "Yes, you may get up. But don't wake Baby José . . . Shh." Before Rachel could turn to leave, her older brother, six-year-old Samuel, had taken his place by his mother's side.

"It is today, *n'est-ce pas,* Mama? It is today we leave?" His dark brown eyes were sober for once, and Eliane read the worry in them.

"Yes, dear, Papa will take us to the boat today."

He wrinkled his brow and peered at her from behind his long brown bangs. "But Mama, I never got to tell El Amin good-bye. I never got to say it!" His young voice was truly distressed.

"I know, *mon chéri,* and I am so sorry. But I'm afraid there is no time. We will be leaving after lunch. We must be at the port by this afternoon."

The baby began wailing in the next room, and Eliane hurried to get him. Holding José, and with the other two children huddled around her, Eliane felt tears forming again in her eyes. She mustn't cry in front of the children. She mustn't. "Come now, it's time for breakfast," she called as she bustled to the kitchen.

As she busied herself with the children, Eliane tried to imagine the streets of France. But she had never once touched French soil. A French citizen she might be, but all she had ever known was Algeria. And now her country was chasing her away. Not safe. Racial hatred. Time to go.

But what did she have to look forward to in France? What would they do? Where would they live? And would anyone help them? Rémi always looked ahead. The men at the church called him a visionary. Not that he saw visions. But he saw and knew something. "The whole *pied-noir* population is going to leave in a big hurry," he had predicted last January. "If we wait till the end, there will be no help left in France. You go on, Eliane. It is best."

"Dear God," Eliane prayed. "Dear God, please help us. Don't leave us now. You have promised. Don't leave us now."

She whistled a happy melody and played with the children as she scurried about packing last little treasures in the two suitcases. But her heart was heavy. She was packing up her life to leave, but would there be orange groves and palm trees and bright bougainvillea in France? What would life be like on the other side of this wide sea?

* * *

The children were playing in the dirt behind the house. Eliane had scolded them once and then decided to let them play one last time. She placed three neatly folded shirts in the trunk that was already overflowing with clothes. She smiled to herself, knowing that somehow Rémi would get it closed.

This was the trunk she was packing for the future. She could not hope to manage it now, along with the children, but Rémi promised he would send it later, when she got settled. In this trunk she would store the rest of her treasures. The photo albums, the silver baby cups, the framed photographs, the children's books, a few favorite pieces of china, the family Bible that traced the Cebrian heritage back to the early Huguenots. Someday these treasures would decorate her home in France, she assured herself. Or perhaps, and this was her fervent prayer, someday they would return to the farm here in Algeria. Once the madness calmed. Surely then they could return.

She knew that Rémi secretly hoped for this too. He had decided to stay behind and protect the farm from the Arabs' looting. His rifles were placed under each window, and he had already used them more than once. She shuddered at the memory. Too many horrible memories of Arab against European and random murders, year after bloody year.

A thick envelope sat on the bed that was now bare except for a pair of worn floral sheets. A heavy sigh escaped Eliane's lips. What was she to do with the testament of Captain Maxime Duchemin? She had been declared the executor of the will, but the Duchemins' only child, the sole benefactress, had disappeared. Four years had passed since the Captain and his wife had died in the massacre.

To think they had been neighbors. And now they too were dead, like Robert Préfet. The farmhouses on either side of the Cebrians' were now empty, abandoned. Eliane remembered the Duchemins' beautiful little daughter traipsing through the orange groves with her Arab friends. So long ago. Later the girl had had a baby when she was barely more than a child herself. And now she too was most likely dead. There had been no word from her since her parents' death.

Eliane closed her eyes to shut out the possibilities. Better think practically now. The best, Rémi had assured her, was to pack the testament in the trunk with their valuables. Perhaps one day the Lord would see fit to reveal to them what should be done. Rémi had said it reverently, full of faith. Eliane laughed to herself. Dear Rémi. He believed the Lord would come down and touch him on the shoulder if he needed. Sometimes with Rémi, it seemed as if the Lord did just that.

* * *

The bags were packed, and time dragged on slowly, filling her with dread. Better that it be over quickly, Eliane thought, than endure this prolonged torture.

She heard Samuel laugh loudly and looked out the window to see his best friend, El Amin, racing across the field to greet him. Eliane's heart stung again, and she could not stop the tears. El Amin, Madira's son, had grown up beside Samuel.

They had shared everything during their short lives. She remembered Madira's words last year as the two young mothers had watched their boys playing soldiers.

"They do not know that they are playing the truth. Friends betraying each other. Friends killing each other. They play with plastic guns, but other friends hold hard metal in their hands and fire at each other." Her eyes had been deep and sad.

"Why must life be so unjust, Mme Eliane, why? Where in the politics is there room for Algerians and *pied-noirs* who are friends? Will they destroy us? Our lives, our families, our homeland, our hope?" She had sat shaking her head and moaning as the sound of little boys fighting and laughing had echoed in the background.

Now El Amin held out his hand to Samuel, and Eliane saw her son's bewildered expression. He shook his head and replaced the treasure, unseen to Eliane, back in his friend's hand. But El Amin was smiling, the bright confident smile of a six-year-old, sure of his gift. Something for Samuel to keep to remember El Amin. Samuel would have other friends in France, surely, Eliane reassured herself as she wiped her eyes. But he was old enough to understand what leaving meant. And his little heart hurt.

From across the field, another figure approached, waving, with a basket on her head. Madira! Eliane left the window and, picking up José, rushed out into the yard.

"I forgot, Mme Eliane, I forgot to give you the oranges! Such sweet oranges for the trip. For the children." She set the basket down, and the women embraced. They both knew the oranges were a simple pretext, a pretext to say one last good-bye. Eliane swallowed but still her throat felt full, as if an orange itself were stuffed in the back and she was slowly choking. This pain! She could not endure it.

Madira read the suffering. "It will be over soon," she said ambiguously.

"I will never forget you," Eliane whispered, her voice

catching. It was pointless to promise letters. Her friend could not read. And a visit? Would she ever return to Algeria?

"El Amin," Madira called to her son. The boys looked up suddenly, their eyes narrowed as if daring their mothers to pronounce the judgment. The end of a boyhood friendship.

Madira nodded, and El Amin came obediently to her. The sun was hot, and a quick wind stirred the sand so that the children shielded their eyes.

"Good-bye, Madira," Eliane said. "God be with you."

Madira smiled. El Amin waved to Samuel. The woman and child turned and walked across the field, past the orange groves and the olive trees. Samuel ran into the house as Eliane cradled the baby in her arms and watched them disappear in the horizon.

Chapter 4

Anne-Marie stood looking miserably out the bedroom window. The streets were silent even though the quarantine had been lifted that morning. There was nothing to see but black sky. A hard knot sat in her stomach and seemed to be growing, like a cancer. She blinked back tears.

She heard Moustafa enter the room, but as he came gently beside her, she could not look in his eyes. She buried her head in his shirt, feeling suddenly sick. *I don't want to go.* She mouthed the words, but he did not hear.

It had been almost simple for all these months. There had been nothing safe around them, so they had built their safety in one another. And she had let herself love him. Separation. That awful, cruel word. That choice. Reunion with Ophélie meant separation from Moustafa.

She sniffed and wiped a tear on his shirt. He was a good man, her loyal friend. Even in betraying her those months ago, he had tried to protect her. To act her enemy so he could be with her. She loved him for his loyalty, for his fierce devotion. She had known he had loved her all those years ago, though she had not wanted to see it.

At first she had dismissed it as a silly infatuation. He was just a twelve-year-old boy. Her best friend. But Moustafa had never once faltered. Every time she had needed him, he was there. Year after year, despite all the times she had run, rebellious and afraid, into the arms of another.

And then the love had simply appeared at the doorstep of her heart one day months ago in that prisonlike room in the Casbah, and she had said, "Of course." So simple. There had really only been one other whom she had ever loved and now, ironically, he was taking her away from Moustafa again.

She looked up at him. "Come, Moustafa, come with me to France. Please." She sniffed again, and he brushed his hand through her hair, his eyes full of the same devotion.

Then he tightened his embrace, lifting her off the ground as if she were a doll. He breathed heavily, burying his face in the nape of her neck. She felt his hot tears. This was worse than torture!

Two months ago they had said good-bye, but fate had brought her back to him. How many times had he saved her? She knew it now, now more than before.

"I want to be with you. I want to be with you always, Moustafa. Please. Please come build a life with me in France."

He set her down, cupping her face in his hands. "Do you mean it, Anne-Marie? Do you mean it, *ma chérie?*"

She nodded and felt a smile cross her lips. "I mean it."

He smiled too, and the simple beauty of his gentle gesture made her ache all the more. He kissed her forehead, leaving his lips there, lost in thought. He took her hands in his and stepped back. She wished then that she was wearing something stunning. A low-cut cocktail dress that hugged her in all the right places. She wanted to be beautiful for him tonight.

"I cannot come with you now." He furrowed his brow, his eyes now sad, like a beagle pup's. He brought her close to him again before she could protest. "But I will come. If you really want me, with all that will mean, I will come. I must help my family escape. You know what independence will mean for the *harkis*. But somehow, somehow I will get my family away. We will try. Surely it will work. If you want me, Anne-Marie, I will come. You are all I have wanted for as long as I can remember."

He brought his lips to hers and when he kissed her, she felt stunning indeed.

* * *

The rumors had started and grown so that no one was sure what was fact and what was fiction. Whole families were being murdered on the way to the ferries at the port of Algiers. The time to leave was in the middle of the night. And carefully. David had only been in Algiers for a week, but he had seen enough to believe anything. He sat beside Marcus Cirou in the front seat of the old Renault 5 with its ripped upholstery. Marcus leaned forward in intense concentration, never taking his eyes from the road.

In the back seat Anne-Marie sat rigid, her hands in her lap, physically distancing herself from Moustafa, whose arm hung limply over her shoulder. David watched them in the rearview mirror as they crept through the alleys of Bab el Oued toward the sea. He could tell she was fighting back tears, and he cursed a war that could so completely destroy hope.

When the car reached the port, David was not prepared for what he saw. An army of people were spread across the docks like frightened nomads. There were hundreds of them. Women with small children asleep in their laps, men pacing nervously around the mass of people, smoking cigarettes and blowing blue puffs into the cool night air. An exodus. Like the Israelites with Moses. The *pied-noirs* were running from Algeria, and only the sea stood in their way.

He climbed out as Moustafa helped Anne-Marie from the car. With a simple nod of his head, Marcus was off. Anne-Marie clutched Moustafa's arm and let out a low moan. "No. No." She set down her small bag and wiped her face. "We'll never leave.

Look at all the people. We'll never get out of here."

There was a faint edge of panic in her voice. David was determined to stifle it. "I've heard it may be a day's wait, perhaps two. But then we will go. Our turn will come. Don't worry." She limped between the two men onto the nearest docks. At their feet, people lay sleeping, oblivious.

"It's still a few hours till dawn. Try to sleep, Anne-Marie. There is nothing to fear." David shuffled around several families huddled together, and found a space near the edge of the dock. He sat down awkwardly. Moustafa joined him, offering his hand to Anne-Marie. She did not speak but, as if in a trance, took his hand and seated herself beside him, staring ahead at the sea that lay smooth and black before them. After a moment, she rested her head against the small suitcase she had been carrying, pulling her legs up beneath her. She closed her eyes. Moustafa pulled off his coat and covered her with it. She did not protest.

* * *

Dawn was just breaking over the city of Algiers when Hussein arrived at the docks, still rubbing the sleep from his eyes. A scowl was on his face, which he hoped covered his fear and that other painful sensation somewhere inside. He had left the house even before his mother awoke as he had done on the three previous mornings. She did not question him but waited worriedly each day. One day he would not come back and, after a while, she would turn mournful eyes toward the other Arab women who wept for their lost sons, and they would understand.

The docks were humming with activity. Hundreds of *pied-noirs* crowded together, clutching children and small suitcases. From the distance it looked to Hussein like victims from some natural disaster, waiting at a shelter for help. He saw their rescuer, looming out at sea, slowly approaching the docks. A *paquebot*, one of those huge ferries that could carry hundreds of people, crawled toward the lost *pied-noirs*. It was a pitiful scene, and he found no pleasure in it. Ali would gloat, but Hussein simply felt drained, weak, and afraid.

He stuck out in this crowd with his soft brown skin, and he could not ignore the cold, harsh stares as he squeezed in and out of the mob, looking for Anne-Marie Duchemin. Ali's instructions were clear. He would find her, show her a drawing of the Huguenot cross, and plead for help. The story was made up in his mind, and he kept repeating it until it seemed more true of his life than what he had actually lived.

Ali's instructions had been explicit. Hussein would wander on these docks day after day until he found Anne-Marie. He shook miserably. It was no doubt hopeless, but he had no choice. Ali was mad, and if Hussein ever returned to the Casbah, he would meet sure death at the hands of his own people.

The day was overcast, and the streaks of dawn gloomy. Large heavy clouds blocked any view of the sky beyond. Hussein wandered among the people, his mood as gray as the clouds.

* * *

By four in the afternoon, the crowds had thinned. Two ferries had already left the port, and there was hope for a third before dusk. "You see, we'll be on the boat by tonight," David said in an almost triumphant manner. Moustafa touched Anne-Marie's face with the back of his hand. She felt the stiffness in his fingers as she placed her hand over his. She tried to smile, but it caught on her lips. She was hungry, and her legs were beginning to throb.

She had tried to push the thoughts away, the thoughts of the last time she stood on these docks. Then they had been deserted, except for a handful of children and herself and one of Ali's snipers. The throbbing in her legs reminded her of the bullet wounds, the fall into the icy water, and Moustafa.

Moustafa appearing out of nowhere. Moustafa, her savior. Moustafa, her lover. In only an hour, maybe two, she would touch his lips with her fingers to seal in the memory, and then she would whisper good-bye.

"I think I'll walk about a little," she managed to say, without looking up at the two young men.

Mingling among the people, she listened to snatches of conversation and felt a stabbing pain for these people. ". . . We've left absolutely everything except what I am carrying in these two bags. . . . No, we have no family in France. Not anymore. . . . No, I have no idea what to expect. It is *catastrophique* . . ."

She brought her thin jacket closer together, fastening a button. The wind had picked up, and the caps on the sea were blowing along rapidly as if in a hurry to catch something. She watched the dull, tired faces of people around her. A young woman was struggling to nurse a baby, calling out to two children who chased each other.

Something in the woman's face looked familiar. Something about its round contour and the lilt of the voice as she called after the children. Anne-Marie found herself staring. A young boy dashed past, stepping on her toe.

"Samuel! *Mais alors!* Calm down!" the young mother called, obviously miffed. She looked up at Anne-Marie. "*Je suis desolée.* Sorry."

"It's nothing." She leaned down to where the woman sat. "Eliane?" she whispered. "Is it you? Eliane Cebrian?"

The woman removed the baby from her breast, startled. She looked quizzically into Anne-Marie's eyes. "Yes, but do I know—" Then she gave a short gasp, and her face lit up in a broad smile. "Anne-Marie! Anne-Marie Duchemin! I would have never recognized you. You're so . . . so changed." Her voice betrayed concern. "How are you?" Before Anne-Marie could answer, Eliane chuckled, but it was a bitter laugh. "How indeed, if you are here with the rest of us, *n'est-ce pas?*" She shook her head. "Anyway, sit down. Are you alone? Is your daughter . . . " She let the phrase trail off.

"My daughter is in France. I'm going to meet her."

"Oh, well, what a relief. Yes. How wonderful. We should make the next ferry, from the looks of it. How good to have a chance to catch up after so long."

"Yes, that will be good." Anne-Marie stood. "I will be back, then. I've only to retrieve my bag. A friend is watching it for me."

Eliane laughed again, and it was the musical, carefree laugh that Anne-Marie remembered from years ago at her neighbors' farmhouse. "Take your time. I'm not going anywhere, as you can well see!"

* * *

When Anne-Marie appeared from another part of the crowded dock, she looked to David suddenly years younger. Although she limped, her gait was stronger and there was the flicker of surprise in her eyes.

"Moustafa! David! You'll never believe it. I've run into my neighbor. The woman who lived next door to us while I was growing up, Eliane Cebrian. Remember her, Moustafa? I haven't seen her in years." She was almost out of breath with excitement. "She's over there with her children. Isn't it wonderful? We'll be on the same boat together. Come with me, Moustafa. She'll be so happy to see you again."

"You go along, *ma chérie.* I'll come shortly," Moustafa said softly. "I want to get you a few things to eat before you get on the boat. From the looks of it, they won't be serving *couscous* on board."

"No, you're right. Not *couscous.* And I am starving. But where will you find anything?"

"I've been watching the crowds. There must be a little *épicérie* and a few *cafés* not far away. Now where will I find you?"

She pointed to the adjoining dock. "You see, near the front. She has a baby in her arms. No, not there—further away. See? And a little boy is running beside her."

"Yes, I see. Who would believe it! Eliane Cebrian. Good. Then I'll be back in a little while."

David watched the young couple. It was as if he were not there with them. Anne-Marie noticed his awkwardness. "Do you want to come with me, David?"

"No, you go ahead. I'll go with Moustafa." He grinned. "From the looks of it, we won't be waiting long." He pointed to the sea where another *paquebot* floated into view in the distance. "Save me a spot if I'm late."

He was sorry the moment he spoke, because the carefree expression left her face at once. "I'm kidding," he said. "Go on. Find your friend. We'll be back soon."

He left with Moustafa, following a handful of men who were heading toward several shops in the distance. Across the wide boulevard that emptied onto the port, they walked behind the chic stores into a small street running perpendicular to the boulevard. He could see a *boulangerie* sign near the end of the street. David was not thinking of anything but a good *baguette* filled with ham and cheese, hoping that the store had not sold out with so many hungry people around.

The youths appeared from nowhere, three Arab boys. They were laughing, but there was anger in their eyes. The tallest, wiry and thin, spoke with disgust in his voice. "Well, if it isn't another *pied-noir*, a hungry *pied-noir* going to stock up on bread before the long trip to France. And he's here with a *harki* boy. Everybody knows what happens to *harki* boys, don't they?"

He motioned to his friend, shorter, sullen, no older than seventeen, who stepped forward, drawing a switchblade. "Aren't we in luck today, *les gars?* Two for the price of one. Doesn't look like you'll be taking that ferry ride after all."

David felt more anger than fear. They were merely boys, threatening with knives. He was ready to fight; his arm was no longer in a sling. But before he had a chance to react, Moustafa pulled out a revolver and fired two shots pointblank, hitting the boy with the knife first in the knee and then squarely in the shoulder.

"Get out!" Moustafa yelled. "Leave us. You think you own Algeria and everyone in it. You think murder is a game. Get out." He pointed the gun at the taller boy who, with the third one, had grabbed their wounded friend and was scrambling to pull him to his feet.

The Arab turned to curse him, "You're done for, *harki* boy. You'll never leave this country alive." They fled, encumbered, down the alley.

David placed a hand on Moustafa, who was trembling violently. "Come on. Let's get out of here. I shouldn't have let you come down to the docks. It's too dangerous. Did you know those guys?"

"No. But they know us. They know every last stinking traitor and their families. That kid was right. We'll never get out of here."

"Good thing you had that gun. I didn't know . . . "

"I never leave the apartment without it." He chuckled, nervously. "A gift from the last guy who tried to kill me. One of Ali's men."

They bought several sandwiches and a bottle of water, but David had lost his appetite. Reality had met him face to face. The *harkis* would be massacred just like the Jews. There was no escape for them. Didn't anyone care?

His mind was whirling now, wondering. If Anne-Marie had a friend on the boat now, a companion to help her make the trip, maybe . . . Could he not finish his mission?

What was his mission? It had been to help Anne-Marie rescue those children threatened by Ali Boudani. Yes, that, but also just simply to help Anne-Marie. This would be his final help to her. She would have Moustafa. She would have her impossible love.

He was unsure, almost angry at himself for thinking of it. Gabriella would not understand. Mother Griolet needed him. But the mission. "Where will you go, Moustafa?" he asked softly.

"I'll be okay. Don't worry. Just get Anne-Marie back to France safely."

"I'm not going back. Not yet." He faced Moustafa and said it with conviction.

"What?" The young Arab wrinkled his brow in disbelief. "What are you saying? What do you mean?"

"I'm staying with you. I'm going to make sure you get to France. I'm doing it for her."

"You're crazy, David Hoffmann. You can't. It's not your problem. The *harkis* aren't your problem."

"You saved my life back there. I figure if I stick around long enough, I might be able to return the favor." He spoke in all seriousness and saw the distrust in Moustafa's eyes. "Please, Moustafa. It's the least I can do for you. It's the least I can do for *her.*"

Moustafa came close to David, narrowing his eyes. "You really mean it, don't you? You really are crazy. A crazy American." He shook his head and cursed, but David saw that a faint smile was playing on his lips.

* * *

It was almost dusk when Hussein saw her. He blinked twice to be sure. She was sitting on a small suitcase, her straight black hair thrown behind her as she talked animatedly to a short, plump woman holding a sleeping baby. Yes! The fine thin face, the small nose and dark eyes, the thick brows. Ali was right. Once she must have been beautiful. Now she looked disheveled, out of place, like the rest of the *pied-noirs*.

Nervously he inched toward her on the dock. She was only fifty feet away. His mouth went dry and his mind blank.

Who was he? The story that Ali had invented for him seemed trapped somewhere in the back of his throbbing head. He reached in his pocket and retrieved the note.

When he reached the two women, it was the other one who noticed him first and motioned with suspicious eyes to Anne-Marie. Even before she had turned around, Hussein was on his knees beside her.

"Mademoiselle Duchemin? It is you, *non?*" He thought of his mother and that brought the necessary tears to his eyes.

"Please, please take me with you. I have been searching for you all these weeks. Please." He leaned forward and whispered. "I am a *harki*. Son of a *harki*. My father has been murdered, my mother too, and my cousin's father. And last week, my cousin and his mother disappeared. I have no one. They will kill me too. Please. I have heard you have a safe place in France for *harki* children. Please." He produced the note with its funny cross and cryptic message.

The woman called Anne-Marie stared at Hussein, her mouth open. It took a moment for her to speak. "Where did you get this?"

"From Mme El Gharbi, before she was killed. She told me if I would only show it to you, you would understand."

"You knew Mme El Gharbi? You know her children?"

For a brief moment, Hussein panicked. He could not remember the names of the children. "I do not know them well." Then it came back. "But Mafoud was in my class at school."

The woman with the baby was staring pitifully at him. "Whatever is he talking about, Anne-Marie?"

The young woman did not look at her friend. "It is too long to explain right now. Perhaps later." She took Hussein's hand, and the gesture startled him. He pulled back in fright.

"No, don't worry. I will not hurt you. What is your name?"

"Hussein."

"I, I don't know what to say to you, Hussein. Perhaps, yes,

68

surely there would be room for you at the orphanage."

Hussein fell on his knees again, head bowed. "I will do anything, anything. Only don't leave me here. Please, please have mercy. They say you are a woman of great mercy. Prove it to me, I beg you. Prove it." He buried his head in his hands and prayed to Allah that she would say yes.

* * *

The giant *paquebot* huffed and steamed into port, crawling slowly to its dock. Its decks were completely empty, and it looked like a forlorn whale that rose out of the sea in a children's fairy tale. David was walking briskly in front of Moustafa and reached the docks first. He contemplated picking up Anne-Marie in his arms, kissing her and wishing her well, and then he could not imagine what had brought that thought to his mind. Oh yes, he remembered. That is how they had parted seven years ago.

Moustafa caught up with him and produced a bag full of sandwiches. One glance assured David that there would be no mention of the incident. But at the right moment, he would tell of his decision. At the right moment.

It was not like him to act impulsively. Something within was propelling him to do so. Something strong and final. Moustafa would get to France. Anne-Marie would have that. He did not consider the other part. The disappointment in Gabby's eyes when only Anne-Marie descended from the train. The betrayal she might feel. He was convinced he could get Moustafa's family on another boat soon. They would all flee within the next weeks, while there was still room, before the rest of the *harkis* turned on their heels and ran. Then there would be time to explain to Gabby.

A young boy was sitting with the women. An Arab boy who looked no more than ten. David saw that Moustafa had slowed his gait and was eyeing the boy suspiciously.

Anne-Marie stood and caught Moustafa's arm. "See,

Eliane. It is as I told you. Moustafa is with me."

The woman called Eliane rose and embraced Moustafa with a kiss on each cheek. "I never expected such a reunion. Between old neighbors." She had chestnut eyes, cheerful, kind eyes.

Moustafa reached out for the baby. "Rémi's littlest son, I suppose?"

"Yes, the other two are over there. Restless." She cleared her throat. "Rémi brought us here last night. He's back at the farm now. Anne-Marie tells me you will not leave." The woman touched his arm. "Moustafa, if you ever need help, go to him. Go to Rémi."

David immediately liked this young mother. She at least had some hope left in her in spite of the war. He glanced down at the boy, and Anne-Marie spoke. "David, Moustafa. This is Hussein. He has only just found me. And look, look . . . " She held out a slip of paper with the Huguenot cross scribbled in the corner.

Moustafa took it quickly. "What does he want?" His voice was brusque.

"He is a *harki's* son. He knew Mme El Gharbi. Went to school with Mafoud. He is orphaned, like so many others, and begs to go with us. Oh, David! What do you think? Surely the orphanage will take one more child?"

David suddenly felt claustrophobic. He had not expected this. His mind was still spinning with his decision. The boy was wiping tears from his face. "Perhaps there would be room at the orphanage. It is so overcrowded now, what would one more child matter?" He said it, but he was not concentrating. He shook his head. "What do you think, Moustafa?"

The young Arab touched the boy's shoulder. "You have lost your parents?" The child nodded. "Let him go. Yes, send him on."

David felt a release of tension and broke in quickly, "Anne-Marie, I won't be going yet. I have decided to stay behind for a week or so. Until Moustafa can get his family out."

Anne-Marie's face drained of color. "You are staying too? But, but what about—"

"Eliane will keep you company on board. If you have any trouble, she will be there to help you," Moustafa broke in as if the lines had already been rehearsed. Indeed they had, David thought.

"Of course. Of course, I will be thrilled to do whatever I can." Eliane nodded enthusiastically.

"Here is the address of the orphanage and the phone number. Call them when you get into Marseilles. Ask for Mother Griolet." David fished in his pocket for some bills. "Here is some money. This will be enough for the boat and the train. We won't be long. Tell them that. Tell Ophélie that Papa won't be long." He thought of Gabriella again and wished he had time to scribble a note.

"And tell Gabby . . . tell Gabriella that . . ." They were all staring at him, the small group, and he turned his eyes down. "Tell her that 'ignorant armies clash by night.' She will understand."

Passengers were rushing to the *paquebot.* "Hurry now, quickly, get on," Moustafa said, but his voice cracked and David shared his pain. He walked ahead toward Eliane and helped her gather the bags and children, motioning for the boy to follow. He left Anne-Marie alone with Moustafa to say what he hoped desperately now would not be their last farewell.

* * *

People were pushing and shoving, children irritable and crying as the line toward the ferry formed. Tickets did not seem to be a requirement for the trip. Just get on and get out. Hussein felt sick to his stomach. Sick with excitement and fear.

Moustafa Dramchini was here too. He wanted to run and tell Ali. Both of them were here. He clutched the suitcase in his hands, hoping that no one would guess that there were firearms within, wrapped amidst his clothes. He was going to France with Anne-Marie Duchemin. It had been rather easy after all. And surely Ali could deal with Moustafa.

They had reached the boat whose plank was lowered. It looked to Hussein like the mouth of a great fish, waiting greedily to swallow these filthy *pied-noirs*. That would suit everyone just fine, he supposed. If they were swallowed up at sea.

Anne-Marie, Moustafa, and David were pushing him along now. An officer stepped in his way. "Who is this?" he asked angrily.

"A *harki's* son, sir. Orphaned. We're taking him with us." Anne-Marie's voice was shaking.

The officer placed a hard hand on Hussein and shoved him out of the way. "No room for *harkis* on this boat. Can't you see we're clear full without one of them?"

Hussein heard the thumping of his heart. He didn't dare to speak.

"Please, please—the child is all alone," Anne-Marie stammered.

"Did you hear me?" the officer exploded. "If you want to get on this boat, come on quickly. But leave the Arabs to take care of themselves. Leave them be. Go on, boy. We've got no room for you."

Hussein turned to flee, but Moustafa caught him. "Hold on, son," he said. Then he looked at Anne-Marie and said with assurance, "I'll bring him with me. Later. Go on. Go. Don't worry." She nodded halfheartedly, blew Moustafa a kiss, and limped up the gangplank after Eliane.

Hussein cursed his luck. But then he smiled to himself. It could be worse. Moustafa Dramchini had just promised to bring him along. Things could be worse.

Chapter 5

Mother Griolet bit her lip to keep from saying something she would regret. She laid the letter down on the mahogany desk, then picked it up again. She considered tearing it into several thin strips and depositing them in the wastebasket. It was the third letter this week. The same polite opening, the same questions in the second paragraph. The same accusation in the third. The handwriting was stiffer, more formal, the signature different, but the message was the same. What is going on in Castelnau and why is our daughters' education suffering? Is this exchange program perhaps too much for you now? The insinuation was not only that she was getting too old, but also that she was involved in "other matters" that took her energy away from the young women.

She sighed heavily. Caroline Harland was no doubt responsible. She had threatened to write her father about M. Hoffmann's long absences, and she had apparently done it. Oh, that silly, pompous girl! Jealous of her roommate, no doubt. Jealous of Gabriella, who had taken David Hoffmann away from her. Mother Griolet felt impatient and a little angry. Caroline complained to her father, and the word had

spread quickly among the wealthy businessmen. Now three
polite, firm, threatening letters sat on her desk with more
sure to come.

It was true she had been distracted lately. They all had—
David, Jean-Louis, Gabriella, and the Sisters. Too many irons
in the fire. She could hear her mother pronouncing that
judgment on her when she was a teenager. It had always been
her weakness. Petite she might be, but Mother Griolet
believed God had given her a strong constitution. She was
rarely sick and had found it easy to rise before dawn all these
years. Sleep was merely an inconvenient break in the day's
activities. And so she worked and gave and seemed never to
need a break.

She rested her face in the palms of her hands and felt
very old. Perhaps she had been wrong to participate in the
plan to rescue the children—but it had seemed so right.
Children who were not merely victims of war, but targeted by
a madman for murder. She had rescued children before, and
God had blessed it.

But during the other war, she had only had the orphanage
to manage. The exchange program had come later. She
frowned, reminding herself that she had had no idea that
David Hoffmann was involved in the operation when she hired
him. It was not her fault. Quickly she reprimanded herself.
She was slipping into self-pity, defending herself. That was not
to be tolerated.

She picked up the files on several of the children, leafing
through them. The adoption prospects were never bright for
her children. Young couples wanted to adopt healthy, cooing
babies, not wounded children. Yet she usually found homes
for them. She had rarely had to send a fifteen-year-old off
alone to the state's care.

But in the past she had been dealing with French children.
Plain French, not *pied-noir*, and certainly not Arab. Perhaps
some of the new children's parents were still alive. Perhaps

74

they would flee to France too, as so many were doing, and find their children. She could only wait and pray and keep working.

She hoped David Hoffmann would be back soon. Maybe that would solve the problem of the angry letters. He would come back for the trip to Paris and charm the girls so that they would write glowing remarks home to their parents. The year would finish successfully, as in the past. If only he would come back.

She thought of poor Jean-Louis, droning along, angering the girls because he was fat and bald and boring. It was as if those girls wanted, needed, David Hoffmann, to help them dream and flirt.

"Bother it all," she muttered to herself. *"Ce n'est pas possible."* The program had thrived for all the years before David had come. He was not the only thing that held it together! The girls must simply grow up.

She glanced at the letter again, then closed her eyes. *Dear God, forgive me, please. I am trying to figure this out on my own. And it is not working very well. Hélas! I can take the criticism from the parents. I can even take the idle talk from the townspeople. But for the children. For the children, please help me find a way. You have always shown me in the past. I need You more than ever now.*

She arranged her desk and stood with difficulty, pushing back the chair and resting with both hands on the desk. She took two deep breaths, straightened up, smoothed her black habit, and left the office.

* * *

Gabriella leaned on the desk and faced her fellow students. She could feel her face going red even before she said a word. "Hi." It was all she could think of.

The girls giggled.

"Go on, Gabriella. Don't be nervous," Stephanie Thrasher encouraged.

Gabriella smiled at her friend. She was thankful for the kind words from the young woman who boarded with her at Mme Leclerc's.

"Well, yes. M. Vidal has kindly asked me to teach M. Hoffmann's class for the next few days. I . . . I have always been fascinated by the work of Victor Hugo. His genius was in poetry, drama, and fiction, and he has been called the greatest writer since Shakespeare.

"Like Shakespeare, he was adored during his life and enjoyed the praises of many. He was a powerful man, with a huge appetite and endless energy. They say he would pop a whole orange in his mouth and eat it without removing the peel."

The girls laughed again, and Gabriella's legs stopped shaking so much. "He was very active politically, using his literary genius to either ridicule politicians or enhance their stature. But of course, he is best known for his collection of novels, *Les Misérables.* They appeared as a continuing humanitarian epic, and held the whole world in rapt attention month by month."

She picked up a paperback copy of the book. "Of course, we will not tackle the work in its entirety, but rather this version that David—" She stopped, horrified at her *faux pas,* and for a moment could not continue. She cleared her throat. Stephanie smiled back nervously, chewing her lip. Caroline Harland, on the other hand, looked delighted with Gabriella's slip, and batted her eyes.

"Excuse me, this version that M. Hoffmann provided. He left a note indicating that we will be studying this novel for the next two weeks."

Caroline raised her hand politely. "Yes, Caroline," Gabriella responded, not wanting to hear her question.

"Gabriella, do you have any idea when M. Hoffmann will be back? I thought maybe since you and he are such . . . such good friends, you might have an idea."

Gabriella felt her cheeks burning with fury that Caroline would humiliate her in front of the class.

"I really can't say," she mumbled.

Stephanie stood up quickly. "Hey, Gabriella, would you like some help handing out the books?"

A wave of relief came over her. "Yes, Stephanie, that would be great." She walked behind David's desk and stared at the neatly written notes that he had left for M. Vidal. She barely noticed as the stacks of paperbacks left the desk and were distributed around the room. All she saw were David's words. His thoughts. Jean Valjean. Cosette. Marius. The characters of the book and yet, it was not even that. It was the rise and fall of each letter, the way his handwriting slanted, the passion behind his written words.

Come back, she groaned inside. *Come back. I can't do this. I need you.* Her throat tightened and even in swallowing, she could not get rid of the feeling, only let it slip further down into her stomach, aching. Less than two weeks ago he had held her, kissed her, handed her the corrected exam. It seemed like forever.

She thought for the hundredth time of his brief note at the bottom of the last page of her exam. *I'm sitting in this hospital bed, barely able to write. I am thinking of you, Gabby. When you wonder, when you begin to question, read this exam again and know that I mean every word. Je t'aime, David.*

She had memorized it, saw the writing now in her mind, the way it looked after all not quite natural, as if he must have strained to write with the sling on his arm.

Gabriella glanced up and realized that the girls were waiting. How long had they been staring at her, letting the silence speak for itself? She ran her hands through her curly mane of red hair and stared back. But for the longest moment, she could not think of anything to say.

* * *

The coffee sat untouched in the dainty demitasse cups that Monique Pons used for her daily visit with Yvette Leclerc. The steam curled between them, but they talked animatedly, oblivious to the neglected morning ritual.

"Well, I am sorry to say it, but she is asking for trouble, bringing all those other orphans here at this time. Imagine the nerve!" Monique declared.

"Yes, but Mother Griolet has been so good for the town. Such a lovely woman. I don't see how she does it all, at her age. *Oh là!* She's a good five years older than I, and heaven forbid that I would have to take care of all those wild orphans and the young women. Three American girls are enough to keep my hair graying!" She chuckled, finally noticed her cup of coffee, and took a sip mechanically, her mind far away.

"But you're right, of course, Monique. Castelnau does not need to be invaded by *pied-noirs*, even if they are only children. I just don't understand why they have to come here. Goodness knows, we've enough problems of our own without them."

"And it isn't just *pied-noir* children, mind you, Yvette," Monique interrupted. "I've heard from a reliable source that there are Arabs there too. Arabs! Absolutely out of the question! They can stay in their newly independent country. There's enough of them swarming around France already, you know, over on the west side of Montpellier. Not one bit safe over there." She shook her head forcefully, and the loose skin under her chin jiggled back and forth, back and forth.

"But Monique, didn't you hear? Surely you realize that these aren't just any Arabs. They're the orphaned children of the *harkis*. They did fight for us, you know."

"Hmmph! It's all the same to me. Let them patch things up between themselves, the Arabs. We don't need them in France. Stealing our jobs, producing a brood of kids that drains the government! It's a mistake, and I don't mind if she hears it from me."

"Oh, don't you worry, Monique. Mother Griolet has already heard it from half the town. *Oh là!* She's gotten an earful, that poor woman. I'm sure of it."

Monique picked up her china cup and regarded it intently. "Do you see any steam coming up, Yvette?" Without waiting for a reply, she stood up and bustled to the counter, where she dumped the coffee into the porcelain sink. Its black color stained the white interior for only a moment before she washed it down the drain. "No good at all, tepid coffee! Useless! Completely useless." She poured herself another cup and sat back down at the table, satisfied.

* * *

The sky was clear, and from the deck of the ferry Anne-Marie counted the stars, laid out brilliantly before her without the lights of a city to obscure them. It looked as if a gleeful painter had taken his brush filled with creamy paint and flicked it time and again randomly across the black canvas of sky.

Every part of her body ached, but especially her legs. She wondered if they would support her when she finally forced herself to rise in the morning. For the moment, six-year-old Samuel Cebrian lay curled in her lap asleep. Once he had cried out, talking to some unseen person in his dream and then laughing loudly so that those seated around her had frowned and stared. But he was silent now.

Eliane sat beside her, propped up against her two lonely suitcases. Her daughter, Rachel, leaned on one shoulder while Eliane held the baby to her breast. Everyone slept.

It was a pitiful sight, Anne-Marie thought to herself. The ferry was crammed with *pied-noirs*, finding refuge in any open spot on the boat. There was no comfort and certainly no *couscous*. Anne-Marie smiled wryly, thinking of Moustafa's comment. She was thankful for the sandwiches she had been able to share with the Cebrians earlier in the evening.

She shivered involuntarily and wished she could fall

79

asleep. The night was chilly, and her coat was wrapped around Samuel. She placed her hand on the boy's hair, stroking it gently. For a moment she imagined it was Ophélie in her lap, and the love of a mother welled up inside her. For just tonight, she let herself think of Ophélie, not with fear and apprehension, but with a hope that seemed sure. A hope that tomorrow she would hold her in her arms.

How long had it been now, she wondered, counting the months in her mind. Seven. Over seven sinister, cruel months of separation. If she thought long enough about Ophélie, she knew the other ache, the painful longing for Moustafa, might disappear.

She was somehow peaceful, thinking of David there with him. Together, those two men represented everything good in her life. She would not believe that she might never see them again. Alone, each one wielded a power that amazed her. Together, surely they would be indestructible.

The small distant spots of white, so silent and steady, made her envious. They were always in their place. Even when light made them invisible to her eyes, they were there. Did they have decisions to make? Did they choose between two places in the universe and blink good-bye to neighboring stars, drifting off to another corner of the sky? She thought they did not. But man was made to choose. It was the constant breath of life, the daily struggle: choice and change.

Always a choice, even in not choosing. And a destiny. They, a pitiful lost flock of humanity drifting on the sea, were being flung out like the stars to fill another spot of earth. But no one was guiding, no one pointed the way. It was as random as the galaxies. Tomorrow light would erase the stars and the *pied-noirs* would be alone to choose and no doubt change.

* * *

When light finally did paint the skies with streaks of orange and yellow, Anne-Marie opened her eyes with difficulty, squinting to enjoy the changing picture before her. Somewhere in the night she must have fallen asleep.

"You aren't too cold?" It was Eliane whispering beside her. "Look at you, Anne-Marie! You're icy to touch! Take back your coat. Samuel will be fine."

Obediently Anne-Marie lifted the light wool coat from the boy's shoulders and wrapped it around herself. She rested her arms on the boy's back, hoping he would not awaken.

Rachel slept still, but the baby José stared wide-eyed at Anne-Marie, a smile forming on his lips. Then he screwed up his face, and his skin wrinkled like that of an old man. She could see the wail of hunger coming, but instinctively, before he uttered a sound, Eliane put him to her breast.

"It wouldn't do to have you wake the whole ship, wee one. *Mais non!* We need all the friends we can get right now." She flashed a smile at Anne-Marie. "Do you know where you'll be going then, once we land?"

"I have a number to call when we get to Marseilles. Ophélie is staying at an orphanage near Montpellier. I . . . I will just go there, I suppose. And you?"

"I haven't the slightest idea! Well, hardly. Rémi said I should stay in a hotel in Marseilles until I can get a place of our own."

"And when will Rémi come?" Anne-Marie asked cautiously. She was not used to exchanging information so freely.

Eliane's face clouded. "I don't know. He wants to try and save the farm from the looters. He will wait till the end, I think, to see. To see what the situation is like after independence on July second."

"You hope to return then, to Algeria?" Anne-Marie wondered if her voice betrayed her surprise.

"Hope, yes, but of course, no one knows." Eliane cleared her throat. "Do you mind if I ask you a question, Anne-Marie?"

"No, I suppose not," she answered softly. There was something in the cheerful, kind voice of Eliane that pleased Anne-Marie.

"I couldn't help but overhear the conversation with the young boy and what he said about you providing a safe place in France. And the slip of paper with the cross. That was the Huguenot cross, *n'est-ce pas?*"

"Yes, but it has no spiritual significance. It was only . . . only a sign for us, you see. A way to communicate." She was twisting her fingers together.

"And the tall young man. He is quite handsome. I have seen him before, haven't I? Years ago at your father's house. He was a good friend to you then?"

Anne-Marie felt the color rise in her cheeks. "Yes, a friend . . ."

"I am sorry. I'm prying. It is a bad habit. Forgive me."

"No, no. It isn't that." Anne-Marie looked into the soft, round face of Eliane, and suddenly she wanted so badly to tell this kind young woman what life had been like for her these past years. She longed for another woman to know her pain, to understand as only a woman could.

"If I tell you my story, will you keep it for yourself?" she whispered.

Eliane smiled and patted her arm lightly as if Anne-Marie were another of her children. "I will not breathe a word, Anne-Marie." Her eyes filled with compassion. "Who should I tell anyway? I know no one in France. Your secrets are safe with me."

* * *

For hours the two women talked. They spoke of the past, of their farms that had been in their families for years. Of the wealthy landowner who rented them the land. Of their Arab friends. Anne-Marie revealed her secrets, and she felt suddenly free as she explained to Eliane what she had never

82

been able to explain before, not even to Moustafa or David. The baby, the pain, the impossibility of telling David.

She spoke of Ali's brutality and how she had become his pawn, collecting valuable information for him. As each detail came back, she let it tumble forth, afraid that if she'd ceased talking she would never again have the courage to tell it. And each time she looked into Eliane's eyes, she saw compassion and, at times, tears.

"So you see, I am a soiled woman. I am ruined and yet, Moustafa loves me still. We know it cannot work, but it is all I hope for. Moustafa and Ophélie."

"And this man, David? You have no feelings anymore for the father of your child?"

"Yes, I do. But they are feelings that torment me, feelings of the past. And he loves another woman. He is not right for me, Eliane. I cannot explain it, but I know."

Eliane looked away, waving to Samuel and Rachel who were perched on the railings, laughing as the seawater sprayed their faces. "Be careful, you two. *Attention, eh?*" Baby José slept peacefully, bundled in a coat on Eliane's lap. She said nothing for a moment. It seemed to Anne-Marie that she was weighing her words, choosing them carefully in her mind before she pronounced them out loud.

"Anne-Marie," she said finally. "There are things that were your fault—you brought on yourself. But there are many other things that happened to you. Terrible things, and you were a victim. You must not carry the guilt. It is over. Don't stay a victim all of your life. It will do you no good." Suddenly she took Anne-Marie's hand, clasping it tightly in her own. "You have a chance to start over. It will be better now. I am sure of it."

She said it with such assurance that Anne-Marie felt she could almost believe it. She wanted to so badly. "Aren't you afraid, Eliane? Doesn't the unknown make you afraid?"

"Oh yes, oh yes." She laughed, and her bobbed hair

swung around her head. "I look at all of us here on this wretched boat, and the rest of the *pied-noirs*, and I think, 'No one wants us.' The French don't see us as one of them. We are different, and somehow, I think, they blame us for this awful war. Yes"—she stared in front of her, but Anne-Marie was sure she was seeing something else besides the sea—"I am afraid at times, but then, I have my faith. You know. Like your father." She seemed embarrassed to say it. "I know you did not agree with him, but it is that faith I trust in now."

"You liked my father, didn't you?"

"Your father was a wonderful man. There was such a tenderness beneath that rough military exterior."

"He gave me this," Anne-Marie said softly, pulling out the Huguenot cross from under her blouse. "We decided to make it our password for saving the children. But it was so much more to him. It was a symbol of what he believed."

"You have your father's courage, Anne-Marie. You are brave. You have helped save lives. I hope one day you will share this faith." She looked at Anne-Marie quietly, penetratingly. Then she changed the subject.

"I have wanted to tell you ever since you found me. Your father left you a will. I was the executor, but you have never seen it because we didn't know how to find you. Rémi will send other trunks as soon as I get settled, and in one of those trunks, I have stored your father's will. I will bring it to you then, just as soon as I find it."

"His will? I never even thought of it. I couldn't even come to the funeral—everything happened so fast." She blinked back tears. "Yes, that would be nice, to have his will. A memento. Although I am sure there is nothing left now."

Eliane nodded sadly. "You are right. Nothing at his farm, nothing in the banks in Algiers. I'm afraid we have lost it all. Not just you. All of us. We have lost our heritage." A sadness had crept into her voice. She brushed it aside. "But we can start over. You will see. It is a chance to begin again. In just a few hours, you will see. A new chance. God will see us through."

Anne-Marie admired the young mother with the sunny disposition. But she knew that no God of Eliane or of her father would stoop down to help her. It was okay. She had gotten used to being alone. She would make it. It was simply a matter of choice.

Chapter 6

The papers ran big headlines on the first of April 1962 in Washington, D.C. Women and men alike still idolized John Glenn for his three orbits around the earth last month. The Americans might beat the Russians in the space race after all.

Troops headed to Vietnam, but rumor had it that the war would soon be over. A little more American support, a few more troops shipped over, and the whole thing would be done with.

But on the home front, here in America, the situation looked sticky indeed. Whites and blacks were not getting along, and the South was protesting any rise toward equality. Crazy freedom riders, intent on having the same rights as whites, were actually pushing their way onto buses. And the white lawmakers didn't respond graciously. Racial problems could be tasted in the air.

Roger Hoffmann slammed down the phone angrily in his office on Capitol Hill. Another belligerent reporter seeking information that Roger could not give. Would not give. He rose from his desk, and his steely six-foot-four frame filled the room.

He was a handsome man for his fifty-four years, and he

knew it. He carried himself with cold, calculated confidence. His smile, though rare, broke through like a sunbeam in a cloudy sky, at just the right moment, when a deal needed to be closed or a woman's favors won. The flecks of silver in his black hair gave him a distinguished look. No one needed to be told to respect Roger Hoffmann. His presence spoke much louder than words.

His thoughts returned to the phone call. Pausing in the middle of his office, he swiveled around and returned to his massive, orderly desk. He spread his long thin hands across the cherry finish and sighed. From behind a tray of impeccably stacked papers, he drew out a picture of a young man dressed in black robes and a mortarboard. There was no mistaking the young man as his son. He had the same lanky yet powerful build, the long, handsome face, the closely cropped black hair. The fine aristocratic nose, the thick black eyebrows and lashes. Only the eyes were different. Roger stared into the eyes of his son and felt a familiar sick rage building. The deep-set black eyes held mystery and knowledge, so different from Roger's own crystal-clear blue eyes.

His son had Annette's eyes. Her beautiful black, brooding eyes. Eyes that hid pain, eyes that mirrored it.

He placed the picture back out of his sight behind the file tray. It happened every time he looked at David's picture. The anger, the rage, and mostly, the dreadful, piercing longing. Annette Levy Hoffmann, his lovely Jewish French bride, had been swept out of his life twenty years ago by the rifle of a cocky, bloodthirsty SS guard. That same gun had murdered little Greta, his three-year-old daughter. He could still see her cherubic face and the ringlets of black hair and the blue eyes. His blue eyes.

He could not bear to remember. For fifteen years he had lived with his son in stony silence, never looking into those eyes that betrayed his mother's heritage. He did not hate David. Not exactly. He only hated the memory that David's presence brought back. Memories of heady excitement and uncalculated risks and a perfect family destroyed. Roger Hoffmann knew that if he thought about it too much, he would remember that it had all, in a way, been his fault. So he never permitted himself to linger on David or life long ago.

Five and a half years had gone by since he had last really looked at David. It was at the train station on a sultry September afternoon when he shook his son's hand and wished him well and, for only a brief second, met his eyes. The eyes were proud, angry, and cold. His son had survived a nightmare, and he would succeed in life. He was brilliant; he was also shrewd. No one would pull the wool over David Hoffmann's eyes.

So it was with little regret that Roger Hoffmann had watched his son board the black, battered train and head north to Princeton, his own alma mater. Roger Hoffmann had been proud to send him there. Proud of his financial status that made an Ivy League school possible. Proud of his son's achievements. The top in his class in each of the four different high schools he had attended in Japan, China, Tunisia, and Algeria. The son of a diplomat. David would do fine at Princeton.

He had never called his son at school and had only visited twice, once for his induction into an honor society and then for graduation. There had been no letters between them, no comparing of notes about the good ol' days, no friendly banter. The wall had been built brick by brick over fifteen years, and the distance between them now only strengthened the stony silence.

Roger Hoffmann massaged his brow. Top of his class from Princeton, and now the kid had disappeared somewhere in Europe. What had the reporter said? The Algerian War. What the heck was David up to now? Roger remembered distastefully his son's passionate affair with the daughter of a captain in the French Army. But that was years ago. Before Princeton. Why would David go back, especially now with the mess that country was in?

He looked down on his desk. From under the neat stack of official government papers, Roger pulled out a newspaper clipping that he had received anonymously two days ago. A remarkable story of a young man falling 160 feet to his death from the top of some ancient Roman aqueduct in the south of France. And another man, a David Hoffmann, falling too, not to his death, but into the swollen waters of a normally placid river. A miraculous survival. There was no picture with the article, but Roger was sure it was his son.

Roger folded the clipping and tucked it into a drawer. He did not have time to contemplate David's audacious acrobatics. Not today. Washington was waiting for him. But if the phone calls persisted, he knew sooner or later he would have to face the last person on earth he wished to see: his son.

* * *

Gabriella stood on *quai* number two at the train station in Montpellier, holding tightly to Ophélie's hand. Her palms felt sweaty, and she hoped the child could not tell how nervous she was. In five minutes the train from Marseilles was due to arrive with Anne-Marie Duchemin and David Hoffmann. Only two weeks had passed since David had kissed her and left, but Gabriella felt it had been years. Try as she might to force them out of her mind, the doubts would not stay away.

Perhaps they would step off the train hand in hand, faces beaming with reunited love. Perhaps David would not dare to look her in the eye, embarrassed for Gabriella to read the truth she would find there. Perhaps . . .

The sound of train wheels screeching pulled Gabriella back from her thoughts. Heart pounding, she watched the train slowly grind to a halt, then she looked down at Ophélie. The child's eyes were shining.

"Oh, Bribri! I can't believe it. Mama! Mama will be here

soon! Mama and Papa!"

The doors to the train opened, and people began pouring out onto the *quai*. Gabriella's eyes searched up and down for Anne-Marie and David. Suddenly Ophélie let out a squeal, dropped Gabriella's hand, and dashed toward the end of the train. "Mama!" she yelled. "Mama!"

Tears formed in Gabriella's eyes as Ophélie virtually tackled her mother on the steps of the train. At once, Gabriella admonished herself for her jealous thoughts. Anne-Marie Duchemin buried her face in the hair of her child and wept.

She was but a wisp of a woman, thin, malnourished, limping badly. Suddenly Gabriella remembered what David had told her. "Moustafa fears she will die."

Indeed, Anne-Marie looked as if she had been battling death for a long time. A wave of pity swept over Gabriella as she watched the feeble young woman caress the cheek of her little girl. Gabriella prayed silently that Ophélie would not be repulsed by the sight of her fragile mother. If she was, the child hid it well.

After several minutes, Ophélie took her mother's hand and led her toward Gabriella. "Bribri, I want you to meet Mama," she announced proudly. Her face shone with love, understanding, and something more.

Anne-Marie's strong grip startled Gabriella. She looked Gabriella in the eyes and behind the tears, Gabriella saw inexpressible appreciation.

"How can I thank you enough, *Mademoiselle,* for all you have done for my daughter? Someday I hope I can return to you the blessing that you have given me." She gently kissed Gabriella on each cheek.

"You have a wonderful daughter," Gabriella said, clearing her throat with difficulty. "It has been a pleasure to get to know her." Anne-Marie looked as if she might collapse right on the *quai*. Quickly Gabriella put an arm around her waist to support her. "We must get your mother to the bus, Ophélie.

She needs to sit down." Only then, as they started to leave the *quai,* did Gabriella realize that David was not there. Where was he?

Immediately she felt a sickening, hollow ache in the bottom of her stomach. Something had happened to him. "David . . . did David come back with you?" she asked weakly.

Anne-Marie met her eyes and shook her head. She spoke softly, with a faint smile on her lips. "He got me to the boat and made sure I would have a place. Oh, the crowds! I met my neighbor there. She was with me on the ferry. But David . . . David stayed behind with Moustafa. Quite suddenly he decided to stay on Algerian soil—to stay and help until it was all over."

Gabriella did not want to hear any more. This was worse than she had imagined. She was not losing David to another woman, but to a country. A country and a cause she could not understand. If he loved her as he claimed he did, wouldn't he come back? She needed him here! He had classes to teach and goodness knows, there was an abundance of work with the orphans. Mother Griolet was completely overwhelmed.

The threesome stopped at a bench for Anne-Marie to sit down and rest. "He asked me to give you a message, *Gabrièle,*" Anne-Marie said, pronouncing her name in French. "He said a strange phrase, but he was sure you would understand. Let me only remember. . . ." She closed her eyes. "*Ah, oui, ça y est.* I have it now. 'Ignorant armies clash by night.' That is what he said." She smiled almost apologetically.

At first, the phrase made no sense at all to Gabriella. Anne-Marie had spoken in French. Then it dawned on Gabriella, as she translated it into English. "But that is from *Dover Beach!*" she said out loud.

"Oh, I do not know it. Is it a poem?" Anne-Marie asked politely.

"Yes, a poem. Matthew Arnold's poem," she replied absently. "The last line." Her voice fell. She didn't want this message from David. This pessimistic poem that she loved and feared. Where was the hope in it? Couldn't he have sent her a line of hope? *Dover Beach* was beautiful in its tragic tone. The doubt and darkness between the speaker and his woman. Why *Dover Beach?*

Ophélie and Anne-Marie were chattering excitedly together. They did not see her pain, and she was glad. She forced *Dover Beach* out of her mind and regarded Anne-Marie with pity. She wore a white blouse and a black skirt that fell to her ankles. A black shawl covered her thin shoulders, and a light wool coat hung over one arm. She looked like a refugee. Gabriella supposed that indeed she was. A French citizen and yet a stranger in this land. A *pied-noir.*

Ophélie snuggled in her mother's lap, talking happily. "... And I can't wait for you to meet the children, especially Anne-Sophie and Christophe. And see my doll and the panties with the lace on them. And Mother Griolet has set up a bed for you...."

"The bus is coming now," Gabriella interrupted softly. She helped Anne-Marie to her feet. Together they walked the short distance to the bus stop. With great effort, Anne-Marie stepped onto the bus as Gabriella and Ophélie steadied her. Mother and daughter found a seat together. Gabriella seated herself behind them, repeating to herself, *Swept with confused alarms of struggle and flight, Where ignorant armies clash by night.*

* * *

For Anne-Marie, the moment she stepped into the halls of St. Joseph she felt sheltered, protected, safe. It seemed to her tired eyes the most idyllic plot of earth imaginable. The nuns stood quickly, beaming, when Gabriella led her into the chapel.

"Welcome, Mademoiselle Duchemin," a small elderly woman greeted her. "I am Mother Griolet. We are delighted to have you among us." The nun kissed her tenderly on each cheek and then bent down toward Ophélie. "*Ma chérie,* would you like to introduce your mama to your friends?"

The scene moved in slow motion before Anne-Marie as her daughter led her by the hand, presenting each child to her. Anne-Marie's eyes clouded with tears as she recognized the faces of the children she had helped flee from Algeria. Several reached out to her and hugged her tightly.

She felt dizzy from standing and seated herself in a pew. "My, how rude we've been!" the elderly nun exclaimed, coming beside her. "Ophélie, run ahead with Sister Rosaline and get a plate of food ready for your mother."

She watched her child scurry off proudly and felt a lump in her throat. Ophélie was healthy, beautiful, happy. It was more than she could have hoped. And now they were together.

"Can I bring you anything here?" Mother Griolet asked. She had pure green eyes that sparkled, nonetheless she looked tired to Anne-Marie. Tired like herself.

"No, *merci.* I will just rest a moment longer and then I will be fine."

"Good, then Gabriella will show you to your room. We are a bit tight on space. I hope you won't mind sharing with Sister Isabelle."

"No, of course not. Your hospitality is overwhelming."

"Well, I hope it will do," Mother Griolet chuckled. Then she shook her head. "And M. Hoffmann has not come back, you say? That is too bad. Do you think he will be long?"

"I hope not, *Mère.* He has stayed to help a friend of mine. I am sorry. It is . . . it is my fault that he stayed. I hope they will both be coming soon."

"Yes, indeed. We will certainly pray that God sees fit to bring them to us." The nun turned to the children. "Come along, *les enfants.* Dinner will be ready soon. *Allez-y!*"

The red-haired woman waited beside Anne-Marie while

the children filed out of the chapel behind Mother Griolet. A
timid Sister Isabelle followed in the rear, glancing shyly at
Anne-Marie.

Everyone seemed kind, she thought. Sorry for her and
kind. She stood up, ignoring the pain in her legs, forcing
them forward. She tripped and Gabriella caught her.

"Hold onto me if you need to," she said.

Anne-Marie obliged. She was a beautiful, angel-like woman,
this Gabriella. It was no wonder David loved her, with her
creamy skin and flaming hair and delicate face. The bright blue
eyes and fine thin eyebrows. The long auburn lashes. She was
sorry that David had not stepped off the train into this woman's
waiting arms. David Hoffmann deserved a woman like
Gabriella.

"Thank you so much for all you have done for us, for
Ophélie and me," she repeated again as they walked through
the building that Gabriella called the parsonage and out into
the courtyard. The red-haired young woman only smiled, a
red flush creeping onto her face.

*   *   *

Jeanette Griolet pulled herself from her bed in the early
morning light. Her silver hair tumbled past her shoulders as
she left one hand on the side of the bed and got shakily to her
feet. She shuffled her toes into a pair of worn gray slippers
and gathered a blue cotton robe around her. Eyes closed, she
breathed in slowly, concentrating. The effort drained her. She
winced, and her pain would have been evident to another, had
there been anyone else in the room.

But Mother Griolet was alone. And yet not really. "Jesus,"
she whispered in a rasping voice as she felt for the bed and
with great difficulty lay down on top of the rumpled sheets.
"Jesus," she cried as a pain stabbed at her. Involuntarily she
clutched at her heart.

She thought of the orphans, too many to count now,

overflowing into every corner of the buildings. Who knew what to do with them? Who knew the right people to contact so that some would be adopted? No one here. Some stodgy old man from higher up would come and assume the leadership of this ancient orphanage when she was buried. Oh, the havoc it would cause.

She sat up straight in bed and said out loud, "No!" The action itself startled her. She felt as if she were wrestling, like Jacob, with God Himself. Her respiration came in long, encumbered breaths as she willed herself to stay right here on earth.

"No, Jesus. Don't take me yet. Not yet. You are right. I have been a foolish old woman, running this place as if I would never run out." She lay back down, propping herself up on one feeble arm, afraid that if she stretched out completely, her soul would rise out of her body.

"I have disobeyed You, Lord. A proud old woman. I thought I could take care of things myself, and so I never prepared anyone to take over. I was wrong. You have been telling me for years now to pass on the baton, and I was too stubborn to listen. But You have my attention now, Holy God. Grant me only time enough to train these women." She listened to her own heavy, labored breathing, but it seemed a stranger's. Surely this could not be her time to die? She forced her mind to practical matters as she prayed.

"Sister Rosaline and Sister Isabelle will stay on. They do not have perhaps the capacity to teach and to work out the administrative details, but the food and the dormitories— those practical matters they handle like a dream.

"And now there is dear Gabriella, such a smart child. All the knowledge to teach and a heart big enough for these little ones. Perhaps she will stay. She is seeking Your will. Will You not call her to stay here? In the world's eyes, it is perhaps a waste of brains and talent. But for the children . . . " She felt herself slipping into sleep and forced herself to sit up.

"And then this young woman, Anne-Marie. She has only just arrived, but I can tell. She has suffered. She has nowhere to go. She understands the children. Perhaps it is she You will choose." Another sharp pain shot through her chest, and Mother Griolet cried out, green eyes shining, "Not yet, Lord! You know I only want to be with You for eternity! You know how I long for it. But Lord! Don't punish the children because of a stubborn old woman's selfishness. Give me time . . . a little time . . . ."

The strength to fight left her, and Mother Griolet slumped back on her bed. From somewhere far away she thought she heard a heavy thumping sound. It echoed in her ears but she could not move.

* * *

Sister Rosaline sat straight up in her bed, sweat pouring down her face. She flicked on the bedside light and blinked her eyes until she could read the antique alarm clock that was propped on the bedside table. Ten minutes to six. The dream was so vivid in her mind that she trembled as she put her arms through the sleeves in her robe and tied it around her. She scurried out of her room, through the hall past the sleeping children, and out into the chilly dawn air of the courtyard. Hands shaking, she jangled the keys in the lock of the basement, pushing hard on the door until it groaned and gave in.

She stumbled through the dark corridor and fled up the steps. The dream's picture flashed before her again. Mother Griolet crying out, grasping her chest, her face deathly white.

She banged loudly on the door to Mother Griolet's apartment, jiggling the keys until she found the proper one. Quickly she unlocked the door and bustled in. "Mother Griolet! Mother Griolet! Are you all right?" Only silence greeted her. The plump nun hurried down the hall to her superior's bedroom. "Oh Lord, have mercy!" she cried, bending down beside the slumped form of Mother Griolet. She crossed herself twice.

Ever practical, Sister Rosaline felt for a pulse. It was weak. She rushed to the office, flipped on the light switch, and dialed the emergency number. In a flurry of words, she gave directions to the orphanage, then hurried back to Mother Griolet's side.

"Oh, Lord Jesus," she prayed softly, "*Seigneur.* Don't take her yet, dear Lord. We need her. These children need her. Not yet, dear Lord. Leave her with me a little longer." She blinked her eyes continually. "I have so much more to learn from her. About this place. About You."

Moments later she heard a siren screaming through the streets, announcing to everyone in the little town of Castelnau that something was wrong. Something was wrong and only God Himself could make it right, of that Sister Rosaline was quite sure.

Chapter 7

The Monday morning paper lay across the bed with its bold headline: EVIAN AGREEMENT OVERWHELMINGLY APPROVED. The day before, in a referendum opened only to French citizens living in the Metropole, voters had agreed to an independent Algeria, that was clear. Eliane Cebrian put her head in her hands and cried.

The children were finally asleep, but she had no idea for how long. Since their arrival in France, bad dreams woke Samuel every night, and baby José at seven months slept fitfully, wailing from swollen gums and a stuffy nose. It was all normal, she reminded herself. Disturbed sleep patterns came with change and babies.

She missed Rémi terribly. She missed curling up behind him in bed and feeling the warmth of his rough legs against her smooth skin. She missed laughing with him after the children slept peacefully and he would come to her, his strong arms encircling her waist.

"It's not so thin anymore, I'm afraid," she would tease him. "I may never get my figure back, you realize. An old milk cow, I've become."

Then she would catch Rémi's eyes, all full of love as he held her and kissed her hair. "Don't change one bit," he would whisper. "Don't change a bit."

But here she was alone in a cheap hotel room with sagging beds and torn wallpaper. Alone with the rest of the abandoned *pied-noirs*. For that was how she felt. Abandoned. Some of the fortunate ones had family to go to and money to spend. But most of them had arrived in France with just one small suitcase. It seemed as though the French regarded them all as spoiled, rich children, fallen on hard times, and resented them for appearing on the doorstep of France. She read it in their eyes. She read it in between the lines of the newspaper. They would never understand. Perhaps she would never fit in.

Even at the church, *le Temple Protestant,* she had felt the cold stares. Harsh eyes, unsmiling faces peering down at her and her children as if they were curiosities in a peddler's shop. "Not here too, Lord," she had moaned.

Now she fiddled with the little paper that held the address of the orphanage. "Please, call me. Tell me how you are," Anne-Marie had begged as they had parted on the docks of Marseilles six days ago. "Thank you for all your help. You are as kind as I remember."

Eliane wiped her eyes and thought that it had been just the opposite. Anne-Marie had helped her. She had held the children in her arms on the ferry ride and watched them once they landed, while Eliane had inquired about a hotel. Anne-Marie had brought a glimpse of light to the frightening trip.

Eliane tiptoed downstairs to the lobby, running her fingers over the French francs. Just to hear a friendly voice. That would be enough. She dialed the number and listened as the phone rang, once, twice. On and on it rang. She let the receiver hang by her side. Eventually, a sound came from the other end. She put it quickly to her ear. "*Allo? Allo, oui?* I am wishing to speak with Anne-Marie Duchemin. Is she there?"

A woman's voice, out of breath, came across the lines, "Yes, just a moment please. It will take a few minutes to fetch her. Do you want to hold?"

"I am calling from Marseilles. Perhaps I shall hang up and call back in five minutes. Would that work?"

"Yes, that will work."

"Well then, *à toute de suite.*"

* * *

When Anne-Marie answered the phone, Eliane suddenly felt foolish. "Anne-Marie? How are you? It's Eliane. I just wanted to see how you are doing. How your daughter is."

"Oh, Eliane, thank you for calling. We are fine, wonderful. I can't explain it—it's like I've found a home for the first time in years." She sounded physically stronger to Eliane, excited.

"And you? And the children?"

Eliane smiled back into the receiver, trying to make her voice sound optimistic. "We are managing okay. We are in a hotel. We have a room. That is good."

"It doesn't sound so good to me." Anne-Marie's voice held concern. "Do you know anyone?"

Eliane sighed and told the truth. "Anne-Marie, it is dreadful. I am sorry to say it, but I will feel better just having shared it with you. We're unwanted, even at the church. I can feel it. Alone."

"Have you heard from Rémi?"

"Nothing yet. I don't want to complain to him."

"Could you call? Sometimes just to hear a voice . . . . "

"Yes, maybe so . . . "

"Where are you, Eliane? Are you in Montpellier? I could come see you, bring Ophélie."

"How kind of you, but we are still in Marseilles."

"And what would keep you from coming to Montpellier? The price of a train ticket? And there are surely hotels here. Then at least we would be close."

Eliane wanted to reach out and hug Anne-Marie through the phone lines. Perhaps, yes, they could take the train to Montpellier. It was only two hours away. Surely she could manage that. "I . . . I'm not sure."

"Call Rémi. See what he says. Someone here will know of a hotel. We could make arrangements. Eliane, anything I can do, anything. Now call me back soon and let me know." Eliane could hear genuine concern in her voice. A heartfelt desire to help. "It will all work out. Remember what you told me. A new start. A new start."

When she hung up the phone, Eliane felt strong again. There was hope. She hurried up the steps and tiptoed in her room. The only sound was the rhythmic breathing of three children. Three *pied-noir* children.

* * *

The news of Mother Griolet's heart attack shocked the whole town. For a few days the gossip had turned from *pied-noir* and *harki* children at St. Joseph's to the terrible shame it would be to lose Mother Griolet. Jean-Louis Vidal contemplated the town's fickleness as he sipped a *pastis* in the *café-bar* on his way home, following the afternoon classes. He had seen her in the hospital that morning, so frail and still.

Jeanette, he thought to himself. He drank the *pastis,* but it had no taste today. *Jeanette, don't leave me yet.* He shut his bloodshot eyes and remembered her as she had been so many years ago. Petite and feisty, determined, charismatic. His brother had loved her during the first war, and Jean-Louis had never questioned why. He knew. A woman of faith and action. A rare woman indeed.

When the war had claimed his brother's life, Jean-Louis, twelve years younger, was not quite an adolescent. Later, he had not dared declare his love for this nun who was so many years his senior. He did not possess the charm and easy speech of his brother. He had been sure that Jeanette Griolet

101

would not turn in her nun's garb for him. But she had always cared for him as if they were united by the same pain that came from loss.

He placed a *casquette* on his balding head and stood up, leaving the *pastis* unfinished on the *café* table. He chuckled to himself. Jeanette would approve somehow. If her infirmity could turn him from so much drink, she would most assuredly lift her hands and sing "God be praised."

The breeze tickled his face as he shuffled out onto the cobblestones. Passing the *café*, he retraced his steps to St. Joseph's. The side door to the chapel was ajar but the hollow church was empty. He took off his *casquette* and held it in bewilderment across his chest, stepping down into the chapel. He blinked, wiping his brow, until his eyes adjusted to the somber interior. Silently, cautiously, he walked to the front of the chapel and knelt before the simple stone altar. Above, a ray of light seeped through the sole small stained-glass window, and he moved to the left, leaving the colored spot of sun unhindered on the stones beside him.

He crossed himself, head bent, and spoke in a feeble voice that cracked with emotion. "She is a fine woman, *Seigneur*. All these years I have loved her, and I have asked nothing of You but to be near her. But now I ask. I ask that You spare her until . . . until I can tell her the truth. You have Your plans, and I am nothing. I would not bother You for so small of a thing. But this, *mon Dieu*, this I ask. A little time. Only a little time."

He rose shakily, eyes still turned down. The spot of light was a kaleidoscope of color. Pale color splashed onto the old, worn stones. He watched it for a long time, until a cloud outside obscured the sun and the patch of color was gone.

* * *

There was a glow about Anne-Marie, and it almost made Gabriella jealous. She observed the young mother plunging into the work of the orphanage, laughing like a child as she carried the heavy buckets of water across the courtyard, following Sister Rosaline into the girls' dorm to mop the floor. A week's worth of good meals, and Anne-Marie looked physically healthier. She was still impossibly thin, limping badly, but her eyes were years younger. She no longer resembled an old woman in a girl's body.

Gabriella carried a high armful of clean sheets into the boys' dorm and began making up the cots. She could hear Anne-Marie talking with Sister Rosaline. "You can't imagine how wonderful it feels to work. To do something again. *Quel plaisir!* It seems most of my life I've been hiding and sick. To work, to work in such a place as this. With my daughter. My Ophélie!"

"She's a bright child, that Ophélie. Full of life," Sister Rosaline's voice chimed from the other dorm room. "But kind too," she added, almost defensively. "She's not one for *bêtises,* you know. Behaves herself very well, that little girl of yours."

They were giggling, as Sister Rosaline had the habit of doing, while she let too much sudsy water splash onto the terra cotta tiles. Gabriella did not see it; she did not have to. She had seen it so often before.

But in the boys' dorm she pulled the sheets on and argued with herself. How could the woman be so happy? Living in an orphanage with no idea of her future. Her boyfriend trapped, perhaps dead, in Algeria. Gabriella envied the joy in Anne-Marie's voice.

She only felt dread herself. Fear that David would not come back. She could not picture what would come next without him. He had stepped into her life, disrupted everything and now, just six months later, might very well step out forever. But everything had changed for Gabriella. She felt a stab of guilt. *You have the Lord. He knows your future. Don't worry. It's wrong.* Wrong or not, Gabriella bit her lip and yanked at a stubborn sheet, tucking the crisp white edges under the mattress.

* * *

The tile floor had dried and the beds were made, but Anne-Marie could not make herself leave the dorm room. She walked slowly to the lower bunk that belonged to Ophélie and sat down. She ran her hand over the clean sheets, then touched the small chest of drawers at the foot of the bed. Opening the middle drawer, she took out a pair of lace panties and could hear Ophélie's voice exclaiming, "These are mine, Mama! Mine!"

She touched the soft, cool nylon to her cheek, letting the stiff lace tickle her nose. The smell was of spring breezes and lavender. She placed the panties back in the drawer and smoothed the skirt she wore. It was a light wool black-and-white herringbone that Sister Rosaline had fished out of the clothes closet in the basement. Some wealthy woman had given it to the orphanage, the nun had whispered. When Anne-Marie had pulled it around her waist and fastened it, she had blushed at the enthusiastic *oh là* coming from Sister Rosaline.

"Well, I'll be!" the round woman had said. "It fits you like a glove. You look like a model." And she had scurried back to the closet, returning with a white blouse and a matching herringbone jacket. "Put it on!" she encouraged. "It's all from the same lady. It's providence! Look at you, Miss Duchemin. You look like you've just stepped out of one of those fancy designer shops in Paris."

It was true that the clothes became her. It was like a small miracle. Even the black leather pumps that Sister Rosaline's sharp eye had uncovered fit comfortably with a little cotton stuffed in each toe. She was clothed like a princess, and she hadn't paid a *centime.* This place seemed made for miracles, just as Ophélie said.

At that instant, her daughter raced into the dormitory,

red-faced, with dirt stains on both knees. "Oh, Mama!" she laughed, throwing her arms around Anne-Marie with such force that they both collapsed backward on the bed.

Ophélie giggled uncontrollably, and the sound of her laughter rang in Anne-Marie's ears, and every part of her body tingled, leaving her warm, content, and laughing herself.

"Can you believe we are here together, *ma chérie?* Who would believe it? It is a fairy tale, *n'est-ce pas?*" She held Ophélie in her arms and drank in the smell of the afternoon on her clothes. "We are in the palace of a kind, aging queen...."

Ophélie interrupted her mother, "Yes, and we must pray, Mama, that Mother Griolet gets well soon."

"Yes, of course, sweetheart. That is true." Even that sad news could not destroy the lyric peacefulness of the orphanage. It was a dream, and Anne-Marie was determined to do whatever she could to make the dream last, for Ophélie, for herself.

* * *

Gabriella slipped silently into the hospital room where Mother Griolet lay asleep in a starched white bed. She watched the old woman in shocked silence. Mother Griolet's silver hair fell across the pillow and over her shoulders, laying sterile and coarse against her dark blue robe. The nun's face looked pale and flat, the translucent glow gone. No color in the cheeks. The skin sagged, pulling her closed mouth down into a frown.

Gabriella looked away. She could not bear to see the frailty of a woman she admired so much. She sat down stiffly in a chair and waited impatiently. She wanted Mother Griolet to wake up. She needed her to open her eyes and listen. At once, Gabriella felt a blush forming on her cheeks. She realized that she was here in this hospital room not so much for Mother Griolet as for herself. She had questions to ask, doubts to discuss with her elderly confidant. It was shameful, she chided herself, to come to a hospital expecting to receive. For once Mother Griolet deserved to be cared for and made a fuss over.

The nun's eyes flickered and opened. She looked around with a bewildered expression on her face until her eyes found Gabriella.

"My child," she whispered, clearing her throat. "How kind of you to come see me." She stretched out her hand from under the sheets, and Gabriella clasped it.

"How do you feel?" Gabriella asked.

The old nun gave a feeble chuckle. "My child, you have the most worrisome expression on your young face. Don't look like that! It will scare me. Do they all think I'm going to die? Nonsense. *Mais alors!* What do they expect? I have a bit of work to complete before I can meet my Maker."

She spoke in her light, kidding voice, but Gabriella saw that each breath came with effort.

"Shh. You rest. Of course we don't think you will die. But you did scare us! We're just waiting for you to hurry on home."

The nun nodded. "Gladly, as soon as the nurses will let me out of here. Terrible, you know, to be confined to a bed like this." A faint sparkle had come into her green eyes. "And you, Gabriella, what makes you sad today?"

Gabriella knitted her brow. "Me? Sad? Nothing. Except, of course, it is disconcerting to see you here. But I'm sure you'll be better soon." She patted Mother Griolet's hand.

"And everything is running smoothly at the orphanage?"

"Yes, fine. Everyone is pitching in to help. Sister Rosaline and Anne-Marie mopped the dormitories this afternoon, and I changed the sheets. The children's lessons are coming along fine. It's all fine."

"Except that something is not quite right with you."

Gabriella reddened and looked down. "Why do you say

that, Mother Griolet?"

"Your eyes, Gabriella. They aren't shining."

She twirled a strand of her hair between her fingers. Then she whispered, "It's Anne-Marie."

"Ah," nodded the nun. "I see. She is not fitting in well at the orphanage? *C'est ça?*"

"No . . . no . . . I mean yes. Yes. She fits in fine. She is doing great. You can't believe how much better she looks in just these few days. Stronger, healthier. And she is so happy. So, so happy. Just to be in the orphanage. With Ophélie . . ." She bit her lip.

"And the problem is, I don't feel one bit happy. I mean, look at her. She's lived through hell ten times over, she has no family, no work. What will become of her? And she has no faith. But she is happy. How can it be?" As usual, Gabriella could not keep from speaking her heart.

"And I'm jealous. Why? Jealous of a woman who is half starved, terrorized, alone with a child. I have a wonderful family. I have lots of possibilities for the future. I even have a young man who . . . who cares for me, I think. And I have the Lord. All this and I don't feel joy. I feel fear. Anne-Marie has dealt with so much more than I. Her easiest day might have been my hardest. And yet she is happy and thankful, and I . . . I am . . ." She covered her face with her hands. "And who am I to spill all this out to you when you're . . . you're so . . ." Flustered, she shook her head, feeling the hot tears on her palms.

"I did ask, after all," the nun said.

Gabriella wiped her eyes with her sleeve, then accepted a tissue from Mother Griolet. "What a mess I am. Making the patient counsel the visitor."

"Gabriella, goodness!" Although weak, Mother Griolet's voice was stern. "Who in the world are you trying to be, anyway?"

Gabriella looked up, confused. "What do you mean?"

"I mean who are you trying to be? Are you carrying Anne-

Marie's problems for her? Do you think you are guilty for her pain?"

"No, of course not."

"And yet because she is happy and you are anxious you have somehow failed?"

"Yes, well, I mean as a Christian. My example. What will she think?"

"She will probably think that you are a human being. That you have a heart. That things bother you. She will probably be quite relieved to find that you aren't perfect." Mother Griolet turned her head on the pillow and met Gabriella's eyes.

"For goodness' sake, Gabriella, just be her friend. Just be yourself. You have been a gift to many. You will be for Anne-Marie too. You don't need to feel guilty that your life has been easier than another's. That is God's business. Do not compare. Oh, it is poison! Remember what our Lord said to Peter. 'You follow Me.' Follow Him, child. Don't look around." She closed her eyes, and Gabriella started to speak, to thank her for her words, to turn and leave. But the old nun continued.

"And you are too close to see it, dear. I'd say you've been dealing with quite enough of your own. Be honest. Be yourself. And ask the Lord to let you love Anne-Marie as you love her child." She reached over and squeezed Gabriella's hand.

"Thank you, Mother Griolet. I'm so sorry to bother you with such trivial things."

"Gabriella, God is . . . how do you say it? Chiseling. He is chiseling away some of the imperfections. Sometimes it hurts. Be honest with Him. You will see. It will all be fine." She closed her eyes again and took a long breath. "Go back now and tell them that this stubborn old woman will be back sooner than they think. Sooner than perhaps they wish. *Mais oui!*"

Gabriella stood up, leaned over, and gently kissed Mother Griolet on each cheek. "*Merci. Merci.* I'm so thankful for you. I pray night and day that you will be back soon."

* * *

The meal had progressed well after all, Gabriella reasoned. She had not looked forward to the evening at Mme Leclerc's with Anne-Marie. But her landlady had offered, and it would have been rude to decline. Fortunately, there had been no awkward pauses or insidious remarks about M. Hoffmann from Caroline.

Anne-Marie had smiled politely and answered Mme Leclerc's questions. She had sat poised and still, reflective, her dark eyes filling up like little puddles of rain when she spoke of her thankfulness to be reunited with Ophélie.

She was only two or three years older than the other girls, yet it seemed to Gabriella that Anne-Marie surpassed them in knowledge and wisdom by many more. Dressed in the smart outfit that Sister Rosaline had rescued from the clothes closet, Anne-Marie was beginning to look stunning and sophisticated. Not like the girls in the program. Anne-Marie had depth of character. She was a survivor, and every word she spoke carried compassion and strength. Never pity. Anne-Marie did not want pity. She wanted to give. To give to others in pain.

Caroline and Stephanie did not see it, of course. They joked and teased with Ophélie as if she were their younger sibling. Ophélie relished their attention and chattered along with them.

"May I see your room?" Anne-Marie asked Gabriella softly.

"Yes," Gabriella stammered, caught quite off guard. "Yes, of course."

Leaving the table Gabriella led Anne-Marie down the hall into her bedroom. "Oh!" she exclaimed. "It is perfect. Cozy, simple." She leaned against the window. "And you have a view of the town. And your very own olive tree to brush the window."

She sat on the bed, lightly, bringing her feet under her, so that she resembled, Gabriella thought, a fine, shining black cat, regal and sure, yet unassuming.

"And are you ever very homesick, Gabriella?" she asked.

Gabriella pulled herself onto the bed beside Anne-Marie. Somewhere a board creaked and groaned. The young women caught each other's eyes and burst into laughter. "I hope it will hold us," Gabriella said. "After all, we are both quite hefty women." This sent them, for some reason, into hysterical laughter as they looked at their almost emaciated shapes.

Gabriella felt a chill run through her as she recalled a time her sister Jessica had tumbled onto her cot in the heat of a Senegal night. "Do you think we'll always live here?" she had questioned Gabriella. "In the bush where we feel we might suffocate from the heaviness of it all?" The teenage girl had sighed. "Do you ever dream of some fascinating man riding into your life—oh, maybe not on a white stallion, but someone coming and carrying you away from *this.*" Jessica had always been the rebel. The beautiful, flirting rebel.

Anne-Marie did not seem to be a rebel as she sat on the bed and stared at Gabriella. Then again, she had gotten pregnant when she was only seventeen. The thought came to Gabriella that this woman, this young mother, the last person she had wanted to get to know, was somehow becoming her friend. It was as if, for that one brief interlude of laughter, the Lord had pulled back the curtain and revealed a future scene. Sisters. Soul sisters. She smiled to herself. Mother Griolet must be praying very hard from that hospital bed. Indeed.

Chapter 8

If weeks could crawl by, the last two had crawled for Hussein. He was staying with Moustafa Dramchini and the tall man, the American called David. He was proud at how smoothly it had flowed, how easily they had believed his story and accepted him into the apartment in Bab el Oued. The men had waited till dark to return to their home that first night after the ferry left. Afraid of the FLN, they were, Hussein thought to himself with satisfaction.

The men did not talk freely in front of him, but Hussein had eyes and a good brain. He noted every detail for Ali. After two weeks, he decided he had enough information to risk his life and climb back through the winding labyrinth of the Casbah. Still, his heart raced. What if Ali slit his throat before he had a chance to explain? The fear made him hesitate and turn instead toward his mother's apartment. When he walked into the kitchen where she worked, bent over the sink, he wished he had not come.

He startled her with his voice, and when she turned around and saw him, her face went pale. For a few seconds she did not move, then she engulfed him in her arms, moaning

"*Mon fils,* my son," while he suffocated against her large bosom. She cried and rocked him, and he never said a word.

When she finally let him speak, all he could say, a bit defensively, was, "Mama, I have been working. I must go again, and I don't know when I will see you. Pray for me, Mama. Allah will protect me. He has, you see. Do not worry. Only pray."

He left her standing with her back to the sink, wadding her apron between her tightly clutched fists, tears running down her face like water from a spigot. Her cry of *"Mon fils"* followed him out the door.

* * *

It was almost time for curfew when Ali returned to his apartment. His stride was quick and angry, and again Hussein hesitated. He pulled his shoulders up and breathed deeply before knocking on the half-opened door.

"Who is it?" the wiry Arab asked, irritated.

"It is I," Hussein replied, coming from the shadows of the alley into the dim light of the room.

"Hussein!" This first word was pronounced almost with warmth. Then angrily, "Why are you here? You are supposed to be in France!"

"I am going ve—very soon," the boy stuttered. He blinked hard, squared his shoulders, and looked Ali in the eye. "But I have been busy here. I have found out where Moustafa lives, with an American who has been helping him in France. M. Hoffmann. David Hoffmann. He is here too." Hussein noticed with relief that at the mention of the two names, Ali's face broke into a smile.

He hurried on. "Anne-Marie Duchemin has escaped to France. The guard would not let me on the ferry. But Moustafa promised to get me there soon. They believe I am a *harki's* son. I have done nothing to lose their trust. You can find them. As soon as I am safely away to France, then you can go and take care of them. It will be easy. And I will . . . will finish the work in France."

Ali rubbed his chin, then lit a cigarette and offered one to Hussein. He accepted, steadying his shaking hand while Ali bent close to him with the fire of the match. Ali took a long draw before speaking.

"This is good, Hussein. Not as I planned, but good. Perhaps better. Perhaps." He twirled around and slapped Hussein hard across the face so that the cigarette flew out of his mouth, landing on the dirt floor. Ali crushed it with his foot.

Hussein stared at the floor as silently blood oozed from his lip and dripped down. He moved his foot forward, so that the blood landed on his shoe. His whole body was trembling. He did not want to see the knife. Let it be over quickly, Allah. Quickly.

"That is only to remind you who is in charge." Ali laughed, and Hussein looked up in surprise and saw the mad gleam in his eyes. "You have done good work, boy. Tell me more."

Hussein spoke quickly, ignoring the blood. "Moustafa is trying to convince his mother and siblings to come with him to France, and this David is staying to help him. It was not planned at first. David came to bring Anne-Marie back, because she was so . . . so ill. But she met a woman at the port, an old neighbor, and they left together. They would have taken me, I tell you, but for the guard.

"And now the two men wait and plan. They are afraid, I can tell. And M. Cirou—that is where they stay, in his apartment. He works for the OAS. They plan to send me on the ferry first, because I am small and easy to conceal. Later they will come, with Moustafa's family. You will have time to do whatever you want. I am not sure when I will leave . . . it may still be a few weeks. I try not to be too eager. I listen and do what I am asked."

"Good." Ali nodded, and there was a cruel satisfaction in his eyes. "Stay with these men. Keep their confidence. And when you are getting ready to leave, then come see me. I will finish the work here, as you say." He dropped his cigarette on the ground and, as he crushed it, he pointed to Hussein's shoe. "Be sure to wipe off the blood before you go back there." He tossed him a dirty bandanna. "Take care of yourself, boy," he said, slapping him hard on the back. "I am a very busy man these days. Don't bother me again until it is time."

Hussein stepped into the alleyway and fled down the street. "Pray for me, Mama," he cried. "Pray for me."

* * *

There was one small spot of blood on the floor, and Ali wiped it clean with a piece of tissue. The surprise of seeing Hussein with his interesting news brought another quick smile to his face. He ran his tongue over his teeth, crooked and stained from tobacco, and thought through the plan.

The warped wooden desk was piled high with documents that he had carried in from the last secret meeting. He found a file labeled "US aid" and opened it. A list of material supplied by the United States to the FLN during the years of the war lay before him.

It had not been free aid, humanitarian though it might have seemed. Oh, no. The U.S. wasn't stupid. They were bargaining for oil when Algeria was finally independent. Oil! And he had instructions from the top of the FLN to continue clandestine negotiations. He laughed, satisfied. It was perfect! Ironic and perfect. He read the names of the men he could call on in the States. Five names. He took a pencil and circled the third one. M. Roger Hoffmann, former ambassador to Algeria, residing now in Washington, D.C.

"Come for a visit, M. Roger Hoffmann. See what surprises await you. Then your son's punishment will be complete, and after he has known, as I have, the agony of losing a father, I will be done with him too."

* * *

114

It was not the first time in two weeks that David wondered why he had stayed. He was impatient to leave. Didn't Moustafa want to be out of here? He knew it would not be easy to get a ferry. The waits were growing longer by the day as more and more *pied-noirs*, convinced of their fate, packed their belongings and headed to the port.

But Moustafa was busy working with his people, stealing about in the middle of the night to deliver messages.

"You aren't going to leave, are you?" David asked him point-blank that night, as they sat alone in the kitchen sipping mint tea and watching the paint flaking from the ceiling.

"I am glad you have stayed, David," Moustafa answered cautiously. "But I do not expect you to understand. It is my people I must protect. We have no one. You saw it at the port. The officer, the French officer who turned the boy away. He does not care that we fought alongside him to keep Algeria French. It is our problem how we will survive in this country when the army leaves. Not theirs. They have enough problems of their own."

His eyes grew dark and somber. "But I tell you, one day France will regret it. Regret our pain. One day."

"And all the officers feel the same way?"

"No, not all. Many treat us like brothers. They will weep, they will try to help. They do try even now. But this is a political war, and we are only a tiny minority. You cannot understand, David. You shouldn't try."

"I want to understand. Then I will know how to help."

Moustafa cursed loudly, staring at David with bitterness that seemed to seep out of his soul. "You can never understand. Perhaps if your skin were black, if you were a black American, then you would understand minorities. But you are a wealthy white American. Your life has not been touched by political squabbles. It is not your fault. It is just what makes it impossible for you to know."

David stood up and turned to leave the room. This

stubborn, proud, loyal Arab had no right to judge him. But he could not leave. "I am an American, a rich American," he said, hovering above Moustafa, feeling the power the Arab accorded him. Then he sat down at the table and said, "I am also a Jew."

The Arab man said nothing. He gathered the coffee cups, rose, and went to the sink. With his back turned to David, he muttered, "So?"

"So . . ." David repeated, "so I understand. She has never told you about me, Moustafa? Anne-Marie has not said that I survived the camps as a boy? The only child in my camp? She has not said that I watched my mother and sister die? You do not know? Don't judge me too quickly, Moustafa Dramchini." Neither spoke for a moment.

"Do you have a cigarette?" David asked, distracted.

"I didn't know that you smoked."

"I don't. Not usually, at least."

Moustafa pulled one from the drawer in the kitchen cabinet and offered it to David, who took a match from a box by the stove and lit the cigarette. "I don't know why I'm here. Not totally. It is more complicated than simply wanting to get you back to Anne-Marie."

He inhaled deeply, then let the smoke escape in a long curl from his lips. "When I saw what shape Anne-Marie was in, it reminded me of my mother in those death camps. I was furious with myself that I had not considered it, not realized the full extent of her pain."

"How could you know? She didn't want you to know."

"I was playing at war. She was living it. You are living it." He watched the smoke float before him like a hazy memory. "I lived through a war a long time ago, and I am only now beginning to accept it. I shut it out because I was helpless to do anything else. The pain would have destroyed me. The pain of doing nothing."

Moustafa watched him with a sort of fascinated gaze. He

did not try to interrupt.

"Now, strange as it sounds, I am learning to accept the past. To forgive." He laughed loudly. "What a crazy word! It was Gabby's idea." He surprised himself as he heard her name. "Gabriella—my friend."

Moustafa only nodded.

"To forgive and to trust again. To trust not only myself, but others." He flicked the butt of the cigarette into the cheap white ashtray Moustafa had placed on the table. "You see those ashes. Look at them, sitting there all gray and burnt. They're useless, absolutely useless." David pressed his finger onto them and lifted it up, examining a few ashes that had stuck there. "Useless unless we learn from them."

He drew slowly on the cigarette. "I stayed here because I want Anne-Marie to be happy with you. Eventually. I want to make that one thing right. And I stayed to prove to myself that I could fight, not out of hatred or revenge, but out of love. Do you understand, Moustafa? Does that make sense to you?"

"Perhaps I was wrong. Perhaps I judged too quickly," Moustafa replied. "But this forgiveness, this love. I don't know what you mean. It is something bigger than what you feel for a woman, *n'est-ce pas?*"

"Yes, bigger. It is a love as big as God Himself. That is why I stayed, and it scares the he—It scares me. Because maybe I don't have the guts to do what it wants me to do."

"You are a strange man, David Hoffmann. You are the kind of man I would not mind calling a friend. Someday, I may call you *mon ami.*"

David crushed out the cigarette and nodded. "So be it then," he said. He reached his hand over to Moustafa, who clasped it. "So be it."

* * *

It hurt to think of Gabriella. Just saying her name out loud to Moustafa had brought back the feeling he got when he was with her. That heady excitement, that quickening wit from being with a woman who could read him. A woman who loved him. A woman he loved. There, he had admitted it. He loved her.

David picked up a pen. "How safe is it to send mail from here?" he questioned Moustafa, who was sprawled on a mattress a few feet away.

"Safe enough if you go through my friends, as we have in the past."

"Good."

"Who do you plan to write? Your girl?"

"You guessed it."

"Write her then. Tomorrow I will take it to my friend. I have a letter of my own to send."

David looked at Moustafa, who held up a piece of paper half-filled with his script. He laughed a bit sheepishly. "Great minds think alike."

"You got that right." He rolled back over on his mattress and started his note. So much he wanted to tell her.

Dear Gabby,

My girl! How I miss you! How confused I feel in this mad country. Did you understand why I stayed? Did you see I had to? I am redeeming the time of my past. I am buying it back so that I can have a future. So that we can have a future, free from bitterness.

I know that you need me there. I hope, I pray that you are managing without me. You should teach Hugo; it would help Jean-Louis. I put a heavy load on you, but I suspect you have already guessed it. You were born to teach, my Gabby.

He chewed on the end of his pen, reflecting. Quickly he wrote about the events of the past weeks. Almost a month now since he had seen her. So much to tell. He only mentioned Anne-Marie briefly. He did not want to spoil the letter for Gabby by trying to explain emotions that could not be explained.

118

The letter ran onto a third, then a fourth page. It was philosophical, he knew, but she would read it and understand. He began his last page.

I will come back, but when, I can't say. This is a hellhole. Murders have become almost mundane. Keep praying for our safety.

It is hard to believe a good God could allow such brutality. It makes me wonder, question. It makes me angry. Somehow, I don't think this God of yours (of ours!) is threatened or surprised by my brash questions. And somehow, too, I see Him in the working out of each day. I can't explain it. But then, you have already understood, n'est-ce pas?

The poppies must be all over the place by now. Pick one for me, my beautiful redhead. I am seeing you in my dreams. I have not forgotten you.

Please give Ophélie a big hug for me. Tell her that I love her, that I miss her very much.

And always remember I love you,

David

He put down his pen, satisfied. Ophélie's picture of the ponies hung on the wall in front of him. He smiled at the thought of his daughter. Why had he stayed? Everything that mattered in his life was on the other side of the sea. He wondered if he could slip out of the apartment and get on a ferry for France tonight.

Then he looked at the picture again. If he left, in his heart he knew that the last pony would never catch up with the others. He glanced over at Moustafa, who was still writing. I care about you, he thought. Miserable Arab. He was not a handsome man. He often looked a little disheveled with his curly, unkempt hair. But he was sturdy, loyal, observant.

David did not allow fear to creep into his mind. There was no need. But he sniffed it in the air. It hung like the smell of cigarettes in every room. Irritating, smoky. He couldn't shake it off. *I want to go home, Mommy!* It was the cry of a young boy with the same fear in the pit of his stomach. The other war, the loss of hope.

But now there was hope!

A door creaked. Hussein slipped into the apartment, mumbling *"Bonsoir"* as he passed the bedroom. David glanced at his watch. The boy had been out late for the first time since they had met him. Where he dared go after curfew, David could not guess. But if he was to get out of Algeria alive, this *harki* kid had better be careful. David felt no loyalty at all to the child. Not yet. But perhaps it would come and surprise him as it had tonight with Moustafa. This was war, and the strangest things happened in war.

* * *

Rebecca Madison was forty-three, but she looked as if she were still in her early thirties. She wore her thick auburn hair long, pulled back into a braid. She was tall and still slim after giving birth to four girls. Her face was tanned from the African sun, and the faintest trace of wrinkles showed by the corners of her eyes and mouth when she smiled.

Her life had not been easy. There was no sign of modern comforts in her thatched hut, which stood amidst other thatched huts in the bush country of eastern Senegal, but she felt no regrets. Years of seeing lives changed gave her more joy than the new kitchen her sister was having installed in her ranch house in Ohio. Rebecca Madison did not know jealousy. She knew sorrow and she knew suffering. But self-pity she had no room for.

Nonetheless she hurt in her heart this morning, sitting at the acacia wood table in the main room of their hut, kicking the dust on the dirt floor. Another letter from her eldest daughter, Gabriella, had come, and she had saved it until the chores were done and the house empty, to savor for herself. But as she read, worry-lines formed on her forehead.

The letter was dated early March, over a month ago. And what Rebecca had guessed from the insinuations of past letters was now confirmed. Gabriella was in love.

She wanted to laugh and rejoice in this news, but it looked like nothing but pending heartbreak. "An impeccable, brilliant guy," was Gabriella's description of David Hoffmann. An American from a wealthy background with an interesting past. "We love the same things, Mom. The same poetry, the same art, the same things about the French. Except that he knows so much more than I do. He is fascinating. And he is searching. . . . "

She put down the letter and sighed. Had she sheltered the girls too much? What kind of social life had they known in the bush? It was not Gabriella's first taste of love, or even of an impossible love. That had been Dimby, the Senegalese boy from the tribe. *Maybe I have set her up for this*, Rebecca reprimanded herself. After all, she had fed the romantic, creative spirit in Gabriella, reading her the classics, the poetry, challenging her to think broadly. Her husband had not disapproved, but he had always called Rebecca a bit of an albatross in the missionary world. While the other ladies mourned their china and silver packed far away in the worn-out attic of a distant relative, Rebecca mourned her books. Mourned them to such an extent that he had had them shipped over for their second term.

All that was so long ago, and yet, on a quiet, thick night, she would pull out Conrad's *Heart of Darkness* and nod because she understood. Or read *Kubla Khan* and feel at peace. She knew her Bible backward and forward, and she loved her God. She loved literature too. And Gabriella was following in her footsteps.

This man, this David, sounded . . . fishy. That was the word, no matter how unsophisticated it was. And her daughter, head-over-heels in love.

Rebecca finished reading the letter, about the orphans

and the discovery that little Ophélie was David's daughter. That caught Rebecca's attention. She had a strong hunch that there was a lot more that Gabriella was not saying.

"Please plan to come in the summer, Mom. Mother Griolet would so love to see you again. It would be a great vacation for you, and Dad and Jessica and Henrietta would have a grand time. Think about it. I'm off with the orphans. More soon. All my love, Gabriella."

It was good that she sounded happy; she had been through a lot since the day she kissed her family good-bye and boarded the plane for France. Rebecca's eyes welled with tears—the tears of a mother for her firstborn, who had to discover for herself how painful and how exhilarating life can be.

Holy Father, may she remember what she has learned under our roof. Don't let her forget, dear Lord. I give her to You again today, as I have every day of her life. And once again, I say, I'm glad You are the one in control. Very glad.

Chapter 9

It was clear to everyone in Castelnau that though Mother Griolet was back at St. Joseph's, she was much weakened. She had to admit that it seemed she worked in slow motion these days. Just putting on her nun's habit was exhausting. Her old heart was slowing down.

She stood in the middle of her office and looked around at the crowded walls. Children's faces smiled back at her from worn photographs in simple frames. She knew the name of each child, and she knew where each child was now. Most had been placed in families. Many had grown up, married, and now had children of their own. Often they would call to share their happy news, for she was "Mother" to them in a real sense.

The picture of one family caught her attention. M. et Mme Cohen with their three children. The parents had been taken to a concentration camp, the children found hiding in a false door behind a huge armoire. They were brought to the orphanage and hidden for months until one day their emaciated, but free, parents, after weeks of searching, stumbled upon St. Joseph's to claim them. The reunion was poignant, bittersweet. They had lost everything, but Jehovah had kept their souls, all of them. With thankful hearts, they had started over again. Now M. Cohen was a wealthy merchant in Geneva. He wrote her often. "Come visit us. The Swiss mountains will do you good."

Never had she accepted the offer. There had not been time. "But Lord, if I do not make time now, I fear I will not have any more time to take at all," she whispered, then promptly pushed the idea out of her mind.

She fingered several worn volumes on the shelves that were stacked sometimes two-deep with books. Here and there, another photograph or trinket sat in front of the books. She reached for a foot-high replica of an old woman with a bundle of branches on her back. Mother Griolet brought the clay *santon* off the shelf and held it in her hands. It was one of her most treasured items. She traced the fine, sculptured lines in the clay face of the *santon*. The old woman looked almost alive, her floral dress and cloak made from real Provençal material.

She thought of the frightened Jewish children who had come to the orphanage in the middle of the night, left on her doorstep with nothing but the santon in their possession. The older child, a girl of eight or nine, had whispered, "It is a gift from our parents for keeping us. Please. Take it. It is very important."

She had taken the *santon* and the children. The parents never returned, lost to the death camps. Somehow the clay figurine had come to symbolize to Mother Griolet the whole of her mission in life. Giving. Giving what you have for the Master to do with as He wishes. The children had given their only possession. In turn, Mother Griolet had given all she could—protection. The children had survived, grown, prospered. And the *santon* had reminded Mother Griolet year after year to keep on giving.

Now for the first time, the *santon* made her consider something altogether different, her own human frailty. Mother Griolet had always assumed that she would stand slightly bent over and otherwise unchanged throughout the years, like the old woman *santon*. Today she knew it would not be so.

She set the *santon* on her mahogany desk, beside another letter from an irate parent threatening to discontinue his support of the Franco-American exchange program. How quickly rumors spread! The stooped clay woman seemed to peruse the letter, but her serene expression did not alter.

"And have you seen this one," Mother Griolet whispered to the *santon*, to herself, as she pulled another letter from a stack of papers. "This one is from my superiors in the church. This one demands that I immediately do something to reduce the overcrowding at St. Joseph's since the *pied-noir* and *harki* children have arrived." She massaged her temples and exhaled. They called it "lack of appropriate space for the proper development of the orphaned children." But Mother Griolet read between the lines. Prejudice. The townsfolk of Castelnau did not want these orphans. They feared what their coming might entail, and they had protested to the higher authorities.

"I protest, too, to a different Higher Authority," Mother Griolet said out loud. "Don't let them take the children away, *Mon Dieu*. I pray that You intervene. Always You have provided in the past. Just what we needed. But now, Lord, I am too old and weak to fight. You are the One who changes hearts. Change the hearts of those dear souls in Castelnau. Whatever it takes. Change their hearts." She replaced the *santon* on the shelf and sank into the thick, black-cushioned chair, feeling suddenly very old.

* * *

A light tapping on the door brought Mother Griolet out of her sleep. She sat up, flustered with herself for having nodded off. "Come in," she said.

Anne-Marie Duchemin walked into the office, looking remarkably changed since the last time Mother Griolet had seen her. Color rose in her cheeks, vitality danced in her eyes, and her hair shone, rich and healthy, falling over her shoulders. The herringbone skirt and jacket that she wore enhanced her small, thin frame. Gabriella had been right. The woman fairly glowed.

"Excuse me for interrupting you, Mother Griolet," she began. Her voice was barely a whisper, soft and velvet. "I can come back if this is not a good time."

"No, no, my child. Come in and have a seat. This is a fine time. How delightful to see you looking so well. You are finding things suitable here at St. Joseph's?"

"Oh yes. Everything is perfect. And that is what I wanted to talk to you about. I know you are tired from your recent ordeal, and with so many new orphans. I want to help in any way I can."

Mother Griolet smiled. "From the reports I hear from Gabriella and the Sisters, you already are helping a lot."

Anne-Marie shook her head. "Just a little here and there. But if there is anything else." She leaned forward. "I can't teach as Gabriella does, but I can entertain the children. I have all the time in the world, you see." She looked up quickly. "I mean if you will allow me to stay here with you."

"Heavens yes, do not worry about that. Of course you must stay, you and Ophélie as long as you wish. And I'm sure Gabriella has told you that I am very good about finding an abundance of work for willing volunteers."

"Yes, she said I should talk to you."

"Perhaps you could keep the children in the mornings, help me with their classes when Gabriella has classes of her own."

"Gladly." Anne-Marie rose to leave. "And I was wondering, if I may ask. Have you had . . . any more news from Algeria?"

Mother Griolet reached out and patted Anne-Marie's hand. "No, dear. Nothing yet. But don't worry. You'll be one of the first to know if I do."

The young woman paused, letting a hundred different emotions wash across her face. She sat back down. "Will you pray to your God for Moustafa? He is a good man. He is responsible for the fact that so many orphans left Algeria. Will you pray that he is safe?" Mother Griolet watched lines of worry form on Anne-Marie's brow. "I do not know how to pray, but Ophélie says that your prayers are beautiful. And they work; you prayed for me, and I am here. Please"—and she closed her hands around Mother Griolet's—"Pray for Moustafa . . . and for David."

"I already do, my dear. Every day I give them to our Father."

Anne-Marie turned away. "I don't deserve your prayers, Mother Griolet. I am not good enough for your God. But these men, they are good. They deserve another chance at life."

Mother Griolet gently pulled her old rough hands out from under Anne-Marie's and reached to touch her face. "Do not be so quick to judge yourself, Anne-Marie. You have perhaps some misconceptions about this God." She stood up and went to the bookshelves. Pushing musty volumes aside, she brought out a small leather-bound Bible. "Take it, child. It is old and well used. I have many, you see. Read what our Lord says in the Gospel of John, at the beginning of chapter 8. Read it and see that perhaps He is quite different from what you expected."

Mother Griolet's eyes were shining again. The power was coming back, the power that ran within her but whose source came from above. It was there, *He* was there whenever a lonely sheep needed to know. And this lovely, broken woman certainly did.

Anne-Marie took the small Bible reluctantly. She smiled almost apologetically. "*Merci, Mère Griolet.* Ophélie will show me. The Gospel of John, you said? Chapter 8. *Merci.*"

As Anne-Marie left the room, Mother Griolet closed her eyes and sighed. "You said it, Lord: 'My grace is sufficient for

thee, for My strength is made perfect in weakness.' Don't I
know it well. May I never feel too weak to offer Your hope,
Holy God. May I say with the Apostle Paul, 'Most gladly
therefore will I rather glory in my infirmities, that the power
of Christ may rest upon me. . . . For when I am weak, then I
am strong.' "

She glanced again at the old *santon*, winked, and
whispered, "The power, old woman. He is not done with me
yet."

* * *

Gabriella caught sight of Anne-Marie waiting outside the
opened door of the children's classroom. She finished her
review of French grammar with the older children as the
younger ones copied vocabulary words from the blackboard.

"Tomorrow we'll have a test on the *passé simple* for the
fourth- and fifth-graders," she said. "And a *dictée* for the
second- and third-graders. Okay, out with you now."

After quickly arranging books and notebooks, the
children scampered out of class. Ophélie saw her mother and
tackled her with a big hug.

"Come on, Mama, it's time for the *goûter!*"

Anne-Marie laughed and played with Ophélie's pigtails.
"Go on and have your afternoon snack then. I'll be along
shortly. I'm going to talk with Gabriella."

"*Salut,* Anne-Marie," Gabriella called, smiling from her
desk. "*Ça va aujourd'hui?*"

"Oh yes, everything's fine. I've just seen Mother Griolet,
and I'm to help with the children in the mornings. She said
she was very good at finding work for volunteers."

"I'll say she is."

Gabriella picked up her books and pulled a gray sweater
from off the back of her chair. She motioned for Anne-Marie
to follow her upstairs. "Would you like to take a walk with
me? I'll just put these books down at Mme Leclerc's and we

can stroll past the village."

"Yes, that would be nice. Let me just run tell Ophélie that I'll be gone for a while."

Five minutes later the two young women walked leisurely along the cobblestones, heading to the outskirts of the village. "I love this scenery. All year long, there are surprises I'm discovering," Gabriella said. "Close your eyes and smell. The hyacinths so sweet, the cypress, the wild thyme and rosemary. And then with those luscious smells in your mind, open your eyes and see the fields. The crooked vines with their sprouting green leaves, and the tall, splendid plane trees whose knobby limbs are beginning to sprout too. And the poppies. Everywhere the poppies."

She had been so caught up in her own descriptions that she had forgotten who was with her. "Oh, excuse me." She felt her face redden as if Anne-Marie might guess the secret of the poppies.

"Whatever for, Gabriella? I think it is delightful to experience all of this with you. You're a teacher even out of the class."

"That's just a diplomatic way of saying that I talk too much!" Gabriella giggled.

"*Mais non!* Not at all. I think it's wonderful that you have such an imagination, that you feel things so deeply." Anne-Marie frowned for a moment. "For the longest time, I have tried not to feel anything at all. It was simply too painful.

"But here, looking at this countryside with your romantic descriptions, life seems to have flavor again." She turned to face Gabriella and took her hands. "Thank you so much for loving my daughter. For caring for her. She has told me all about it. All about the incident in Paris and David rescuing her... and you being here to care. And the crosses." She turned and stared toward the open fields and breathed in deeply. "It is such a beautiful story."

"A tapestry," Gabriella commented.

"What do you mean?"

Gabriella shrugged. "Just a phrase Mother Griolet uses. She says God weaves lives together to make a beautiful tapestry. We can't see the finished work, but He does. And I think she might be right."

They began to walk again.

"That is a lovely philosophy, but it is hard to believe," Anne-Marie commented. "My life is not like that at all. It is a long, tangled piece of yarn, hopelessly knotted and unfit for use."

"That's an awful thing to say," Gabriella blurted out, then felt bad about speaking so impetuously.

"I suppose it is. Maybe it's hard for someone like you to understand. It's just that my life has been so . . . different from yours." She smiled. "You are so good. So kind and thoughtful. I am glad David loves you. He deserves you."

She did not seem to notice how bright Gabriella's cheeks grew as she continued. "I have done so many awful things. The only good I think that has come from my life is Ophélie. It is a miracle that from something . . ." Her face grew red. "That fate could bring me such a wonderful child."

"But you see, Anne-Marie," Gabriella said softly, "that is what Mother Griolet means by a tapestry. She says God specializes in bringing triumph out of tragedy." They were silent for a moment. "That is what has happened to me."

"Really?"

"Yes," and Gabriella related the story of her mother's rape and Ericka's birth, and how she died. "I only found out a few months ago. Sometimes it makes me so angry. But then Ophélie came into my life, and it was as if God said, 'You see, life continues.' She is showing me what a healthy six year old is like. It probably doesn't make sense, but she is helping me heal."

"Helping you heal? What a strange thing to say."

"Heal my heart. My memories. That's what I mean."

Gabriella suddenly knew she must confess. "I was so afraid that when you came back you would steal away Ophélie . . . and David from me." She blushed. "You see, I'm not so kind after all. I was so jealous of you."

"Of me?" Anne-Marie asked, incredulous. "Oh, Gabriella. I am happy my daughter loves you. I would never steal that love away. Someday, when you have children, you will know that assurance that your child will always love you. You wonder why, but it is so. Even after the most awful things. I am happy she has other adults to love her too, like you and Mother Griolet. . . and David."

She met Gabriella's eyes. "David loves you. *Non*, do not be afraid of me. I hope he comes back and marries you and you have lots of children. . . ."

Gabriella chuckled. "You're the kindhearted one around here, Anne-Marie. But I can't think of marriage and children right now. Too many things are uncertain. And I have enough children on my hands now to keep me plenty busy."

"Don't you ever get tired of being with them? I don't quite see how you do it all. You have the classes you are taking yourself. And then Sister Isabelle says you've been teaching a class for David. And then with the children . . . you are so busy."

They had reached the edge of a hill and stood observing the vineyards below. "Oh, I'm not really all that busy. And I love everything I do. It's just when I get tired and start feeling sorry for myself that things go wrong."

"Does that happen a lot?" Anne-Marie asked, fascinated.

"Often enough to keep me humble. When you see all the garbage inside you, the pride and self-pity, you can't get a very big head."

Anne-Marie sat down on a large rock and folded her arms around her knees. "I'm sure your 'garbage' is nothing compared to mine. What are a few well-justified selfish thoughts compared to a . . . a girl who has slept with cruel, filthy men?

Who has condemned whole families to be murdered? I wish my sins were as small as yours."

"But you've survived!" Gabriella exclaimed. "You are different now. You are strong. I'm just a little naive goody-two-shoes."

"Well, I hope you're not ashamed of that!"

"No, of course not." Gabriella brushed back her hair. "Anyway, in God's eyes, sin is sin. I mean, any sin is big enough to keep us away from Him—a bad thought or a murder. And yet no sin is so big that He won't forgive it. That is the remarkable thing about God."

Anne-Marie wrinkled her brow. "That's not what I've always heard. Anyway, confession seems so pointless. All the people I've ever known just confessed to the priest so they'd feel okay long enough to go out and do the same *bêtises,* the same sins, again. Didn't seem to do much good."

Gabriella patted her hand. "Well, just see what God has to say about it. Sometime read the story in John 8."

Anne-Marie narrowed her eyes. "Have you been talking to Mother Griolet about me?"

"No! I mean . . . what do you mean?"

"That's just what she said to me this afternoon, before I came to see you. Read John 8. Now that is strange." She seemed lost in thought.

"Tapestry, Anne-Marie. Tapestry. Read it then. You'll see."

Gabriella watched the young woman huddled on the rock and knew she had found a friend. She reached over and hugged her tightly. "That's what Americans do," she said quickly, feeling Anne-Marie stiffen to her touch. "That's how we welcome a friend."

Anne-Marie glanced up and softly touched Gabriella's face. "Tapestry," she whispered with a smile.

* * *

Yvette Leclerc placed ten francs on the counter as Pierre

Cabrol handed her three *baguettes.* She leaned forward and whispered, "I hear that Mother Griolet is having problems from the church. You know, her superiors. Such a pity for that good woman, but really it just won't do to have all those *other* children at St. Joseph's."

She strained even closer as Pierre's wife, Denise, came out from the back of the shop and listened intently. "They are so loud. Lucie Lachat lives right next to the church, and she says the noise is deafening. At all hours of the day and night. *Oh là là!*"

Denise nodded. "It's exactly as you say, Yvette. The Sisters take those children on a walk in the afternoons, with your little redheaded boarder, I might add. And oh, the racket. It's all the little Arabs. *Mal élevés,* they are. No manners at all. I hope someone will talk some sense into that dear nun before they just take over the place."

"And that is a danger," Yvette chimed in. "You know how Sister Rosaline and Sister Isabelle have always kept the place immaculate. Well, I hear"—and she lowered her voice and leaned so far forward that she almost touched noses with Mme Cabrol—"the children from Algeria have brought *les poux.* Can you imagine? Lice in Castelnau. *Oh là là!*"

Pierre cleared his throat and grumbled, "You women! Leave the poor lady alone. Good grief, she almost died two weeks ago of a heart attack. Why don't you go over there and offer to help her with the wild little Algerians, if they bother you so much. It's a fine thing she's doing. A child is a child. And an orphan, an orphan."

"Hmmph!" snorted his wife, who swished her handrag across the counter and disappeared into the back of the shop.

Yvette Leclerc shrugged and bid him good day. Now what has gotten into Pierre, she wondered. Everyone knew what those Arab kids would do to the reputation of Castelnau.

* * *

"I just don't know how we could manage it," Sister Isabelle was saying, her timid eyes growing wide. "But it is a wonderful idea, Sister Rosaline. A wonderful idea."

"Oh, nonsense, Sister Isabelle. We'll manage just fine," stated Sister Rosaline cheerily, as she placed her plump hands on the table in the refectory.

Sister Isabelle giggled nervously. "It's so exciting. . . I mean planning like this, in secret."

Sister Rosaline rolled her eyes. "Well, for the moment, it has to be a secret, until we arrange for all the details. Then we can let her know, and she won't be able to argue a bit."

"Right," Gabriella added. "Now let's go over what each of us is doing. Sister Rosaline, you are going to contact the family in Geneva, right? The Cohens, you said?"

"Yes, and I'm sure they'll be delighted to have her. A fine Jewish family. M. Cohen begs her to come every year. The children are all grown now, but I'm sure they'll come back for the occasion."

"Well, we want it to be a real vacation for her. She needs rest. Be sure to specify that," Sister Isabelle said.

"And two full weeks," Gabriella interjected. "Now Anne-Marie, you think you could teach the children in the mornings, with Sister Isabelle's help, right?"

Anne-Marie bit her lip. "Yes, I think so. If Mother Griolet will leave her lesson plans. And if that is okay with Sister Isabelle." She looked questioningly at the nun.

"Oh, yes. I'm sure we'll manage just fine. But that will leave you alone in the mornings until 11:30 to prepare for lunch, Sister Rosaline. That won't be too much on you?"

"*Mais non. Ne t'en fais pas!* We've been preparing the same meals for all these years—I think I could do it with my eyes closed. You peel the potatoes and boil them and make your *purée*. You broil the fish, you set out the yogurts and fruits. I may be well-padded, but I can work fast. It'll be just what I need!" She laughed, patting her thick sides. "And you,

Gabriella, will teach in the afternoons. You're sure you don't mind missing out on M. Vidal's history class for two weeks?"

"Well, it will be one of the hardest things I've ever had to give up." Gabriella burst into laughter, and the other three other women did the same.

"*Quel dommage! Ah oui.* Such a shame," Sister Rosaline said playfully, her eyes dancing. "Well then, it's all set. As soon as Mother Griolet goes to the girls' dorm for devotions, I'll slip into her office and make the call."

"Perfect!" Gabriella grinned.

"Oh, it is just so exciting!" said Sister Isabelle again as she stood up. "I've got to get back to the boys' dorm and make sure they're getting into pajamas." She scurried out of the dining hall.

"And I'm late for dinner at Mme Leclerc's," said Gabriella. "See you tomorrow everyone. It's a great idea you've had, Sister Rosaline. A great idea."

"And I'll go help with the girls, I guess," Anne-Marie replied meekly. "Unless you need help with the dishes, Sister Rosaline."

"No, go on to the girls. The dishes. *Oop là!* It's just like with the dinner. I can do them with my eyes closed."

* * *

Anne-Marie curled up on her cot, trying to get comfortable as she leafed through Mother Griolet's worn Bible that night. She was intrigued to find the story that both Gabriella and Mother Griolet had recommended.

"What are you reading?" Sister Isabelle inquired timidly, peering at Anne-Marie from her bed in the tiny room.

"I'm not sure. I haven't found it yet. Something in the Gospel of John. I've never read the Bible before." She noticed Sister Isabelle's shocked expression and laughed. "No, I wouldn't be a very good candidate for a nun, I'm afraid."

Sister Isabelle blushed as her eyes widened. She cleared

her throat uncomfortably. "Well, don't worry about that. I mean, everybody has to start somewhere. At least that's what Mother Griolet says."

"Do you like being a nun?" Anne-Marie asked bluntly.

"Me? Well, yes. Yes, I do."

"And you truly believe all the stuff written in the Bible? Even the most farfetched?"

Sister Isabelle squirmed in her bed, pulling her sheets around her. "Yes, I believe it. Mother Griolet says—"

"I don't want to know what Mother Griolet says," Anne-Marie interrupted. "Forgive me, Sister. I don't mean that the way it sounds. I just want to know what *you* think."

Sister Isabelle's cheeks were crimson. She stuttered, "I'm... I'm not very eloquent, you see. But I know I believe. I have seen so many things in my life. I have found that what the Bible says is true."

"Like what? What things?"

"Oh, I don't know...." She thought for a moment. "Like when the Germans, the SS came here, when we were hiding Jewish children during World War II. They knew the children were here. They were going to shoot them. But we prayed and prayed that God would blind their eyes. And in the end, the SS guards couldn't find the children.

"And another time, when one soldier was questioning Mother Griolet and God gave her the exact words. Something she had no idea about, but God gave her the words to answer his trick question correctly. And he went away.

"And surely Ophélie has told you what happened most recently? That awful madman came and tore the place apart looking for her and the Arab children. Opened every closet and room, looked under every bed and in every corner. But when he got to the closet where they were hidden, well, he said, 'Never mind!' A miracle! All kinds of things like that happen, so that you really can't say it is coincidence. You know it's because you've prayed.

"And little things too—like having enough clothes for the children. At just the right time a warm coat will be donated, or socks or a sweater. And the food. Out of the blue one time, it was during the war when we had no food left. Well, a carton of *pâtes* and flour appeared. At just the right time." She looked wide-eyed again. "Oh dear, I am talking so. Excuse me, please." She blushed. "I guess I can be long-winded after all when I get going."

"I don't mind. It is good, interesting to hear. Those are incidents where you believed prayer helped. But what about the Bible? What about the things it says?"

Sister Isabelle sat up taller in her bed before answering. "Christ died to forgive us, and rose again to have victory over death and offer us a life of freedom—spiritual freedom. And all the Bible is like an intricate tapestry showing us that God's plan is good. A Savior is what the Bible promises." Sister Isabelle spoke reverently. "And a Lord. Someone who is in control of your life, not because we are puppets, but because we have chosen it to be. And that is when the adventure begins."

"What adventure?" Anne-Marie asked, intrigued by that word *tapestry* again.

"The adventure of Christ changing your character so that it becomes more and more like His. It's like we are all scrunched up in our pain." She pulled herself into a ball. "Until He transforms us into healed, healthy people who can walk tall in spite of the pain." She stretched out her legs under the covers to illustrate the point. "Anyway, that's enough theology for tonight. I'm afraid you will probably hear a lot more if you stay at St. Joseph's. Radical theology, Mother Griolet says." She covered her mouth. "Never mind that now. You read. I'm going to sleep. Good night, Anne-Marie." She reached over and turned off her bedside lamp. "I'm glad you're here."

"Me too," Anne-Marie whispered.

She found the eighth chapter of John. It was a story of a

woman caught in adultery, and the religious leaders wanted to
stone her to death. But when they brought her before Jesus to
be sentenced, He said the strangest thing. "He that is without
sin among you, let him first cast a stone at her." One by one,
the religious leaders left until it was just this Jesus with the
woman.

Anne-Marie could hardly read the words. Her eyes were
blurred with tears. She felt as if Jesus were in the room now
with her, asking that question. She read it, "Woman, where are
those thine accusers? Hath no man condemned thee?" And
the woman had said, "No man, Lord." And then Jesus had
replied, "Neither do I condemn thee: go and sin no more."

Anne-Marie closed the Bible and flicked off her lamp. She
lay down, staring into the darkness. She heard it again,
Neither do I condemn you; go and sin no more. What a
strange, wonderful thing for that Jesus man to say. She turned
over, pulled her covers around her and drew her legs up
tightly against her, shivering. Gradually she relaxed,
stretching her legs out until they almost touched the end of
the cot. With the words of Christ still in her head, she fell
asleep.

Chapter 10

The gray-haired Arab woman was crying, her head hidden in her arms. Moustafa sat beside her, gently shaking her shoulders. He spoke to her in Arabic. "Mother. Mother, please listen." He sighed and cursed silently to himself. Every encounter with his mother in the past month had ended the same way. Her wailing, his waving his arms in exasperation, shrugging, and leaving the apartment.

He never explained his long months of absence, and she never asked. He saw that she did not want to know. War did strange things to boys. Neither did he speak of Anne-Marie, but sometimes he wondered if his mother had guessed the truth years ago.

Tonight he tried to remain calm. "Mother, we must leave. Can't you see? The murders are increasing daily. Seventy-three this week alone. All the *pied-noirs* will be at the ferries by the middle of June. Let's go now, now before May is upon us. While there is still room."

The woman wrung her hands together, moaning. "Your brother is fighting in the Army. He will not leave until they leave at Independence. And I will not leave until we can all leave together. That is that."

"But Mother, think of Rachida and Saiyda. Your daughters deserve a chance. Please! I will stay for Hacène, but please go to the boats. There is help in France. You go first and find a place for us. Please, Mother."

The older woman, round and strong, looked up at her son. The skin beneath her eyes was dark and sagging. "You ask to break a mother's heart. Is it not enough that I have seen my husband slain? For months I thought you were dead too. Now you ask me to abandon my sons to the same fate. I would rather die with you!"

Moustafa ran his hands through his curly hair. He sighed again, "I will not argue any more tonight. You keep doing your part. You keep a list of the orphaned *harki*s. When I find out if I have the permission, I will send for them. These children will need a chaperone, Mother. Wouldn't you go then? Will you?"

"Perhaps, my son. Perhaps I would take my daughters and flee with the children to France . . . where I would wait every day with my prayers rising to Allah until you and Hacène join us there . . . in this other country that does not want us. This other country where there is perhaps no future. Exiled to a life without meaning."

"It will be better than that, Mother. I promise." He grabbed her hands. "It will be better than that, because nothing could be worse than this."

* * *

Eliane Cebrian waited until baby José was fast asleep to open the letter from Rémi. On the phone two weeks ago he had been distracted. "Yes, perhaps it would be better for you in Montpellier. I'll write. Let me think it all out. I will write and tell you what to do."

She had wondered if the mail was not leaving Algiers now, but Rémi had laughed. He said he had ways to get letters out easily enough. He told her to go to a *boulangerie* down the street from the Port de la Joliette and ask for a *pain de campagne*. Sometimes Rémi said the strangest things, but ten years with this man had taught her not to question. Rémi always had a logical reason, even if he didn't explain it.

Samuel and Rachel wiped their soup bowls with the delicious wheat bread that had moments earlier held this letter. Amazing! A letter hidden in a loaf of bread.

She let her eyes dart quickly down the page, looking for a hopeful phrase, willing that there be no bad news.

Dear Eliane,

I miss you, my little orangier!

She smiled at the term of endearment. An orange tree. Rémi had always said that she was as fertile and fragrant as an *orangier* that grew in their groves.

I pray night and day that you are safe and managing there in Marseilles. I have considered what you said. Yes, go to Montpellier. Let Anne-Marie Duchemin find a reasonable hotel for you. To have a friend would be invaluable for you, my dear.

I cannot say when I will be coming, but things don't look promising. Seventy-three murders by the OAS this week. And two farmers a little farther out—you know the Fraises and the Rampons—have received the warning this week in their mailbox. La valise ou le cercueil. You know what that means. The FLN is offering them one week to get out of Algeria. It is their choice. A suitcase or a coffin.

If it comes to that for me, of course I will have to leave. But so far the farmhouse is fine. No cryptic messages in our little mailbox.

I was surprised to hear you had met the Duchemin girl. And relieved. How good of God to give her to you and you to her for that long crossing. I have not seen Moustafa, but have indirect news from him. Don't worry.

We'll take care of each other. Amazing to find our old neighbors after so long, n'est-ce pas?

About the trunks. I will send one of them along as soon as you have an address. I've got an idea about how to get it to you safely. All your heirlooms, my sweet. Then even an old hotel room will begin looking like home.

And I'm sure that Anne-Marie will be anxious to get her father's will. You have told her, I assume. That will be a nice memento for her.

How is José? And the teeth? I'll bet he has a whole mouthful by now! And Samuel and Rachel? Oh, Eliane, give them such hugs! Tell them Papa misses them so much. Tell them I would love for them to draw me pictures. A castle from Samuel and a garden of flowers from Rachel.

If you have news to send, take it to the boulanger. Say it is for me. He will understand.

I'll leave you now. Don't forget, Eliane. Isaiah 42. He is leading even if we cannot see right now. Don't forget.

And never forget l'autre chose.

Je t'aime,

Rémi

She placed the letter on her lap and smiled. *L'autre chose.* Their little code. When Rémi raised his eyebrows and looked at her and whispered *l'autre chose,* it meant . . . well, it meant that tonight they would share more than just a bed together.

She felt a quickening pulse at the thought. She hoped it would be soon. How she missed that man! But he had agreed for her to go to Montpellier. That was a bright spot in the day. She would call Anne-Marie tonight.

"Rachel, Samuel! We've gotten news from Papa! Good news from Papa," she sang out, coming to the table.

"Read it, Mama! Read it please!" Rachel begged.

Samuel looked up from under his long bangs. He ran his

142

finger over the small knife that sat by his soup bowl. "Did Papa say anything about El Amin, Mama?" When his mother shook her head, his eyes fell. "I'm saving the knife he gave me. I will give it back to him when he comes to France."

Eliane saw the hope in his eyes.

"Won't he come to France, Mama? With Madira? Won't they come to France too?"

"I don't know, Sammy. I can't say. But you know El Amin is happy that you have it. With the knife, you think of him often."

"I would never forget El Amin. Even without the knife."

Eliane nodded. Of course not. There were so many things they would never forget about life in Algeria.

* * *

Sister Rosaline left her bedroom at 6:45. She was the early riser of the two Sisters and had been for all these years. She crept past the adjoining bedroom where Sister Isabelle and Anne-Marie were doubtless still asleep, and let herself out the door in the hallway that opened into the courtyard. She was always first in the kitchen to warm the milk for the hot chocolate and take out the butter and jelly for the *tartines*, the long slices of bread the children ate in the morning.

She walked through the basement of the parsonage and out into the dark streets of Castelnau, as had been her custom for years. All the heavy wooden shutters on the houses were still closed. Nothing at all stirred as she walked briskly through the village to where one light shone from the *boulangerie.*

Good old Pierre. He was always ready when she came to pick up the bread for the day. Lately she had almost doubled her order, with the arrival of the new children. Today as she slipped into the shop, the old *boulanger* was in the back, whistling as he removed bread from the ovens.

She pressed a small bell that sat on the counter. Pierre had placed it there years ago especially for her use, so he would not have to leave his work and wait for her in the wee hours. It was hardly necessary, Sister Rosaline thought to herself. She was always on time.

This morning the graying baker came out of his shop, covered in flour, a sheepish look on his face.

"*Bonjour*, Sister Rosaline," he greeted her. "I believe today I have a little *cadeau* for two of your friends."

"A *cadeau?* What kind of present are you talking about?" she asked, narrowing her eyes.

He laughed as he brought out a large paper sack full of warm *baguettes* and placed them on the counter. "Your regular order, Sister Rosaline. And there is this *pain de seigle* for Mlle Madison and a *pain complet* for Mlle Duchemin." His eyes were merry, as if he had just played some trick and was trying to hide it.

Sister Rosaline nodded, "I understand." Business. A matter of business. She didn't need to ask questions. She was just a simple link in the chain. But as she picked up the bag filled with *baguettes,* she could not help quipping to the proud Pierre, "Just like old times, *n'est-ce pas?* Just like old times."

She was back at the orphanage in five minutes, and everyone still slept. Except for perhaps Mother Griolet. She was an early riser too. Or at least she used to be. These days, Mother Griolet moved a bit slowly.

Sister Rosaline unlocked the door to the refectory, flipped on the light switch, and began placing bread in the long, straw containers on the tables. Yes, Mother Griolet was tired, she mused with a smile on her face. But today she would announce the news to the old nun. Today she would tell her that she was expected for a two-week vacation in the Swiss Alps in the very near future. Sister Rosaline felt satisfied with that thought.

She tucked the *pain de seigle* and the *pain complet* under her arm and stashed them in the kitchen in a cabinet. So there was news for the two young women too. Good for them.

News all the way around today.

* * *

It was after lunch when Gabriella finally had a chance to slip back into the refectory and pick up the bread that Sister Rosaline had told her about. Her hands trembled as she broke it apart and dug inside the soft part. She felt a piece of plastic and triumphantly brought out the small cylinder, then pulled out the tightly rolled miniature scroll. Four sheets of extremely thin paper covered from top to bottom in David's handwriting! She felt light-headed with happiness.

She glanced at her watch. Twenty minutes until classes started. She stuffed the letter into her green backpack and hurried through the basement of the parsonage, slipping out into the sunshine only long enough to reach the old oak door of the chapel. Inside the hollow nave, she quickly sat in a pew and withdrew her treasure.

Dear Gabby,

My girl! How I miss you! How confused I feel in this mad country. Did you understand why I stayed? Did you see I had to? I am redeeming the time of my past . . . so that we can have a future.

She breathed a sigh of relief. *So that we can have a future.* The hope was still there. It was going to be okay. David loved her and he would come back.

She frowned to read of the increasing murders. She had heard, but with David's gift for writing, she could almost see the carnage, graphic, horrible. She could feel the restlessness in David's mind, pacing, waiting, almost desperate to get out.

She nodded as she read of his questions. It must be so very hard to believe in a good, orderly God when all around lay bedlam and death. But David wasn't afraid to question and complain. This was healthy, necessary for spiritual growth, she reminded herself. Before, hers had been a blind faith, intimidated by the unanswerable questions. Now she felt confidence in not having to have all the answers. "Trust," she whispered.

Imagine, my dear Gabby, who I was thinking of last night? Well, you of course. But then T.S. Eliot. I hear these lines from "The Waste Land" and I can only think of you.

> Who is the third who walks always beside you?
> When I count, there are only you and I together
> But when I look ahead up the white road
> There is always another one walking beside you
> Gliding wrapped in a brown mantle, hooded
> I do not know whether a man or a woman
> —But who is that on the other side of you?

It all begins to fit together in another way in my mind, as I recall the poet's words and allusions. There will be time again to speak of these, ma chérie.

Send me news of you, dear Gabby. Send it through Pierre. I do not know where I will be next. This hiding is long. But Moustafa is a good man, and he deserves to be with Anne-Marie. If it is within my strength to do so, I will bring him back.

Please give Ophélie a big hug for me. Tell her that I love her, that I miss her very much.

And always remember, I love you,

David

She glanced at her watch again, surprised to see how quickly the minutes had passed. She was happy. So happy. She could write him back. She knew the protocol now.

There was so much to tell. So much to understand. She folded the letter and placed it between the pages of her history book. Leaving the church, she ran behind the stone building to a little square that opened into a small park. An ancient stone wall enclosed one side, and a wooden bench had been placed in front of it for mothers watching their children at play. A tiny fountain built into the stones bubbled up water

146

that then trickled into a moss-covered basin. And out of the stone wall, three poppies grew. She picked one quickly, far down on the stem, and tucked it in between the same pages in the history book. By the time her letter was written, she thought, satisfied, the flower would be ready to send a message of its own.

* * *

The girls' dormitory sat empty and quiet. No sound of children's voices echoed out into the hallway as Anne-Marie stepped into the building from the courtyard. She came to Ophélie's bed, fluffed the pillow, then opened the second drawer of the small dresser. The blue velvet bag inhabited a corner of the drawer. Anne-Marie touched its soft material and remembered the evening nine months ago when she had given the bag to her daughter.

She stretched out on Ophélie's bed and withdrew a letter from her skirt pocket. The crusty, oblong loaf of *pain complet* had held a priceless treasure, and she unfolded the wispy sheets of paper.

Anne-Marie,

I am sending this as we have sent messages to that lonely orphanage for so long. Are you safe? Are you happy to be with your daughter? Are you stronger? And your legs? I think of you constantly and hope that you and Ophélie are well, laughing together. I miss you, ma chérie.

There is no laughter here. The madness only increases. The FLN continues to terrorize the pied-noirs with threats of 'a suitcase or a coffin.' The OAS has killed nearly a hundred Muslims in just this week. Innocent victims.

I am glad David stayed. He is careful and smart. We have many plans. Mother refuses to leave until Hacène comes, but I am going to propose to her a plan to chaperone other harki *children coming to the orphanage. For that she will come with Rachida and Saiyda. The boy you met at the docks, Hussein, is staying with us. We hope to send him along soon. I am in contact with Rémi Cebrian, and he has several ideas.*

Write to me, Anne-Marie, through the boulanger. *I will get your letter. I dream every night of being back with you. A new life in France. This I imagine. I am not good with words, but you know my heart. You know I love you. Give my love to Ophélie.*

A bientôt, j'éspère

Moustafa

She closed her eyes and tried to imagine what it would be like to have Moustafa here with her. She could not see it. The thought sent a chill up her spine as if in warning. She should not expect too much happiness. She did not deserve it. A tarnished woman.

Hath no man condemned thee? She heard the phrase in her mind. Those words were spoken by the enigmatic Christ. But was He to be trusted? How could she be sure? If she were not condemned, perhaps she dared hope for a future—for Ophélie, for herself, even for Moustafa.

Everyone at this orphanage said the same thing. Trust. Well, of course, they would. They were religious. But even David believed something now. That had puzzled her. Why would a sworn atheist believe? She almost wished she could ask him the questions of her heart. She wanted to probe his sharp mind for answers.

These women had to answer with faith. It was their job. Still their stories rang true. And even her daughter was telling her what to believe. She longed for the simple faith of a child.

Neither do I condemn thee, she whispered to herself and left the dormitory, holding the letter tightly in her hands.

Chapter 11

Spring had come to Washington, Roger Hoffmann mused as he walked along the Potomac, admiring the blossoms on the cherry trees that were reflected in the Tidal Basin, looking like snow on the twisted branches. The Washington Monument stretched before him like an elongated finger pointing to the heavens. Daffodils tossed their yellow heads in the mild breeze at the foot of the Lincoln Memorial, as if to entice the president to come down from his pedestal to play.

He'd better enjoy the scenery now, Roger Hoffmann reminded himself, because in three short weeks he'd be leaving for another part of the world whose landscape would doubtlessly provide a sharp contrast. Of the five Americans whose dossiers had been presented to the FLN, he had been chosen.

He had balked at the idea of going to Algeria now, before the country was officially declared independent on July 2, but the word from the FLN was adamant. *Important negotiations about oil needing immediate attention. Russians have expressed similar interests.* The note from the head of the FLN made their point clear: first come, first served. If he

wanted to keep his present job, Roger had better pack his
bags and go.

He felt a gnawing apprehension, which perhaps was not
even directly related to the war. It was that blasted journalist
asking questions about his son. And the newspaper clipping
from mid-March. Somewhere in the recesses of his
conscience, he wondered what David was doing in the south
of France.

Might as well look him up while you're over there. He
scoffed at the idea. He had no clue where David was. *Get the
work done and get out, if you know what's good for you.*

In the meantime, Roger had plenty to keep him busy.
Details to handle. Conferences to attend. Counsel to be
sought from a few men in the know. And a plane to be caught
in the middle of a warm afternoon to take him to a country
whose gaping wounds had surely swallowed up any hint of
springtime renewal.

* * *

The train slowed at the border between France and
Switzerland, and the *conducteur* stepped into Mother
Griolet's compartment, asking for a passport. She held hers
out, smiling, and the heavyset man with the large, graying
mustache took it, touching her hand as he did.

"A wonderful time of the year for a visit to Switzerland,
Ma Soeur," he commented. "Of course, it is always beautiful
in our *pays.*" He left the compartment, giving her a wink.

"Men these days," Mother Griolet fumed. "Making eyes at
an old nun. Honestly!" The train pulled into the *quai* in the
Geneva station. She listened to the loud whistle and the
incomprehensible announcement that came over the
intercom.

"So," she thought. "I'm here." The women's scheming
had worked out perfectly, and she was glad for it. A forced
rest. She had felt excitement, anticipation this morning when

Jean-Louis had driven her to the train station. But after five hours on the train, she had no energy to move from her seat.

"A good thing this is the end of the line, old woman," she reprimanded herself, "or you'd just stay in your seat and take off to some unknown destination without the strength to protest."

As if hearing her thoughts, a tall, silver-haired man in a dark blue business suit stepped into her compartment. "There you are, Mother Griolet! How wonderful to see you again." He bent down and kissed her cheeks. "You look just the same." His voice was enthusiastic. "But I imagine you're exhausted after the trip. Here, let me help you up. I'll have someone fetch your bags." He held her arm as she stood shakily.

"*Merci*, Joseph. How kind of you to come to get me. I'm delighted to be here." She straightened up with difficulty, holding tightly to Joseph Cohen's arm as he called out to a porter, "*Ici! Oui, les bagages pour Madame.*"

"Emeline has everything ready for you. Tonight you will stay in Geneva, and tomorrow we'll have a short drive to our chalet near Montreux. It is quite comfortable, and Emeline will stay with you. I'll be there off and on. The perfect spot to rest. Just the lake and the mountains to charm you. Two weeks of complete rest—that's what the Sisters ordered, and we intend to see that you get it!"

* * *

It happened every time she came to Switzerland, which had not been frequent. Mother Griolet felt as though a burden had been lifted from her shoulders and any dark clouds had dispersed. She let her eyes drink in the scenery. France's beauty was wild, almost untamed. But Switzerland looked to Mother Griolet as if someone had mowed the mountains so that every blade of grass was in place.

They had followed the shoreline of Lake Geneva all along the drive, and the contrast of the deep blue, placid lake with the tall caps of the mountains reminded Mother Griolet of a psalm. *O Lord, our Lord how majestic is Thy name in all the earth!* Majestic was the word to describe the picture that moved outside her window.

Emeline parked the car by a chalet that sat perched on the mountain like an ornate triangle high above the lake. The narrow dirt driveway continued down at a steep angle where the lower part of the chalet was built into the sloping mountainside. Mother Griolet took Emeline's arm, and they walked in the front door on which had been placed a brightly painted hollow little box with balls that jingled as they touched the strings. The word *Volkommen* was written underneath the strings, stretched taut across a hole in the box.

Beyond the entrance hall unfolded a spacious sitting room with a stone fireplace and a picture window that encompassed the entire side of the chalet. A sliding glass door led to the balcony with its finely sculptured wooden railings. Four oblong planters blossomed with bright pink and red geraniums that cascaded down from the railing.

The view of the lake and the mountains beyond startled Mother Griolet. As she slid open the glass door, she cried out in spite of herself, "A taste of paradise! It is more than I could have hoped for." She took Emeline's hand, squeezing it as they stared into the bright sun.

"Yes," whispered Emeline with a catch in her throat. "Much more than we ever imagined. Jehovah Jireh—the God who provides. Who would have thought that after the hell of the camps, we would ever live to see these exquisite mountains." She cleared her throat and said, "Let me get your bags. I'll be right back."

Mother Griolet watched her leave. Elegant at forty-five, Emeline Cohen carried her tall frame with grace and poise. A woman of standing, the French would say. Her blond hair was swept back in a soft *chignon*. Such a contrast from the skeletal woman who had appeared at the orphanage in 1945, at the end of the war. "My children," she had asked pitifully. "I am looking for my children."

It was a dark memory, yet it shimmered with hope, because the three Cohen children had survived. Mother Griolet could still hear their squeals of delight as they ran into the arms of their mother and father. Jehovah Jireh.

"I've given you the room just off the den here," Emeline called out as she crossed the spacious room. "That way you won't have any steps to manage. I hope you'll find it comfortable."

Mother Griolet left the balcony, following Emeline through the den into an immaculate bedroom. "Oh, Emeline. *C'est trop beau. C'est magnifique!*"

"*Mais non!* Nothing is too good for you."

The furniture was all light pine, crafted in simple Swiss symmetry. A fluffy white down comforter covered the bed, and a porcelain vase filled with wildflowers sat on the bedside table. The large window opened to the same view of the lake and mountains as that from the den.

"We are so glad that you are here," Emeline said, and Mother Griolet saw that she meant it. "You must be tired. Why don't you lie down for a few minutes while I get lunch ready?"

Mother Griolet did not argue in her typically feisty manner. Instead, she unlaced and removed her black shoes, pulled down the comforter, took off her headpiece and lay down on the bed. She had one flickering thought—*the whole earth is full of Thy glory*—before she drifted off to sleep.

* * *

The evening air turned chilly as the sun left the mountain in shadows. It touched the lake, making it glisten with a few waning rays, and disappeared. Joseph had lit a fire in the fireplace and sat down in a comfortable chair, puffing on his pipe. "The children will be coming over this weekend. They're dying to see you. But don't worry, they know the rules. A quick visit. That's all."

"You spoil me. It will be delightful to see them. How is Sarah?"

"You know she has a baby now? I did tell you in the letter, *n'est-ce pas?*" Emeline chimed from the kitchen.

"*Non!* A baby! In my mind, she's hardly more than a baby herself," Mother Griolet replied.

"She's quite the little mama. Twenty-four years old. She and her husband live in Geneva, only about ten minutes from our house."

"And Jacob? He can't be married yet."

"No, Jacob is in his last year at the *université* in Geneva. He plans to attend medical school next fall," said Joseph proudly. "And you saw our youngest last night."

"Yes, beautiful Rebekah. You must be quite proud of her accomplishments on the piano. She is really talented."

Emeline entered the room, beaming. "*Mais oui!* We had to get this little treasure for the chalet so she could keep up her lessons when we come here on *vacances.*" She patted the baby grand piano with its mahogany finish. "You'll see her again soon enough, too. Now let's eat."

Emeline brought out plates of sliced cheese, bacon, ham, tomatoes, and boiled potatoes. "It's a bit late in the year for *raclette,*" she apologized, "but I seem to remember how much you like it."

"It is my favorite—the melted cheese with the potatoes, ham, and bacon. *Vraiment, vous me gâtez trop.*"

"You deserve to be spoiled a little," Joseph teased.

They talked freely, laughing often. The Cohens knew how to appreciate life, Mother Griolet observed silently. They had narrowly escaped having theirs cut short, and now, with generosity and warmth, they welcomed beauty and laughter into their chalet. There was a certain inexplicable depth to the luxurious atmosphere. It felt, Mother Griolet mused, heavenly.

Later in their conversation, Joseph's voice became more

serious. "And how are things in Castelnau?"

"*Ça va bien*. Just a few matters of concern."

"Tell us, Mother Griolet," Joseph said, as they placed the squares of cheese into little cupolas that were set under a grill to melt. "Rumors have drifted up even to the Swiss Alps. Tell us."

She sighed. "I'm afraid the town is turning against me—not that I care for myself. But for the children. People are so narrow-minded and fickle!"

Joseph nodded. "Did you expect them to be different?"

"Of course not. You know it was like this before. They lauded me for helping in the Resistance, then they turned up their noses at the Jewish children."

Emeline nodded solemnly. "At our children and so many others. But you didn't! You have never turned up your nose at anyone. And look how Jehovah has taken care of you! And there are others who help you, *n'est-ce pas?*"

"Yes, *bien sûr*. I am not alone," the old nun replied. "God has given me a group of compatriots." She laughed at her choice of words. "Compatriots from different countries! Senegal, America, Algeria, France. And I suppose you've heard about the *pied-noir* and Arab children?"

"Only a quick résumé from dear Sister Rosaline," Joseph chuckled. "It didn't surprise us a bit. You're still rescuing . . . ." His voice caught.

Quickly, before haunting memories from the other war could destroy the evening, Mother Griolet explained Operation Hugo from its inception until the present situation, with the overcrowded dormitories and the complaining townspeople. "I suppose I could understand if these children were just Arabs. But they're *harki* children. Their fathers died for France. Ah, well, prejudice is prejudice. But of course, you understand all about that."

Emeline nodded. "Jews, Arabs, *pied-noirs*. What's the difference? Unwanted."

155

"So the problem is that the church is unhappy with me. The people have complained, and I'm afraid the church may cut off its funding. And the parents who support the exchange program are equally irate. I let one of our best teachers—the most handsome and eligible—go to Algeria to help in a terrible situation, and one of the young American ladies is mad or jealous. Unfortunately her father has quite a lot of influence with those businessmen who support the program.

"Dear Jean-Louis is taking up the slack, but . . . well, you know Jean-Louis. He doesn't exactly fit the part."

The Cohens nodded sympathetically. "So you're lacking funds all the way around," Joseph summarized.

"Well, not yet. I can finish out the school year, but if the parents cut their support and spread rumors of incompetence, we'll have to close down the exchange program. And you know I've been on shaky ground with my superiors for years. If I retire and there is no one to take over, I'm sure they will just shut the orphanage down too."

"So you're thinking about retirement?"

Mother Griolet chuckled as she poured the bubbling cheese over a potato. "I should have considered it years ago. Not quitting, but training someone else. I got my theology confused—thought I would be immortal on this side of heaven.

"Actually, there are a few young people who could possibly take over, if they were properly trained. One is the daughter of Protestant missionaries in Senegal, another is a single-mother *pied-noir* with no religion whatsoever, and the third is this intellectual young American who is off in Algeria. Each has the energy and the heart for such a job, but I'm afraid the church wouldn't approve of a one of them."

Joseph interrupted her. "If the orphanage had proper funding, could it be privately run? Or could it be taken on by the state?"

"I don't know. I've never considered it. Perhaps."

He wiped his mouth with a napkin. "Let me think about

156

these things. Give me a little time to investigate your possibilities."

Mother Griolet smiled at the couple, her eyes grateful. "Thank you, thank you both. And Joseph, I have another little matter of interest to discuss with you. It is about my will."

"Mother Griolet, you're not planning on leaving us yet!" Emeline scolded.

Mother Griolet laughed. "I hope not. Nevertheless, things must be in order, and I have a few changes that need to be made concerning my will. I thought you might have a lawyer friend who could look at it."

Joseph squeezed her hand. "I have a dear *ami* who would like nothing better than to spend an afternoon looking out on the lake with a charming lady."

"You flatter me, Joseph," she laughed, her eyes twinkling. "Well, then, I can see why the Lord sent me here. You will help me solve all my problems. I'm afraid I've burdened you enough for one night. Forgive me."

"Anything we can do to help," Emeline said emphatically. She glanced at her husband, who nodded his approval. "Anything."

"*Merci. Mille fois merci.* You are so good to me." Mother Griolet rose from the table, feeling very old. "I think I will turn in now."

"*Bien sûr.* Let me know if you need anything."

"Everything is perfect. The dinner was delicious. *Bonsoir, mes amis. Et merci.*"

Snuggled beneath the warm comforter, Mother Griolet watched the bright white moon so stark against the pitch-black sky. By its incandescent light the snow-capped tips of distant mountains were barely visible, looking somehow surreal. She peered through the window, watching for an unseen star as her silver hair hung over her shoulders. "Give me only a little while longer, Lord. Only a little while. I am coming soon."

* * *

The new terror in the month of May spread from the bowels of Bab el Oued into all of Algiers. Teenage *pied-noirs*, aligned with the OAS but now uncontrolled, exploded into complete madness. The death count in the first week climbed toward 200. Seven Arab women were shot in the back of the head as they walked from their domicile to the *pied-noir* residences where they had worked for years. A thirteen-year-old youth interrupted a young couple in the road, pulled a trigger, and shot the man in the face.

A few days earlier a booby-trapped truck blew up at the docks while hundreds of Muslim men waited in line to be hired for the day. Over sixty perished.

A priest watched twenty Muslims murdered within the church, while he stood by helpless. Postmen, store owners, street vendors, housewives. Random and terrifying, *pied-noirs* and Muslims alike watched and wondered when the horror would end.

Rémi Cebrian thanked the Lord every day that his wife and children were safe in France. Perhaps not happy, but safe, he thought, recalling his phone conversation with Eliane. But by now she would be in Montpellier, near Anne-Marie Duchemin. Having a friend would help her deal with the solitude, he was sure.

It seemed ironic that their lives were entwined again with their old neighbors. The Duchemin girl in France, the Dramchini boy here in Algiers.

Rémi brought a tray of steaming mint tea into the main room of the farmhouse. The two young men who sat before him looked intent on their business.

It was Moustafa Dramchini who spoke first. "So you understand the need for a safer way to get the children onto the ferries."

Rémi listened as Moustafa and the American, David Hoffmann, explained how their rescue operation had worked in the past. They told him of the orphanage in Castelnau and their conviction that more war orphans could be saved using the same means.

"It won't be easy to get the *harki* kids onto the ferries," Rémi commented.

"Yes, we have already realized that," the lanky American said wryly. He related an incident of a *harki* youth trying to board the ferry with Eliane and Anne-Marie. "Is there no other way?"

Rémi thought for a moment, letting his eyes fall on the two trunks in the corner of the room. "I have an idea," he said softly. "Just an idea, so bear with me. Eliane is moving to Montpellier soon. She is supposed to send me her address. And I have these trunks to send her. Large trunks." He caught the eyes of the young men and went over to lean on one of the heavy wooden containers. "Perhaps we could smuggle a child in one of these."

David frowned and Rémi forestalled his argument. "No, look. If we cut holes in the insides, enough for a little air. Once the trunk is on the ferry, the child could get out—at night while everyone slept. No one would throw him in the water once he was already on board."

"And how do you propose to get a trunk on the ferry?" Moustafa said skeptically. "The people are fleeing with tiny suitcases."

"We'll think of a way. There has to be a way." Rémi had already opened one of the wooden trunks and begun taking out the contents. "Yes, a child could fit in here. Have a look. How old did you say this boy is that is staying with you?"

"Around ten, I think," David said.

"Would he fit?" Rémi asked, hopefully.

David pursed his lips. "Possibly. Uncomfortably, but it is possible."

"Good! I'll start working on it tomorrow!" Rémi patted Moustafa on the back. "Give me two weeks. This first boy will leave in two weeks. That gives you time to warn your people at the orphanage and me time to inform Eliane." He grinned. "And time to get this old box fixed up for transportation of important matters and make some contacts about getting it on an overcrowded ferry."

The men stood up and shook hands. "Two weeks then. It is settled."

* * *

In the adjoining bedroom Hussein could hear them talking in hushed tones. Planning his escape. He frowned at the thought of being stuffed into a trunk and smuggled onto a boat. He suddenly felt claustrophobic. But he had no choice.

"Should we tell the boy yet?" Moustafa was asking.

"Better wait until a little closer to the date," responded David. "I'm glad we can at least get that poor kid out. And to think that here in Algiers, it's kids only a little older who are doing all the killing now. Senseless!"

Hussein frowned again. David was wrong. The youths were his very own age. Fourteen. It was only that he looked much younger. He felt a slight twinge of guilt to think that these benefactors were sending him to do exactly what many of the Arab and *pied-noir* boys were involved in here. Murder.

Pity was not allowed. He tried to think of something that would stir up his hatred for the *pied-noirs*, so that he would not consider the kindness of these two men. He remembered seeing the dead Muslims yesterday at the *café*. That worked. With plans to appease Ali's desire for vengeance floating in his head, Hussein fell asleep.

* * *

It was long past midnight, but neither man could sleep. They stared at each other from their mattresses.

"Are you ever afraid?" Moustafa's voice cut through the silence.

"Rarely," David stated. "Sometimes. Maybe. It depends of what."

Moustafa considered the American's words. He shifted on his mattress, throwing off the sheet. "Of having been loyal to the wrong thing. To something that has no meaning."

He watched David struggle with the idea, turning it over in his mind, hesitant to speak. "Yes," he said finally. "Maybe. For the longest time I wasn't loyal to anyone but myself. I had a neat little philosophy worked out that protected me from being hurt."

The idea intrigued Moustafa. "And does it work? Does it keep you from fearing yourself?"

David chuckled. "I don't think I'm a very good person to ask that question of right now. I'm in the process of changing philosophies. But I haven't figured the new one out yet."

"What kind of philosophy is it?" Moustafa pressed him. He wanted to pick the brain of this American intellectual. He wanted to know what someone so far removed in culture from this hellish war thought in his soul.

"Nothing that would interest you. Christianity."

Moustafa sighed, disappointed. "Ah yes. Catholicism."

"No. Not Catholicism. Not Protestantism. Not Orthodoxy. At least not for right now. Just the Christ. I'm trying to figure Him out from the Bible, without a myriad of religious traditions attached."

"That is good. Go to the source." This was what Moustafa wanted to hear about. Another man's searching. "I read the Koran."

"And do you find it helpful? Spiritually? And practically?"

"Yes, at times I have. But now . . . " He did not want to state his opinion. He wanted to hear David's.

"What?"

"I wonder if truth exists. My religion says that if you die a martyr in a holy war, a *jihad,* this is the only sure way you will get to heaven. It says in the holy book that a husband should beat his wife if she is unsubmissive. The hope it offers is through violence."

David laughed, holding up his thick Bible. "This book tells of violence too. It seems full of contradictions. Jesus says He comes to bring peace. And then in another Gospel, He claims it is not peace but a sword. Strange." He set the book down. "But I can't get around it now, for all my questions. I think I'm stuck." He laughed again.

"Stuck?"

"Yes, stuck with this Christ. I've recently understood that Christianity is all about relationship with a higher power. Being known by God and knowing Him. Without the need of all of the religious traditions or the intermediary of a priest or prophet."

"And how does that make you stuck?"

"Perhaps I did a foolish thing. I gave in to this God in a moment of weakness. I bared my soul to Him and gave Him my life. And even if I want to take it back, I have the feeling I can't. Oh, I can turn away from Him, but He's sealed me for eternity. It says something like that in the New Testament. Sealed for life by His Spirit. I don't own my life anymore."

Moustafa was fascinated by his discourse. "That is a terrible shame. Unless of course, you find purpose in this religion . . . this relationship."

"Yes. It is a religion of forgiveness and trust. And freedom. Kind of paradoxical. You choose this God, and He forgives you. Frees you to live without guilt. But binds you to live in obedience. And this obedience is freeing. Very strange."

"And does it work?" That was the question burning in his soul. Did anything work?

"I'm very new at it, Moustafa. At first, I felt a sort of freedom—emotional freedom. And I even found it stimulating intellectually. But now . . . now I am only angry that a God who claims to be in control of all life could watch this around us and do nothing." He cleared his throat. "So give me a little while.

You see, I am only just starting to figure it out. I have the feeling it will take me a long, long time."

"My religion is simpler. You pray five times a day. You fast. You follow the laws. But there is no freedom. What I want is an oasis. An oasis here." Moustafa pointed to his heart. "Have you ever seen one? A real oasis?"

"No."

Moustafa closed his eyes, imagining. "It comes to you out of nowhere, like a mirage in the desert. Only it isn't a mirage. It is real. It is there. In the middle of the unbearable heat, the loneliness, the dust that fills your lungs, your whole being, it opens up before you, fertile and green. And you are suddenly satisfied." He ran his hands through his curly hair, measuring his words. How much could he say to this American? "That is what I am searching for. An oasis for my soul."

David rubbed his chin. In the shadows his face looked almost misshapen, long, thin, skeletal. The American seemed vulnerable and insecure. "Do you have a copy of the Koran?"

Moustafa looked at him, surprised. "Not here. But at home, yes. Mother does."

"Could you get it?"

Moustafa laughed sarcastically. "Sure. On my next futile trip to try to convince Mother to leave, I can get it."

"And when will that be?"

"Soon, I guess. Now that we have a plan. Or at least Rémi has a plan."

"Good. Get the Koran. I have this Bible. We'll compare. We'll look and see what these holy books say. Maybe I'll even find out if I've made the right choice."

Moustafa shrugged. "Maybe I will see if there is a choice to make after all." He pulled the sheet over himself and rolled onto his side. The night was still, but he was afraid. Displaced loyalty. All he wanted right now was a place on a ferry and a chance to see Anne-Marie, coming to him with the warmth of her love for him in her eyes. An oasis.

Chapter 12

Gabriella's nose was pressed against the glass window of the train as she watched the scenery rush past her. The whistle screamed and the train wheels screeched as it slowed and entered the Gare de Lyons. Paris! Something awesome and grand danced within her. Paris! For a moment, she forgot that forty-one other young Americans were on the train with her, and that she and Sister Rosaline were supposed to be in charge.

David should have been here. He had been the guide for the Paris tour last year, and every girl on the program had fallen in love with him. How could they not? She could imagine them listening as he led them through the Louvre, the young women lost in a trance, ignoring Da Vinci's *Madonna of the Rocks* and instead, inspired by the big-chested women who flirted in Fragonard's paintings, wishing to be caught in an embrace with the professor.

Why couldn't David be here now, with her? She should have the kiss in the Tuileries gardens as flowers bloomed and fountains splashed around them. She should be held in his embrace on the *bords* of the Seine as they stared at the flying buttresses of Notre Dame and admired the green foliage that tumbled down toward them from walls beside the giant cathedral.

She thought of the letter she had given to Pierre two weeks ago. Surely David had received it by now. Was he thinking of Paris as he read it? Did he want to be with her? *Why aren't you here?*

The girls chattered excitedly, grabbing suitcases, laughing and causing everyone else on the train to stare. *"Les filles,"* Sister Rosaline called out, exasperated. *"Un peu de silence!* You're acting quite rude." She rolled her eyes. "We must catch the Metro to the hotel. It is not very *compliqué* if you will only listen. There are tickets for each of you. You only need one, but keep it to use when we change stations. *Comprenez?"*

The girls nodded, only half-listening. Sister Rosaline caught Gabriella's eye and shrugged. Gabriella imitated the movement and they laughed. Forty-two American girls in Paris with equally as many daydreams in their pretty little heads. What had Gabriella gotten herself into, she wondered.

* * *

The hotel was not a hotel at all, but a convent that each year housed the Americans from Castelnau for their stay in Paris. In previous years this had lasted two weeks, but due to the circumstances this year, their visit had been shortened to five days. The furnishings were sparse, mattresses on the floor of the chapel and hard bread and coffee for breakfast. But no one was looking for comfort. The convent was only a place to come to at the end of an exhilarating day, a brief pause before rushing back out into the wonder of Paris.

After the first disastrous morning when it had taken three hours to get everyone from the convent to the Eiffel Tower, Gabriella grew impatient. "Must we always stay together?" she asked Sister Rosaline. "We'll never see anything."

"Ne t'en fais pas, Gabriella. They aren't children. They

each have an itinerary and two books of Metro tickets, a map of the city, and their own money. Let's leave them alone, let them enjoy. If they need help from us, we'll hear about it."

"That is an absolutely great idea." Gabriella breathed a sigh of relief. There was so much she wanted to see, and she secretly hoped no one else would tag along behind her.

As the girls stretched their necks to see the fascinating latticework of iron from their position under the Eiffel Tower, Sister Rosaline called out to them, "You're on your own now, everyone! Just remember, if you want the student discount, show your cards. And curfew is at 11 P.M. You'll be locked out after that."

In no time at all, the girls had scattered with their friends, and Gabriella was left standing at the base of the immense tower with Sister Rosaline and Stephanie Thrasher.

"Well, what are we waiting for?" Stephanie called. "Let's go up!" She found a place in line, chattering to Gabriella as if the Eiffel Tower were nothing more than a huge Ferris wheel at a country fair.

* * *

Gabriella and Stephanie walked through the Latin Quarter on Rue St-Germain-des-Prés at dusk. Paris by night. Student artists displayed their pastel prints on the sidewalks beside beggars and vendors. The *quartier* was littered with theaters and sidewalk *cafés.* They sipped a *chocolat* at Aux Deux Magots, and Gabriella imagined Sartre or Hemingway sitting at the same table, scribbling notes for a novel. They admired the majestic eighteenth-century architecture, still well-preserved, and they watched the city bustle by.

Then they took the Metro to the Right Bank, where they listened to a violinist playing Pachelbel's Canon within the recesses of the subterranean passages. Its melancholy melody echoed in their ears as they hopped onto the subway and emerged at the Place de la Concorde where Gabriella could imagine in all its grisly detail the guillotine falling down to decapitate the king, the queen, and countless others in the year of 1789. By the lights of the city, they left the Place and strolled up the majestic tree-lined Champs-Élysées. Gabriella felt the magic of one of the most famous avenues in the world, where everything was grand, large, splendid.

"Oh, look, Gabriella! Godiva chocolates! Let's just have a look," Stephanie said, pulling Gabriella toward the richly adorned store, whose window front displayed ornately decorated boxes filled with deep, rich chocolate. "Too bad it's closed."

They walked to the end of the avenue, then took the underground passageway to the Arc de Triomphe. Stephanie and Gabriella stood in respectful silence before the tomb of the unknown soldier under the immense Arc. "It was commissioned in 1806 by Napoléon to commemorate French victory," Gabriella told Stephanie, reading from her guidebook. "And there are twelve avenues that radiate from the Arc. It's called L'Étoile."

"The star. That makes sense."

"Can't you just imagine the uniting force of the French as the troops marched in procession after the Liberation of Paris in 1944? Wouldn't you have loved to have been here on one of the grand occasions when all of Paris turned out on the Champs-Élysées?"

"Hmmm. Sure, why not?" Stephanie shrugged, nibbling a fingernail. "If you ask me, just being here tonight is pretty wonderful."

"You're right." Gabriella smiled, interlocking arms with her friend. "Of course, you're right."

* * *

Stephanie was fun and energetic. Seeing Paris with her was easy. But at every new monument Gabriella would stop and say to herself, "You should be here, David. You should be here beside me."

She said it the next morning as she stood at the base of a flight of hundreds of steps leading to Sacré Coeur. The impressive white Byzantine basilica with the gold dome loomed proud and picturesque on the green hill, surrounded by a blue sky with billowing clouds. Halfway up the steps they paused, panting, to take in a brilliant view of Paris.

Inside, the church was filled with mosaics. Gabriella lit a candle for David and prayed for his safety. On the chancel vaulting, she admired the immense mosaic of Christ, the Sacred Heart. She wondered how many of those who stopped in reverence before the glorious Christ really understood. It moved her to tears.

When they left the church, the sky had turned gray, and it was raining. "Oh, look, Gabriella," Stephanie exclaimed, pointing to her right. "Isn't that just what you'd expect to see outside of Sacré Coeur?"

A magnificent rainbow arched across the gray sky in yellows and blues and reds and oranges. *A promise*, Gabriella thought, watching the rainbow. "You should be here now," she whispered again as they headed out into the rain.

* * *

Gabriella was determined to see the museums, even if she had to do it alone. "Sorry, Gab, but I get bored in those places," Stephanie apologized after breakfast on their third day in Paris. "Anyway, Caroline and I are going to check out some of the shops on rue St. Honoré. Remember, I need a new wardrobe. I've outgrown the one I have," she chuckled, patting her thighs.

Sister Rosaline declined her offer as well, preferring to chat with another Sister at the convent. Everyone else had plans, and Gabriella felt a sudden relief to be alone. Except that Paris was meant to be shared . . . if not with a lover, at least with a soul mate. Someone who would run with her through the rain, entering the Jeu de Paume Museum sopping wet, and stand, bedraggled but mesmerized, before the painting of Degas' ballerinas.

As it was, Gabriella stood there alone. She shivered, not so much from cold as from pleasure, as the graceful ballerinas danced off the canvas in the first room of the Impressionist museum. She reached out, as if to touch one of Degas' sculptures in its glass case. It was the small bronze figure of a young girl, dressed in a tutu with a faded pink ribbon tied in her braided hair.

In every room of the museum, she found herself talking to David as if he were beside her, commenting on a certain painting as he had done while showing slides in class.

When she reached the room where Monet's poppies spread across the far wall, she stopped. *Les Coquelicots.* Without thinking she whispered "Exuberance that softly spread to capture fields of dreams and hearts." A line from David's poem to her, inspired by this painting. "Why aren't you here?" she said, her soul aching with the distance.

And then she knew. She *was* sharing Paris with him. In her mind, he was here beside her. Now she must simply put it on paper. She would write him every thought and impression, every fragrant wisp of the perfume in the spring flowers, every detail of this tableau.

* * *

It was raining again, and Gabriella watched the colorful array of umbrellas from underneath the awning at a clean little *café* across the street from the Rodin museum. It reminded her of Pissaro's painting of Paris in the rain, which she had seen at the Jeu de Paume. She scribbled every thought in tiny script on thin paper as she sipped a cup of tea. Every thought for David.

She blushed then, describing to him the intimate, delicate, sensual sculpture of Rodin. Somehow she could tell him in a letter. "My favorite sculpture, David, is, of course—you have guessed it—*The Kiss. Le Baiser.* And I am not afraid to tell you that I stood there and wished it were you and I sharing that eternal moment, chiseled into the marble."

Then later in the afternoon, when the rain stopped and the streets glistened with oil and water, she walked leisurely from the Faubourg St-Germain to Ile de la Cité, the island between the Left and Right Banks where Paris was born 2,000 years ago. When she arrived at the Cathedral of Notre Dame, she stood for a long time outside, studying the facade as she read of its history in her guidebook. Then, almost reverently, she went inside.

Later in another *café* she wrote to David, "As I stood there, awed by the beauty of the south rose window, I prayed that I would return there someday and stand in that very place, staring at man's magnificent expression of God's glory with the one man He will have given me to share His perfect love with on earth."

Then, afraid of her words, she hurried on to tell him of walking up the narrow little winding stone staircase to the top of the cathedral and standing among the gargoyles for a pre-sunset view of the Paris skyline.

As she wrote of how this great city overwhelmed and surprised her, she suddenly felt a pang of homesickness. Perhaps she had been too honest with David. Perhaps her wild, romantic dreams and prayers were just that, the dreams of a silly schoolgirl. Nine months had passed since she had seen her family. In only two more she would be back in Senegal, or maybe moving to America. She wanted to hold on to Paris, never letting it slip through her fingers. Hold on to something stronger than herself.

She remembered what David had said Hemingway had supposedly written to a friend. *If you are lucky enough to have lived in Paris as a young man, then wherever you go for the rest of your life, it stays with you, for Paris is a moveable feast.*

Yes, that was it. A moveable feast. Even for the visitor, at least for her, she was sure she would carry this time alone in Paris, sharing her secret emotions on paper with David, for the rest of her life. Then, wherever she ended up, she would be rich with the memory.

As she thought of home and France, the conflicting emotions translated themselves into a simple sonnet, and she added it to the end of her letter to David.

Taut-stretched these strings within my heart
An ocean spans betwixt this war
Of sentiments, unknown before,
Each warrior proudly plays his part:

Antiquity claims precedence
"Vieilles villes are new to foreign eyes."
From yonder shore my Homeland cries,
"Regain your peaceful residence."

This ancient world fresh joy invites
To youthful heart, Adventure's friend.
Yet memories wakened, quickly send
Deep longings for familiar sites.
Fast home! before strings severed, break,
While Present must new memories make.

She reread the poem, satisfied. Now he knew everything on her heart.

* * *

It was their last evening in Paris and the only one for which everyone's attendance was required. They had eaten at La Bonne Fourchette, a charming little restaurant hidden in an alcove off the rue St. Honoré. Then the whole troupe had literally danced through the streets of Paris, singing songs from Broadway musicals, until they arrived on the Ile de la Cité and came to the Sainte Chapelle. *Exceptionellement,*

Sister Rosaline told them, the Chapelle was offering a concert of Vivaldi's *Four Seasons* this night, and they had been fortunate enough to get tickets.

Once inside, there was still enough light in the sky to shine through the superb stained-glass windows in the upper chapel. "It is a jewel," Gabriella whispered.

"Yes, indeed," Sister Rosaline agreed, as the girls took their seats and strained to hear the nun's whispered commentary. "The chapel was built in the thirteenth century, supposedly to house the Crown of Thorns. The stained-glass windows are the oldest in Paris and among the finest produced in the thirteenth century. They catch the faintest hint of light, you see. The tall, brilliant windows illustrate in vivid color and detail the whole of the Bible."

The ceiling arched above them with its royal *fleur-de-lys* embedded between the stained glass, and while Gabriella studied a scene from the Book of Exodus, the violins burst into play. Her eyes followed the windows as she listened to the familiar music. The violinists drew their bows frantically back and forth, back and forth, filling the chapel with Vivaldi's *Spring*. Sitting in the world's most beautiful chapel, her eyes feasting on the play of light through sublime windows, her ears tuned into the lyrical harmonies of one of the world's favorite composers, Gabriella absorbed the superlatives with delight. This was a night to inspire. This was a night when the heavens were singing out themselves to applaud creation. Tonight it was perfect. Tonight she was sure that wherever David was, he could hear it too.

* * *

The letter had arrived in the bread and as David unrolled the paper, a flattened poppy fell out. He held it in his hand, a boyish grin on his face, as he read the letter. Gabriella wrote as she lived, words tumbling out faster than she could put them together, covering page after page of onionskin paper.

She wrote of receiving his letter, of the orphans, of Anne-Marie's appearance, of David's absence, and her fears. Of her sudden bonding with Anne-Marie. She wrote of Mother Griolet's heart attack and their plan to send her to the Alps. She wrote of their scheduled trip to Paris.

She wrote as a woman sure of his love, and he was glad.

And now, she was surely in Paris with the rest of the young women at the program. He wished he could introduce Gabriella to Paris himself. He was sure that the two of them, the girl and the city, would get along quite well. Gabriella would not be a simple tourist. She would feast on the city, as Hemingway described it.

She would find meaning in the paintings in the museums and the stained-glass windows in each cathedral. He thought of what it would be like to stand in the Sainte Chapelle and gaze with her at the exquisite windows, while music played around them. He wished for it and yearned to take her in his arms.

For a moment, he forgot about the war that was ripping apart this little universe that had parenthetically become his home. He thought of Gabriella and Paris. Sisters in their depth, in their beauty and vitality. He would give anything to share it with her. Someday, he promised himself. Someday he would.

In his mind, a bar of music played softly, amplifying, until he heard it as if the orchestra were there before him. Vivaldi. He caressed the poppy with one finger. In the deepest part of him, David Hoffmann knew that he was sharing Paris with Gabby even now.

* * *

She and Sister Isabelle had managed the orphans fine for the two weeks that Mother Griolet was in Switzerland, but with Sister Rosaline and Gabriella now gone, Anne-Marie felt less capable. Mother Griolet was back, looking healthier. But they must not let the old nun tire herself. As it was, Anne-Marie felt exhausted. She collapsed on her cot while Sister

Isabelle watched the children in the courtyard.

"You're an answer to prayer," Sister Isabelle had confided to Anne-Marie before the American girls had left for Paris. "Mother Griolet is determined not to cancel the trip, but if you weren't here, we'd never be able to manage it. Not with Mother Griolet so weak."

Anne-Marie did not believe in answers to prayer and today, she thought, she didn't feel like the answer to anything. The children were frazzling her nerves. Another morning with them and she might snap.

It did not help that she had received another letter from Moustafa. Not a love letter at all. Just the news of that little *harki* orphan, Hussein, coming to St. Joseph's. "Well, isn't that just wonderful," she had said to herself. "Just what we need." Immediately she felt guilty. How could she be so quick to give up, when only a month ago she had been the one fleeing Algeria? Couldn't she still see the fear in the young boy's eyes as he pleaded with her?

She was embarrassed by how quickly she could let herself be pampered by a safe lifestyle. A few short weeks ago, St. Joseph's had been to her an idyllic haven. Now she longed to escape from its confines with her daughter in search of a little peace.

How selfish, she chastised herself. This was peace compared with Algeria. She put her head in her hands and sighed. What was really bothering her, besides plain old fatigue, was the note from Moustafa. She read it again.

New orphan scheduled to arrive. Jeudi 24mai 19h30SNCF. That was all. David Hoffmann would have written something else to Gabriella, she was certain. David . . .

She hit her pillow with her fist. Maybe he didn't care. Maybe all of Moustafa's kind, loyal words were only that. Empty words. Were they true? She felt him being pulled by his people back into the heart of the war. He would never come.

It was as one of the *pied-noir* authors had said: "And

that's why even if the Algerians and the *pied-noirs* speak of the same landscape, they aren't speaking of the same Algeria. Their two countries are juxtaposed one against the other without ever truly mingling, separated by the barrier of the language."

It was true. Moustafa spoke French as well as he spoke Arabic, but his culture was completely different. How had she believed he could put that behind him? He was an Arab ostracized by his people. A tiny microcosm of a culture that had turned inside out.

Why did I let myself love you? Why do I feel the torture now? I could have been free. Truly free. Now you weigh me down, Moustafa. I am weighed down by your love, and it will suffocate me. She sobbed into her hands. *Weighed down by love. By an impossible love.*

* * *

"Mama," Ophélie said softly, entering her mother's bedroom. "Mama! Why are you crying? What is the matter?" She watched her mother brush the tears from her face, and then she rushed into her arms. "Oh, Mama! *Je t'aime!* My beautiful mother. Sometimes, when I wake up in the night, if I've had a bad dream, do you know what I do, Mama?"

Anne-Marie shook her head.

"I tiptoe into your room and kiss your cheek, and then I thank Jesus that we are here together. I can always go back to sleep after that. Knowing you are here."

She sat down in her mother's lap, wrapping her arms around Anne-Marie's neck. She did not like to see tears in her mother's eyes. There should be no more tears. "Why are you crying?"

Anne-Marie hugged her daughter tightly. "It is nothing, my precious little one. Mama is just tired. Sometimes, when I am tired, I forget how wonderful everything else is." She ran her fingers through Ophélie's hair.

Ophélie snuggled even closer. She loved the feel of her mother's fingers in her hair.

"I know why you are crying, Mama. You miss Moustafa, right?" Her mother looked down. "It doesn't hurt my feelings, Mama. I know you miss him." She studied her mother's face, thinking hard for something to say.

"When Papa came to get you in Algeria, didn't he show you the picture I drew him? The picture of the ponies?"

"I . . . no, I haven't seen it. Tell me about your picture, sweetheart."

"Well, I drew it when I was going to meet Papa for the first time. Well, not the first time, but the first time after I knew he was my father. I wanted to take him something, and when Bribri suggested a picture, I just saw it in my mind. Saw what I should draw. Ponies, different colored ponies. All running to Jesus. There was me and Bribri and Mother Griolet and Papa, all running, and then you, you were the prettiest pony of all. And behind you, there was Moustafa. He was behind you." She knitted her brow. "But I am sure he was coming. I saw it."

Anne-Marie smiled, but it looked to Ophélie as if tears were still in her eyes. What else could she say to make Mama feel better?

She took her hands and held them, as Bribri had done to her when she was sad. She looked straight into her mother's face. "Why don't we pray? When we are tired and afraid, Bribri says we must pray. She says that's when Jesus comes to our rescue. He loves to be strong for us when we are very weak." She frowned. "I think that is hard to understand, but I am glad that He said it. Now let's pray." She closed her eyes and waited. Then she opened one eye, squinting up at her mother, who had a faraway look in her eyes. "Mama! Close your eyes," she reprimanded. "And pray."

Anne-Marie lifted Ophélie's chin and brushed her fingers across the child's face. "I do not know how to pray, *ma chérie.*

176

I am sorry to disappoint you, but I don't know how."

"Oh! Is that all?" Ophélie exclaimed happily. "Well, that's no problem. I'll teach you. Just like Bribri taught me. It's very easy. You just say exactly what I say. Okay?" She closed her eyes again. "Are you ready?"

"Yes, dear," her mother said softly.

"Dear God," Ophélie said. After a moment's silence, she whispered, "Mama, you're supposed to say the same thing I say."

"Yes, Ophélie . . . only . . . "

"What?"

"Nothing. I will follow you. Go ahead."

"Dear God."

"Dear God."

Ophélie folded her little hands together, and in a voice full of innocent faith, she began to pray. "You see that Mama is tired and sad."

"You see that I am tired and sad."

"And You say that You are strong when we are weak."

"And You say that You are strong when we are weak."

"So please be strong for my mama now. Oh, please, Jesus. Oh, please, bring Moustafa back to Mama. And Papa too. Oh, please. I know You can do it. I know You can." She had forgotten to wait for her mother to copy her prayers, but when she peeked again, her mother's eyes were tightly closed and tears streaked down her face.

Ophélie hurried on with her prayer. "Please, God, make Mama happy again. Thank You so much for bringing her back to me. You listened when I prayed for Mama to come back. Please listen again. Amen."

She sat with her head buried in Mama's lap as her mother stroked her head. Sometimes, Bribri had said, sometimes the best thing is just to cry. So Ophélie let her mother cry while she prayed the same prayer over and over again in her mind.

Chapter 13

Eliane Cebrian reread the letter with the mayor's signature, then held it out for Anne-Marie to see. The government was promising the repatriating *pied-noirs* housing in the near future. Construction would begin immediately on the HLMs, the government housing. And loans were being offered to help the *pied-noirs* get on their feet.

Eliane sighed. News could be worse. The hotel that Anne-Marie had found for them on the west side of Montpellier was adequate and its owner sympathetic to *pied-noirs*. He provided them with two little rooms with an adjoining door and breakfast and dinner served at the hotel, all for a reasonable price. And the government promising housing. Things seemed brighter.

"I'm sorry I haven't been more help to you," Anne-Marie apologized. "But we had our hands full with the orphans last week."

"*Au contraire,* you've been of great help. This is so much better than Marseilles, I assure you."

"Well now." Anne-Marie sat down on the bed, and the mattress sank under her weight. She laughed. "You're right.

This isn't so bad. And you've got the little park across the street for the children."

"It's really fine, all things considered," Eliane agreed. "And with you and Ophélie here today, everything is just perfect. Shall we go outside?"

Ophélie, Samuel, and Rachel enjoyed a game of tag in the park, while Eliane strolled José. "There are Arabs everywhere in this neighborhood," she said. "Most have been here since the end of World War II. They came over to France as cheap labor and live in these HLMs."

"Are you afraid of them? Are they hostile?"

"No, not really. We just keep to ourselves and so do they. Classified as separate populations, living in our own little worlds. It makes me sad. I wonder if any of us will truly integrate into the French population."

"You mean like we were in Algeria before the war, a happy hodge-podge of people. Or at least we thought everyone was happy," Anne-Marie commented. "It's too early to tell what will happen. For now you are here, we are closer, and Rémi will be coming soon."

Eliane laughed a high, nervous laugh. "I don't know about that. He's wrapped up in saving children. You got a letter too, *n'est-ce pas?* They're sending the *harki* child. In my trunk, of all things!"

"Your trunk?"

"Didn't Moustafa say? Yes, they are smuggling him in a trunk, my trunk, filled with all our treasures. Well, I suppose the treasures won't be coming after all. Not all of them. But Rémi is sending the most important. The baby things, a few scrapbooks, and your father's will." She gave Anne-Marie a wry look. "And a young boy."

"I know you'll be happy to have a few things to make this place seem like home. But in a way, I've found it's almost freeing to have nothing."

"Yes," Eliane agreed. "I much prefer this life to the

absurdity of what's going on in Algeria. We may not have much, but at least the children are safe." She reached over and squeezed Anne-Marie's hand. "And pretty soon our men will be here too. You'll see."

Anne-Marie shrugged, and Eliane knew she did not sound very convincing.

* * *

Lodève was a small village west of Montpellier with a rich and secret past. From the sloping hills surrounding the town, Henri Krugler liked to look down on his adopted city. The thirteenth-century Cathedral of Saint-Fulcran in the center of town still displayed its Gothic tower and some of the original fortifications. The whole region surrounding Lodève was dotted with chateaux, ancient abbeys, and remarkable geological monuments dating back, some said, to the Neolithic period.

Five years ago, Henri Krugler had moved from a picturesque village in Switzerland to Lodève not in search of archeological ruins, but simply out of conviction. A pastor, a direct descendant of the Huguenots, proud of his heritage and undaunted by rejection, Henri had a dream straight from the heart of God.

No one had understood his move except the man himself. A widower with grown children, Henri needed another mission in life to give him a reason to wake up in the morning. Even the lush mountains of Switzerland had lost their charm when his Louise had died. And so he had prayed, and God had answered. Lodève. *Centre aéré.*

The small Protestant church he presided over in Lodève was home to no more than two handfuls of old people. The youth of the city were mostly Arabs. Lately several *harki* families had fled to the village, with more sure to come. Henri's dream was integration. Catholics with Protestants and Arabs. And the means was a *centre aéré,* a recreational center for children. All children. A place to draw families together. After two years of French paperwork, the center was ready to open, the dream ready to begin.

The townspeople, suspicious at first, loved the white-haired giant with the blazing eyes and the kind heart. He was a robust man, a man of endless energy and passion. With his white hair and white goatee, he resembled a huge mountain goat. The stooped Arab women smiled at him from behind their white scarves, and the fragile ancient *fidèles* at his church called him "Pastor" with the assurance and comfort that should anything befall them, he would be there.

It had not been out of the blue that God's finger had led him to Lodève. Years ago his friend, Captain Maxime Duchemin, had recommended the village. "A stone's throw from Montpellier, a perfect place to retire. Which is what I intend to do."

Henri Krugler did not like to think of Maxime's retirement. He shook his white head and muttered "retired unto the Lord." This was true. And it sounded somehow more hopeful than "murdered by the FLN," which was also true. And that made integrating anyone that had anything to do with the Algerian War into society in France a very delicate problem.

* * *

Hussein found Ali examining papers at his desk. "It is time for me to go. Everything is arranged," the boy stated.

"And your housemates?"

"Staying behind until Moustafa can convince his mother and sisters to leave. They hope to send other *harki* children along as well." He fished in his pocket. "Here is their address. Smack in the center of Bab el Oued."

Ali spun around in his chair. "You have everything you need? The guns, the explosives? You remember what I have taught you, Hussein?"

"Yes, sir," he whispered, cowering as Ali reached out and

grabbed the collar of his shirt. "I remember."

He did not need to ask any questions. He knew his mission. Destroy the Duchemin woman and her child and anyone else in the way. He tried to make his face look hard, set with hatred. But the thought that worried him broke forth. He cleared his throat and asked in his deepest voice, "And what shall I do when I have finished this mission?"

Ali released the boy and smiled. "Allah will guide you. Do not worry." He handed Hussein a wad of French bills. "This is all you will have. But if the work is well done, then you will see how well I can reward you."

"Yes sir."

Ali grabbed him again and pulled him close, so that Hussein inhaled the taste of Ali's rancid cigarettes. "You aren't afraid, boy? There are many younger than you who have already killed half a dozen people in broad daylight in this city." He softened his voice. "What could be easier than a few timely explosions in a peaceful little orphanage? It will be simple. No one will even know to be afraid." He burst into laughter. "They won't know to be afraid until it is all over and much too late. Go on now, my boy. Allah be with you."

* * *

There was no life left in the farmhouse with Eliane and the children gone. Rémi felt the house growing distant and cold around him, as if it were preparing itself for his departure. He watched out the window as Amar and Abdul continued harvesting the oranges. It had been a good year for them. The groves spread out in every direction, almost surrounding the small farmhouse. He had always felt a type of virility at the farm, with the fertile trees all around. Life had been good here.

But the nightmare had become reality. The end was blowing toward them like the fine, stinging sand from the Sahara that forced them to take shelter during a dust storm.

There was no shelter in Algiers. So everyone was leaving. All the *pied-noirs*. The engineers, the store owners, the doctors and nurses, the farmers like himself.

He recalled the scene at the airport yesterday where he had taken a neighbor who was fleeing with his family. Babies slept in boxes on the floor of the overcrowded terminal. Flies flitted on sleeping children's faces. Mothers cried. Suitcases supported the backs of the elderly. The wait was lugubrious.

The official limit for each traveler was two small suitcases. Rémi patted the heavy wooden trunk that sat in the den, where he worked on it day after day. The trunk was three feet high, four feet long, and two feet wide. Nobody would call it small.

Why didn't he leave now? What could he gain by staying and waiting by his window at night with a gun in his hand? In six weeks, Algeria would be independent. Then he would lose everything. Why wait for the inevitable?

Even now, many departing *pied-noirs* burned their belongings rather than leaving them to be looted by the Arabs. So this was how the war would end. Mass exodus, terror, flight, and a razed countryside. And every plot of land, Arab and *pied-noir* alike, stained by blood.

Glancing out the window again, Rémi saw David and Moustafa approaching. Relief flooded him as he opened the door and invited the men in. They declined drinks, and he read the determination in their eyes.

Rémi proudly displayed the trunk. "The boy will crouch in the center, knees tucked under him. I've made two boxes to fit on either side of him. They're filled with a few of Eliane's favorite things. When the trunk is closed, the boy can control the lock from the inside. So he will be able to free himself once it is dark and the ferry is at sea."

He pointed to little barred openings at the front and back of the trunk. "And the air holes are here."

Moustafa patted Rémi on the back. "It is good work." He stepped into the trunk and carefully lowered himself into a crouched position. "Yes, the boy will fit. He will have plenty of room. I think I might even make it for a few hours." He eyed David. "Good thing you're not an Arab. With those long legs, we'd never conceal you."

"I've written the address of the orphanage on the top and bottom of the trunk," Rémi continued. "Looks pretty convincing, *non?* An innocent trunk heading to Castelnau, France. But you must go to the right guard, the one my friend has paid. The others will never allow this monstrosity on the boat. Families are waiting for two or three days to get on.

"You must be there at precisely 9:30. He will be watching and take the trunk on." Then he added, "He has no idea, of course, what is inside."

Moustafa ran his hands over the large box. "This chest will carry a treasure, like a pirate's chest. A priceless treasure."

"One life. It is worth it," David stated.

"Of course it is worth it. I only wish I could climb in there too."

Rémi nodded. The *harkis* were slated to be killed. If he could help a few more, well then, perhaps he could make some sense out of the end of this war. The men standing before him still had some sort of hope in them. He did not want to extinguish that.

"And once the ferry leaves the port in Algiers, no one will care. He can let himself out and be inconspicuous. Then in Marseilles, he must simply hire a taxi driver to take him and the trunk to the train station. From there you say he will have someone to meet him in Montpellier."

"Yes," David confirmed. "He only needs to call them to give his time of arrival. They've already been told of the date."

Rémi looked skeptical. "You are sure this boy can handle it? I don't want Eliane's things lost. Or Captain Duchemin's will." He pointed to a thick envelope pressed tightly between two large photo albums.

"He is a responsible lad. Quiet and smart. He has nowhere

else to go. He is afraid, and for fear, he will do whatever we ask. Don't worry," Moustafa assured him.

"Good luck to you then," Rémi concluded. "I hope you won't have any trouble at the port."

"Pray for us," David said. "We'll let you know how it turns out. If it's successful, you may have a lot of work ahead of you, Rémi."

"I wouldn't mind a bit. Keeps my mind off other things."

The three men carried the trunk from the house to Marcus Cirou's waiting car. When they drove off, Rémi stood motionless, letting the dust blow into his eyes and settle on his clothes. He was not leaving yet, but time was running out. Soon it would be his turn. He brushed the sand from his eyes and whispered, *"Bon voyage."*

* * *

It was the way they had spent every evening for the past two-and-a-half weeks, and tonight the added advantage was that it eased the tension as they waited. With two hours before them, Moustafa and David took out the holy books and read. Because the Koran was approximately the same length as the New Testament, they had decided to read each through once, then compare their findings.

Tonight David questioned Moustafa. "So Islam includes some of the prophets of the Bible, yet maintains that Mohammed is the greatest. And wherever the Koran contradicts the other inspired books—that is the Pentateuch, the Psalms, and the Gospels—the Koran supersedes them all."

"Yes, this is what we believe."

"But what I don't see in the Koran is the provision for sin. What has Allah done for his people? How do you communicate with him? In Christianity, there is the sacrifice of the Christ— God who dies for mankind and resurrects Himself to conquer death."

"Islam is submission to the will of Allah. It is total

185

submission. The prayers five times a day show one's devotion."

"But where is the guarantee of eternal life?"

"The only guarantee is through *jihad.* Soldiers who die in a holy war are assured of their entrance into heaven."

"But, Moustafa," David argued, "can you accept a religion of laws and recitations? Where is the meaning?"

"There are many who find great meaning in the tenets of Islam. I, as you, have questions. I am still searching. You agree there is one true God, *non?*"

"Yes, I agree."

"But you see, for the Muslim, the Christians' belief in a trinity is polytheistic. Christians worship three gods."

"But that is not how they see it. One God with three distinct aspects."

Moustafa shrugged. "My mind is not on it tonight. We should get the boy ready."

"You are angry?"

"Not angry. Restless. Restless to know the way it will all turn out." He grimaced, then said sarcastically, "The will of Allah." Moustafa placed the books on either side of him. "Which holy book is right? These two books, these two testaments, are like Algeria. The Arabs hold the Koran, the *pied-noirs* the Bible. There are two cultures and two religions and two languages, and we are eternally separated by this. Who dares to step over the line?"

He picked up the Koran and held it out to David. "Algeria's end was inevitable. You cannot reconcile two cultures if one people feels repressed. The Europeans have been wrong. And I, my family, we too have been wrong. We chose the wrong side."

David saw Moustafa's face in the shadows, obscured. He could have been anyone. "You believed in *algérie française.* You fought for that."

"We were wrong. And now we have nowhere to go." He spoke fatalistically. "No hope for the future."

"You are thinking of Anne-Marie?"

Moustafa gave David a hopeless smile. "When am I not? When we were young, we did not see the invisible line that separated us. Then we grew up and acknowledged it. At least I did. She didn't need to fear it, for I was just a childhood friend. And then we had these months together." His eyes flashed. "To awake a forbidden love. And now she waits and worries.

"If only she had no hope, then she would forget me and build her life again. Why am I such a coward as to give her hope when the whole world separates us?" He reached in his pocket and took out an envelope. "But I can't help it. I have to let her know I love her, no matter what. I'm going to put it in the trunk."

"You are right to send it. I tell you, I'm no expert on faith, but there is something about this God of the Bible." David smiled, showing the dimple in his cheek. "He seems to have a penchant for love stories. For the most impossible ones." He winked at his friend. "No more worries tonight." David patted him on the back. "Call the boy. It is time."

* * *

When the men lifted the trunk from the back seat of the old Renault, Hussein felt butterflies dancing in his stomach. Fear and excitement mixed together, kneading themselves into a tight ball. Above all, he must not panic. He reminded himself that there was no fear of suffocation. The air holes were large and sufficient.

Already that afternoon he had sat in the trunk, with the top closed, for more than an hour. Then at Moustafa's bidding, he had slipped the small key into the inward lock and freed himself. The top had opened without difficulty.

But now, as they carried him, stopping and starting, bumping a railing, setting the trunk down only to pick it up again a moment later, Hussein felt queasy and nervous. Eyes were staring, he was sure, burning their questions through the little barred holes where, despite himself, he pressed his nose against them and stared back.

The crowds had grown since his last visit to the port nearly two months ago. People occupied every open space, making transporting a trunk almost impossible. With a thud, the trunk was placed in the midst of the quiet bedlam. A small girl came and sat on it, and her long, thin legs obscured the barred hole. Hussein shrank back, placing a thin blanket over the hole and holding it in place with his feet. He breathed deeply.

Why had they set him down in the middle of the crowd? Surely a guard would come and order the trunk removed, or worse, opened. In his lap, Hussein clutched his small oblong sports bag. Every grenade, each gun, and the explosives had been wrapped with minute attention within his underwear and shirts. Two small *plastiquages* were tucked in the pocket of a pair of pants.

David had insisted on going through his little bag of possessions. To empty his mini arsenal and conceal it in the apartment while David searched the bag, and then to rewrap each article, well, it had not been easy. He smiled to himself, pleased; he had done it. And now, if he could only sit still for another hour or two, then he could release himself from the prison. The prison that was bringing him to liberty. A twisted liberty.

Up went the trunk again, and this time David's voice came through the bars in a whisper. "Now's the time, my boy."

Hussein closed his eyes tightly, as if in not seeing, he would not be seen. He counted the seconds, listened to Moustafa talking in hushed tones and David saying gruffly, "Go on. Hurry!"

Then the trunk came to rest once more, and David was bending down beside it. "You're on the ferry. All went smoothly. I can't tell you exactly when to come out, but wait until at least an hour after the ferry pulls out of port. You will hear the announcement. You are near the toilets on the upper deck. Hide in there if need be. Cover yourself with the blanket and sleep. You are in no danger, now. Remember, call the orphanage from Marseilles. Take the taxi. And don't forget the trunk."

Hussein thought he heard David laugh before he whispered, "God be with you, Hussein."

Then he was alone. Waiting. His palms were sweaty and every muscle stiff. He rested his head on his bent knees, breathing deeply, forcing himself to remain calm. Telling himself that the wet tears that seeped into his pants were nothing more than a simple reaction to adventure.

* * *

Somehow, in the heavy, closed atmosphere of the trunk, Hussein had fallen asleep. When he awoke with a start, he momentarily forgot where he was. Immediately his claustrophobic quarters reminded him and he panicked. How long had he slept? Was it light outside? He listened, but could hear only the low rumble of the ship's engine.

He winced with pain as he tried to straighten one arm that had fallen asleep and was now numb. Eventually he succeeded in removing the small key from his shirt pocket. Waiting again until the tingling sensation left his hand, he turned the key in the lock.

He pulled back the latch and slowly pushed up the lid of the trunk. It rose easily. Hussein breathed in a mixture of sea air and gas. He strained to hear voices. Nothing.

He lifted the lid higher, until he could stand hunched over. Quickly he stepped out of the trunk, ignoring the stiffness in his joints. He almost stepped on a child's arm and realized that most people were sleeping outside, strewn across the boards of the boat like victims from a natural disaster. At any rate, Hussein thought grimly, they were victims.

He reached back into the trunk, retrieved his sports bag, and closed the top. His first thought was to find the toilets that David had said were nearby. That done, he observed some people, looking like shadows, huddled together by the railings. Many slept with their heads resting in others' laps or on suitcases.

The night air was cold, and Hussein quickly took the blanket from the trunk, secured the lock on the outside latch, and slid down beside it. He wrapped the blanket around him, covering his face. For some reason, the scene of this mass of *pied-noirs* made him want to cry. He swallowed, trying to force the lump out of his throat.

Freedom, a strange, knotty freedom, lay before him. He could not stop thinking about his mother. For days he had refused to let himself dwell on their last encounter. But now, with no recourse, it was safe to think of her. "Good-bye," he had whispered, petrified that he might tell her too much, yet desperate to see her one last time. "Pray for me, Mother. Pray that Allah's will be done."

He was small, and this endless black sky so big. But the task that lay before him seemed bigger than the universe itself. It was a task for Ali, and Ali had assured him that Allah would be there to guide. When the first wrinkles of light rose in gentle rays along the sea on the horizon, Hussein knelt and bowed his head. "There is no God but Allah," he recited the Shahadah in his mind, "and Mohammed is his prophet."

* * *

As the ferry docked in Marseilles, the *pied-noirs* stood confused and melancholic, waiting to debark. They looked like a huge flock of sheep, Hussein mused. Sheep without a shepherd. Sheep who would perish in the arid Sahara if left alone. Would they fare better in France?

The wait seemed interminable. When at last the people were freed onto the docks, they wandered aimlessly, with a lost, vacant expression in their eyes. Of the hundreds who got off the ferry, only a few handfuls were greeted by waiting friends and family at the port.

Hussein took it in as a spectator, telling himself that he was not lost. He had a job and a place to go. The thought brought a feeling of relief, if he did not think about what he had come to do. He clutched the sports bag closer to his chest.

A taxi. That was the first order of business. He squeezed through the jam of *pied-noirs*, pitying their predicament. He could not laugh like Ali. He had seen the blood that soaked the sidewalks in every *quartier* of Algiers. It was human suffering on a large scale, and Mother said that Allah wept over all human suffering. He must be weeping now, Hussein thought.

With his bag tucked under his arm, he left the dock. Hundreds of nameless *pied-noirs* stood resignedly in lines behind signs marked taxis. Hussein cursed. Never mind the taxi; he could reach the train station by foot. The map David had given him showed the station only twelve blocks away. It would do him good to walk, to break away from the suffocating masses, to use his muscles after the confinement of the trunk. The trunk! He considered it only for a moment. What did he care about an old trunk? He would be quite happy if he never saw his wooden prison again.

* * *

The docks at the Bassin de la Joliette in Marseilles had finally cleared of most of the *pied-noirs*. The way they arrived in France was a pitiful sight to see, mused the old *concierge* as he shuffled throughout the huge ferry, picking up a stray scarf, a lost mitten, an empty carton of cigarettes. People fleeing for their lives with nothing but a suitcase in their hand and a hollow, hopeless look in their eyes.

And what the devil was France supposed to do with them? Mighty fine fix that President General de Gaulle had gotten them into now. The papers claimed the president had not expected such an exodus. Already over 200,000 had left Algeria, with hundreds of thousands more expected to follow. And where would these *pied-noirs* end up? On the doorstep of

France. As far as he was concerned, they should have stayed in Algeria. That was their home, they had insisted all throughout the war. They might be French citizens, but everyone knew that the *pied-noirs* were different.

His trash sack was almost full, the fifth one from this ferry. He came near the toilets and paused for a breath, wheezing. "Now what do we have here?" He tapped a large wooden trunk with his knuckles. "*Bon sang,* how in the world did this get on the boat? And now someone's just left it here for me to deal with. Ignore the regulations and then leave the treasure." He laughed, thinking of "treasure," and tried to lift the lid. A small lock held it in place.

"And how in the heck am I gonna get this stinking box off the ferry? Break my back, hauling it around. *Punaise!*" He pulled on a handle, and the trunk slid awkwardly toward him. "Not too heavy, mind you," he grumbled, surprised.

Ten minutes later the old trunk sat on the dock, surrounded by overflowing bags of trash and lost clothing. It sat in the sun, waiting for someone to come and claim it. "Let it sit there till it rots," the *concierge* laughed. "Or maybe I'm supposed to pay the postage to get it to some little village in the Midi. Ha! Not me. Let it sit."

He flung a trash bag into a waiting bin. As he left the port, the *concierge* looked back to see the massive ferry preparing to return to Algeria. Another ferry loomed at sea, heading for harbor, ready to empty more of France's unwanted citizens onto French shores. And the old treasure chest, as he thought of it, sat alone on the empty dock. "*Punaise,* nobody's comin' back to get you," the *concierge* spat. "Must not be worth much."

Tomorrow they would haul it away to the warehouse where all the other lost luggage was stored. After the sailors had finished their looting, he suspected there wouldn't be much treasure left in that old trunk for anyone to claim anyway.

Chapter 14

The rest in Switzerland had done her good. Mother Griolet closed her eyes and saw the perfectly manicured green slopes outside the Cohens' chalet where the cows grazed, shaking their big, lazy heads at the flies, causing the thick bells that they wore around their necks to go *thunk, thunk.* She recalled the vivid colors, the crisp air, the landscape so perfect it looked as if an artist had painted it, covering up any faults with his paintbrush.

Two weeks there had brought back a little vigor to Mother Griolet's steps. Mostly, she felt her burden lightened. Her will had been changed, and M. Cohen had offered several suggestions for the orphanage. But her best idea lay within the hands of the fiery redhead who at any minute would burst into the office, full of enthusiasm and energy. She hoped that somehow God was preparing Gabriella for this encounter.

Confirming Mother Griolet's thoughts, Gabriella arrived moments later, out of breath, eyes shining. She fell into the chair and pulled her long, curly hair into a thick strand, lifting it off her shoulders. "Whew! I'm burning up. Those kids are wild at tag!"

She wiped a bit of perspiration from her forehead and straightened in her chair. "Sister Rosaline said you wanted to see me. Is everything all right? There aren't any problems with the new orphan who will arrive this afternoon?"

Mother Griolet smiled serenely. "No, my child. Jean-Louis has just left to get him. Everything is fine. I was just remembering the scenery of Switzerland, and thanking the Lord for that vacation. You girls have spoiled me."

"Oh no! Not a bit! Sister Rosaline says she should have forced you out years ago. You deserve a break every once in a while. I don't see how you keep going."

"Yes, well, it is precisely about this that I wanted to talk to you. About my future." The old nun leaned back in her black cushioned chair, touching her fingers to her lips. "I have realized recently. . . . The Lord has brought it to my attention through these last incidents that I have neglected to prepare myself and the orphanage for my eventual retirement."

She smiled, watching Gabriella for a reaction. The girl sat still, intense, a look of concern on her face.

"I have ignored the problem for many years because I didn't want to admit that I was, shall we say, mortal. Quite foolish of me. Disobedient. Selfish." Gabriella opened her mouth to protest, so Mother Griolet hurried on. "Don't defend me, child. I have been wrong. Proud. Thinking I was indispensable, God's answer for the orphans. But He is the One with the answers."

She looked away. "And I suppose I never really felt there was anyone capable of taking my place. I mean, anyone with the heart for the children. I was so afraid that the church would send a strict, rigid woman to replace me, and I would have no say in the matter. It terrified me. I have seen it happen before. An orphanage completely devoid of love. Of course, I was wrong to assume. Eventually I just chose to ignore the problem."

Gabriella interrupted. "But Sister Rosaline and Sister

Isabelle are perfectly capable!"

"Yes, they are. Please don't misunderstand me. They are wonderful women. But they cannot teach. And this orphanage has always been a school too."

"Oh," Gabriella mumbled. "I see."

"I have been praying for these weeks, asking the Lord to show me what to do." The nun hesitated, moistening her lips. "And I have come back again and again to you."

"Me?" Gabriella laughed. "Me! What do you mean, Mother Griolet?"

"I mean, *mon enfant*, that I want to ask you to consider becoming my apprentice, with the eventual goal of taking my place as director of the orphanage."

Gabriella's face went white. She stared at Mother Griolet with a look of total disbelief on her face. Silence invaded the room.

"I am sorry to shock you, Gabriella. Please, take all the time you need to consider it."

Gabriella turned to the nun, and Mother Griolet saw that she was dazed, a hundred questions running through her mind. "Me, the director of the orphanage? But that's impossible! I'm not Catholic. And I'm certainly not a nun and, and excuse me for saying it, but I don't want to be one. I'd make an absolutely awful nun! And I'm only twenty-one. I haven't finished school. My parents would, well, they might not approve of me leaving my studies. And as for teaching, well, I enjoy it, but I've only had two years of studies in Dakar. This is my first practical experience—"

"Hold on, dear! Slow down." The old nun chuckled. "You sound like Moses in front of the burning bush. My, wasn't he full of excuses?" She stood and came around her desk, placing her hands on Gabriella's shoulders. The young woman looked up at the old nun, her blue eyes full of questions.

"My child, do not be afraid. I would not throw this in your lap all at once. You would be my apprentice for the next year, maybe two, learning the ropes. A *stage,* you know. How do you Americans say it? Ah yes, an internship. A paid internship. We will have time to discuss the finances involved in such an arrangement later. At the same time, you could finish your teaching degree at the Faculté des Lettres in Montpellier. Get your teaching degree and let me train you at the same time."

She saw that Gabriella was not at all convinced. "Dear child, God will provide. He has always provided in the past. Perhaps I am wrong, perhaps it is not you He has chosen. All I ask is that you consider it. Ask the Lord what He wants of you. Do not be afraid to tell me no. But before you answer at all, I simply ask that you talk to Him about it."

Gabriella frowned. "Mother Griolet, I'm not sure I will know what He says. I am not afraid to ask, but how can I be sure that what I hear will be from Him?"

"Trust, Gabriella. God does not change. Neither does His Word. Through all the changes in our lives, He does not change. He is truth. Seek Him. He is perfectly trustworthy."

"And what if He says yes and I say no? What if I don't want it?"

"Trust. The God who made Moses, who had been raised as an Egyptian and did not even know the one true God, into a dynamic leader of God's people, that God is perfectly capable of convincing you of His will, if you listen. He is also perfectly capable of redirecting a stubborn old nun."

In those few minutes, Gabriella's whole appearance changed. Worry lined her face, and her shoulders slumped as if a real weight had been placed on her back. "Why are there so many decisions in life? Why won't they just go away and leave me alone for a while?"

"Shh, now, my child." Mother Griolet caressed Gabriella's hair, and the young woman rested her head in the nun's skirts. "We will talk again soon about all your fears. For now, let's leave it with Him. Shall I pray for you? For us?"

Gabriella nodded, her head still bent, and Mother Griolet

prayed. "Holy Father, today we humbly ask that You show us Your will for St. Joseph's and for Gabriella. May nothing I have said be of consequence in her life, if it is not from You. Guide Gabriella..." She paused. "And our dear David. You call us in the midst of our humanity to do things that are beyond us. Help Gabriella discern Your will. Amen."

Gabriella rose slowly to leave, still in a sort of trance. *"Ne t'en fais pas,"* Mother Griolet whispered. "Do not worry. Only trust."

She shut the door as Gabriella left the office, then stood for a moment in the middle of the small room. The faces of the orphans smiled down at her from the walls. Hundreds of faces. So many, many years ago, when she had been a young woman, she had stepped into a calling that left her scared and unsure. But God had been faithful every step of the way. "Teach her to trust You again, even more fully, Lord," Mother Griolet prayed.

She took the *santon* off the shelf, brushing away the dust. The clay figure, ever bent in her burden, had nonetheless an expression of bright determination on her wrinkled face. Mother Griolet thought of the beautiful redheaded American and chuckled to herself. Gabriella was right. She would make a poor nun. "But that is not what I am asking," Mother Griolet said softly, replacing the *santon* on the shelf. "I am only asking her to be herself. That will be quite enough for this old orphanage, I am sure."

* * *

The balding, heavyset old man who met Hussein at the train station wore a foolish grin on his face. *He would not be smiling if he knew why I am here,* Hussein thought. The boy said nothing. He must act polite and very, very thankful, oozing appreciation. But not too happy. There must be grief in his eyes too. It was a role for an actor, he thought, not a fourteen-year-old boy.

"Well, we are certainly glad to see you," the old man was

saying. "I believe they said your name is Hussein?"

The boy nodded.

"Good. I'm M. Vidal. Pleased to meet you, Hussein. You'll find the orphanage is a bit crowded—a mixture of French children and *pied-noirs* and, of course, *harki* children like yourself."

He talked on and on in the dullest voice. Hussein hung his head sullenly, glancing up at the man from time to time to nod or mumble an answer to a question. All the while he took careful note of every detail of information that the man provided.

When they arrived at the orphanage, M. Vidal explained that the other children were in class, and led Hussein across a courtyard that was enclosed by buildings. "Here is the boys' dorm. Your cot is there in the corner, right beside Hakim's. You'll like the boy. An Arab, like you." The old man rubbed his chin. "How old are you, Hussein?"

"Fourteen."

"Ah, fourteen! Just like Hakim. Really. Would never have guessed from your size. . . . " M. Vidal grew flustered, as everyone did when they realized that they had mistaken him for a much younger child. Hussein wished the boring old man would leave him alone.

"You must be tired. Perhaps I should let you rest?"

"Yes, that would be good. *Je suis vraiment crevé.* Exhausted."

"Yes, well that's to be expected." He rubbed his bald head. "Hmm. I see you've brought a few things with you. You can keep them right inside this dresser. I'll tell Mother Griolet that you're here. Someone will be over in just a moment."

"*Merci, Monsieur,*" Hussein grumbled. "It was very kind of you to come and get me."

"*Pas de quoi.* Good luck, my boy. I'll be seeing you around."

As soon as M. Vidal left the dormitory, Hussein opened

every drawer in the dresser. They were filled with clothes. He cursed, then laughed. Extra clothes meant extra hiding places for his weapons. He started to unpack his sports bag, then hesitated, wondering if the nuns around this place checked through the kids' belongings.

The room was crowded with eight bunk beds and three cots. Each bed had an old mismatched dresser beside it. A few of the dressers were really oversized trunks. Hussein thought of the trunk left on the ferry. Maybe it would have been a good idea to bring it after all. Too bad.

He walked into the hall. A bathroom with three shower stalls and several toilets and urinals was just outside the main room. Beside the bathroom were two other rooms, their doors locked. At the end of the hall, he found the girls' bathroom and dormitory.

As he headed back into the boys' dorm, he saw an old nun approaching across the courtyard. Quickly he emptied the contents of one of his drawers into another and stuffed his sports bag into the first, sitting down on his cot as she entered the dorm.

"*Bonjour*, Hussein," she huffed, out of breath. "God be praised, you are here. I'm Mother Griolet, the director of the orphanage. I hope you will be comfortable here. Sister Rosaline has put some things in the drawers for you." She walked toward the dresser.

"Yes, I already saw. Thanks," he answered quickly.

"Well, fine. Now if you find you need anything else, you just let one of us know. The children are just finishing up afternoon classes. They're eager to meet you. Would you mind coming with me now?"

Obediently, Hussein followed the old nun through the courtyard and into the basement of the building that M. Vidal had called the parsonage. In the classroom, he stared at the children, counting silently to himself. Over forty of them. Kids of every age. Each one rose and introduced himself. Hussein met eyes with the Arab boy called Hakim and almost smiled, before he caught himself. He wasn't here to make friends.

"Ophélie Duchemin," a little girl was saying. The carbon copy of her mother. A cute kid with pigtails. Hussein felt sick to his stomach.

When all the introductions had been made, Mother Griolet dismissed the children for afternoon play. "The children have thirty minutes of *récréation* before they do their chores. Dinner is at seven. Would you like to rest for a while?"

"Yes, *merci*. I would like to be alone."

"Go ahead then. Tomorrow I'll fill you in on our rules, chores, the way school works."

Hussein hung on the edge of the courtyard, watching the kids at play. From the corner of his eye, he saw a young woman waving at him. Leaving a group of children, she walked over to him. Anne-Marie Duchemin. The emaciated woman he had last seen at the port in Algiers looked healthier. Healthy was the polite way to put it. His friends in the Casbah would call her a *nana*. A real number. Shining black hair, and dark, bright eyes, with thick lashes and full, parted lips. And, he thought, moving his eyes down her body, a shape that any teenage boy could not help but notice.

"Hussein! You're here!" He stiffened as she took his shoulders and kissed him on the cheek. "I'm so glad you made it."

"Yeah, me too," he mumbled. "Thanks for all your help."

She ruffled his hair. "Welcome to St. Joseph's. I think you'll like it here." She turned and called out, "*Coucou*, Ophélie! Come over here and meet Hussein."

The pretty little girl skipped across the courtyard to her mother. Hussein longed to disappear. If he didn't know them, if they were just things to be eliminated, then he could do it.

"I've already met Hussein, Mama, in class." The child beamed up at him. "Mama said she met you when she was leaving Algeria. I'm glad you're here." She touched his arm

200

with her delicate hand, and suddenly her big, brown eyes
looked imploring.

"Did you see them? Papa and Moustafa? How are they?
Please, how are they?"

Again the sick feeling overtook him, and his skin felt
clammy all over. "Fine. Moustafa and David are fine," he
stammered. They wanted more details, he could see in their
eyes. His head was swimming. More details about the men
who had sheltered him and arranged his escape. More details
about the men he had betrayed to Ali.

"I feel sick," he moaned, and he didn't have to act to
make it seem real. "I need to lie down."

"Oh, of course, of course." Anne-Marie touched his head
with her warm hand. "How rude of us. You must be completely
worn out. Do you want me to show you to the dormitory?"

"No, thanks, I've already seen it." Hussein left, almost
running, hearing Anne-Marie Duchemin explaining to her
daughter, "Honey, it's all right. He'll tell us about Papa and
Moustafa later."

On his cot, Hussein fell facedown and wept. He hated
himself for his tears. He had to be brave, like his Arab
brothers. Not a coward! If only they wouldn't be kind to him
here. And not ask him questions about those young men.

He knelt on the floor beside his cot. "There is no God but
Allah, and Mohammed is his prophet."

He collapsed again on the cot, but his head was still
spinning, his stomach cramping. He made it to the boys'
bathroom, and, hanging his head over the sink, he vomited.

* * *

Gabriella's head ached. The pain had begun near the nape
of her neck, working upward until her whole head was
throbbing. She lay on her bed, the shutters closed, in
complete darkness. Feeling nauseated, she had declined
dinner with Mme Leclerc, Stephanie, and Caroline. A

migraine, Mme Leclerc had assured her with several *oh là làs* to go with it.

In the darkness of her room, Gabriella relished the silence. The clanking dishes, the silverware being set on a plate, the burst of laughter from the girls around the dinner table, every sound had been like a shrill, piercing siren meant to drive her mad. But now the meal was over, and the girls were studying quietly in their rooms.

"You're just worried," Caroline had commented matter-of-factly as she gave Gabriella two aspirins. "You're doing too much—with those orphans and teaching David's class." She raised her eyebrows when she pronounced the word David. "You're just worn out, that's all. You should have some fun."

Gabriella groaned, recalling her shapely blond roommate's words. Maybe Caroline was right. Maybe she should just hop a train with the other girls in the program and see the sights of France. Paris had been a real break. Even without David, Paris had been fun.

But now, responsibility was crushing her. Why, why in the world had Mother Griolet asked her to be her apprentice? It angered Gabriella, as if her youth had been stolen in those brief words, and a weight much too heavy for her dropped with a thud on her shoulders.

There were certain advantages, of course. Agreeing to the internship would ensure that she would still be near David. That was comforting. Otherwise, in two short months, she was planning to fly to the States with her family for their furlough, and she might never see him again. If only he would come back from Algeria so she could know his thoughts. At any rate, taking on such a job just to be close to David was surely pretty pitiful reasoning.

She tried to sleep, but her mind was racing. She flicked on the lamp by her bedside. The light made her wince with pain. She took her Bible from the night stand and wondered where she should read to find the answers to her questions.

She fumbled through the pages, reading from her favorite psalms, but her head hurt too much to concentrate.

Mother. Mother could help her with the answers. For all these months, Gabriella had turned to Mother Griolet as a type of spiritual mentor. But now, she needed advice from someone else. Someone who was removed from the situation.

She slipped out of bed, got a piece of stationery and a pen, then cuddled once again under the thick comforter. She started with news of the orphans and Anne-Marie. Then she cautiously mentioned David, knowing from her mother's letters that she was already worried about their relationship. Finally she mentioned the proposal by Mother Griolet.

"Mother, I am so confused! How can I know if God wants me here in this little village? It seems confining, crazy. I'm not patient enough to deal with the children all the time. And there is so much else I want to do and see. Maybe that is selfish. If I say yes, will I regret it later? And if I say no, will I feel guilty that maybe I missed God's will?"

She answered her own question. *No one has said I would have to do this for the rest of my life. Maybe I could have a contract for a few years. Until someone more suitable can be found.*

Suddenly she knew what Mother would do: make a list of the pros and the cons. Her head was still throbbing as she wrote furiously in the column under "cons": too much responsibility, not what I had dreamed I'd be doing, unable to finish education, too confining with the kids, far from family, too young, too inexperienced, not Catholic or a nun. The list went on and on. In spite of her headache, she laughed. It was easy to see that the cons would win out.

But then she thought of Moses. Well, yes, he had balked at the idea. Surely his list of cons had been longer than hers. Yet in the end, he had gone because he was convinced that God had called him to the task.

But he had heard the living God speak to him, she

reminded herself. Seen the burning bush and his rod changed to a snake. And his hand made leprous. He had had all those signs. It would be easy to know what God wanted with all those signs!

Gabriella put down her pen and prayed silently. "I don't want this. It's too big, too hard, too *everything* for me. But You're the One who is in control, and I do trust that You see beyond my feeble reasoning. Show me, Father. In Jesus' name. Amen."

She picked up the pen again and wrote under the side of the page marked "pros": I would have to depend on God because it is too hard, I would be close to David, I work well with children, I like the Sisters, Mother Griolet would be here to train me. By the time she finished the list, an entire page was filled.

She thought of her mother. She had left comfort and a promising future to follow her father to the lost country of Senegal when she was barely on the brink of womanhood. Her mother's life had been hard, painful, isolated. But she knew what Rebecca Madison would say to all that. "Phooey! When you are doing what God has called you to do, there is something that goes way beyond all the trappings of the world. It's the beauty of sacrifice. I can't explain it, Gabriella. You'll have to discover it yourself."

She leafed through the pages in her Bible until she came to the Gospel of Mark, chapter 10. Verses 29 and 30 were underlined in pen, and out to the side was written *Mother's promise from You when she left for Senegal.*

Gabriella looked at the words, blurred at first, until they came into focus. It was Jesus who was speaking. "Verily I say unto you, there is no man that hath left house, or brethren, or sisters, or father, or mother, or wife, or children, or lands for My sake and the gospel's, but he shall receive an hundredfold now in this time, houses, and brethren, and sisters, and mothers, and children, and lands, with persecutions; and in the world to come, eternal life. But many that are first shall be last; and the last first."

Already she had received in nine short months so much. Mother Griolet, David, Ophélie, the Sisters, Anne-Marie, and all those little orphans. A hundredfold. She closed the Bible, feeling a warm peace running through her being. When she turned off the light, her headache was gone.

* * *

In the middle of the heavy Senegal night, Rebecca Madison woke with a distinct feeling that she must pray for her daughter in France. She fell to her knees beside her cot, careful not to wake her husband, whose large chest rose and fell peacefully under the sheets.

Decisions. That was the word that came to mind. Rebecca imagined Gabriella agonizing over her relationship with the American teacher. She thought of her daughter surrounded by orphans, teaching, telling stories. That was her gift, with children. Gabriella had the knack, more so than Jessica and Henrietta.

Rebecca had no idea exactly what Gabriella was struggling with, but she was certain God had awakened her for a good reason. For an hour she knelt by the bed praying silently for Gabriella, remembering all the while her own fears when she was young and contemplating the future.

As she climbed back into bed and snuggled beside her husband, she no longer felt worried. This God had proven time and time again that she could trust Him with her life and the lives of those she loved. She fell asleep, reassured.

Chapter 15

A heavy fog hung over the runway as the small aircraft touched the ground in Algiers. Roger Hoffmann breathed a sigh of relief. At least he had made it into this war-ridden country without a bomb exploding within the plane's cabin. He had read enough of the gruesome details of the final showdown between the OAS and the FLN to expect the worst.

Yet despite all he had read, the atmosphere inside the airport shocked him. Hundreds, maybe thousands, of *pied-noirs* waited for their planes, sitting on suitcases, pacing aimlessly on a small patch of floor. The expression on their faces showed sorrow mixed with relief. There was not an Arab in sight.

The smells of tobacco and perspiration caught in the muggy afternoon air, suffocating Roger as he made his way through the crowds. *My God,* he thought. *These are the saddest looking people on the face of the earth.* He had not left the airport, but already it told the story of a country destroyed by war. Human misery and displaced citizens were common to Roger Hoffmann. Thirty years as a diplomat had opened his eyes to many things in many countries.

But this was Algeria! Eight years ago, when he had lived among the people, the country was in peace. Of course, the grumbling was becoming louder. Rumors of a small terrorist group among the Algerians had spread. But no one had imagined it would grow and gain such force as to become the powerful FLN of today. He had left at the right time, he told himself. Before the destruction.

Outside the airport, lines of cars were stopped in traffic, ready to deposit the *pied-noirs* and their few belongings. The brief telegram that he had received in Washington just before departure instructed him to look for a red Peugeot by the northernmost exit. With suitcase and briefcase in hand, he strode confidently through the crowds, ignoring the stares. A six-foot-four American in a pin-striped business suit would stick out anywhere in Algeria. Still, his hands trembled involuntarily as he set down his luggage and waited, trying to look inconspicuous. He hoped the negotiations would go quickly. Washington would look tranquil after his stay in this Sheol.

Ten minutes later, the Peugeot appeared at the appointed location. Roger half expected a turbaned Arab to emerge from the car with a machine gun in hand, opening fire on the restless throng of people. No one got out. As he approached the Peugeot, the front window was lowered. A smartly dressed, middle-aged Arab nodded to Roger.

"*Bienvenue dans notre pays.* Welcome, M. Hoffmann," he said politely. He nodded to the back seat. "Please get in."

"*Merci,*" Roger replied. Experience had taught him to be on his guard. In a moment's time, he had sized up the situation. Simply the driver and the older Arab. The revolver concealed cleverly within his suit jacket was enough insurance for the ride. He opened the car door, placed his luggage beside him, and pulled the door closed. The Arab turned around. His skin was the color of weak tea, his eyes dark and hard.

"We are very glad that you arrived safely, M. Hoffmann. Allow me to introduce myself. My name is Ali Boudani. I am looking forward to working with you in the next few weeks."

"Likewise," Roger answered. Boudani smiled, revealing two rows of yellow, crooked teeth. Otherwise, he was a handsome man. He kept his poker face, radiating confidence and calm. No Arab would see him tremble. But the revolver reassured him, nonetheless.

* * *

Five Arabs welcomed Roger Hoffmann to their headquarters in the Casbah. The headquarters consisted of a twenty-by-thirty-foot room concealed behind a cement wall within the recesses of a crumbling apartment. A low round table surrounded by richly embroidered cushions sat in the center of the room. After handshakes and official greetings, the men sat down on the thick cushions.

"I hope you enjoy *couscous*, M. Hoffmann," Ali Boudani commented.

"Indeed, I do." He had been looking forward to such a meal. The typically Arab dish was a favorite of Roger's, and he smiled unconsciously, thinking of steaming lamb and vegetables heaped on top of the tomato-tinged wheat grain.

Two women, their heads covered with scarves, brought out an overflowing enormous round porcelain bowl. He understood the etiquette immediately. They ate from the "common bowl," as it was called, each dipping his spoon into the mound of couscous that sat in front of him.

The men ate hungrily, loudly, speaking in Arabic. Roger followed little of the conversation. As the bowl was taken away and a green salad brought out, Ali Boudani spoke in French, addressing him. "The FLN has appreciated the aid your country has given to our refugees during the war. It has not gone unnoticed."

"I can assure you that the American aid will continue after independence."

"Very helpful, yes. Independence is only five weeks away."

Ali raised his eyebrows, and the other Arab men nodded approvingly.

A bowl full of large oranges was set on the table, and the men attacked them with eager, greedy hands. Ali held one up to Roger. "See what beautiful fruit we produce in this land? We have much to offer the world."

Roger began cautiously peeling the fruit, as if with one wrong move, it might explode on his plate. "I have several proposed plans to present to you during these few days together."

"Excellent."

"And several U.S. executives are ready to negotiate prices on oil and gas in the southern Sahara."

"Yes, we have heard. The oil is most attractive to you Westerners." He bit into the orange, and its juice sprayed forth in a little gust. Ali laughed.

The meal ended with a rich cake for dessert. Roger was glad to finish his piece, thankful that the meal was almost over. He was beginning to feel the time difference.

Ali wiped his face with a cloth napkin. "Tomorrow morning we will meet again. For now, I am sure you are quite tired from your trip. Mohemmed will show you to your room."

Roger did not protest. He was exhausted, his head spinning from an evening in Arabic and French. The other four Arabs rose, bowed slightly, and filed through the door that transformed into a kitchen cupboard as it swung outward.

"You understand that secrecy is of utmost importance," Ali confided, as they stood alone in the hidden room. "Many things in this country are best kept secret. Our little negotiations included."

"Of course."

"Well then," he said, pushing the door outward, "we'll meet again tomorrow. Good evening, M. Hoffmann. A pleasure to see you here." He gestured to the elderly Arab who waited by the entrance to the apartment. "Mohemmed, M. Hoffmann is ready. Oh, and M. Hoffmann. I am sure you recognize the . . . shall we say . . . the risk of wandering around the Casbah alone? You are a bit conspicuous."

"Don't worry," Roger spoke smoothly. "I'll stay put until one of your friends comes to get me."

"Very good. *Bonsoir.*"

Roger followed Mohemmed through the whitewashed apartment and into the alleyways of the Casbah. He was sure he would not sleep. There was much too much to think about. Images of what he had seen driving from the airport flashed before him. Hollowed-out buildings, carcasses of cars that had been bombed, shattered glass in the window fronts of neighborhood stores, filthy slogans painted on the sides of buildings, empty apartment buildings. Algiers was a skeleton of what it had been. The Algerians would need plenty of aid from the U.S. if they hoped to build it back. Plenty of American aid.

* * *

"You cannot simply murder the man, Ali," the older Arab insisted, talking in a frenzy. "We must do nothing to endanger our valuable relationship with the Americans. You are crazy."

Ali, who had displayed a dignified, refined behavior throughout the evening, now felt the anger in him building. "Shut up, Mohemmed!" he screamed. "Who are you to tell me what to do! You are nothing to the FLN!" He paced back and forth in his cubicle, inhaling on his cigarette and then tossing it to the floor. "Anything can happen in Algiers. Anything. The blame will not fall on the FLN, rest assured! Do you think I am stupid? Have I worked all these years to gain the respect of my people, only to ruin it in one afternoon? Of course not." He removed another cigarette from his shirt pocket. "The OAS will do the job for me. Ha! Don't worry. Timing is the word. Simply a question of timing. Your job is to find the men in Bab el Oued. Leave the rest to me."

He flipped off the lamp and struck a match. Lighting the

cigarette, he inhaled. The cigarette glowed orange in the dark. "Leave the rest to me," Ali whispered again, letting the smoke curl upward into the older Arab's face. "See you tomorrow."

* * *

When Gabriella's second letter made its way across the sea and into David's hands, he devoured every word, hungry for some happy news. He thought of her standing before him, her creamy white skin, the bright blue eyes and long, blond lashes, and her fine, small nose. He imagined her shaking her thick red hair, sending it dancing in every direction. He imagined these things, and his heart ached.

Life came through Gabriella's erratic penmanship. On the first page she wrote slowly, neatly. A few drops of rain had blurred several words. Then her writing erupted into excited scribble on the onionskin paper as she described the paintings in the Jeu de Paume, her delight at seeing Monet's poppies and the sculptures in Rodin's museum. He closed his eyes and sighed. To hold her and soak in her life, her exuberance. How he needed her! Algiers was dying in front of his eyes, and David felt as though a part of his soul was dying with it.

He read her words and let himself be carried away by her enthusiasm for Paris. Each scene floated off the page and played in his imagination. It moved him that she had caught every thought and detail and saved it for him. She was right. He *had* been there with her.

He read her sonnet, and the teacher in him nodded approval. A simple sonnet, a promising example for a future poet. And a window into her soul. She was struggling with her emotions, wondering what was next. *I know what is next for us, Gabby. I hope I know.*

As she described the Vivaldi concert in the Sainte Chapelle, a chill ran through him. He had seen it in his mind's eye. He had been there with her. Was this a meeting of souls? Was this knowing someone intimately?

He finished the letter and started it again. He needed to feel the hope that radiated from Gabby's writing. Hope was fleeing fast in Bab el Oued. Death was stalking the streets. He wished he could paint the blood of the lamb on the door posts, wished that Almighty God would promise him protection, as He had the Israelites. He wished this God would promise protection for Moustafa too, from whatever death angel had landed on this country.

Last week it had been the postmen killed. Ten of them. This week the *boulangers*. Shot down in cold blood. No one was safe. He heard the clock ticking in his mind. A few more weeks, a month at best. And if they did not leave by July 2, the clock in the bomb would stop ticking for Moustafa, and his life would simply be blown away.

David picked up his pen and started a reply. What could he promise her?

We must be out before July the second. Of that I am sure. Pray that I can convince Moustafa to leave. His mother and sisters may leave with other harki *orphans soon. That will mean only his brother remains. Rémi Cebrian is helping us. Please pray for us.*

Gabby, dear girl! I am afraid that I am having a hard time trusting in your God over here. Nothing makes sense. Pray that I will understand and, if it is not to be understood, that I will not persecute myself with trying to figure it out. . . .

Life is heavy and morose here. I wish you could see it, and I am so glad you cannot. Do you know what a man looks like when his throat has been slit? Or a café after a bombing? It is people's bodies in the wreckage. You vomit and you curse and then gradually you harden yourself so that you can simply survive. That is all these people want. Any of them. Arab and pied-noir. They simply want to survive. Let the nightmare be over. Survive.

He was sorry for the anger and bitterness that had crept

212

into his letter. He changed the subject.

> *By now Hussein is among you. I can't imagine much of a future for him in France, but at least he will survive. That is something.*
>
> *You say you have enjoyed teaching Hugo. Have the girls written their essays yet? Final exams are coming soon. Another month and the girls will be gone. Have them write on the dignity of human suffering seen in* Les Misérables. *Write on it, Gabby.*

It scared him to think that school was almost over for her. What was she planning next? They had never discussed it. Never had a chance to see past that blissful, fragile moment when they acknowledged their love.

> *I am coming back as soon as I can, Gabby.*

He wanted to add: *And the only prayer I can pray is that you will wait for me.* But that was not fair. He could not ask her to wait when he himself had no idea what was next.

David signed the letter with a heavy heart. Too many unanswerable questions. Waiting. It had always been for him the hardest part.

* * *

The whole neighborhood of Bab el Oued had dried up like a withered vine. With the massacre of *pied-noirs* at the end of March, the dream of *algérie française* had died. Now what was left of the *pied-noir* population huddled inside their apartments, terrified of what would come next. That news had pleased Ali, Mohemmed mused.

It was late afternoon when the old Arab crept through the silent streets with a young Arab girl at his heels, following him like a faithful puppy. It was not a safe time for an Arab to roam through Bab el Oued, but Mohemmed knew Ali too well to argue. He was paid to obey orders. A quick visit to make sure Hussein's information was good was all that Ali requested. The child went along to lend credibility to his task.

He found number 28 on the second floor of a nondescript building that sat in the worst section of Bab el Oued. He knocked quickly on the door, eyeing the child. "It's almost time for you to play your part."

A middle-aged man, pudgy with greasy gray hair, answered the door. He looked at the two visitors suspiciously. "What do you want?"

"Please, sir," the young girl pleaded. "Please let us in. I am a daughter of a *harki*. Please! This is my grandfather. Hussein gave us this address."

The stocky little man opened the door reluctantly, looking about the hall. "Come in. Just wait here in the hall."

Mohemmed patted the child on the head approvingly. Presently a tall man, of striking resemblance to Roger Hoffmann, strode into the hall. He was no more than twenty-five, almost as tall as his father, black hair and eyes, with the same angry, confident look on his handsome face. There was no question in Mohemmed's mind. This was David Hoffmann.

"Yes?"

The child repeated her plea. The young man's face did not change.

Mohemmed cleared his throat and bowed slightly. "Sir. Please forgive the imposition. We have taken a great risk in coming here. For me, I will stay and face my fate. But for the girl. For Fatima. She deserves a chance like Hussein. He has told us how good you were to him. He thought perhaps—"

"Who has he told?" David demanded.

"Us. Only us."

"I told him to speak to no one. I do not believe you."

The child looked up at Mohemmed, worried. The old Arab spoke softly, "You must understand, sir. They have been closest friends. For years. Do not be angry with the boy. He has not told others. He hesitated to tell us, but you must understand. We are like family."

Fatima grabbed David's wrist and began to sob. "Please,

Monsieur! Please take me to France! They will kill me here! Please give me a chance, like Hussein. He said you were kind. He said it!"

Mohemmed watched David Hoffmann closely, and noted with satisfaction that his face softened. Fatima was a pretty child, almost ten, already skilled in the ways of her real grandfather, Ali Boudani. She could be very convincing. She would grow up to be a beautiful, dangerous woman, Mohemmed thought.

"Let me think about it. How can I reach you?"

Mohemmed quickly spoke. "Do not trouble yourself, *Monsieur*. May we call again in a few days? Would that give you enough time to decide?"

David rubbed his chin, his eyes flashing angrily. "Two weeks. I'll expect you in the afternoon. Good-bye."

He showed them into the corridor and closed the door. Mohemmed squeezed the young girl's hand and smiled. But they did not say a word until they were safely out of the neighborhood and climbing back through the alleys of the Casbah.

* * *

Ophélie saw many things that she never spoke about. Her life had taught her to observe and keep quiet. Even now, in the safety of the orphanage, even with so many who loved her, she did not always reveal what she saw.

She watched the new boy, Hussein, carefully. He was not a handsome boy. His dark hair was wiry and unkempt, his nose flat and wide. He had large, round eyes and thick lashes. Mama said he was Hakim's age, but he looked much younger. Perhaps he was ashamed of his size, Ophélie concluded. He did not seem one bit happy to be in France, even though Mama said he had begged her to take him with her at the port.

He kept to himself and only spoke when directly asked a question. Even then he would turn his eyes down and give a one-word response. He needed a friend, Ophélie decided, and she was determined to be that friend.

She sat beside him at supper and smiled brightly. "How are you today, Hussein?"

She watched his face darken. "*Ça va,*" he mumbled.

"Are you very mad at me, or is it just because you are in France?"

He looked up at her, surprised. "Mad at you? No, it's not that."

"Don't you want to make friends?"

He nibbled a piece of bread. "I don't need anyone."

"Oh." She furrowed her brow, thinking. He was a very stubborn boy! "Would it make you very angry to tell me about my papa and Moustafa? I miss them so much, and I know you have seen them. Could you just tell me that? It doesn't mean we'll be friends. Please."

He glanced at her out of the corner of his eye and scowled. "Yeah, I guess." He wiped his plate clean with the bread, then stuffed it into his mouth. Ophélie waited quietly as he chewed and swallowed.

"They're okay. David and Moustafa are okay." His voice caught, and he took a drink of water.

Ophélie smiled brightly. "Did Papa show you the cross I gave him? And the picture of the ponies? Did he say anything about them?"

"We didn't talk much."

"But did they say anything at all about when they will be coming back? Surely they said something."

Hussein lifted his eyes and stared at her with a tortured face. He looked angry and sad and afraid. "Can't you see I don't know anything? I told you we didn't talk much!" He stood up abruptly, picked up his tray and after depositing it, left the dining hall.

He made her afraid. But more than that, she felt sorry for Hussein. As she put up her tray and walked into the courtyard, she whispered a prayer, "Help me be his friend, God. He really needs a friend."

* * *

Hussein fell on his cot, breathing deeply. Why did that kid have to be so darn persistent? And cute? She was bright and sympathetic and years ahead of herself in her heart. He didn't want to like her. He had to hate her. Hate the compassionate six-year-old and her beautiful mother.

But the only person he felt hatred toward was Ali Boudani. Hatred and terror. Five times a day he said his prayers to Allah, and every time he begged him to spare David and Moustafa.

He felt so confused. He had thought it would be easy to hate the *harkis* and the *pied-noirs* after all the horrible years of war. But what he had seen when he had gotten to know them was kindness. Bewildered people, just like him, caught in a war that divided and killed. That was what war was supposed to do, he argued. His people deserved freedom from the condescending Europeans! They had rightfully gained their independence!

But freedom at what price? The word sounded grand and heroic until he attached faces, human faces that he knew, to those who must be eliminated. Ali said these people were traitors, spies, murderers. They must die!

But all Hussein saw were kind young men who had sheltered him, and a mother and child who wanted only to befriend him. *If only you knew,* he moaned, thinking of Anne-Marie.

He had no choice. The sooner the better. Allah, through Ali's orders, had sent him on a difficult mission. He had been entrusted with a high calling in this war. He opened the second drawer in his dresser and fingered the revolver tucked beneath his clothes. At least he need not worry that the Sisters would snoop in his belongings. Mother Griolet had assured

him of privacy, and Sister Rosaline had stated matter-of-factly
that anything that needed washing had to make it to the dirty
clothes bin. She did not have time to sort through the drawers.

He must rid himself of this sentimentality. He needed a
plan. He contemplated using explosives in the dorms. No, not
first. First he should deal with the little girl. She would be the
easiest. To do something so incredibly hard, Hussein had to
progress logically. Start with Ophélie. With that settled in his
mind, he felt reassured. Allah would be with him.

Chapter 16

A dark cloud hung over St. Joseph's, threatening rain. A similar cloud seemed to have perched itself above Mother Griolet's head. Her hands trembled as she skimmed through the letter. Her mouth was set in anger, and her bright green eyes shone with rage.

"*Seigneur, ce n'est pas vrai!* It is not fair! How can we go on?"

She let her eyes fall on the second paragraph of the letter stamped with an official seal from her superiors in the church.

Even though we most heartily applaud your efforts at caring for the misplaced war children, it has come to our attention that their conduct is causing trouble in your village. The townspeople have supported the orphanage and exchange program with their money and their willingness to take in boarders for many years. Without their financial support, we cannot guarantee the continued functioning of St. Joseph's. To jeopardize this because of unwanted children would be foolish.

Several camps are being set up to keep these harki

*children. They will doubtlessly be happier in their own
communities. . . .*

Mother Griolet felt sick to her stomach. Couldn't they see
what the government was doing to these people? Parking
them in camps, away from society. They would never
integrate. She was sure the memory of what they were doing
to the *harkis* would one day come back to haunt the French.

The letter continued.

*We must add that unless this problem is resolved
soon, we will have no other choice but to close the
facilities, dispersing the French children to other
orphanages throughout France. It has always been our
belief that the support of the community is essential for
such a program as yours. . . .*

For years she had been considered a renegade, a
troublemaker. But she had never lacked the money to run the
orphanage and exchange program, and so the church had not
complained. She was left alone, as long as she kept quiet and
the village people did their part.

But it wasn't fair. The rumors simply weren't true! Yes, the
orphanage was overcrowded. But the children did not make
noise in the middle of the night. It was glaring prejudice, and
it made her sick. Why had the people of Castelnau so quickly
turned against her? Didn't they understand that her whole
goal in life was to help the helpless?

The old nun buried her face in her hands. "Lord God, I
am tired and angry. Forgive me for this anger that burns in
me. Life is so unfair! Please remind me that You are in
control. You are bigger than any organization, and if You want
this little place to keep running, I'm sure that You will find a
way to do it.

"But, Lord," she sighed, "I can't see how You will do it.
People are afraid that these children will infiltrate Castelnau
and ruin the village's image. Prejudice is so ugly, and yet, I
too have let it pull me along. May I not hate those who are

against me. It is human nature to be fickle. You have shown me that I am only a small, old woman. I am not indispensable. Your will be done, Father. For the children."

The old nun set down the letter. This was a very delicate problem, not like that of the exchange program. That could be resolved quite simply. David Hoffmann must come back before the school term ended. His presence at the school would reassure the girls and their parents. He had already missed Paris, but there was still time. Caroline and the others would stop complaining, she felt sure, if only M. Hoffmann could be here to teach the last two weeks of school.

It was her fault, Mother Griolet told herself. She should have never permitted David to leave. At the time, the urgency of the matter and the revelation of his selfless work for the *harkis* had influenced her decision to let him go to Algeria. She had not imagined the consequences.

But how could one man's absence bring such chaos to the place? One man's absence and a dozen *harki* children's presence. People just looked for excuses to complain, and this had given them a golden opportunity.

In a sense she did not blame them. The whole country was in upheaval as masses of *pied-noirs* poured in daily. This region of France was especially scrambling to provide housing. People were hesitant, worried, suspicious.

She sifted through the mail. A letter from the government implied that the Franco-American school would not be permitted to reopen for the next year if the parents withdrew their support. She did not finish reading it. Mother Griolet did not have the heart to keep going, but one letter remained. Doubtless another angry parent. She flipped the envelope over and slowly opened the seal. The return address was Senegal.

Four sheets of stationery fell onto her desk. Before she had read the first word, Mother Griolet felt tears brimming in her eyes. How well she knew the handwriting of Rebecca Madison.

These months have been hard for Gabriella. She has discovered the pain in her past and tasted what she thinks is love. It is difficult to be so very far away, to read of her struggles and feel a certain powerlessness to help.

I am so thankful she has had you, Mother Griolet! Her letters bring you back to me in full color! God has touched many, many lives through you. You know the joy and the pain of serving Him.

And you have served us. I realize it has not been easy. In a sense, you were left to pick up the pieces after she discovered the truth about Ericka. That was unfair of me. You received the brunt of her anger. Forgive me. Forgive me and thank you, for being there for me so long ago. And now, for doing the same thing for my daughter.

Please receive our kindest regards. We are hoping to be able to come in July to spend a few weeks in Montpellier before going on to the States for our furlough. . . .

The letter went on. The old nun smiled as she read. God's timing often surprised her. He had inspired a woman in Senegal to write this letter weeks ago, so that on this day when she needed it so desperately, Mother Griolet would have a word of encouragement. That was her God. It was not coincidence, she was convinced. It was tapestry. Thunder grumbled outside, but the dark cloud had completely disappeared from Mother Griolet's heart.

* * *

Anne-Marie looked in the mirror in the bathroom and saw a healthy, vibrant face smiling back at her. *Funny I should look so well,* she thought to herself. She stared at the reflection of her dark, wide-set eyes and fine nose that turned up ever so slightly, and thought that she did indeed look like the delicate, well-bred Arabian mare in Ophélie's imagination.

Her exterior was soft and smooth, but inside she churned,

like the same Arabian mare pacing nervously in her stall, anxious to escape. Anne-Marie had hoped against hope that Hussein would bring a letter or note from Moustafa, but there had been nothing. The boy was silent and reserved, giving no explanation of his time in Algeria. She wanted to grab him by the arms and beg him to tell her everything. Was Moustafa well? Did he speak often of her? Had his mother consented to come to France? Was there a reason to hope?

She chided herself. The boy was alone and terrified. She expected too much from him. Maybe she even expected too much from Moustafa. She told herself there was no reason to doubt Moustafa's love. And she didn't. But she doubted his resolve to come to France. His loyalty, the trait she most admired in him, might keep him away from her forever. Moustafa was loyal to his people, to his idealism. She must convince him that she had been serious when she begged him to join her in France.

She wanted Moustafa to see her now. Even her limp was hardly noticeable. She could run into his arms, those solid, strong arms, tousle his unkempt hair, and look into the soft chocolate brown puppy-dog eyes. She could, but would she? Would Moustafa return?

She took out a sheet of stationery and wrote quickly, pouring out her heart on the pages. She told him of Ophélie, of the kind people, of the strange way they looked at their faith, and of her certain love for him.

A soft rap came on the door. Anne-Marie swung around, almost embarrassed to see Gabriella standing in the doorway.

"Did I interrupt something?" she inquired.

Anne-Marie blushed. "No, just my feeble attempt at a love letter. I wish I could write like you. It seems so trite and ..." Her eyes filled up with tears.

"Anne-Marie!" Gabriella sat beside her, putting an arm around her shoulders. "Are you all right?"

She shook her head. "I just wish I had what you have. A

faith, an assurance that somebody cares and is in control. And a man who is coming back for you." She was sobbing now. "I have nothing. A weak dream. Don't you see? I have nothing at all." She held Gabriella tightly. "What is Ophélie's future with me? I have nothing—no family, no country, no hope." She covered her face with her hands. "I'm sorry. It is just, just that I miss him so much. I had hoped so for a word from him. I am afraid, Gabriella. So very afraid."

Gabriella held her for a long time without saying a word. "Did you finish your letter?" she whispered finally.

Anne-Marie sniffed and nodded.

"Let me have it then. I know just how to get it to Moustafa." She squeezed Anne-Marie's hand. "I'm sure it will be exactly what he needs to hear." She stood up and faced her, and Anne-Marie saw that Gabriella's face was streaked with tears.

"You are *une vrai amie*. Why in the world do you care about me?"

"I care because God has knit my soul to yours. And I am crying because, even though my life is very different, I think I understand how terribly much it hurts to love someone."

When the two women left the dorm room later, a flicker of hope had returned to Anne-Marie's eyes.

* * *

"Would you look at this, Monique!" Yvette Leclerc jabbered, setting down a basket full of fruits and vegetables with a huff. "Did you get the same thing in the mail yesterday? A petition from Denise Cabrol."

"I got it," Monique Pons replied sourly, "and I don't like it one bit. She's scheming, that woman. She wants to close the exchange program. That's fine and well for her—she doesn't have her income tied up in it. Do you realize, Yvette, that we'd lose a third of our monthly revenue without the American girls? A third!"

Yvette nodded. *"Oh là là!* I know it. That would be a real shame. *Catastrophique!"* She furrowed her brow, revealing a half-dozen fat wrinkles. "But didn't you approve of the measure to rid the town of the Arab orphans?"

"Of course I did. But Arab and *pied-noir* orphans have nothing to do with the exchange program. Denise is overzealous. She never liked Mother Griolet in the first place." She leaned over the kitchen table and whispered, "If you ask me, she's been jealous all these years that her Pierre and Mother Griolet get along so well." She winked. "She's just been waiting for an occasion to get back at her!"

"Really! Some people! And after all the good that nun has done for us! Well, what did you do? Did you sign it or not?"

Monique stood up, retrieved a folded piece of paper from the counter and set it before her friend. "There's what I did. Read it for yourself."

Yvette scanned the paper. Monique had signed her name at the bottom and underneath the signature had scribbled, "I am most heartily in favor of the removal of the disruptive children from the orphanage which has, up until the present time, run quite smoothly. I cannot, however, approve the termination of the exchange program, as I do not see that it in any way reflects upon the problems the orphanage is now experiencing, being a completely separate program."

"Well said, Monique!" Yvette cooed enthusiastically. "Do you mind if I copy it?"

"Go ahead. You know, it is after all your boarder, Mlle Caroline, who started all the rumors about there being problems with the Franco-American program. Can't you talk any sense into her?"

Yvette shrugged. "She's jealous about your M. Hoffmann. But what can I say? She claims, along with many of the other girls, that the classes are not up to college level. You know she's referring to the two classes Jean-Louis teaches. She's probably right. It was a bit foolish of Mother Griolet to let M.

Hoffmann go away again. He's hardly been at school at all during the second and third trimesters. What can I say?"

She stopped talking, intent on copying every word of her friend's objection. Monique prepared the coffee, clucking merrily to herself. "Did you see the latest statistics from Algeria, Yvette? Read it in this morning's paper. Over 200,000 of the *pied-noirs* have left Algeria so far. City governments all over the south here are starting housing projects for them. Pouring into our country without an inkling as to what they'll do. Left everything behind in Algeria and jumped on the boat. Can you imagine?"

"Shh for a minute. I've got to concentrate." She scribbled for a moment longer and then set down her pen. "A mess. A huge mess is all I can say. Send them to the west side of Montpellier. They'll be happy over there with the Arabs for neighbors. Maybe that'll make them feel a little more like home, *n'est-ce pas?*"

Monique nodded. "Sounds like a good idea to me." Picking up her cup of coffee, she asked, "Now what did you decide to fix for the girls' supper tonight?"

Yvette's eyes twinkled. "The asparagus was on sale and beautiful, so I'll have that *au gratin* for the *entrée* and then a leg of lamb with macaroni." She laughed. "They're always surprised when they taste the real thing. You know those Americans. They eat everything from a box. *Quel horreur!* Macaroni and cheese from a box. And I found the most delicious strawberries today. Seven francs a kilo. Now you know you can't beat that."

The ladies laughed and planned and, before separating, stuffed their petitions in an envelope and sealed it shut.

* * *

A light rain was falling, forcing Henri Krugler to send the children inside for recess. He blew two sharp blasts on the whistle around his neck. "*Les enfants!* Time to go in!" Thirty pairs of eyes watched him with a mixture of admiration and amusement. Whistles were not commonplace in *centre aérés*.

"He's Swiss, my mom says. You know how they are," a young boy whispered to his neighbor, loud enough for Henri to hear. "He likes order."

Henri chuckled to himself. The *centre aéré* was finally open, and the children stared in awe at the white-haired giant. He doubted he would have many discipline problems with these kids. "Martine has an activity planned for the four- and five-year-olds, so please join her in the *salon*. You older ones can come with me."

He led fifteen girls and boys up a winding tiled staircase that emptied into a vast hallway. Rooms branched off from the hall in every direction. "We'll be removing wallpaper this afternoon."

Henri's announcement was met with a series of groans.

"I know, I know! No fun. But it has to be done if this place is going to be usable. So"—he gave another puff on the whistle—"I am hereby giving a *pain au chocolat* to the child who removes the most wallpaper in the next thirty minutes." He held up the chocolate bread for the children to inspect.

Immediately eager hands reached out for trowels and buckets of sudsy water. Henri directed his crew into the bedrooms, indicating a separate wall for each child. "You may begin!"

The ancient farmhouse was never intended to be a children's center. But the house had been left in his keeping for these five years, and it appeared that he would have it forever. His apartment, a few minutes down the road was plenty adequate for his needs. So when his requests to buy other buildings for the *centre aéré* were turned down, Henri decided to transform the house into a center. The additions were actually minimal: another bathroom added, insulation for the basement, an enlarged eating area.

With great satisfaction, Henri observed the children,

French and Arab, working side by side, squealing proudly as
they peeled off long strips of soiled wallpaper. He knew the
predictions. Soon Lodève would be flooded with Arabs, more
specifically *harkis*. The parents' prejudice had grown and
ripened over the years. He could not change that. But two
afternoons a week with the children might just start
something in Lodève. He was betting his life on it.

* * *

"What do you mean I have to call another depot? You're
the tenth person I've talked to today, and every single one of
you is giving me a different story!" Eliane Cebrian could not
conceal the anger and frustration in her voice. She shook her
bobbed head and slammed down the phone so hard that
Samuel and Rachel looked up from their game in surprise.

"Mama, what's the matter?" Rachel asked innocently.

Eliane bit her lip, fighting back the tears. "Nothing,
children. *Ça va.* Mama's just a little bit tired today, that's all."

She stood by the window and watched the rain drizzle
outside. She hated this hotel room. She was tired of being
cooped up with the kids all day, especially on Wednesdays
when Samuel and Rachel didn't have school.

School was bad enough for them. They reported with sad
eyes that the other children made fun of their accents and
wouldn't play with them at recess.

And now this. The *harki* kid had left the trunk in
Marseilles. Her trunk! With her belongings. When Anne-
Marie called to tell her, Eliane cursed out loud, shocking the
children. Another loss. The things that mattered most to her—
baby pictures of the kids, their silver cups, the old family
Bible with the family tree inside, her grandmother's set of
Limoges china—all lost. Eliane felt sick just thinking of the
heirlooms the trunk held. And of the stupid Arab kid who
had left it there. How could he?

The porters in Marseilles gave her little hope of finding it.

No one could even direct her to the right warehouse where lost items from the ferries were stored. They just laughed and said it was probably pretty well picked over by now anyway. Behind the laughter, she could hear the sarcasm. "Serves her right. Nutty *pied-noir*, sending a trunk over at a time like this. Serves her right."

She knew that if she hoped to find the trunk, she would have to go to Marseilles herself. But the thought of dragging her children around on buses in that chaotic city overwhelmed her. She would just have to wait for Rémi. His last letter had sounded very pessimistic. He had not yet received the cryptic warning—the suitcase or the coffin—but plenty of others had. With one month until independence, she doubted he would hold out much longer.

"I want to go home," she whispered to herself. "Oh, God, how I wish I could go home." With the trunk lost, every memory of their life in Algeria was gone. She closed her eyes and pictured Madira and El Amin coming toward her in the orange groves. She saw Rémi hefting a heavy sack on his shoulders, followed by Amar and Abdul. She could almost feel the fine, biting sand on her skin, and she wished for it with all her heart.

She remembered that night on the ferry, crossing the Mediterranean. She remembered clasping Anne-Marie's hand and assuring her that she had a chance to start over again. That God would see them through. Eliane had believed it then. She truly had.

She groaned to herself and felt that anger lurking again, below the surface. Normally good-natured and bright, Eliane was repulsed by her own emotions. Like it or not, she was being forced to start completely over, and nothing was easy. "Why should life be easy when you can make it hard?" That was her new motto for France, and she disliked the bitterness that was creeping into her soul.

Even at church she felt it. The stares, the cold, formal

politeness. *Good grief,* she had thought. *We're few enough Protestants as it is. Can't we at least get along?* But every week it was the same—an aloofness that screamed "You're different and we don't care to get to know you." Finally she had stopped going to *le Temple Protestant* altogether.

Thank goodness for Anne-Marie and Ophélie. Their weekly visits were the bright spot in an otherwise dreary but complicated existence.

"Come over, Rémi. Give up your dream and come on over. I need you." She picked up the phone and dialed another warehouse in Marseilles. The phone rang on and on. No one answered.

* * *

Jean-Louis Vidal gladly gave his position in front of the class to Gabriella as he took a seat in a chair beside the desk. He was relieved that the pretty redhead had agreed to handle the lecture on Baudelaire and *Les Fleurs du Mal.* He personally considered the poetry nasty, no matter how beautifully it was written, and he did not relish the thought of explaining it to these young women. As it was, he fixed his gaze on Caroline Harland's shapely legs and let himself daydream.

He realized he must have nodded off when he was awakened by a thin ripple of laughter in the classroom. He straightened up in his chair, pushed his wire-rimmed glasses back on his nose, and turned his attention to Gabriella, whose face was bright red.

She smiled weakly at Jean-Louis. "As I was saying, some of Baudelaire's poems were censured and had literally to be cut out of the collection of verses before the volume was put on sale. Soon after that event, Baudelaire died of paralysis at age forty-six. He was considered to be insane at the time of his death."

He thought she was handling a delicate subject extremely well and continued contemplating Caroline's figure. At one point, the seductive blond looked over at him and raised her eyebrows. Jean-Louis was sure he blushed all the way to the top of his bald head.

He reprimanded himself for letting his mind wander, especially to Caroline Harland. After all, she was the girl responsible for starting all the rumors about the exchange program. She despised him, he was sure. He was too old and fat to care much what the young ladies thought. But out of respect to Jeanette Griolet, he ought not to daydream about Caroline.

When Gabriella asked the young women to read several poems silently to themselves, he slipped out of the room, giving Gabriella an appreciative nod. He walked down two flights of steps into the basement and stood outside the children's classroom.

Jeanette was going over multiplication tables. He did not enter the room, but contented himself to stand outside and listen to the nun's firm, happy voice. Something tugged within his heart. Something much different than the quick rush of excitement that the sight of Caroline's legs brought him.

He told himself that Jeanette's voice sounded as strong as ever. He told himself that she was in fine shape. He listened and thought of her as a young woman with sparkling, mischievous eyes and a wonderful, ringing laugh. He reached into his pocket and brought out a yellowed envelope. The ink was faded, but her name was still legible on the outside.

Jean-Louis turned the envelope over and over in his hands. He could not bring himself to give it to her. Perhaps the time had not yet come. He walked back through the basement, up the stairs, and out into the gray drizzle, tucking the envelope safely back in his coat pocket.

Chapter 17

It was near the middle of the night, and Hussein was weary from fighting off sleep. Long ago the other boys had closed their eyes, and their peaceful breathing testified to the fact that all were asleep. He got out of bed and, with shaking hands, pulled on a pair of pants over his pajamas. He reached into the drawer and fumbled through the clothes until he touched the revolver. His throat was dry. He tried to swallow, but it made him gag.

The silencer was in place. He had prepared it in the afternoon. He tucked the gun into his pants, his pajama top concealing it. Not that it mattered, he told himself. Everything was perfectly quiet. Hussein made his way down the hall and slipped into the girls' dormitory. He found Ophélie's bed. She was sleeping so peacefully, a smile on her lips. Her brown hair fell over the covers, and one arm hung outside the sheets. Hussein touched it lightly.

"Ophélie," he whispered. "Ophélie. Wake up. It is Hussein. Wake up." He shook her lightly, and after a moment, the child's eyes fluttered open. Immediately Hussein put his hand over her mouth. "Shh. Don't make a sound. It's the middle of the night.

Come with me. I have the most beautiful thing to show you. Outside. Don't be afraid."

Ophélie rubbed her eyes, a frown on her face.

Hussein smiled weakly. "I thought of you. How much you love to imagine. I wanted to . . . " He swallowed again. ". . . To share this with you since you've been so kind to me."

The little girl's eyes brightened as she slipped out of bed. Hussein took her hand and led her through the hallway. He pushed on the door leading out to the courtyard, but it was locked. Panic seized him. He had forgotten the door might be locked.

"Oh, *zut alors!* We can't get out." His head spun.

Ophélie tugged on his sleeve. "Hussein," she whispered excitedly. "We can get out. Through the bathroom window. Hakim did it once. It's too high for me to climb up, but if you help me, I can do it." She looked like a mischievous puppy ready for adventure.

He felt his resolve slipping. "But how would we get back in?"

"Oh, that's easy. You just get Mother Griolet's chair. It's always in the garden. Hakim put it under the window and climbed back in. Come on." She grabbed his hand, leading him toward the boys' bathroom. "This is fun!"

Hussein saw that she was right. If he stood on the toilet, he could open the window and then hoist himself up. He hesitated a moment. He had been so sure that it must be done in the courtyard. Now he wished he had just shot the child in her bed, in her sleep. Her eager, trusting eyes made him feel all the sicker.

"Okay, Ophélie, you come first. Just stand on my shoulders and see if you can open the window." She did so easily, climbing through the opening and dropping lightly to the ground outside. Hussein followed quickly.

The sky had cleared after the afternoon showers, and the stars flickered by the hundreds. In the middle of the dark expanse sat a bright white full moon. Hussein sighed with relief. For some strange reason it mattered that he had not lied to her. Not yet.

"It is sooo pretty!" she laughed, almost forgetting to whisper. She strained her neck upward and stared at the scene. "Thank you for letting me see this. It is so quiet and peaceful. I hope Papa is well. I hope tonight he is staring at the same sky and remembering how much I love him."

She was whispering as if in a dream. Hussein slowly backed away from her, pulling the revolver out of his pants. His hand shook violently. Tears blurred his eyes. He wondered how many shots he would have to fire to make sure she was dead.

He brought his other hand up to steady the first. "There is no God but Allah . . ." he repeated silently, desperate to regain his concentration. "This is for Ali, for Ali, for Allah." The child still stood with her back to him and head upturned, as if mesmerized by the beauty of the night. Sweat poured down Hussein's face. He had to do it now! Now!

"Do you ever think about heaven, Hussein?" she asked, still looking at the stars.

Fire! Kill her now before she turns around and sees and knows what you will do.

"I can't wait to go there and be with Jesus. Where there is no more crying or war or bad guys."

She wants to go to heaven, and I will send her there with one pull of the trigger. He aimed. He touched his finger to the trigger. Everything in him trembled, and tears ran down his face. "I can't do it," he said out loud, and a wave of relief ran through him. He dropped the gun in the grass.

"Can't do what?" Ophélie turned around to face him. "Go to heaven? Oh, Hussein. Don't worry. Jesus loves you. He'll take you to heaven when you die, if you ask Him."

She walked over to him. She was like a ghost or an angel, standing there in her white gown. Her fine, small features looked so fragile and delicate. A soft breeze blew through her hair. Hussein could not move. He stared at her, trembling, crying.

"Whatever is the matter, Hussein? Don't you find it beautiful?" She wiped a tear from his face. "Oh, I know. It is like Bribri says. Sometimes you cry with happiness. Sometimes your feelings get all mixed-up, and you can't think if you are sad or happy or both."

Suddenly Hussein laughed out loud. She was right, this child of six. His emotions were strained, wild. He was terrified at what he almost had done and equally terrified that he had not done it. But mostly, he was relieved and ecstatically happy that this pint-sized angel was standing before him, alive.

"We must go in now," he whispered hoarsely.

"Aw . . . well, okay. I'll get the chair." She ran over to a corner of the courtyard. As she did, Hussein stooped and picked up the unfired revolver, tucking it back into his pants. He had the strangest feeling that the heavens were blinking down their approval.

* * *

"One of the children has been playing with my chair again," Mother Griolet commented good-naturedly. "Right under the bathroom window. Dear me, I hope none of the new children are trying to run away. You could hardly blame them if they did. I assume they found the orphanage and grounds rather well secured."

Gabriella picked up the wicker chair and brought it into the shade of an olive tree near the wall of the courtyard. "Sit down, please, Mother Griolet."

"Thank you, child." She leaned over and touched a pansy. "Poor thing. It's getting too hot for them now. They'll soon be dying out. Ah well, they've been so very helpful, haven't they? Got us through the winter cheerily, with their bright splashes of color. Can't expect them to last forever."

Gabriella brought a chair from the dining hall into the courtyard and sat down beside Mother Griolet. "I wanted to talk to you, while the children are out on their walk about . . . about your offer."

"Ah *oui, ma fille.* Of course." She spoke with difficulty, as if her mind were on something else.

"Are you still interested, Mother Griolet? I've been thinking about it a lot—praying too, of course. It scares me to death. I don't possibly see how I could do it." She turned her hands in her lap. "But I'm willing to give it a try."

Mother Griolet said nothing, staring lamely in the distance. Gabriella watched her carefully. She had expected the nun to be ecstatic, or at the least enthusiastic.

"Are you all right, Mother Griolet?" She touched the old woman's hand.

The nun looked around and smiled at Gabriella, but her eyes were filled with tears. Gabriella thought that perhaps she had not heard her. She started to speak again, but the old nun began talking.

"Have you noticed the vines on the parsonage? When I first came here almost fifty years ago there wasn't a single leaf on the building. Look at it now. Back and front completely covered. I think it gives such a lovely look to the place, don't you?" She breathed deeply, then she laughed.

"Forgive me, dear. A bit reflective these days. Thank you, Gabriella. Thank you for being willing to stay. You are quite a spunky young woman. The Lord will do many things through you, I have no doubt." She patted Gabriella's hand. "But I am not sure it will be here."

"What do you mean?" Gabriella had wrestled with this decision for two weeks, and now it sounded as if there was no decision to be made after all. "You mean you don't want me?"

"Of course not, Gabriella. No, that isn't it." She shook her head slowly back and forth. "We've been receiving a lot of disturbing mail lately, and it seems the church and the government both agree that this place should be closed down."

"What? That's crazy! There's not a better orphanage in all of France. And the exchange program! What about that?"

"The parents are withdrawing their support. You must understand that a good deal of the funding comes from a handful of wealthy Americans who have supported this program since its inception. Without their money, well, it can't go on."

"But why? Why are they withdrawing support?" She answered her own question. "It's Caroline, isn't it? She wrote her dad."

"Yes."

"And all those important businessmen believed her? That's crazy!"

"Her father is very influential. I'm afraid little St. Joseph's has gotten caught up in a political game of power that really has nothing to do with us."

"And the orphanage?"

"The townspeople have worked up a petition demanding that the Arab children be sent away. They are no happier about the *pied-noirs*, but what can they say? The church feels that the place cannot stay open without the town's support— they do provide a good bit of the financial backing. Some of the more prominent families have always been extremely generous . . . until recently."

"But they can't just close it down! What will happen to the children?" Gabriella felt faint, angry.

"Some will be adopted, the rest sent to other orphanages. The *harki* children will doubtless go to the refugee camps that are being set up in the region."

"And you can't do anything?"

Mother Griolet laughed. "I am not a very popular person in the higher echelons. People have put up with me, but few will be sorry to see me go."

"Go! Go where?"

The nun shrugged.

"It is impossible! I won't let it happen! Surely Sister Isabelle and Sister Rosaline can do something! No! We won't give up. It's not like you to give up."

"My fiery little redhead! I appreciate your zeal. Of course I don't want to give up. But it seems God is closing the door."

"He can't be. Not when I'm ready to step through it." Gabriella stopped herself, realizing that she had been shouting. She lowered her voice. "Aren't you the one who said to trust? That God always provides? You've said it to me a hundred times. Please don't give up." She grabbed the nun's hands. "Please teach me. Teach me everything. School will be out in a week. I'll have all my time to learn. All summer to see your files, to understand how you have done it."

"I don't deserve you, Gabriella. If you wish, I will show it all to you. But I can't promise you or David a job for next year. I must be honest with you. Our Lord can do as He pleases. I've been stubborn enough in the past. He's got my attention now, and I'm not sure where He's leading."

"I'm not afraid of whatever comes. You will be here to show me. I'm sure God will do the rest."

* * *

The talks about oil were leading nowhere, and Roger Hoffmann had a strange feeling that they never would. He could not put his finger on it, but something was amiss. For the past two days he had felt sluggish, unable to think clearly. His flight was scheduled to leave tomorrow, to his immense relief. His suitcase was packed. Official good-byes had already been said. He decided to find a taxi and ride to the airport tonight to make sure nothing changed his plans.

When his hotel door was forced open and two hooded men rushed in on him, he was completely unprepared. He reached for his gun, but one of the men hit him hard across the face and sent him reeling.

"What in the —?" he mumbled.

"This is a message from the OAS, Hoffmann. No more dealings with the FLN. You shouldn't be here. We're gonna make sure you never come back."

The hooded man brought a revolver crashing down on Roger's head. Everything went black.

* * *

The letter had come through his friend Marc at the *épicerie* just this morning, and Moustafa tore open the envelope with trembling hands. A letter from Anne-Marie. He knew that he was grinning foolishly. He couldn't help it. Today he had two reasons to celebrate.

Moustafa grabbed David by the shoulders, shook him hard, and laughed. "It's a miracle! Mother has agreed to leave with my sisters! A miracle. And here's a letter from Anne-Marie. Maybe your God is smiling down on me today."

David patted him on the back. "Go enjoy your letter, *mon ami.*" He raised his eyebrows. "And afterward, I want to hear all about it."

The young Arab stretched out on the mattress in the bedroom, letting his eyes soak in the reality of Anne-Marie's penmanship in her first three words, *My dear Moustafa.* The doubts that had plagued him for the past two months seemed to fade away; the future was suddenly bright with possibilities.

I do not know how I can tell you how much I miss you. I am happy and safe in this little haven. It is so perfect, and yet I am sick for missing you. Even the joy of being with Ophélie is marred by my worry for you.

I am surprised at how selfish I can be. All is well and yet, when the harki child came and would not speak of you, I was so frustrated and angry. Poor Eliane, he left her trunk in Marseilles, and I doubt she'll ever find it. And I'll never see my father's will. Not that its value was anything other than purely sentimental, but I was so disappointed. I was wanting to keep that last treasure from him and Mother. And of course, I had so wanted a word from you.

Moustafa frowned at the news of the lost trunk. She had not received his letter.

Forgive me for whining like a child. It is only that in being far from you I realize how desperately I want us to be together. I don't care how impossible it is. We will make it work, in spite of all the hatred and prejudice in this country. I can't write poetry, but I can tell you the truth. I love you, Moustafa. Please, please come here to this safe place. I am sure these kind people will help us. Come back with David.

Gabriella is becoming a true friend, Moustafa. You will like her. You will think she is perfect for David. She has the strangest way of looking at life. Perhaps it is because she is Protestant. But then Mother Griolet and the Sisters see things in a similar manner. It is very different from the Catholicism and Protestantism I have heard about. Maybe it is what Papa believed. I am sorry now that I never even went to church with him.

These people read the Bible, for themselves. Even Ophélie can quote verses from the Holy Book and explain them to me. I hope I am not shocking you, but I am reading it too, just to see. These are things we will discuss when you are here.

Moustafa shook his head in wonder that Anne-Marie was also discovering the Bible. It made a chill run down his back, as if maybe Allah, or whatever this God's name was, actually wanted them to be together. How he longed for a safe place, away from the suffering, away from the pain.

He let himself think of her as he read on. Even when she had been near to death, he had found her beautiful. Now she said she was stronger, the limp barely noticeable. He imagined

Anne-Marie with a smile on her lips, her fine, slightly up-turned nose and high cheekbones, the wide brown eyes. Maybe she was right. Maybe there was a life for them in France . . . if only he could get there!

Rémi Cebrian had another trunk at his farmhouse. But one trunk could not conceal his brother and himself. There was talk blowing around, his mother had whispered to him this morning, that a French officer was renting a whole ferry to take his *harki* troop, of which Moustafa's brother was a member, to France on July third. If his brother could secure two places on that boat, they would be guaranteed safe passage. But one boat was only a drop in the bucket for the hundreds of thousands of *harkis* and their families who needed to escape. He had two and a half weeks to find a way.

A knock came on the front door, and by the sound of David's voice, Moustafa knew it was the Arab girl calling. Two weeks to the hour. He tucked Anne-Marie's letter under his mattress and came into the den. The girl and the turbaned man nodded politely.

"We've come to see if Fatima will be able to leave with you."

"I'm sorry to be unable to give you more information. We are in the process of working things out with a friend," David explained. "Could you come back in a few days? The details should be firmed up by then."

Moustafa shot him a glance. "Yes, is there a way to reach you in a hurry, in case it comes together quickly?"

"No, that is impossible. We are in hiding." The turbaned man did not try to hide his frustration. "We will come back in three days."

When they had left the apartment, Moustafa showed Anne-Marie's letter to David. "She said Hussein left the trunk in Marseilles. Why in the world would he do that?"

"Maybe it was too much of a mob."

"But he knew it contained valuables."

"What are you getting at?"

Moustafa thought out loud. "I don't know. Anne-Marie says he wouldn't tell her a thing about us. Don't you find that strange? What has the kid got to hide? He's an orphan."

David's eyes narrowed. "I don't have any idea. He never was very talkative anyway. But it's a shame about the trunk."

"Yeah, a rotten shame."

* * *

They squatted in the fine sand around a bucket of ripe black olives, eating the fruit and spitting the seeds out on the ground. Rémi was shaking his head as he listened to Moustafa. "How could the kid do it? Leaving Eliane's trunk? It had her favorite heirlooms in it. I thought you trusted him."

"We did. He seemed happy to help in any way." David stood up, stretching his legs. "Look, Rémi, I don't know what to say. We miscalculated. I'm sorry."

"How could you know? It's just for Eliane. She's already been through enough, and with this. Well, she must be heartbroken."

"Surely they wouldn't destroy the trunk. There must be a warehouse where lost items are stored." Moustafa threw a seed into the sand.

"You're right. It is all the more reason for me to leave here soon." Rémi rose. "I've been fixing up the other trunk like the first. I've put the rest of her favorite things in it, and there's plenty of room for another child. But now I wouldn't trust anyone." He laughed bitterly. "Maybe I'll hide in it myself. Maybe that's how I'll get to France."

The men talked on. A worry line crept over Rémi's face as Moustafa spoke of securing a place on a ferry for his mother and sisters so that they could leave immediately.

"I tell you it is impossible to get them on the ferries. Have you been to the docks lately? It is claustrophobic. Hundreds of panicked *pied-noirs*. The wait is days long. No room for

Arabs. I am afraid your mother and sisters would be left sitting by the sea when independence comes. It is much too dangerous." He saw Moustafa's face fall. "I'm sorry."

"There has to be something we can do," David said, tossing an olive seed forcefully into the yard. In a second, his face lit up. "Of course! Why haven't we thought of him before? Jacques and the *Capitaine!*"

"We haven't thought of him," Moustafa said sourly, "because you told us he refused to make any more trips. Too dangerous."

"Yes, yes, you're right. That is what he said. But you've worked with him. You know Jacques. He needs a lot of coaxing, a feeling of importance. One last trip. We'll fill the boat with the *harki* women and children and tell him he'll be a hero. Which is the absolute truth."

"And how will we convince him? It's not like we can trot on over to Marseilles tomorrow."

"Your friend, Moustafa. At the *épicerie.* He's sending and receiving mail with the ferries. Jacques could have the letter in a matter of days." David sounded confident. "If I word it right, I am sure Jacques will not fail us. We'll get the children ready. Tell them it will be in less than two weeks. I'll write the letter today, and you will leave with your mother and sisters."

Moustafa shook his head vehemently. "I can't. I have promised Mother that I will stay until my brother goes. She will not leave unless I stay. But don't worry. I am planning a trip to Philippeville on the second of July."

"That's three hours away. What will you do there?" Rémi asked, narrowing his eyes.

"My brother and I will be on the *harki* ferry. Protected by the French Army. I will do anything to be on that boat." He smiled at the men, but his eyes were solemn. That same determination, that loyalty was fixed on his face. "Will you drive us there, Rémi?"

The basket of olives was almost empty. Rémi reached

down and pulled out one last small black fruit, turning it over in his fingers. "Some of the finest olives anywhere in the world. Grown right here. *Chez moi.* How I hate to leave it." He tossed the olive up in the air and caught it in his mouth. "I'll take you, Moustafa. Nothing would give me greater pleasure than to watch you ride away from this putrid place to find a future in France."

Chapter 18

The sun was hot and forceful as Henri Krugler straddled the roof of the farmhouse, working on a few loose tiles. He wiped his forehead to remove the perspiration. His back was burning, he could tell, and reluctantly he pulled a white T-shirt over his thick torso.

For a moment he looked toward the rolling hills surrounding Lodève. These were not the majestic mountains of Switzerland, yet the rugged, wild beauty of the Cevennes pleased him. He liked to think of his Huguenot ancestors hiding in these mountains, refusing to abdicate their faith to the cruel King Louis XIV. That same zealous, fervent blood ran in his veins. The Huguenot persecutions in the seventeenth and eighteenth centuries had been gory and ruthless. Because of the atrocities, the Huguenots had fled to many other countries, notably Switzerland. There his ancestors had prospered and multiplied, and he felt proud to be among the offspring of a people with so rich a heritage.

And now he was back in the same Cevennes mountains carrying his message of hope and reconciliation to the French and especially to the Arabs.

The sun could not bleach his already white hair and beard, but it gave him nonetheless a look of power, sitting like a huge troll on top of the farmhouse. He waved down to the pedestrians who walked by and gawked up at him.

"Une belle journée, n'est-ce pas?" he roared down to the elderly women who watched him in awe, and they nodded back, their old eyes twinkling.

After only one month, the *centre aéré* seemed a great success. Every afternoon after school, forty children, ages four to twelve, invaded the farmhouse. On Wednesdays, when there was no school, Henri had the children for the entire day. And soon, during the summer break, he would fill this little farmhouse with children every day of the week.

The children loved the friendly giant. Lonely Arab teenagers hung around the center in their free time, offering to help with the handy work, content to be in the presence of Henri Krugler. Henri seized these opportunities to build friendships and raise questions about the meaning of life. During the hours that the *centre aéré* was open, he could not talk religion. But afterward he spoke to the children, who stared at him with eager eyes, of a gentle prophet who was also a priest and a king.

So it seemed that quite naturally God was guiding Henri Krugler in the next step of his dream. A *centre aéré* met the needs of the children, helped the parents, and provided nonthreatening integration. The next step was to form a group for the teenagers and young adults. A group that spoke of faith, but that respected culture. A group for the Arab kids. A safe place to come and talk. An oasis.

This afternoon, in only thirty minutes, the first meeting of *Oasis* would take place. Henri climbed down from the roof and headed for the shower. Afterward, he dressed and towel-dried his white mane so that it stood up on his head in every direction as if to demonstrate the power of an electrical current. He let himself into a newly wallpapered bedroom upstairs and sank to his knees.

"Father God," he prayed out loud in a rich, booming voice made for a pulpit. "Thank You for making the dream a reality. Thank You for this house. You provide in the strangest ways. And thank You for the children who will come today. Give them the courage to attend despite their fears and prejudices. And, dear Father, give me the words today—the words and the actions to show them that this is indeed a safe place to come to. An oasis for their souls. Amen."

* * *

The warehouse smelled of mildew and rotting fruit. A young French soldier, weary from his journey and a few too many bottles with his departing comrades, stumbled through the large building that was packed with newly delivered boxes fresh from the ferries. Beneath the grime and stubble of a beard, he looked to be barely more than a teenager. Other soldiers had already picked through the good fruit and the clothes. What was left was junk. Plain old junk. The soldier laughed to himself, recalling a saying his father had often repeated: "One man's trash is another man's treasure."

He glanced at the boxes. Nothing of value today. Absentmindedly he walked through the warehouse, running his finger over suitcases with broken handles, split umbrellas, a doll with one button-eye missing, boxes of mildewed clothes. Why didn't someone throw out all this rot?

And it was all rot, everything that had to do with this stinking war. But he was home now. Home. Could it be real? Was this really French soil? Friendly French soil. Four years in Algeria had made him doubt that any place was friendly. Too much blood, too many tortures, too many men behaving like raving lunatics. He might still be there if it weren't for the bullet that had grazed his head. He touched the bandage. Thanks to the bullet, he got to go home a whole two stinking weeks early.

The old wooden chest was squeezed in beside a larger container and a metal trash bin. The soldier bent over to inspect it. Now that was a nice piece of work. A trunk. A treasure chest fit for Robinson Crusoe, he thought, chuckling to himself. He ran his fingers over the rounded top with its black metal casing. His mother could surely use such a chest to store their blankets and quilts during the summer months. He lifted the lid, and a broken lock fell to the floor. Yep, other soldiers had been here first.

He felt a tinge of disappointment. Papers and china and old dolls and a big family Bible. Pictures of children, knickknacks. It was strange though. The contents had been picked through, laying randomly in two compartments in the interior of the trunk. But the center space was empty, with a grilled-in open window in the front and the back. It looked like, well, it looked like somebody had been in the trunk. Now that was an ingenious way to get to France. Hidden in a treasure chest. He let the lid fall back in place and noticed the address written in bold letters on the top. Castelnau. Never heard of it. But the postal code meant it must be near Montpellier. Too bad for whoever was looking for their treasure. They'd never find it in this old warehouse. Just a piece of junk.

He rubbed his stubby chin thoughtfully. He'd ask his mother about it. If she seemed remotely interested, well, he could find his way back to this warehouse. It wasn't so far from where he lived. Yeah, if that would make dear old Mama happy, he would take it home, clean it up, and give her a nice surprise for her birthday in July. He left the warehouse, muttering to himself, "One man's trash is another man's treasure."

* * *

Gabriella did not know how she felt as she stepped out of the parsonage after her last exam. A few more days and the program would be officially over. She heard a small voice in her head. *Now is when the adventure begins.* She winced involuntarily. What adventure? All the nights spent wrestling and praying over the decision had been for naught if Mother Griolet was right. No more exchange program. No more orphanage. She swallowed hard.

Little Castelnau. The town had welcomed her, delighted her, instructed her patiently in the ways of the Midi. She took one of the tiny side streets that led away from the church. This was perhaps her favorite part of town, crammed with small stone houses that were joined together and hidden behind the main roads and could only be reached by foot through the narrow alleyways.

Vines were clinging to the stone walls where palm trees poked their long-leafed heads over the top. Potted geraniums and petunias decorated every ancient windowsill. An old woman sat in front of her house on a tiny cement verandah, the vines above her making a living canopy to shade her from the strong June heat. A parakeet sang to her from its cage. A few white T-shirts hung from the upstairs window.

Gabriella followed the twisting passage, climbing up and down its wide steps. Every corner held a new surprise: a jubilant daisy bush, bright white with its green shoots pointing in every direction; a low-tiled wall that gave a view into the town below, a rounded little alcove with a stone bench hidden inside. *This is where I'll bring David,* she thought, *when he gets back.*

She sat down on the bench and took his latest letter out of her backpack. She had already practically memorized it. They would leave by July second, he had said. She was counting the days. Thirteen of them. That wasn't too long to wait.

But what was she waiting for? A job in an orphanage that might be closed down, and a man who had promised her nothing. Did he even consider the possibility that she might not be here when he got back? Had the thought even entered his head?

He sounded so angry, so despairing. The biting tone that had put her off so many months ago had found its way into his letter. She understood, or at least she tried to. Trust. What a huge word for its single syllable. How did you trust when the whole world was exploding in front of you?

The sun felt so soothing on Gabriella's face. Castelnau was oceans away from the war, and yet she did not feel peaceful. She closed her eyes. She had made the hardest decision of her life. She had agreed to stay in this tiny town, to take over an orphanage. She had decided without consulting David, in faith that her God would work out the details. She thought that it would be easy after the decision had been made. No, not easy. Clear. But Gabriella could not see anything at all.

Suddenly she sat up straight. Maybe God was making things clear. Originally she had planned to travel around Europe with her family during the month of August, and then go with them to the States where they would spend a year's furlough. She was already enrolled in a college there. Maybe she was supposed to do just that.

Those plans seemed centuries old. Or maybe, maybe it was *this* that was the dream. Was she really considering giving up travel and a year in the States for this? For an aging nun and a cocky Ivy League grad? She blushed with the thought. It sounded crazy when she thought about it. Maybe God was rescuing her from wasting her life in a little lost village in France. She had tried to reason it out, and she had been wrong. The answer was no. Now she must simply get on with her life.

She reread the letter that had arrived this morning from her mother, informing Gabriella that her whole family would be arriving in less than a month. Could she find a place for them to stay? Gabriella groaned inwardly. She didn't even know where to look. Everything seemed so extremely complicated. The knot in her stomach returned. She would ask her landlady. Mme Leclerc would have an idea.

She left the bench and walked down the steps that let her out onto the main cobbled road of the town. The fountain sprayed beside her. Across the street, a small island of velvet green grass harbored some bright pansies and two tall cedars.

Her heart ached. *But I love this town,* she whispered to herself. *I could live here for a long time and be happy.* It thrilled her to walk on the cobblestones and touch the fruit displayed in a worn cart outside the *épicerie,* to contemplate bunches of purple grapes that had been painted on the stone wall by the liquor store. A hair salon came next, tucked inside an ancient vaulted room. She passed Pierre's *boulangerie* and smiled at the graying baker. Gabriella loved the flavor of France. She wanted to walk past these stores every day for a long, long time. She couldn't explain it. She just knew. She belonged in Castelnau.

She had made a wide circle through town and now came back to St. Joseph's. Anne-Marie stepped out of the chapel.

"There you are! I've been looking for you. *Félicitations!"*

"Congrats for what?" Gabriella asked, surprised.

"For finishing your last exam. Don't you feel relieved?"

"Oh, that." Her voice fell flat.

"You mean it doesn't matter?"

"I don't know."

Anne-Marie fell into step with Gabriella, and they walked on through the town to where the road became paved.

"I guess I should feel relieved, but I only feel confused."

"About David?" Anne-Marie asked gently.

"Him and everything else. I told you Mother Griolet had asked me to stay on at the orphanage—to be trained to take her place?"

"*Oui.* I remember."

"Well, it looks like it's going to be closed."

"*Non! Ce n'est pas possible!"*

"That's what Mother Griolet thinks. Everything shut down. And I had just told her I'd stay. Doesn't make sense, does it?"

Anne-Marie shrugged. "I don't think much in life makes sense. It doesn't seem like much of a tapestry to me."

They walked past the stately homes of Castelnau, which stood proud and private behind thick walls and high, neatly trimmed hedges. Further out on their walk, some poppies tossed their heads beside the road.

"A tapestry always appears confused and tangled if you look at the back. I have a feeling that is all I'm seeing right now." Gabriella stopped to pick a poppy. "But surely God knows what He's doing, even if I don't."

"May I ask you a question?"

"Sure, go ahead."

"You are struggling with your God, *n'est-ce pas?* I wondered if it happens often. And if it does, who wins?"

Gabriella chuckled. "That is a very good question, Anne-Marie. You have a way of seeing things, you know?" She bent over and pulled a few more tenacious poppies up by their roots. "Yes, I guess I struggle with Him a lot. I don't know who is going to win this time."

Gabriella pointed to her left where the fields and vineyards opened out below them. "Could anything be more beautiful than that? An ancient countryside with stuccoed houses and vineyards and tall cypress and little flocks of sheep and goats." She looked down at her watch. "Oh my! We've got to get back for the orphans!"

They turned around and headed back into town. "I still have a question," Anne-Marie remarked. "Do you mean that your God is not strong enough to convince you that His way is best?"

"God doesn't work that way. How can I explain it? He gives us a choice, never forces us. And His Spirit guides us. If we listen."

"But you have tried to listen, and you are not sure. Now what do you do?"

Gabriella turned to her friend, admiring both her dark,

natural beauty and her honest questions. "You wait. That is the hardest part. You just wait."

* * *

The letter from Rémi helped to soothe Eliane's frazzled nerves. He wrote that as soon as he arrived in Marseilles he would try to locate the lost trunk. He said he missed her. And he explained that some other *harki* children would be arriving within the next two weeks.

"Great. More *harkis*," she groaned. Then she felt ashamed. Poor people. Slaughtered in Algeria.

At the end of the letter, Rémi gave the slightest hint that he would be coming to France soon. Was she reading it into the letter? No. It was there.

I have done all I can do here. The situation is hopeless. Time is running out.

He closed by promising that he would see her soon. If she held on a few more weeks, then Rémi would be here and maybe she would stop feeling as though her life had been put on hold.

"Come on, children! Time to go. The bus will be here in five minutes."

She placed José on one hip and locked the hotel door, letting Samuel and Rachel go in front. The bus stop was just across the street. For their first visit to the orphanage in Castelnau, she didn't want to be late. She only hoped she didn't see that *harki* boy. She might just give him a piece of her mind.

* * *

Some of the children were doing chores in the parsonage. Others played in the courtyard. Ophélie was chasing Christophe while Anne-Sophie and André ran after her. Anne-Marie watched her vivacious daughter. Today that was enough. She wouldn't fret over what Gabriella had said. She wouldn't show that she was terrified.

If the orphanage closed, where would she go? She had no money. Not one *centime*. Maybe she could get a job cleaning houses. Perhaps that would be the future for a *pied-noir* in France.

Mother Griolet motioned to her from her office window. "Anne-Marie! Your friend is here to see you."

"Ah, *oui! J'arrive.*" She had almost forgotten about Eliane's visit. She caught Sister Isabelle's eye. The timid nun smiled and waved her on.

"I can handle them for a while."

She found Eliane standing in Mother Griolet's hallway, talking with the old nun. "Eliane! Good to see you. Did you have any trouble finding us?"

"No, not at all." She sounded out of breath, but her round face was happy as she shook her bobbed head. "It just took us a little longer than we'd planned. I hope we haven't inconvenienced you." She glanced first at Anne-Marie and then at Mother Griolet.

"Not at all, my dear," the nun reassured. "What fine children you have. What are their names?"

"I'm Samuel!" the boy stated proudly. "And I'm six!"

"Well now, that is just grand. We have many six-year-olds here."

"And I'm Rachel," the little girl whispered, barely audible. "I'm four."

"Good. We have a four-year-old too. Christophe will be thrilled to know there is someone his age."

"And this is José," Eliane said, turning the baby to face the nun. He cooed happily.

"Lovely baby. Well, go on along then. A few more children in the courtyard won't hurt a thing."

"*Merci*, Mother Griolet," Anne-Marie said. For an instant she had the feeling that the last thing the nun wanted was another child underfoot.

* * *

When Hussein saw Eliane Cebrian, he lowered his eyes. A feeling of shame washed over him. He thought of the trunk and how much David had said it meant to this woman. At the time his private mission had seemed much more important than an old trunk. Now he wasn't sure what his mission was.

He slipped into the dormitory. He certainly did not plan to talk to her today. What could he possibly say? Better to remain aloof and angry. Let them think what they wanted at this orphanage. Anything was better than having them discover the truth.

* * *

Today had been the last day of the exchange program. Tonight the young ladies, Mother Griolet, M. Vidal, and the Sisters were celebrating out with dinner in Montpellier.

Anne-Marie was relieved that she and Elaine were left to watch the children. With all the clamor of the kids, plus keeping an eye on baby José, Eliane did not have time to ask her any questions. Anne-Marie did not want her to know how afraid she was.

In the late afternoon Sister Rosaline came across the courtyard, waddling like a mother duck in her white apron. "Listen, Anne-Marie. Do you think you can handle all this, just you two?" She addressed Eliane. "M. Vidal has offered to drive you and your children back to the hotel after we return from the restaurant."

"Perfect. We'll be fine," Eliane assured the nun. "It will give us more time to visit. You and Sister Isabelle go on with the rest of them. And have a wonderful time!"

"It's very kind of you." The nun hurried away, humming happily to herself.

When the children were settled in their dormitories for the night, including Rachel and Samuel, Eliane took Anne-Marie's arm. "We could take a little stroll here in the

255

courtyard, if you want. I'll just put José in the stroller."

Reluctantly Anne-Marie agreed. They walked slowly around the empty courtyard. The silence was heavenly. "Something is wrong, isn't it?" Eliane probed.

Anne-Marie nodded. "I didn't want to mention it. The new boy. He didn't bring any news of Moustafa. I think it is strange. It makes me afraid. That boy is strange."

"He's a selfish little tramp," Eliane said. "I'm sorry he's had a rough life, but he could at least have had the decency to bring me my trunk. After all, it did grant him his freedom. Hmph. I'm sorry about your father's will."

Anne-Marie shrugged. "I'm afraid, Eliane. Gabriella has said that the orphanage may be closed soon. What will I do? I have nothing. Not one *centime*. What will happen to Ophélie and me? I'm so afraid. And I'm afraid that Moustafa won't be coming back."

Eliane took her friend's hand and placed it on the buggy handle, with hers on top. "It's hard, isn't it? I'm afraid too. It feels like my life has stopped. It feels like we're in another hostile environment. Not the terror of war, but the prejudice of racism."

"You talked about a new beginning, Eliane. Do you still believe it?"

The cheerful young mother with the ready smile looked suddenly pensive. "I do believe it." She measured her words. "But it isn't going to be easy. I am trusting God to show us. It is awfully hard to wait, though."

"You sound like Gabriella. She said that was the hardest part, the waiting. But at least you believe Someone is there to answer. I have no one to call on."

"Do you want to have Someone?"

"What do you mean?"

"If you want God to be your God, He's there waiting. Membership is not reserved for some elite group. It's open to everyone who truly believes."

Anne-Marie felt uncomfortable. "I hope you won't take this wrong, but I'm just not convinced. It seems so easy for you, for Gabriella, for Mother Griolet and the Sisters. But you all grew up believing. I did not. Papa didn't start attending church until he was over forty."

"Yes, I remember. We were all surprised to see the well-known captain walk in the door of the *temple*."

Anne-Marie got up her courage. "Tell me what he was like there, Eliane. At home he was so strict and aloof. He tried to explain his new beliefs, but I didn't understand."

"Did he act differently?"

"Not really. Not at first. And then the war came and he was gone so much. When he would come home, he had this urgency in his eyes, but I couldn't understand. I was in my rebellious years. I didn't want to hear. But now I do."

The extreme guilt that had weighed her down years ago rushed back upon Anne-Marie. "We weren't exactly on the best of terms when Mama and Papa were killed. I was living at home with them with Ophélie for a while. It was awkward. They did their best. But I was awful." She covered her face with her hands. "Finally I moved out. And then they were killed. It was terrible, Eliane. I never really knew him. I never knew my father. Mama and I were close, but . . . "

They were leaning over the end wall of the courtyard, staring out at the leafy trees and the tiled roofs of the village. Anne-Marie found no comfort in the landscape.

Eliane's voice was quiet, soothing, her hand gently squeezing Anne-Marie's. "It's okay. Your father loved you very much. You and your mother and your baby. Whenever he came to a prayer meeting, he would pray for you. He loved you so much. Maybe he couldn't say it, but it was written on his face. He wanted you to know the peace he had found. It was so tragic, their deaths. So pointless and tragic."

"Did you read his will, Eliane? Did you at least read it?"

"Yes, as executor, I read it. He left the house, his

possessions, everything to your mother, and then, of course, to you if she were not alive. But there is nothing left to claim now. The house has been looted many times. It stands empty, waiting for the Arabs to take it over. But there is a letter for you with the will. I didn't open that. I'm so sorry the trunk was lost."

Anne-Marie suddenly longed for that letter. Anything in her father's writing. To know he loved her, to know he forgave her. Something. Anything. But Eliane's trunk was lost, so it looked as though what Anne-Marie would have was nothing at all.

* * *

The girls pored over the menu at *Le Ménestrel,* one of the oldest restaurants in Montpellier, debating between the *saumon fumé,* the *magret de canard aux figues,* and the *foie gras aux épinards crus.* Candles flickered on each table of four, and soft strands of Haendel and Bach drifted in the background. The young women talked in hushed tones, only occasionally bursting out in a ripple of laughter. It didn't matter. They occupied the entire restaurant.

Later, they enthusiastically sampled different cheeses, undaunted by the strong smells that had become so familiar to them over the past months. Stephanie chose a goat's cheese and a *bleu* as well as St. Marcelan.

"You're brave!" whispered Gabriella, who took a wedge of Brie and a slice of *Pyrénées.*

"It's my last chance," Stephanie confided to her happily. As the cheese plates were being cleared off for the dessert course, the *maître d'* stopped by each table, explaining that the stone vaulted ceilings in the ancient room where they sat dated back to the fourteenth century.

Gabriella closed her eyes briefly, soaking in the peaceful ambiance, so different from the bedlam at the orphanage. She wished that Anne-Marie could have joined them. As it was, the young *pied-noir* and Eliane had stayed behind with the passel of children so that both Sister Isabelle and Sister

Rosaline could take part in the elegant dinner. At least the children would be tucked into bed by now.

Gabriella noted that the Sisters were enjoying every minute of "indulging the flesh," as Sister Isabelle called it. Even M. Vidal seemed lively and talkative tonight, sharing stories of the war with an astonished group of young women. Mother Griolet's voice sounded almost carefree as it mingled with M. Vidal's, adding a detail here and there to an adventure.

When the group finally rose and left the restaurant, it was well past eleven. For Mother Griolet's sake, Gabriella felt extremely thankful that the evening and the program had ended on a happy note. Even without David.

* * *

After breakfast the next morning, Gabriella and Mme Leclerc helped Caroline and Stephanie gather their bags and take them down the winding staircase to where a taxi waited. "Well, we're off to the train station and three weeks of travel," Caroline said happily. "You sure you won't change your mind, Gabriella? We're gonna see seven countries in three weeks. It should be a real adventure. Take your mind off other things."

Gabriella hesitated. It would be so nice to escape for a few weeks. But she had already made up her mind. Mother Griolet needed her. "No, I'm going to stay."

"Waiting for David, huh?" Caroline eyed her slyly. "Well, I hope for your sake it's worth it. Good-bye. *Au revoir,* Mme Leclerc." She stepped into the taxi.

Gabriella turned and gave Stephanie a warm hug. "Have a good time on your travels. And be careful!" she admonished her friend playfully.

"Don't worry about me. It'll be a blast. And then I'll have to get back to the good old U.S.A. fast." She giggled. "Otherwise I'll just float across the ocean on all my newly acquired blubber."

Gabriella was sorry to see her go. Stephanie looked at life so simply, taking whatever came without reading into it a deeper meaning. Gabriella gave her a kiss on each cheek. "I'm going to miss you. Thanks for everything."

"We did have some fun times, didn't we?" She laughed again, then whispered, "And don't pay any attention to Caroline. She's just jealous. Promise me you'll tell me how the story ends!"

"I promise."

The taxi drove off over the cobblestones with Caroline and Stephanie waving from the back seat. Mme Leclerc stood beside Gabriella, wiping her eyes. "It is always so *difficile* to see my girls go. *Oh là là!* Thank goodness you're not leaving me yet."

"Thank you for letting me stay. I promise I'll know something soon."

"I'm not in any hurry. And your family is welcome to stay here when they arrive. I'll be leaving for a month starting on July the 23rd. When did you say they would arrive?"

"On the 16th."

"Ah, well, you see. It will work out just fine. It will be *un vrai plaisir* to meet them."

"Yes. And thank you, Mme Leclerc. I don't know what I would have done with them otherwise. It's not as if they could stay at the orphanage."

"*Oh là, non!* That's for sure." Mme Leclerc rolled her eyes. "I'm delighted to have them here. And don't you worry about that Miss Caroline. I'm sure your M. Hoffmann will be coming back."

"*On verra,*" whispered Gabriella. "I hope so. We'll just have to wait and see."

Chapter 19

David had been right. Reluctantly Jacques came back for one more run with the *Capitaine*, agreeing to bring a last load of *harki* women and children to Marseilles. Within the week, Moustafa had rounded up fourteen children as well as his mother and two sisters, all of whom were now ready to leave. They stood on an otherwise abandoned dock ten kilometers outside of Algiers. The sky was dark.

Jacques looked proudly at the assembled little group. "You done right to ask me, M. Hoffmann. You done right. You sure you won't be coming with me now?"

"No, Jacques. Not yet. As I told you, I have to get Moustafa to Philippeville on Tuesday. The *harki* boat is leaving then. Once he and his brother are safe, then I'll go too." He patted Jacques on the back. "Thanks for coming back, Jacques. You don't know what this means."

Jacques flashed him a timid smile, shook his hand, and bellowed to the group, "Time to go, folks. Let's get outta here!"

Mme Dramchini hugged her son to her breast. "You come soon, with your brother." Before Moustafa had a chance to answer, his mother was scurrying about, counting children, memorizing names.

A real mother hen, David thought, amused. Moustafa had said she would be perfect for the job, and he was right! His two teenaged sisters followed the orders of their mother, gathering up luggage, wiping tears from little faces, whispering words of encouragement to frightened children.

"Did you get the message out soon enough?" Moustafa questioned David.

"I certainly hope so," David chuckled. "I'm not sure what Jean-Louis will say when he sees this load of passengers." He suddenly looked very serious. "There's no room for them at St. Joseph's. Gabby has written that the townspeople are protesting the arrival of Arab kids."

"What will they do?" Jacques asked.

"If there is no place at St. Joseph's, they will be sent to the camps, the refugee camps that are being set up for the *harkis*," Moustafa replied grimly.

Jacques cursed under his breath. "A prison in France."

David shrugged. "At least they will live. Don't worry, Moustafa. They'll be safe. And when you get to France, your family will be waiting for you to start over. A new beginning. You'll see."

David knew that his words did not sound convincing to Moustafa as the young Arab waved good-bye to his mother and sisters. Yes, at least these few would get away. But Hussein's friend Fatima had not shown up. David thought it quite strange. She knew the day and the time. She had been so adamant about going. But there was no sign of her. David hoped she did not lie dead in some forgotten side street.

They could not wait any longer. He motioned for Jacques to leave, and the *Capitaine* cast off from the docks and floated peacefully out into the Mediterranean.

For an instant, David felt the peace. He wished to high heavens he was on that boat. But everything was going to be okay. There was less than one week to wait. That was no time at all.

"Come on, Moustafa. Relax. They're safe. Let's go find Rémi and get home." David yawned. "It's past midnight."

Moustafa nodded, and he and David walked through the heavy brush without talking, listening to the crickets' incessant chirping. Somewhere a twig cracked as if stepped upon. The two men stopped. David put his finger to his lips. Nothing.

Moments later, coming out of nowhere, three men in ski masks appeared. There was only a brief scramble. Caught from behind by one of the hooded men, David looked around for Moustafa. The Arab lay on the ground, unconscious.

One of the men held his hand over David's mouth, twisting his arm behind his back.

"Where's your car?"

David did not reply. Somewhere nearby, Rémi was waiting in the car.

There was a blow to his stomach, and David doubled over. "Answer me if you want to live."

"A friend let us off at the road," he gasped. "He'll be back soon." Then everything went black.

* * *

Rémi Cebrian waited in his car, three kilometers from the dock, concealed in the bushes. He was the eyes of this mission, his job to watch and warn if anything looked amiss. Another car, a dark colored Peuguot, had driven by twice, slowed to a crawl, and parked five hundred meters up the road, near the path. Rémi flicked a match and read his watch. After midnight. The rendezvous for the children had been an hour ago. Why would someone show up so late?

He touched the rifle on the seat beside him, hesitating. Slowly he stepped out of the car, shutting the door with the slightest of sounds. He jogged through the bushes, toward where the car had disappeared.

There was a faint rustling of leaves. He stepped farther

into the foliage and heard David's voice. "A friend let us off at the road. He'll be back soon." A curse. A thud. Then silence. From the path two masked men carried Moustafa and David over their shoulders and pushed them into the back seat of a car, while a third let himself in the driver's seat. The doors slammed shut, and the car screeched on its wheels as it backed around and flew through the night.

Rémi felt his muscles go weak with fear. Then with some strange strength, he ran to the car and pulled into the road. He did not turn on the headlights, but drove recklessly, terrified, in pursuit of the gray Peugeot. The stretch of road was deserted. Within five minutes, he could pick out the car, still careening madly in the distance.

It was a brief prayer he sent to the heavens. "Give me eyes to see. Give me eyes to see."

*   *   *

When David came to, he was afraid to open his eyes, afraid to see Moustafa's lifeless body beside him. He was aware of a terrible throbbing in his head. His mouth was gagged with a cloth, his throat parched. Through blurred vision, he took in his surroundings. He was lying on the floor in a basement. There was no light.

Eventually his eyes adjusted to the darkness. Someone else was in the room. He heard the heavy breathing of someone who slept. David's hands were secured behind him, his feet bound tightly. He tried to turn on his side, and a piercing pain shot through the same shoulder that had received the bullet wound in March.

Cold fear overpowered him. Were the hooded men here too, waiting? Waiting for him to wake up so they could torture him? That could be the only reason for leaving him alive. His mind was foggy. He couldn't think.

Even darkness is not dark to Thee. That same verse. At once the debilitating fear left. He was not alone. Trust. In his mind he prayed, "Help me, God. Help us. Help me see a way of escape, dear God. Help me." With the psalmist's words in his mind, David fell back asleep.

* * *

The faintest light of predawn broke through a small, barred window near the ceiling of the room. Moustafa blinked his eyes, hoping to shut out the nightmare, but this was real. He sat in the same dingy basement where he had spent five weeks with Anne-Marie last fall. He was sure it was the same place. The same filthy prison. He wanted to cry out, but the sob stayed in his throat, held in place by the thick handkerchief secured in his mouth.

David Hoffmann lay stretched out uncomfortably on the floor nearby. Moustafa watched him intently. Yes, he was breathing. Relief flooded through him. Together there was hope.

He rolled over awkwardly and caught his breath. They were not alone. An older man, unshaven and wearing a white T-shirt and suit pants, slept, his head resting against the cement wall. His hands and feet were bound, as were Moustafa's and David's.

Somehow Ali had caught up with them. How? Moustafa knew the answer immediately. Fatima. The girl had not shown up for the boat. She was the only other person who knew where the meeting was to take place. And if Fatima had led Ali to them, then what about Hussein?

He swallowed hard. Now it all made sense. Hussein showing up, begging, leaving in the trunk, and then abandoning it at the port.

He could not speak. He could not move. Moustafa lay flat on his stomach and felt his tears form a small, wet patch on the ripping mattress. A low moan echoed in his soul. *Anne-Marie. Anne-Marie.*

* * *

When David woke again, the room was bathed in gray shadows brought on by a single barred window. Moustafa lay on a mattress nearby. Their eyes met, and they read each other's thoughts: sorrow and relief. They were both alive.

Moustafa motioned with his head toward a corner of the room. A man sat with his back against the wall, still asleep. David scrutinized him carefully. His legs were tucked up against his chest, bound. *He must be very tall,* David thought. His forehead was bent forward, resting on his knees. His hair was peppered with gray.

David scrambled to sit up, and the noise caused the older man to stir. Slowly he lifted his head, blinking his eyes.

David could not cry out. Only his eyes registered his terrible surprise. Sitting across from him, ten feet away, was his own father.

* * *

There was nothing to do but sit and stare. It was his father all right, but much changed. He was unshaven and gaunt. The proud allure that had always been part of Roger Hoffmann's appearance was replaced by a type of subservient gaze, as if, as if. . . . David felt sick to his stomach. It was the gaze he had seen on the faces of the prisoners at the death camp. He would never forget that hopeless, defeated gaze. The look of a tortured man, a man who had been to hell and back and whose life was nothing but bare survival.

How could his father be in Algeria, in the hands of whom? The FLN? Was it another level of Ali's sadistic revenge? The madman had won. His last victory would be for David to watch his father die. Then Moustafa. Was that the plan?

David felt the tears in his eyes, and they surprised him. This man he had hated, this distant father, sat weak and helpless before him. David did not want to feel sympathy. He did not want that part of his heart exposed. It was too painful.

But with arms and legs tied, unable to move or speak, unable to control his emotions, he sat and let the tears fall down his cheeks.

He swallowed hard. *We are going to die here together, and I've never once heard you say you care about me.* But in that pitiful gaze from his father, he read something, perhaps not love, but concern. He brought his head to his knees and wiped his face on his pants. Still the tears came.

Roger Hoffmann, bound and gagged in the same manner, stared at him with an expression of deep sorrow. One tear, then another. A wet gleam in his eyes. It trickled down his cheek.

David heard Mother Griolet's words. *Your father wept.* Perhaps it was true after all. Perhaps his father had cried when he had found him at the orphanage all those years ago. The tears on his face at this moment suddenly made anything possible in the past. Anything.

* * *

Rémi Cebrian had worked frantically through the night, but light was coming too soon. Now his little band of men raced through the Casbah, looking for the building where he had seen Moustafa and David imprisoned in the night. The tiny white bits of material he had left on signposts had been the only way he could possibly retrace his steps in the labyrinth of the Casbah. He whispered a prayer of thankfulness that it had worked.

Now Abdul and Amar, his friends and farmhands, stood panting beside him. Their Arab faces would be accepted in the Casbah if dawn broke before they could free the prisoners. Rémi admired their courage, their willingness to risk their lives for him, for his friends. That was the Algeria he knew and loved. Friendship, not betrayal.

Each man carried a rifle over his shoulder. After one last turn into a tiny alleyway, they reached the building where the prisoners had been enclosed. *Let them still be there,* Rémi prayed. Abdul and Amar climbed with Rémi onto a low roof beside the building. From his perch, Rémi peered into the barred window. Three men, bound and gagged, sat in the room. Abdul dropped to the ground and tried the door. It was bolted with a lock. They would have to use the small explosive to free the men. Time was of the utmost importance.

Rémi tossed a small stone through the window. Immediately three pairs of eyes looked toward him. Pressing his face against the bars, he whispered, "We are going to have to blow it open. Move back, and be ready."

The men nodded, relief in their eyes. But before he had taken the explosives from their bag, Abdul climbed up beside Rémi. "Someone is coming," he whispered.

Rémi felt a sinking in his heart. Four men approached in the predawn light. What to do? Shoot them now? But that would awaken the whole neighborhood. They crouched out of sight, hearing their own hearts pounding in their ears.

The tallest man, older than the others, inserted a key in the locked door and threw it open, motioning to his men to follow him inside. Then the door was closed behind them, and Rémi watched the scene through the window, dizzy with fear.

The tall man slapped David across the face, then rammed his head with the butt of his gun and laughed. "So! At last you are here." His voice was soft and seething. "It could not have worked out better for me, David Hoffmann. You are all here. Our dear Moustafa—" He nodded to one of the men, who kicked Moustafa in the stomach.

"Easy," the tall, angry Arab muttered. "Don't kill him yet. I want them to know every last grisly detail."

He turned back to David, who was crumpled on the floor, blood seeping from his head. "And your estranged father, Roger Hoffmann. Brilliant to have you all here together. You will watch him die slowly, painfully, as my father did. This will be my final revenge.

"Yes, final! No one has escaped. Not one. Have you not

guessed? Could you not read the mind of my prodigy, Hussein? Of course not! We are too smart! He is even now accomplishing his task in Castelnau at the little orphanage." He laughed madly. "I have word! The timing! The incredible timing! Today I have word that Hussein has successfully completed his little task. What is that, you ask? Ha! I will tell you. He has eliminated your friends."

Moustafa stirred, crying from within the gag, but it was only a muffled sound. Rémi saw the anguish, the hatred in his glare.

The tall man continued talking about the boy, Hussein. So this was Ali Boudani. Rémi had heard them talk of the revenge-obsessed man. Everything they had said was true.

He was snickering, "Not only Anne-Marie, mind you. Her daughter! Yes, her daughter was the first to go. And then the redhead. And all the children. They are all gone. Explosions in the night in both dormitories. Nothing left of that place but an old nun, and she will die soon enough as it is." He paced gleefully around the room as the three bound men turned their eyes down and wept.

Ali Boudani was momentarily distracted by his own sickening pride. The sun was rising over the stack of buildings in the Casbah. Soon people would awake. Rémi sensed that it was now or never. With a quick whispering, the men were ready.

Abdul and Amar dropped to the ground without a sound. They kicked open the door and fired. Several bullets sprayed forth, hitting two of Ali's henchmen, who fell to the ground, stunned and wounded. Rémi fired from the window, and his shot lodged in the back of the Arab who held Moustafa.

Enraged, Ali turned his gun toward the window and fired twice. The bullets ricocheted off the stone. He turned his gun on Moustafa and fired two more times. Moustafa screamed and fell to the ground. Amar came at Ali. From close range, Amar's bullet hit Ali in the gut. Ali cursed, clutching his stomach and dropping his gun. Abdul struggled to cut away the prisoners' ropes. "Hurry, run!" Rémi urged.

Ali lay dazed beside Roger Hoffmann. He reached for his gun, while the older American struggled to stand. Rémi fired another shot. Ali never reached his pistol.

Supporting the prisoners, the three rescuers half-ran, half-stumbled into the streets. Doors opened; people screamed.

Abdul looked at Moustafa. "Can you get us out of here?"

Moustafa was losing blood. "Yes, I know the way," he moaned.

"Good. I'll stay behind and divert them. No one will know I am not an inhabitant of the Casbah myself."

"Thank you, friend," Rémi said. "Be careful. God be with you."

*   *   *

Abdul watched the little band disappear down a tiny, steep alleyway. By now Arab men were emptying into the streets, guns in hand. Several had discovered the men in the basement.

"It is Ali Boudani! He is badly injured. Quickly! Get help for him and his men."

Chaos reigned. Abdul shook with fear inside but composed himself enough to shout, "There!" He pointed in the opposite direction from that which the group had taken. "Do you have a gun?" He grabbed a young Arab by the arm. "Down that street. Come with me. We must find them."

Immediately six or seven men charged ahead of Abdul, with a dozen others following in their nightshirts. "Spread out!" he cried. As they separated, Abdul lost himself in an empty sidestreet. Maybe Rémi and the others would have time to escape. His chest heaved up and down, heart racing. He had shot his own countryman. Another Arab. He prayed to Allah that he had not killed him. How he hated this war!

With the shouts of angry men ringing in his ears, Abdul crept quickly through the tiny, twisting streets of the Casbah.

Much later, he found his way through the arches that separated the Casbah from the rest of Algiers. He was safe. More or less.

* * *

Rémi had parked the car in an alleyway in Bab el Oued. The men reached it in broad daylight, piling in on top of each other. Rémi sped through the streets, panic racing through his brain. Moustafa was badly injured. David and the other man had lesser wounds, still serious. But what hospital was safe? The angry Casbah mob would search for them. His only hope was to get to his farmhouse, care for them the best he could, and get to Philippeville in four days. Moustafa had to make the boat. It was his last chance.

The men said nothing. Exhaustion, pain, and sorrow filled their eyes. He cringed. Could it be true? The orphanage destroyed. Eliane. His thoughts turned to Eliane and the children. He shuddered. Surely not. Surely this madman was wrong. God protects His own.

* * *

No one had spoken since they arrived at Rémi's farmhouse and collapsed inside. A pretty Arab woman called Madira was attending to Moustafa. Rémi explained that she was Abdul's wife. She had cried with relief when her husband entered the farmhouse, hours after the others.

David tried to make sense of the turn of events, but he could not think straight. He could only hear the crazed Ali explaining the fate of the orphanage. Surely, surely he was wrong. Hussein? With bombs? It seemed so impossible, and yet it made perfect sense. That was why Fatima had never shown up at the docks. She was also working with Ali. Fatima and Hussein. Children. Mere children were malicious murderers.

David would not believe that they were gone. Gabriella, Anne-Marie, Ophélie. The others. It was too grotesquely impossible to imagine.

But he feared with everything within him that it was true.

No God would not permit it! Every ounce of faith was drained away. Bitterness engulfed him. If it were true, then all he had left was this dying father. He did not want him. It was not a fair trade. Gabriella for his dad. It wasn't fair.

* * *

The doctor was a friend of Rémi's, a *pied-noir* who had practiced in Algiers for thirty years. He examined the wounded men without any commentary, then quietly addressed Rémi. "I can remove the bullets from the Arab here. It will be painful, but there is too great a risk in taking him to the hospital. Do you have any alcohol?"

Rémi nodded.

"Get him drunk, then. Good and drunk. It is the only way he will stand the pain."

Two hours later, Moustafa floated in and out of consciousness. Through persistence, Rémi had gotten half a bottle of whisky down his throat. The doctor was ready to begin.

David lay on the couch in the den. The doctor had diagnosed a broken rib and advised him to have it x-rayed as soon as he got to France. David also had a nasty head wound, from the butt of Ali's gun. His head was now covered with white gauze. His whole body ached.

His father slept on a mattress hauled from one of the bedrooms. Starvation and torture, the doctor had whispered. He needed medical help badly. It would have to wait until they got to France.

David was glad he could not see the procedure the doctor was performing on Moustafa. In spite of his rage and grief, the only thing that seemed to make any sense was prayer. He closed his eyes. "God, I don't understand what is happening. I am too afraid to learn the truth. Gabby has always said You are a good God. She says that the righteous will prosper. I have read it in Your Word. Please, bring Moustafa through." David shut his ears to the low moans coming from the other room. "Bring him through, God. And . . . and give me a word, a simple word to say to my father."

Before he had finished his prayer, Roger Hoffmann whispered, "David?"

"Yes?"

"Are you badly hurt, son?"

"No. No, Father, I don't think so." The words were like glue in his mouth. "And you?"

"Fine," he sighed. "The plane has already left." He sounded incoherent, delirious.

"Father?"

"Be sure, Annette, to show your American passport if there is any doubt. I'll be back in three days."

"Father! Father, what are you saying?"

"Detained, David. I was detained for questioning." He looked at his son, his eyes dull. "It was the SS. They found out our work. Took me to a camp. It was the torture, David. I thought I would say nothing. The torture. All my fault. For you, for Annette and Greta. All my fault."

His father's voice was cracking with emotion. "I had forgotten what you say when you are tortured. Until recently." His breath came in sporadic sighs. "I'm so sorry, David. It was all my fault."

Roger Hoffmann was sobbing like a baby. At first David could only stare, wide-eyed. Surely this wasn't his father, confessing in tears before him. Why had he never explained it before? Why had he not said that he too had been taken to a camp?

David felt he would vomit. He put a hand on his forehead. "You were in a camp?"

"Only for a few months. My passport worked for me. But there was no word of you and your mother and sister. By the time I traced you, it was to that orphanage in France. And you were alone."

"You hated me for surviving, didn't you? You wanted it to be Mama, not me." There was no accusation in David's voice. He might have been asking a question about the weather.

His father did not answer. At first David thought he had fainted. His breathing was slow and with effort.

"I didn't hate you, David. I hated myself. For all these years, I have hated myself. And your presence in my life has been a constant reminder of the fool that I was, of the lives I destroyed. Annette. Greta! Why did I leave that day? I have asked myself that question a thousand times. And the only answer is self-hate. I contaminated you with it, David. I thought I had ruined your life, as I had my own.

"But you were strong and smart. You survived in spite of me. You didn't need me. And I couldn't bear the sight of you. Your very presence accused me."

David did not want his father to see that he was crying again. With difficulty, he asked, "And now?"

"Now." He spoke resignedly. "Now the nightmare has come back to haunt us both. Another war. Another chance to betray the one I love." He did not look at David. The words floated in the stifling air. Roger Hoffmann fainted.

* * *

When Moustafa awoke, he was aware of incredible pain. It was more than physical. It was psychological, invading his being. He wished he had died from the bullet wounds. Now the torture was only prolonged.

There was no reason to leave for France. Anne-Marie was dead. His thoughts spiraled down to despair. He thought of his mother and sisters arriving in France with all the children. What would they find? A shelled-out orphanage? A crazy kid tossing *plastiquages* as if they were stones? Who would warn them?

Another thought came to him from the corner of his mind. *He's lying.* Ali could be lying. He had done it before, months ago, telling Anne-Marie that they had captured Ophélie. The thought made his heart soar with hope. Of course! A lie. Hussein would not murder. *But how can I be sure?*

Trust. What was that word? Trust? Whom? There was no one to trust.

The Christ. He heard the words in his mind. He fought to push them away. Impossible! No God could save them from this hell.

And yet, for now, they were alive and safe. It stung him to think of it. Despair or hope. He could choose. He closed his eyes, wincing with pain, and, reciting something he remembered reading in the New Testament, Moustafa whispered, "I believe. Help Thou mine unbelief."

Chapter 20

The petition from the townspeople of Castelnau was quite conclusive. *Get the Algerian kids out and now.* Only Pierre Cabrol, the *boulanger,* and Jean-Louis had voted to keep them. Every other person had expressed, some vehemently, dissatisfaction with the overcrowded, understaffed, and integrated orphanage of St. Joseph. The situation already looked grim, and now another fourteen *harki* children had arrived in the night with three Arab women.

The petitions had first gone to Mother Griolet's superiors and now lay on her desk, beside the letter she had received from her superiors several weeks ago and another polite though pointed letter from the church.

Due to grave complaints from the citizens of Castelnau, we hereby recommend that all Algerian children be immediately sent to the refugee camps being set up for the sole purpose of housing this unfortunate population. If they are not removed from the orphanage within the next thirty days, the church superiors will take firm action and close the orphanage of St. Joseph until the problem can be resolved and a new Sister

*appointed. This would mean, regretfully, the resignation
of Mother Jeanette Griolet. . . .*

Mother Griolet leafed through each petition, reading the
angry notes. She could almost feel the embarrassment of her
friends and neighbors as they scribbled their signatures in
barely visible ink. People she had loved and trusted and helped.
People who had given their money to the church of St. Joseph.

Denise Cabrol was tricky. She'd added the exchange
program in for her own purposes, knowing that most people
would agree with the Algerian problem and not consider the
loss if the exchange program closed too. Monique Pons and
Yvette Leclerc were quick to note it on their petitions, as were
a handful of other widows in town who gained a salary
through the *demi-pension* program with the students.

Denise was a jealous woman who had never understood
that her husband's sympathies for St. Joseph's had nothing to
do with an interest in Mother Griolet and everything to do
with an interest in the Christ. It didn't matter really. If
Mother Griolet left, the Franco-American program would
close at once. So there she was. The choice was hers. Send the
Algerian kids away or be sent away herself. She laughed in
spite of the grim letter. There really was no choice at all. She
would not send orphaned *harki* children to be cloistered from
French society. Here, at least, they could learn to function
within a small village, find some safety, integrate. With all her
heart, Mother Griolet knew that the answer to the *harki*
problem was not refugee camps.

She fingered a letter from Joseph Cohen. Dear Joseph.
She wished for a moment that she were back at the chalet in
Switzerland, sitting by the roaring fire with Joseph and
Emeline there to advise her. As it was, they counseled her
now through a letter. In this one, Joseph urged her to get in
touch with his Swiss friend, Henri Krugler, who now lived in
Lodève, an hour's drive from Montpellier.

He will be sympathetic to your cause. A giant of a man

whose heart in every way matches his size. He is very keen on integration. . . . Mother Griolet reread Joseph's description of Henri Krugler's *centre aéré* in Lodève, which had recently opened to both Algerian and French children. She knew that the ancient city in the hills of the Cevennes was now being flooded with *harki* refugees. Perhaps indeed Henri Krugler could help her find homes for the children before the church dispersed them to the camps.

With great determination, the old nun picked up a pen and began to write a letter to this intriguing stranger. She hummed the tune of a hymn that Rebecca Madison had taught her years ago. *My Jesus, I love Thee, I know Thou art mine. To Thee all the follies of sin I resign. My gracious Redeemer, My Savior art Thou. If ever I loved Thee, my Jesus 'tis now.* Sometimes those Protestants had a very simple, beautiful way of expressing their faith.

She smiled as she heard the words in English. Then, with a catch in her throat, she began to sing another verse of the hymn. "I'll love Thee in life, I will love Thee in death. And praise Thee as long as Thou lendest me breath, And say when the death dew lies cold on my brow, if ever I loved Thee, my Jesus 'tis now." Then she switched to French and sang the last two lines in her native tongue, loudly with a mixture of joy and pain. *"Ma voix expirante ne s'entendra plus. Sachez que je chante, je t'aime, O Jésus."*

The words made a chill run through Mother Griolet as she continued writing. "Lord Jesus, may this dear man know what to do next. Time is running out." In more ways than one, Mother Griolet had the feeling that time was indeed running out.

* * *

It was love that propelled Mother Griolet to enter the empty chapel in the late afternoon. A strange kind of love. She stepped slowly onto the stones, relieved to escape the brutal heat of the sun in the cool interior. She placed her hand on the back of the last row of wooden pews to steady herself. She felt so dizzy. She closed her eyes briefly.

With labored steps, Mother Griolet walked toward the west side of the chapel into a small alcove. She paused in front of a stone pillar, one of several that supported the roof. Then she touched the simple stone monument that rested on the pillar. She read the words through blurred vision. *Nos frères, nos fils, nos maris qui ont donné leurs vies pour notre pays. 1914-1918.* There on the plaque were listed all the names of the men from Castelnau who had died during the First World War. It was almost an act of self-pity to look, Mother Griolet chided herself. She ran her fingers over the stone, feeling the rise and fall of the chiseled letters. Thirty-eight names. Her hand came to rest on the last one. Sebastien Vidal.

She let the memories come, let the emotions rise as she remembered the soft kiss on her lips and the terrible searing in her heart when he left. The bittersweet agony of knowing he loved her and knowing he must leave. The scene rushed upon her in three dimensions, and she leaned against the stone to keep her balance. "Sebastien," she whispered, covering her eyes with one hand.

She shuffled to a wooden pew and sat down. "Dear Lord, my Savior. This has been my calling. This place, this life. I have never accused You of taking Sebastien. There are things too hard to understand. I have known Your power and grace for all these years. And now, this place is being taken away from me. But it is not mine. It is Yours. Work Your will, Divine Father, and may I accept it. You have always provided for every need, for me, for the Sisters, for the children. I trust You now."

She closed her eyes and pictured the orphans in the courtyard, laughing. She thought of Gabriella and Anne-Marie and the cold stone pillar with Sebastien Vidal's name carved into it. "Please Holy God, give these women Your courage to face the future. I understand the pain of waiting. Give them courage. And show me how I can help. Surely You will not forsake Your own. We are the people of Your pasture and the sheep of Your hand."

She did not hear Anne-Marie enter the chapel, so that when the girl sat down beside her, the nun let out a small gasp, then smiled. "My child!"

"I scared you. I'm sorry." Anne-Marie sat down. "Am I bothering you?"

"No, of course not. I was just finishing my conversation."

"Your conversation?" Anne-Marie asked, looking around the empty chapel.

"With the Lord."

"Oh." Anne-Marie lowered her eyes. "Excuse me." She rose to leave.

"My dear, don't go. Please. The Lord and I have been talking for many years. He understands interruptions. Especially those that He ordains."

Anne-Marie blushed.

"Sit down, please."

The young woman could not look the nun in the eyes. "I am so afraid, Mother Griolet."

"Afraid?"

"Afraid of the future, if the orphanage is closed. Where will I go? You and the others, you have saved my life and that of Ophélie. We have no one. I don't want to return to the life of fear and hiding. I long to start a new life with Ophélie. I even had hope. But now."

Mother Griolet turned toward Anne-Marie, blinking back a stubborn tear. "Life takes many turns and twists. It bruises and burns and rips apart. But it also loves and heals and forgives." She took the younger woman's thin, smooth hands into her own. "Perfect love casts out all fear. And there is only one perfect love. It is in Christ. In seventy-two years, He has yet to let me down. He is in control when life is completely out of control." A smile spread across her face.

She searched Anne-Marie's eyes for understanding. Perhaps there was a gleam, a hint. Mother Griolet sensed an urgency to open her heart to this brave young woman. "It's the truest word in all of time. If you are in Christ, nothing, nothing, my child, can separate you from Him ever again. Not life, nor death, nor persecutions, nor nakedness, nor peril, nor sword."

Her words were melodic and powerful as she sang the Scripture as much for herself as for Anne-Marie. The lively little nun recounted the promises of God to Anne-Marie and as she did, God's peace flooded into her own soul once again.

* * *

Jean-Louis Vidal found Jeanette Griolet dozing at her desk. The sight of her, mouth opened, face braced in one hand that leaned precariously on the desk, embarrassed and frightened him. He had never known Jeanette to nap in the middle of the day. He fidgeted with his hands, running the yellowed envelope between them, back and forth, back and forth. Perhaps he should turn and leave. Taking a deep breath from the hallway, he rapped softly on the office door, which stood ajar.

There was a shuffling sound, then Jeanette cleared her throat and called, *"Oui, qui est là?"*

Jean-Louis took two steps into the office, keeping his eyes turned to the floor. His temple pulsed. "I just had a little matter to discuss with you," he mumbled.

The nun straightened up, flashed him a tired smile. "Of course, Jean-Louis. Of course, come in and sit down."

Always a shy man, he was often embarrassed in the presence of women. But life had forced him to overcome some of the timidity. Normally his conversations with Jeanette were pleasant and unhindered. He sat stiffly on the edge of the chair, still clutching the envelope.

"Whatever is the matter, Jean-Louis? You look positively moribund!"

He removed his wire glasses and ran his fingers around his bloodshot eyes. "I have something for you." He held out the envelope. "But before you read it, I must tell you one thing. I have kept this letter all these many, many years, not out of hurt, but out of love. I have loved you, Jeanette, as much as Sebastien did, and more."

His hands were shaking violently. He could not look her in the eyes, but his voice was steady. "It has been my greatest pleasure and joy to know you, to work beside you, to watch you. We could not be man and wife. I knew that so long ago. But you have been my sister." He smiled bashfully at the pun. "A sister closer than blood. I admire your tireless work for the children, for this town, for American women, for me. You are a fine servant of our Lord. Don't let those letters get to you. I will do everything I can to keep St. Joseph's open. I had to tell you now, so there would be no doubt. Whatever you need, I will help you. I will always help you."

He stopped talking abruptly, feeling the sweat on his forehead. He placed the envelope on her desk. "I could not give it to you sooner. Forgive me." With a slight bow of the head, he rose to leave.

"Jean-Louis," Mother Griolet said softly. She took his hand and squeezed it. "Thank you. You have always been here for me. You are a blessing in my life."

He squeezed her hand in return, turned and left the office.

* * *

Jeanette rested her face in her hands and stared at the yellowed envelope. Her name, Jeanette, was written across it in a handwriting that she recognized immediately, even after half a century. The envelope had been ripped open, then taped shut, and the tape, equally yellowed, no longer held any stick.

A letter from Sebastien.

Her hand shook the slightest bit as she pulled out two pieces of paper, one yellowed, one white. She opened the yellowed sheet and felt a tightness in her throat. Fifty years could not make her forget the way her heart leaped when she had received a letter from Sebastien. This one was barely legible, but nonetheless his hand.

Ma chère Jeanette,

I fear I will not see you again on this earth. I cannot bear to tell you the extent of my injuries or the nightmare we face. I only want you to know that I have loved you for two years. I could not love you more. But I must release you to God. Go forth with strength, examine your heart for your service. It is worthy. More worthy than I. I wanted to share life with you. If not me, let God lead you into your calling. Only please care for Jean-Louis. He will miss me so. And his love for you is as strong as mine.

Sebastien

The clean white sheet was scribbled by Jean-Louis and dated several weeks ago.

Forgive me, Jeanette. This letter was found on Sebastien's body. I could not give it to you all those years ago to place an extra burden on your heart. Somehow you fulfilled his wish without knowing of it. God is gracious. Merci.

Jean-Louis

It had startled her to see Sebastien's handwriting. Why now? Why after she had permitted herself that brief moment of memory in the chapel? She thought about the letter, and then she thought about Jean-Louis' note. Dear Jean-Louis. He had seen it lived out before him. There was no burden in the task. Surely he had understood what had been evident to her for years. His absolute devotion and her complete love.

* * *

To say that people seemed frazzled at the orphanage was a gross understatement. Fourteen new Arab children and three Arab women were, as the French said, the drop that makes the vase run over. The children had slept on mattresses on the floor of the dormitories. The three women had spent the night in Mother Griolet's den, but as soon as more mattresses could be found, they planned to move into one of the classrooms on the third floor of the parsonage. With almost sixty children at the orphanage, the buildings seemed to somehow shrink. Room was running out.

At least the girls from the exchange program were gone, Gabriella thought as she pushed several straggling children into the refectory. The din of silverware clanking on plates and voices shouting greeted her ears. One of the new Arabs screamed and another threw his food. Gabriella observed Sister Rosaline's displeasure. She snapped at them, then asked Hakim to see what they needed.

Sister Isabelle wrung her hands together, completely overwhelmed. Gabriella caught Anne-Marie by the arm and whispered, "This is pure bedlam. We've got to do something."

"I agree, but what?"

Suddenly Gabriella had an idea. Grabbing a soup spoon and a pot, she stood on a chair, raised the pot above her head, and banged it with the spoon. The noise was deafening. Immediately all was silent.

"*Eh, les enfants! Taisez-vous!* Quiet down, won't you? Everyone find seats. Now." Three of the boys who had been flipping peas across a table scrambled to find a chair. They clamped their arms between their legs, looked down, then caught their friends' gaze and giggled. "This is not how we behave at St. Joseph's. Manners are a must if we are to all get along.

"I think it would be appropriate for those of us who have been at St. Joseph's for a while to welcome our new guests. As I call your name, come stand in three rows beside me. Anne-Sophie, Christophe, André, Ophélie, Hakim, Jérémy . . ." Gabriella called all forty-three names, and one by one they came, grinning sheepishly, and stood before the newly arrived

Arab children. Quietly and yet with great animation, Gabriella drew the children around her. "First we'll sing *'Pour ce repas'* in a round. Then *'Eclate de Joie'* and finally, *'Je t'aime, O Jésus.'"*

A short time later, Sister Isabelle and Gabriella were sitting in chairs facing the group of orphans. As they began to sing, a chill ran through Gabriella. The voices of angels. She turned around and saw that the Arab women and children were mesmerized by the different melodies. When the song ended, silence reigned. Then a wide smile formed on one of the Arab woman's face, and she began to clap. Soon all the others joined in. By the time the impromptu program was over, order had been restored to St. Joseph's.

* * *

Mother Griolet had not come to dinner. Gabriella was worried and slipped out as the orphans sat back down to be served dessert. She found the nun in her office, writing letters.

"Mother Griolet, are you all right?"

"I'm afraid that I'm being buried by all this paperwork," she replied, not looking up. "And perhaps I don't quite have the strength to face all the children. There are several possible adoptions I'm working on. I must finish them before, before . . . " She set down the paper. Her eyes fluttered closed briefly, and she ran her hand across her forehead. "The petitions arrived today. All ninety-three of them. And the final warning from the church. We have thirty days to get the Arabs out. I'm afraid I am going to lose my post, Gabriella. I'm just trying to get as many children situated as possible before that happens."

"You mean there is no hope for St. Joseph's?"

"My dear child. I am so sorry to have misled you. I asked you to make a tough decision, and now my control over it has been yanked away. Of course, there is always hope. But not as I had imagined. I will not be staying around unless I agree to send the Arabs away to refugee camps. I don't intend to do that."

"It's not fair! They can't force you to go away. It's wrong!"

"It is not as I had hoped and prayed, but my superiors see it differently. My responsibility is to stand up for what I believe. But I cannot convince others that I am right."

"But the townspeople love you. The church has admired your work. How can they not see the good?"

"It is a dangerous thing to want everyone's approval, Gabriella. You must be willing to stand firm and take the risk of being misunderstood. We must find our approval at the feet of our Master." She closed her eyes again. "It's a lesson I have learned over and over. We're to expect suffering, in whatever form it comes—physical, emotional, spiritual. The Holy Book promises suffering for those who follow Christ."

She placed her unfinished letter in a stack of neatly folded papers. "Come now, Gabriella. They will be needing us at the refectory." Mother Griolet gave a soft groan as she tried to rise from her chair. It shocked Gabriella. Helping her up, she interlocked arms with the nun and walked slowly down the steps into the basement and through the hallway. She felt her mouth go dry. Thirty days. That was all the time they had. It seemed much too short.

* * *

Anne-Marie regarded the big-bosomed, gray-haired Arab woman who was now patting the heads of the children who had crossed the sea with her. She had not seen Mme Dramchini in years, nor her daughters, Saiyda and Rachida. Now they were here. In the confusion of the day she had not yet gotten to speak to them. Now she could have news of Moustafa. She approached them slowly.

"Mme Dramchini, *bonjour.* Do you remember me, Anne-Marie Duchemin?" The gray-haired woman nodded and took Anne-Marie in her arms, kissing her cheeks. *"Ma fille,"* she exclaimed, with a heavy accent.

Knowing that Mme Dramchini had never mastered French, Anne-Marie addressed her daughters. *"Bonjour,* Saiyda and Rachida. How very good to see you." The young women embraced. Politely Anne-Marie answered their questions about how she had arrived with Eliane Cebrian on the ferry. Of course, they remembered Eliane. Yes, yes, Rémi had followed them to the dock. Anne-Marie's head was swimming. She did not know what Moustafa had shared with them. She did not want to seem too eager for information. As glibly as possible, she asked, "And Moustafa. How is he?"

Good! Oh, very well. He and the American had taken them to the little sailboat with the funny Frenchman for a captain. Moustafa was coming with their other brother, Hacène, remember Hacène, the day after independence on a boat just for the *harkis.*

They babbled on, smiling, and Anne-Marie knew then that Moustafa had never mentioned a word about what had happened during the months that he was missing. They did not know she loved him. Not yet.

She could not help but smile with great relief to hear of his plan to come to France. Yes, he was coming! With his mother and sisters here, right here at St. Joseph's, and a boat waiting to bring him. It was a miracle. Moustafa would be coming. The day after independence. Tonight was June thirtieth. She had only four more days to wait.

* * *

Hussein spoke in Arabic with the new kids, placing himself within hearing distance of Anne-Marie and the three Arab women. It took every ounce of concentration for him to keep up a conversation with the children and still make out what the women were saying. He gathered that these Arabs were the mother and sisters of Moustafa. He heard, yes, he was sure that the younger girl said that Moustafa would be

coming on a boat in a very few days. A hint of a smile crossed
his lips. Allah be praised. They were alive! He had heard the
women say it. Moustafa and David had seen them off. He let
out a long sigh.

It scared him slightly to think of seeing David and
Moustafa. It also relieved him greatly. His betrayal had not
meant their deaths. With them, he was sure he could find
protection. Protection until the will of Allah was revealed to
him more clearly.

Chapter 21

The mood in Algiers on July third was one of joy and celebration for the Arab population. In the referendum to determine Algeria's independence, the vote had been 200 to 1 "Yes!" Hundreds of thousands of jubilant Muslims packed the streets of Algiers, singing, waving flags, raising their arms in a cry of victory. Rows of women with white-veiled heads marched behind FLN army men. Today the heavens were raining down not mortar and bloodshed, but a bright ray of peace. Mohemmed and Fatima celebrated with their countrymen, the young girl screaming and waving her body back and forth to the sound of the music that played in the streets.

Ali was in no shape to join in the festivities. He was lucky to be alive, the doctor had told him somberly when he had regained consciousness yesterday. So he had sent Fatima to be his eyes, to take part in the merriment and report every detail back to him.

Fatima craved the approval of her grandfather. For months she had jealously watched him dole out the hardest assignments to Hussein. Who was Hussein? A piece of trash.

Certainly no relation to Ali Boudani. Why Ali had chosen him, trained him to be his apprentice, she could never figure out. But today, with the sun shining and the masses of people singing and dancing together, she did not care. Hussein was far away in France. She had informed Ali of the boat leaving with the *harkis*. She had performed flawlessly! That the men, David and Moustafa, had escaped was no fault of hers.

Algeria free! She could taste it in the air, smell it in a breeze coming in from the sea. Her grandfather stood to gain more power in the new government. She had observed his tactics for a long time now.

* * *

Philippeville was a small port city next to Constantinople, a good 400 kilometers from Algiers. That morning of July third a thick tension hung in the air on the Place as one after another, the Arab soldiers from a Muslim auxiliary troop of the French Army walked up the plank of the ferry that waited for them at port. French officers stood guard, brandishing arms as they welcomed their *harki* brothers aboard. These Arab men, most of them carrying no more than a duffel bag, hurried onto the boat. Their faces read pain, sorrow, and relief.

FLN officers milled around the square, looking disgusted as the *harkis* prepared for departure. When the old Renault pulled to within sight of the ferry, Moustafa squinted, searching for Hacène. It was impossible to make anything out with the crowds.

"He'll be there. Don't worry," David reassured him.

Moustafa nodded. He fixed his thoughts on the feat before him, walking the 500 yards to the boat. He had not walked more than a few yards since the shooting four days ago. The two bullets had been removed. The one from his shoulder had come out easily; the other had lodged itself stubbornly between two ribs. He did not dwell on that painful memory. Through the ordeal, he had lost quite a bit of blood. No infection had set in, but Moustafa felt weak, terribly weak.

"I guess I'd better be going," he mumbled to David and Rémi. The thought of leaving Algeria left him numb, and the uncertainty of the situation ahead in Montpellier made him sick with fear. He chose to imagine a different scene.

First there would be Anne-Marie running to him as he stepped onto the dock in Marseilles. She would run with no effort, laughing, as she had when they were teenagers playing in the fields, hiding in the orange groves, letting the sweet scent of the fruit make them heady with their power and youth. He could almost feel her arms around him, holding him, and her soft voice whispering, "Everything is fine now, Moustafa, my love. It is fine." Behind her, his mother and sisters would be huddled like a peck of hens, cackling with pleasure. Hacène would go toward them and all would be well.

He stepped from the car. The sun was blazing hot. His head swam. He leaned on the Renault for a long minute watching the sea that glistened in the port. The smell of gas fumes and seaweed greeted him as he turned from the car. "Good-bye, David. Rémi." He shook their hands. That gesture was numb as well.

"We'll see you soon in Montpellier," David called after him. "It will all be fine." His optimism sounded canned, but there was nothing else to be done. One foot in front of the other, Moustafa inched along toward the ferry. He shivered as he walked, despite the fierce heat. He sensed the eyes of the enemy on him. His people, these newly independent Arabs, were burning their hatred for the *harkis* through a hard stare like the sun on the back of his neck. His ears were ringing constantly. The noise unnerved him.

"Allah or whoever You are, God. Whoever You are, have compassion on us," he said out loud, but it was as if the words were not his own, as if this whole scene were unreal. *Harki* soldiers climbed up the plank, hurrying, tasting, he imagined, for the first time, the hope of safety as they stepped off the

soil of this country gone mad. This country that was not safe
for so many of its former inhabitants.

Approaching the boat, no more than a hundred feet away,
he stumbled, fell, and caught himself with his hands,
touching the slimy hot pavement. Then he saw Hacène. His
older brother smiled quickly and motioned for him to hurry.

"What is the matter, Moustafa? You are injured!" Hacène
grabbed him around the waist, dragging him forward.

"Never mind that now. I'll explain everything as we
cross."

"Yes, that will be good." His brother was nervous, his eyes
darting from side to side. "Moustafa. I . . . I have had a hard
time getting you a right of passage. You must understand that
this ferry has been hired by our top French officer. There are
so many, so many who have fought in the war." There was an
edge of panic in Hacène's voice. Moustafa shivered again. He
felt lightheaded and placed one hand on his forehead. "I must
sit down," he groaned.

"Yes, of course." Hacène knelt down by him as Moustafa
collapsed on the dock. "I'll get a stretcher and tell them you
are wounded. They'll let you on," he whispered, his voice
shaking. "They must."

Moustafa realized his mistake at once. He was not a part
of this Muslim troop. How foolish to have believed he could
simply slip on the boat unnoticed when all the others wore
their military uniforms. Hacène had seemed so sure. But as
Moustafa turned to look out at the square that swarmed now
with Algerians, he cursed to himself. How idiotic to think
anything would be easy. The Algerians, giddy with their new
independence, circled the ferry like a pack of hungry wolves.

"God, don't leave me here to die." He pulled his body to
the edge of the dock. The oil on the sea reflected a rainbow of
colors two feet below. Moustafa looked up. The gangplank was
almost within his touch. *So close,* he thought.

* * *

From the car, David strained to see what was happening on the ferry. "We must leave," Rémi insisted. "It is too dangerous here. This place is crawling with FLN. Moustafa is with his brother; he's safe. Safer than we are right now."

David watched as the French officers motioned to one another to pull up the plank. Had Moustafa gotten on the ferry? He could not be sure. There was a brief discussion, and then an officer of the FLN approached the ship. Hundreds of Arabs now surrounded the ferry, chanting in angry Arabic. David could barely see past them to the officers, still arguing by the plank. Something was grotesquely wrong.

"Rémi, there's trouble. Something's not right. I'm going closer to see."

Rémi grabbed his arm. "Are you crazy? What can you do? Look at you, all bandaged up like a mummy. There's nothing you can do."

David swung around. "I promised Anne-Marie he'd get there. I'm just going a little ways. Just to see."

Rémi nodded. "You're right." They left the shelter of the car, walking toward the ferry, then stopped before entering into the crowded square. Jubilant Arabs carried guns and knives, looking, David thought, like cruel barbarians. Looking like everyone looked in Algeria. Crazed, half mad.

In the distance, there were loud shouts. A chilling scream. Another. David felt a cold sweat drench his body. Now the French officers, the same ones who had moments ago welcomed the *harkis* aboard, were forcing them to get off the boat with guns at their backs. And the *harkis* were clinging to the Frenchmen, begging, screaming in anguish. They were being pushed off the ferry into the angry Arab mob who yelled "*Les traitres! Egorgez-les!* Traitors!"

First a dozen *harkis*, then twenty more, then a whole tangled group of them, staggering, lurching, cursing, helplessly being fed into the violent crowd. It couldn't be happening, David thought, trembling. Rémi gagged beside him, crying,

"No, God, no."

A massacre. They were witnessing the beginnings of the *harki* massacre that Moustafa had been so sure of. The ferry promising safety had turned into a cruel, taunting decoy. David could not bear to see more, and yet his eyes were riveted on the scene. The *harkis* grabbed onto railings, flooring, other men, pleading. It was useless. The Arab mob surged upon them, pulling them down and then stabbing, shooting, and finally slitting their throats.

"No!" David cried out. "No!" He started forward, but Rémi caught him from behind.

"David!" he yelled. "David, listen to me. It is hopeless. This whole stinking world has gone crazy. The French are betraying their comrades."

David put a hand to his head. His face was a pasty white.

"There's nothing we can do but be murdered as well if we stay." Rémi was sobbing. "We cannot help Moustafa now. It is too late."

David stumbled backward, eyes glued to the horrific scene. No hope. His throat constricted. The muscles in his chest tightened. He could not swallow. Still backing toward the car, he cried, "Moustafa! Moustafa!"

Then he broke into a run. "The sea!" he cried. Rémi seemed to understand as they raced to the water's edge. Hidden by a thick-leafed plane tree, they kicked off their shoes and dived into the murky water. They swam furiously underwater toward the ferry. When they surfaced, the sound of their heavy breathing was swallowed up in the chaotic babble on shore.

"God, let us see him," David prayed. The screaming men, sobbing and groping, slid down the gangplank that was forty feet away. He watched the knife of a muscular Arab find its target in a *harki's* neck. He closed his eyes and threw up into the dark water.

Recklessly he cried, "Moustafa!" And again, "Moustafa!"

Two Algerians ran toward the edge of the dock. "Who is

there?" one spat angrily. David and Rémi dived down again underwater, watching a spray of bullets above on the water's surface. Rémi shook his head slowly in the water, pulling at David's shirt, swimming back away from the dock.

Thirty seconds later, lungs burning for air, they emerged. "It's no use," Rémi heaved. David heard his heart throbbing in his ears. He looked back again. The slaughter continued. The two Algerians were kneeling by the dock, peering into the sea.

Rémi pulled himself out of the water, then caught David under the arms and dragged him out. They lay on the grassy shore for a moment, their chests rising and falling. Everything in David's body burned.

"Can you get up?" Rémi stood, offering David his hand. They stumbled to the car, crawling inside and slamming the doors as several Arabs, detoured from their butchery, ran in pursuit. Rémi stamped on the gas, and the tires squealed. A bullet grazed the back window as they sped toward the road. David glanced back. The whole square was engulfed in red. "Moustafa," he groaned again.

* * *

The veiled Arab woman and her elderly father surveyed the massacre from their window overlooking the square. All was quiet now. Mangled bodies, twisted and bleeding, lay strewn across the Place. The heat was unbearable and flies swarmed overhead, landing in puddles of blood. Slaughtered. Every one of them. Dead. Men with silver hair and leathered faces lay still, their eyes open, beside young men with thick black curls and smooth skin.

The woman rocked slowly back and forth, moaning. The father turned away. "So," he said reverently. "We are free. But the price we pay is very high. Very, very high."

* * *

Philippeville was but a drop of red in the bucket of blood filled up on July third, 1962. Throughout the cities in Algeria, FLN troops and their supporters stormed the houses of the *harki* traitors. Men, women, children were murdered, whole families, thrown down on the floors of their houses and slain.

Farther out in the fields, busy soldiers dug deep, wide graves into which the dead bodies could be rolled. The fresh dirt was pushed back over the lifeless Arabs, covered with leaves and sand, camouflaged from the world. No one could count the number. No one cared to know. Not President de Gaulle, not Ben Bella. No one.

Yet it was simple to calculate. In the weeks and months that followed independence, there would be no *harki* families left in Algeria. Some would flee, the stinking lucky ones, Ali mused. Some had already fled. But that could be no more than 10,000, 15,000 at best. The vast majority, and this made a sick smile flicker across his pain-ridden face, perished with their throats slit. France would not know, would not care. No one in the outside world would question. But inside Algeria, he and his comrades would exchange knowing glances. One hundred thousand murdered. One hundred fifty thousand easily.

Ali lay in his bed draped in a sheet and gave the orders. Mass graves to be dug and bodies to fill them. The vegetation would grow over them in some areas. In others, the fine, hot sand would drift on top. The world would not know. He felt in that a type of satisfaction.

It served the stinking traitors right! They had abandoned their homeland to support the French Army. Traitors every one. He only wished the punishment, the terror, and the unbearable pain would last a bit longer for these filthy *harkis.*

Suddenly Ali slammed his fist on his bed, and it sank into the soft mattress. Hussein! He did not doubt that the boy had made it to France, although he did not have word yet. No, that had been a lie to turn his captives to despair. Perhaps it had worked for them, but he wanted to be sure. Hussein was quite capable. What was taking the boy so long?

But there was not time to worry over Hussein, Ali told himself. No, he must reserve every bit of his strength for the future of Algeria. The new government. He intended to be part of it! He cursed his wounds and sank down in his bed, and his thoughts returned to the skirmish in the Casbah. Perhaps David Hoffmann and his father would find a way out. But the *harki* boy, Moustafa. If he hadn't already died from the wounds he received in the Casbah, there was no worry. He was a *harki* boy. Dead meat.

Ali closed his eyes and imagined the throngs of happy youth invading the streets, celebrating freedom. Fatima was surely among them now. The confetti, the loud horns, the dancing. Ali Boudani chose to think of the celebration. The graves would be forgotten. A just end for those who had betrayed their country. Algeria was free!

* * *

David and Rémi did not leave Philippeville that night, but instead, parked among the thick foliage ten minutes out from the port. Rémi had agreed to go back to the Place after dark to see. The thought now made David gag and sweat. What did he hope to find? Moustafa lying among the carnage with his throat slit?

Earlier in the afternoon, they had driven recklessly through the town as if their mad flight might somehow bring Moustafa back. Then Rémi had stopped in another thicket on an unknown road and turned to look at David. Bedraggled and shivering, they had sat listening to the radio reports throughout the afternoon. Tears mixed with sea water. Disbelief and fury. Again and again, Rémi cursed the fact that he had not brought his rifles. Why had they been so naive as to think things would go smoothly?

The radio did not speak of the massacre. Its airwaves were filled with victory announcements and news of Ben Bella's return after five years of imprisonment.

Now they drove back through the night without saying a word. Perhaps he had gotten away. Perhaps they were not all dead. Little phrases of hope. Make-believe hope. They had seen the massacre with their own eyes. No one had gotten away.

Rémi saw the trucks first. Covered, camouflaged trucks leaving the port, driven by silent Arab men. He stopped the Renault by the Place, shutting off the engine and headlights. In the dark of the summer sky, Rémi and David watched the men at work, lifting bodies, tossing them into the back of the trucks. The chirping of the *cigales* was all they could hear.

Later, Rémi turned the car around and followed one truck, keeping his distance, driving without headlights. David dozed off and on, unable to keep his eyes open. His dreams came in little clips. Guns, knives, red. He woke with a start, blinking to get his bearings. Rémi had stopped the car. "Would ya look at that," he murmured. "Just like the rotten Nazis. Dumping them into the ground."

David leaned forward to gaze out the windshield. Far off he could make out the forms of men emptying their human cargo into wide holes. He choked, opened the car door, and vomited.

Moments later, they retraced their path to the Place. The last truck had gone. David stepped into the open air, which was thick, oppressive with the stench of death. The bodies had all been removed from the Place. Nothing but dark splotches of dried blood remained on the cobbled stones. For a long moment, David walked as if in a trance, a defeated man, encircling the square. Moustafa was gone. Murdered. And he had done nothing to stop it.

* * *

When they finally pulled up to Rémi's farmhouse in the wee hours of the morning, David could not bring himself to go inside. Somewhere in the house, his father lay asleep. He felt more allegiance to Moustafa than to his father. He had no strength to work through that messy relationship. His father was not doing well anyway. Maybe he'd wake to find that Roger Hoffmann was dead, like the rest of them.

When he finally did go inside, he did not sleep, but turned and thrashed on the mattress in the den, cursing this country, this war, this life. David felt the tiny sprouts of faith that had barely broken through the soil begin to wither and die within him. There was no God. It had been a hoax, a cruel joke, a fantasy. The emptiness he felt in his soul overwhelmed him. It was an ache at the core of his being, and he could find no comfort.

He tried praying, several times, but in the end, his prayers ended up being angry accusations at God. "You can't be omnipotent! Or if You are, You are evil. You are either a cruel master or a powerless king," he accused. "You are not the kind of God I want in my life!

"You are a God who takes. You want my undying devotion while You strip me of all those I care for. I hate You, God! Was it not enough with Greta and Mama? Was that not enough? You must take Moustafa? And Gabby and Anne-Marie? Are they too dead? Where is the hope?"

Gabriella's Bible lay by his mattress, retrieved from Marcus Cirou's apartment two days earlier. He took it and walked to the farmhouse door. Stepping into the moonlight, David flung the heavy leather-bound book as far as he could toward the orange groves. It landed with a soft thud in the sand.

"I hate You, God! Can You hear me? Do You understand? I hate You. Go away! Get out of my life! I was doing just fine without You."

He cursed the tears that came to his eyes. The black sky would soon be bidden awake by the first touch of sun. David walked out through the groves, past the spot where the Bible lay open, facedown on the soil. He walked for a long time, coming up to the shell of a house he had known all those years ago. The

Duchemins' place. He felt his pulse quicken, remembered his first encounter with the Captain, stiffly shaking his hand with his other arm around Anne-Marie's shoulder. He remembered the proud allure of Captain Duchemin, and his determination to be equally proud and aloof.

He rammed the door with his foot, relieved to do something with his anger. The door swung inward. Windows were broken, leaving jagged glass edges. He ran his fingers over the dining room table, tracing a deep gash drawn through the wood, perhaps by a knife. Fine layers of sand covered the few pieces of scattered furniture.

He walked into the kitchen. Broken china lay on the floor. Drawers hung open, empty. He went down the hallway and into Anne-Marie's bedroom. The sheets had been stripped off the bed and the mattress slashed. In the opposite corner sat an overturned crib with most of the slats broken. And everywhere, the sand, the fine whitish powder, blown in from the Sahara.

David walked back into the dining room and hit the table hard with his fist. Every bone in his body ached. His head wound began to bleed. He fell to his knees and sobbed, "I hate You, God. I hate You." Then, covering his face with his hands, he whispered, "But help me. I have no one at all if You leave me too."

Chapter 22

Henri Krugler put a paintbrush into a jar of turpentine and wiped his blue-stained hands with some of the potent liquid, until the fleshy color was once again visible. He washed his hands thoroughly, dried them on a damp towel, and ran his fingers through his thick white hair. He removed his T-shirt and replaced it with a clean, starched button-down, which he tucked into his pants. The contrast of the clean shirt with the paint-splattered work pants was laughable, but he didn't seem to notice.

He glanced at his wristwatch. Two-fifteen. Locking the door behind him, Henri hurried through the streets of Lodève, nodding politely at those he passed on his way to the train station. He reread the letter that had come in the mail two days ago. A nun called Mother Griolet from an orphanage outside Montpellier asked to come and discuss urgent matters. The handwriting was a bit shaky, but the tone of the letter was serious, businesslike.

He remembered the description Joseph Cohen had given him of Mother Griolet years ago: "the feistiest little nun you'll ever meet. A remarkable mixture of determination and commonsense compassion."

It was for this reason that Henri looked forward to meeting this nun. Everyone had always called him a rare bird. It sounded like another of the kind was about to land on Lodève. "Birds of a feather flock together," he said to himself, smiling.

The train from Montpellier pulled into the station and screeched to a halt. Several minutes later, a small woman with wrinkled skin, dressed in a black nun's habit, emerged from the train. By her side, helping to steady her, was a striking young woman with long, curly red hair. The nun looked more feeble than feisty.

"Henri Krugler," he introduced himself, walking up and offering his hand. He felt suddenly big and awkward.

"*Enchantée*, M. Krugler. I am Mother Griolet." She squeezed his hand firmly, then looked toward the girl. "And this is Mademoiselle Madison, a dear friend of mine."

The redhead smiled, though she looked at him suspiciously. He put out his hand, and she touched it briefly without meeting his eyes.

The old nun cleared her throat. "Thank you for agreeing to see us on such short notice."

"The pleasure is all mine. Joseph Cohen has spoken highly of you for many years. It is an honor to finally have the privilege of meeting you."

The nun chuckled. "You flatter me, M. Krugler."

At this point, the young woman spoke. "Excuse me, M. Krugler. Mother Griolet has recently suffered a heart attack, although she would never tell you herself. Is there a place where we could sit down?"

Henri felt the blood rise in his cheeks as the girl regarded him with her bright, clear eyes. "Of course. *Mais bien sûr.*" He motioned to a bench nearby. "I'll go fetch my car. You just wait here. I'll be right back."

The nun nodded, and he gathered she did not have the

strength to protest. Henri chided himself for not thinking of the car. He had been so wrapped up in his work that he had forgotten the time and then rushed off without considering that an elderly nun would need a ride back to the house. He felt equally embarrassed about his attire, and for a moment, considered changing pants, then decided that would be even more awkward. Ever since Louise had died, his clothes were poorly matched. Ah, well.

It took no more than fifteen minutes for Henri to return to the farmhouse, drive his gray Citroën to the train station, pick up the nun and the girl, and be back at the house-turned-*centre aéré*. Henri congratulated himself for at least having remembered to dust off the couch and chairs in the *salon*.

"Please have a seat, Mother Griolet. Mlle Madison. Can I get you anything to drink? A cup of coffee?

"A glass of water would be just fine," Mother Griolet responded.

"Yes, for me too," the young woman echoed.

Once the drinks were given and he had taken a seat, Henri felt much less nervous. "What exactly may I do for you, Mother Griolet?"

The nun smiled, and he saw that her eyes were a lively shade of green. Feisty. Yes, perhaps.

"I am interested in what you are doing in Lodève with the *centre aéré*. Your vision for the *harki* children. I would like to hear what is on your heart, and then I will tell you what is on mine."

No nonsense. Joseph had described her well.

"I'd be most happy to comply." He scooted forward in his chair, resting his hands on his knees. His fingernails were stained with blue paint. "I am Swiss-French. For many years, I was a pastor in a small town a hundred kilometers north of Geneva. Before becoming a pastor, I was a businessman." His voice drifted off for a brief moment.

"My ancestors were French Huguenots. Some were

murdered here in the Cevennes. Many escaped to Switzerland at the end of the seventeenth century. In the period of fifteen years, from 1685 until 1700, 14,000 Huguenot refugees came into Switzerland. They arrived with nothing, half starved and naked. And the people of Switzerland welcomed them with open arms—in Geneva, Lausanne, Zurich, Neuchatel, Berne. My ancestors arrived in Geneva. At the time, the city had only about 16,000 inhabitants. Every day they took in hundreds of refugees. I'll never forget what one of my ancestors wrote: 'It seemed as if the walls of their houses expanded of their own free will. That is how openly they welcomed us.' "

He stopped himself suddenly. "Forgive me. I tend to get carried away when I talk of these things."

Mother Griolet said softly, "Please continue. It is always a blessing to hear of God's provision for His children."

"Amen," Henri said heartily. "Yes, well. After my wife died several years ago, I felt the call of these mountains where my ancestors had suffered for their faith.

"My dream was to reach another group of refugees, the Arabs. By establishing this *centre aéré* for the French and Arab children, I hoped at the same time to offer them the opportunity to understand the truth. God's truth.

"But you understand French bureaucracy," he chuckled, and the nun nodded. "It has taken longer than I had thought. Perhaps the timing is the Lord's after all. With the way things are going in Algeria, we expect many more Arabs here.

"This house has been transformed, if you will, into the *centre aéré*. As of right now, we have thirty children who come on Wednesdays when the schools are closed. Most of the children come after school on the other days for snacks and activities. And we have a group for the teenagers." He flashed a quick smile. "It is my belief that these different cultures must learn how to live side by side, to integrate, so that Arab children, who are really more French than Arab in their lifestyle, will feel at home, welcomed into this society. So they will have a future here."

"Ah, yes," the nun said, nodding her head in approval. She smiled. "Very good, M. Krugler."

"And you, Mother Griolet. Tell me how I can be of help to you."

She massaged her temples, touched her black robes, and said, "I run an orphanage in a small village on the edge of Montpellier. Normally we house between twenty to twenty-five children. Their schooling is provided. However, due to the extreme circumstances of the war, we have lately accepted many more children at the orphanage. I forget the exact number."

"Fifty-eight. Fifty-eight children now," Mlle Madison broke in. "These new children have all arrived within the last six months, refugees from the war. *Pied-noir* and *harki* children. Escaped by the skin of their teeth. Mother Griolet has taken them in, and now the townspeople and the church are demanding they be sent away to refugee camps or the orphanage will be closed."

"Gabriella!" the nun reprimanded. "Dear, let me explain."

The girl blushed, bit her lip, and folded her hands in her lap. "Sorry."

Henri forced a chortle to stay in his throat. Quite feisty herself, this Mlle Madison!

"Yes, as Mlle Madison has said, we face a difficult time. We have fewer than thirty days now to solve this problem or be closed down. When Joseph Cohen wrote me about you, well, I thought it would be a good idea to meet you."

"Yes, it is so unfair!" the girl broke in again. "If you knew of all that Mother Griolet has done for that town, for so many children. Why, during the Second World War, she saved many Jewish children. Surely M. Cohen has mentioned it." The young woman stopped suddenly. "Excuse me, Mother Griolet. May I tell him some of your stories?"

"Yes, Joseph has spoken briefly of that time. But I'd be

delighted to hear more," Henri volunteered.

The nun shrugged. "Go ahead, Gabriella. But no embellishments, please. Just the facts."

They made quite a pair, the wise nun and the enthusiastic girl. Henri listened, spellbound, for an hour as they shared remarkable stories from both wars as well as their present troubles.

He thought of families moving into the area. He thought and wondered if there were those Arabs, *harki* families, who would be willing to take in another child. It was possible. Anything was possible. He had seen much stranger things happen in his lifetime.

* * *

Gabriella found Henri Krugler fascinating. Hearing him talk of the Huguenots, she fingered her cross as she looked around the large farmhouse. It held a certain charm, even if it lacked a woman's touch. And the scenery out the window was breathtaking. There was a small field, and then the Cevennes mountains rose up beyond. Imagine having the mountains in your backyard! Then she thought of David. The trip to Lodève had served a double purpose—to help out Mother Griolet and to get her mind off of the clock. The fourth of July. In America they would be celebrating with parades, apple pie, and fireworks. All she asked for was David. Today he should come home.

Bring him home, she repeated in her mind. The prayer was never far out of her thoughts. *Bring him home. Bring them home.* Maybe even now the ferry was pulling into port in Marseilles. Suddenly she wanted to leave Lodève.

As if reading her thoughts, M. Krugler said, "I'm afraid we must leave for the train station a little early. I hope you don't mind, but I need to be back by 4:45, when the *centre aéré* opens."

"Of course," said Mother Griolet. She struggled to stand,

and Gabriella helped her to her feet. "You have been most kind to receive us."

"I admire your work, Mother Griolet. I will do whatever I can to help you out. I'll be back in touch within the week." He shook her hand and added, "Pray for open hearts. Yes, open hearts."

* * *

Hussein splattered a brushful of bright green paint onto the mural in the classroom. He watched the thick blobs run down the paper. Just when several threatened to run off the edge, he gave a swish of his brush and stopped them.

"What are you making, Hussein?" Ophélie questioned, coming to his side.

He shrugged. "I don't know. Nothing."

"Sister Isabelle says that you can even make mistakes into something pretty. She helped me—"

"It's not a mistake!" he answered gruffly. He wished Ophélie would leave him alone. He felt all tense inside. Worried and tense.

He wasn't alone. The tension vibrated throughout the orphanage. They were all trying desperately to busy themselves so they wouldn't have to think about it, but it wasn't working. Not for him, not for anyone.

When were they coming? Two full days had passed since independence. If Moustafa had gotten onto that *harki* ferry as his mother had explained, well there should be some word soon.

Hussein saw the hurt expression on Ophélie's face. He felt rotten and reached out to touch her hand. "You're right. I'm sure I can make something out of this."

The child pushed her pigtails behind her. She headed back to her spot on the wall, picked up her paintbrush, and then paused. "And don't worry about Papa and Moustafa. They'll be here soon. You'll see."

She was the strangest child, Hussein thought. The image of her staring up at a full moon in the black courtyard haunted him. To think he had almost . . . Allah be praised, he had not followed through.

Hussein had decided what to do next. He would wait until David and Moustafa returned. They could help him compose a letter to Ali. One that was believable.

"Hurry home," he whispered, and began painting the random spots of green, turning them into long, delicate leaves on a weeping willow tree.

* * *

When Gabriella returned to St. Joseph's, she ran to the classroom in the basement where Anne-Marie was teaching art with Mme Dramchini. Mme Dramchini patiently painted thick red lines on the paper of the youngest children, then they tried to imitate her. The older children were busily covering a mural on the wall with bright paint as Saiyda and Rachida encouraged them. Sister Isabelle nervously gave little pointers. The children, draped in oversized shirts retrieved from the clothes closet, were enjoying themselves thoroughly.

When Anne-Marie saw Gabriella, she shook her head slowly. Gabriella's hope fell in her breast. No word from Marseilles. Gabriella did not let herself dwell on the disappointment. Instead she joined the other women as they painted with the children. The classroom was in shambles, but everyone seemed to be having fun. No one spoke of the ferry.

At the end of the afternoon, Sister Rosaline bustled into the classroom, rolling her eyes as she pointed to the multiple drops of paint covering the floor. *"Au boulot!"* she sang cheerily, handing rags and mops to children. "Let's get this place clean." Eager hands grabbed for the mops, begging for a turn to slosh water onto the tiles. Anne-Marie and Mme Dramchini herded half of the children to the dormitories to wash up and start on their chores.

Anne-Marie grabbed Gabriella's hands on the way out. "I can't stand the waiting any longer. We're all going crazy with it. There must be news!" She searched Gabriella's face. "I am *praying* for it night and day. For protection for Moustafa and David." She pronounced the names cautiously, painfully.

"The crowds at the port must have been even worse than before. They may still be waiting, but it won't be long." Gabriella's voice did not sound optimistic.

The radio played continuously in the kitchen of the refectory. During the evening meal, the women huddled around it, eager for news from Algeria. The talk was of celebration, the new Algerian government, the exodus of the remaining *pied-noirs*. There was talk of a group of *harkis* moving to a little village near Arles. Anne-Marie leaned closer, motioning for complete silence.

"Should I go there, Gabriella? Do you think he is there with Hacène?"

Mme Dramchini spoke in worried Arabic to Saiyda. The young girl translated. "Mother thinks that the men are there. If not, she fears they have perhaps been forced to the refugee camps. She wants to go with you, Anne-Marie, to Arles."

"Should we wait one more day?" Gabriella suggested. "If they are there, David will know. Give them one more day." She squeezed Anne-Marie's hand.

"One more day, then," Anne-Marie whispered.

* * *

On July the fifth, Rémi encouraged David to leave for the ferry with his father. "Go back to France. You heard what the doctor said. You both need medical attention. You'll be better off there."

David doubted it. Was there an orphanage still in Castelnau? Moustafa had believed Ali was lying. Moustafa . . .

David was overcome by fear and dread. He had failed in every way. Moustafa was not coming back to Anne-Marie.

Maybe there was no one to go back to. The thought made his head swim. The only choice was to take a ferry back to France and find out. And what if it were true? Then there would be nothing but an awful gaping hole in his heart . . . and his father standing there to watch.

David slipped into the back bedroom to check on Roger Hoffmann. He was sitting in bed, pillows propping him up. The gray stubble that had covered his face had now become a thick beard. It did not fit his father. He looked sick, pale, vulnerable. He stared into the room with a vacant expression.

"Father. Are you about ready to go?"

The older man nodded, but made no effort to move.

"I'll be back in a sec for you."

Curse it all, David thought. His head throbbed. The wound was not healing properly. Blood and pus oozed onto the bandage. He unwrapped the gauze and changed the dressing again. Maybe he was simply losing his mind.

Rémi came into the house and handed him the Bible. It was covered with sand. "I found this. Didn't figure you wanted to leave it here."

David took it and said nothing. He set it by his briefcase.

"You did everything you could, David. It's a crazy war."

"Why don't you come now, Rémi?"

"There are things to tie up." He picked a ripe olive from a bowl on the table.

"You don't want to leave!" David accused.

"No, you're right." He twirled the olive between his thumb and forefinger. "Once I leave, I'll never come back. We'll never see this old place again. It's mighty hard to say good-bye to all you have ever known."

"When will you come to France?"

"A few weeks. Tell Eliane it'll be a few weeks. After we finish with the oranges."

"It's dangerous to stay, Rémi."

"I know." He took another olive. "The *pied-noirs* were

supposed to be able to stay in Algeria, you know. It shouldn't end this way. If the OAS, if they hadn't committed so many unspeakable atrocities in these past months. . . . It's their fault we're leaving. The *pied-noirs* are afraid of what the FLN will do to get revenge, now that Algeria is free." He shrugged. "There are many who don't agree with me, but that's what I think."

They did not speak of what they had seen. The mass graves, the bodies. They did not have to say it. The genocide in Philippeville had been complete, and they had stood by and watched. What had their feeble effort mattered? They had not rescued Moustafa or anyone else.

Rémi placed a hand on David's shoulder. "Don't live with guilt. You did what you could. Get on with life."

"Do you think it will be that easy?"

Rémi grimaced. "No. We'll wake up in the middle of the night, sweating and screaming. And only those who have lived through it will understand."

"And that isn't guilt?"

"Scarred. Scarred but healing," Rémi said. "Come on. We've got to get your dad in the car. You'll have your hands full with him, David. It'll be all right. You'll see."

* * *

They had waited twenty-eight hours before they found a place on a crowded ferry. It was now far out at sea, and David could not help thinking of his last crossing. He had stood alone, hopeful, confident in his new faith. Sure of his mission. Now he slumped over the railing, casting a glance behind him at his father, who slept with his back against a cabin door.

Rémi had thought having charge of his father would help David get his mind off other things. But all David heard in his head was *Why are you here with me? Why must I care for you? Why didn't you die, instead of him?* It filled him with an incredible sadness and guilt. But his anger was stronger. This man had tried to ruin his life! What right did he have to reappear and ask forgiveness? What blasted right did he have? And now, as a new convert, was David supposed to smile a sick, sweet smile and say, "Sure, Dad. I understand. It's fine"?

Well, it wasn't fine. Oh, he understood about the dreadful mistake and the concentration camp. How his father had left him with his mother and sister, and they had been taken to a camp where Greta and his mother had been murdered. How his father himself had been detained in a camp, unable to help them. But how could he forgive him for that? For leaving everything up to him, a six-year-old child? Why had his father placed him in charge? It was so David could harbor the guilt, the blame for their murders. The coward! How could he dare to think it would be all right?

I don't want to forgive you, and I certainly don't want to get to know you, he admitted. *I hate who you are, Father. I hate what you stand for. So why must I drag you along in my pain? Why must you be here to complicate what is already too heavy to carry?*

Oh, the anger! It crossed his mind to pick up his father while he slept and throw him into the sea. The thought repulsed him. He held his head and moaned, "You're messed up, David. Really messed up."

He cursed the sea and then cursed God Himself. It was His fault. Why was He showing Himself so helpless when David needed Him most? Why was He allowing this anger and hate, this blasphemy to well up within His child? David felt he would go mad with the questions.

His father called for him, and David knelt down beside the weakened man. Roger Hoffmann's eyes looked clearer. That icy blue stare, softer now, met his son's gaze.

"David."

"Yes, Father?"

"We are on our way to France?"

"Yes."

"To your friends?"

"I hope."

His father closed his eyes, and David thought he had fallen back asleep. "Son, I'm sorry about Moustafa."

David cringed. What right did his father have to pronounce that name? To pretend to care? He was in the way. Out of place. "Yes. It is tragic."

"Thank you for bringing me along."

David gritted his teeth. He did not want to make conversation. *Leave me alone, old man.* He stood up quickly. "I'm going to walk about a little."

Walking was next to impossible. Every space was filled with the men who had stayed behind until now. Their large suitcases and bags stuffed with every imaginable possession gave evidence that the two-suitcase rule was being completely ignored. David pushed past a young man who held a rocking horse under his arm. The sight made him think of Ophélie. For the past few days he had almost forgotten that he had a daughter.

He thought of Ophélie, and the hate for his father diminished. He tried to remember the good things that had happened before the *harki* massacre. He thought of Gabriella and relived every long conversation with her. Tomorrow he could hold her to his chest and let life start again. Surely there was a future out there.

But even as he imagined Gabriella coming to him, laughing, running, eyes dancing, he saw Anne-Marie behind her with a question in her dark, mournful eyes. *Where is Moustafa?*

"What am I supposed to say to her, God?" A chill ran through him. And if there were no Gabriella or Anne-Marie or Ophélie? No response. Just darkness all around in the thick, balmy air. He could not acknowledge the beauty of it. The colors faded into one another, the black-green of the sea and the white caps blending into the indigo sky, which was tinged with purple and the faintest shade of crimson.

He had the feeling that this was his chance to talk to his father. The chance to listen and begin to settle the pain of the past seventeen years. Instead, he stood for another hour or maybe two, watching the wake the ferry made in the water, analyzing every movement of the sea against the boat. When he finally walked back to where his father sat, the older man was asleep.

Chapter 23

The train from Marseilles to Montpellier seemed painfully slow, and yet David was afraid it would arrive too fast. He had resisted the urge to call the orphanage from Marseilles. What if Anne-Marie answered? What if no one answered at all? No, it was better to show up in person and face the questions head on.

His father was in no shape to wait for a bus, so David signaled a taxi. It was a lazy summer day in Montpellier. People sipped cool drinks in sidewalk *cafés* and old men played *pétanque* beneath the shade of the plane trees. The mood was calm. No bombed-out buildings or shells of cars littered the scenery as they drove by.

He could not calm his racing heart in those few minutes driving to Castelnau. He rolled down the window; the heat was blistering. Sweat ran down his face.

Suddenly the cobblestones of Castelnau were bumping under the taxi's tires, and St. Joseph's tall spire, and then the whole stone facade, came into view. It was there, sitting peacefully at the back of the square as it had done for hundreds of years. The same fountain sprayed forth water, the same shops offered fruits and wines and bread and cheeses, their doors flung open. All was well. David sighed.

The taxi driver let them off in front of the church. For a brief moment David hesitated, one arm supporting his father. He set down his bags and knocked forcefully on the parsonage door. Blood pumped in his ears. Nervous, he said, "Someone will be here soon, Father."

"*J'arrive,*" came the sound of a jolly voice from within, and the door swung open.

Sister Rosaline stood wide-eyed before them. She looked from one man to the other, her expression changing from surprise to delight to confusion to worry.

"M. Hoffmann. God be praised! Come in, M. Hoffmann!"

David followed her into the hallway. "Sister Rosaline, this is my father, Roger Hoffmann. It is a long story."

"Well, I'll be. Do come in. Do come in." She led them in to Mother Griolet's den; they sat on the faded brown couch while Sister Rosaline brought them each a glass of water. The plump woman, obviously flustered, said nothing, but kept staring at the two men, shaking her head.

Finally she spoke. "Let me go tell the others."

David touched her arm. Leaving his father on the couch, he walked with her into the hallway. "Sister Rosaline, I, I . . ." His voice caught. "I don't know how to say it, but . . . Moustafa did not come with us. He didn't make it." David broke into a sweat, caught the door, and felt his knees buckle under him.

"M. Hoffmann. M. Hoffmann!"

He pulled himself back into the den and collapsed into a chair.

*   *   *

Few things rattled Sister Rosaline anymore, but she was obviously rattled as she hurried through the basement into the courtyard. It *was* David Hoffmann up there in the den. But so changed. He was unshaven, and his clothes were wrinkled and dirty. His black hair was long and unkempt, and a bandage covered the left side of his head above his ear. He looked thin and sad. Terribly sad.

Sister Rosaline wrung her hands. This was not the homecoming they had envisioned. An afflicted M. Hoffmann with an even weaker man in tow and no Moustafa at all. No Moustafa. What was she to do? She had immediately understood what David Hoffmann could not say. There wasn't going to be any Moustafa. Ever.

Everyone was eating dinner in the refectory. She reflected that it was a good thing she had been in the basement of the parsonage, or no one would have heard M. Hoffmann's knock. She entered the dining hall without making a fuss, thankful for the noise. Mother Griolet sat at a table with Gabriella and several children. Sister Rosaline fiddled with her headpiece, casually approaching the table.

"Mother Griolet," she said in her lightest voice. "Could I see you for a moment?" The others must not guess. Already they sat on pins and needles, desperate for news. But this was not the time to have it.

"Yes, Sister. Is there a problem?"

"Not at all, only I'm afraid I need a little advice." She helped the old nun up, wishing she did not have more distressing news to share.

As soon as they were in the courtyard, she whispered, "M. Hoffmann has just appeared looking *affreux*. And he brought with him his father, of all things!" She lowered her voice to where it was barely audible. "But it's not who he brought with him that matters. It's who did not come." She met the nun's green eyes. "Moustafa . . . the man they call Moustafa is no more."

"Dear Lord," Mother Griolet said. "Dear Lord."

"They are in your den. I thought it not wise to announce it."

"No, of course not. You were right. Take me to see M.

Hoffmann."

They hurried off, their black robes swishing together in the hallway.

* * *

Sister Rosaline did not mince words. David Hoffmann did look terrible. Mother Griolet shook his hand, wrinkling her brow, then took a seat next to him.

A wave of dizziness came over the old nun. She mopped her brow. "Dear David, how thankful we are to have you back. And this, I understand, is your father." The other M. Hoffmann was sprawled out on her couch, his eyes closed. They both looked like the pale, weak Jewish parents who had wandered back to the orphanage after escaping death in the camps back in 1945.

She remembered then that M. Hoffmann *had* been one of those parents all those years ago. He had stood before her, a tall, distinguished looking man, well dressed yet completely distraught. She remembered his tears when he learned that his son was at the orphanage.

Now he lay almost helpless before her. These men needed medical attention. "Let me call *les urgences.* Your father must get to a hospital at once. From the looks of it, you must see a doctor, too."

"Yes, of course," David mumbled.

"I'll make the call, Mother," Sister Rosaline said and scurried to the nun's office.

The young man was so obviously shaken, so completely exhausted that he hardly resembled the capable young teacher she had known.

"I am deeply grieved to learn of Moustafa. It is a terrible tragedy," Mother Griolet said.

"Yes. Terrible." David's face was ashen underneath his black stubble.

Sister Rosaline came back into the den. "An ambulance

318

will be here shortly."

"Thank you." Mother Griolet smiled softly at the Sister, then turned to David. "Do you wish to see Gabriella alone?"

He held his head in his hands. "I don't know what to do."

Mother Griolet placed her hand on his head, praying silently. Then she gently said, "I am so very sorry for you, David. Let me call Gabriella. The others will not have to know yet." She stood shakily, and David stood with her, offering his hand. "David," she said at last. "God does not waste our suffering. It always serves a purpose."

Then slowly she left the den.

*　*　*

It was not at all the reunion Gabriella had expected. When Mother Griolet whispered for her to go to her apartment because David was there, she caught her breath. Then Mother Griolet cautioned, "He is not well and his father is with him. An ambulance is coming to take them to the hospital. Go alone, just for a moment."

She tiptoed through the basement hall, her mind racing, asking herself a hundred questions. When she came to Mother Griolet's den, she stopped short. An older man, looking like a hobo, lay asleep on Mother Griolet's couch, his clothes torn. And David, yes surely it was David, sat with his head in his hands, fresh blood seeping from a bandage around his head.

For a moment she could not bring herself to speak. She swallowed hard. "David?" she whispered.

He sat up quickly and looked at her. "Gabby," he said, and a weak smile came to his face.

She covered her mouth with her hand, but the gasp escaped. It was not so much the way he looked that shocked her. She had seen him badly injured before. It was the hopelessness in his dark eyes. She stood frozen, unsure of what he needed.

But then it was stronger than herself. She loved him. That

much had not changed, whatever else had. She came to him and carefully cradled his head in her arms, as he leaned against her breast. "David. You're here. It's going to be fine now."

"Dear Gabby." He took her hands and softly kissed them. Outside, the sound of a siren shrilled.

"Shall I go with you to the hospital?"

"Yes, come. Come."

* * *

The emergency room was crowded with pitiful, desperate-looking people. A father held a screaming child with a gash in his leg, covered only with a handkerchief. An elderly man slumped forward in a wheelchair, murmuring something incomprehensible to a nurse. A young woman, covered with sheets and moaning, was wheeled in on a stretcher. David felt for a moment as if he were back in Algeria.

One look at Roger Hoffmann, and the young doctor on duty had sent him immediately to intensive care. After two hours, he was installed in a private room. "He will be here for a while," the doctor warned, motioning for David and Gabriella to follow him.

"*Et vous, Monsieur.* Let me take a look at you." David stiffened as the young intern removed the bandages and inspected his head wound. "You needed stitches," he stated. "When did it happen?"

"I don't know. About a week ago. Maybe a little longer."

"You should have come to the hospital immediately," the doctor reprimanded.

"I was in Algeria."

"Oh." There was silence. "It's a nasty wound. Infected."

David winced as the doctor cleaned it with antiseptic and covered the wound with a new bandage. "Thanks, Doctor," he said gratefully. "Could you just check out the rib here? The doc in Algiers thinks it's cracked."

X-rays revealed two cracked ribs. "We'll need to bind you

up. You'll have to undress."

"I'll, I'll wait in the hall," Gabriella stammered.

The intern shrugged. "As you wish, *Mademoiselle.* But he only has to take off his shirt."

Immediately Gabriella's face turned bright red. She stayed with David. In spite of the pain, David could not suppress a throaty chuckle. *Gabby,* he thought to himself. *All innocence and imagination.* He was glad she still held a few illusions of propriety. His had all gone down the drain in Algeria. Every last one.

*   *   *

They had spoken only a few phrases during their afternoon at the hospital. Gabriella felt so far away from him, from his pain. She dared not touch him for fear of hurting him worse somewhere deep inside. When they left the hospital and stepped out into the suffocating heat, he took her hand in his. "Let's go somewhere and get a drink. I can't go back there yet."

He called a taxi, and it amazed her how quickly David seemed to regain control. He was stiff, formal, rigid. Only his hand in hers gave a slight indication that he cared for her.

He took her to the Comedie, and they sat in the shade of the large, thick-leafed plane trees with their gray patchwork bark.

The waiter came. "A *pastis* and a *citron pressé,*" David ordered without asking Gabriella, and for the first time she saw a sparkle in his eyes. "You see, Gabby, I haven't forgotten your favorite drink." His dimple showed as he smiled wearily.

"Does it bother you at all that everyone is staring at the unshaven weirdo with the white turban who is seated beside you?"

"Not a bit," Gabriella whispered. "I hadn't even noticed." They held hands across the table.

He stared at her for a long, long time. She studied his face. The rough black of his beard covered his face and neck like a thin layer of pepper. The bandaged wound was far up in his hairline. His coarse black hair curled over the gauze and at the back of his neck.

"My gosh, it's good to see you, Gabby. I didn't know if I ever would again." He touched her hair, twirling the red strands around his finger. "I didn't think we'd ever be back here."

He fell silent again, letting go of her hands when the waiter brought the drinks. She forced the hundreds of questions she wanted to ask him back in her mind.

He watched the people milling on the Comedie, and it seemed to calm him. He was far, far away. Finally, he looked at her, his eyes shining with tears, and said, "Moustafa is dead."

* * *

When they returned to St. Joseph's, David stopped outside the chapel. "Can you bring Anne-Marie here, alone?"

Gabriella nodded and left him seated in the chapel's cool interior. She felt, as at other times in the past, like his child, expected to obey. She could not reach him, and she dared not question him. He wanted to break the news to Anne-Marie.

The children were resting in the dorms. She found Anne-Marie stretched out on her bed, reading.

"Come in!" she said brightly, seeing Gabriella. "And where have you been?"

Immediately Gabriella knew she had betrayed it, simply meeting her friend's eyes. Anne-Marie frowned. "You have news?"

"Come with me." Gabriella could not say more. She could not pronounce the word *dead* to Anne-Marie. She held her hand and led her through the basement and out into the street, then stood beside the doors to the chapel. "David wants to talk to you alone," she whispered, swallowing hard. She caught Anne-Marie in her arms and hugged her tightly. She did not let go for a long time.

Then Anne-Marie stepped into the chapel. Gabriella did not wait, could not wait. She ran to Mme Leclerc's apartment, let herself in, and collapsed on her bed, sobbing.

* * *

David looked up to see Anne-Marie standing in the doorway, her dark eyes full of questions. He stood and watched her as he had done in Algiers three months ago. He studied the contour of her face, the high cheekbones, the olive skin that glowed from the incredible heat, the slight flush in her cheeks.

He held out his hand, and she took it. He did not have to speak. She understood him perfectly well. He squeezed her hand tightly, closing his eyes and silently cursing this moment. She did not cry, although her bottom lip quivered ever so slightly.

He pulled her to his chest, held her there, stroking her hair. "I'm so sorry." It was not his voice that spoke. It was as if someone else were forcing out the words through the tightness in his throat. "I'm so, so sorry."

* * *

David had decided that he would tell her whatever she wanted to know. He would not hide anything from her. He sat in the hard pew and held her as he spoke of Moustafa. Somehow the telling of it brought with it comfort.

He told her of the teenagers at the port who had attacked them, and of Moustafa's courage, and why he had made up his mind to stay. He spoke of Hussein and the trunk and Rémi and the *Capitaine;* of Moustafa's mother and the orphans. He explained the ambush in the night and finding his father and being imprisoned in the same dank basement as she had been months before. Then he told her of Ali's pronouncement of her death and the explosions at the orphanage.

"We didn't know. We could only wait and hope."

"Funny how we must do that, isn't it, David? Wait and hope." Her voice was calm, and it amazed him. Softly, she asked, "And how did it end?"

He described the slaughter at Philippeville, reliving the moment in his mind, not looking at Anne-Marie. He did not realize that he was crying until she reached over and brushed away a few tears with the tips of her fingers. She had not yet shed a tear.

"He was a good, brave man, Anne-Marie. He loved you with everything within him. I can tell you that. He should be here now. It is not right!"

When he had nothing more in him, they sat in silence. He held her hands, clutching them as he repeated again and again, "Why? Why?"

The sun lowered itself in the sky and brought the chapel into shadows. She had not uttered another word, but sat with a numb expression on her face. Perhaps not numb, he thought. Composed. Carefully he spoke, "I won't let anything happen to you, Anne-Marie. I'll care for you and Ophélie. I promise."

She cleared her throat, a softness in her voice. "There is so much that is unclear. Dear David, thank you. Thank you for being there with him, for trying, for telling me. I, I need to be alone now."

He left the chapel, left her sitting in the dark, staring at the small stained-glass window behind the altar. The sunlight blinded him. He felt disoriented, unsure of where to go. He wanted desperately to rest. He remembered Mme Pons' apartment and his room there. It was a short walk through town. The sun beat down on him. Finding the key in his briefcase, he let himself into the apartment and fell into bed. He slept straight through the night.

* * *

Anne-Marie could not explain her reaction. She only knew that something was pulling her to the front of the chapel. She knelt on the hard stones, caressing the cross around her neck. She did not feel angry. She did not feel anything except a strange peacefulness that enveloped her, as if invisible arms were cradling her. She stayed kneeling, letting the quiet, the gentle breath of life wash over her. She was afraid to move because with the slightest movement perhaps the blissful calm would pass.

She thought of Moustafa and saw him smiling at her, his head covered up with curls. She could not cry for him, and she didn't know why, only that his memory came to her with joy. A slight breeze touched her hair; the door in the side of the chapel creaked. When Anne-Marie looked around, no one was there.

The bell in the tower chimed seven o'clock. Some time later she realized that she had been praying, but she was sure the words were not her own. "Nothing can separate us from the love of Christ. Not life, nor death . . . " She whispered it over and over again, took the cross to her lips and kissed it softly.

She rose from her knees, felt the stiffness, and brushed them off. For some reason, she crossed herself as she had seen the nuns do. Then she said simply, *"Merci, Seigneur"* and "I love you, Moustafa."

* * *

The Dramchini women moaned and wept through the night. Anne-Marie sat with them and spent her tears in their presence. She knew how Arab women mourned. She thought it tragic and beautiful. The weeping, the wailing, the tears, the swaying bodies, and the silence.

Later the women talked in quiet tones of Hacène and Moustafa, recalling many happy memories, remembering what their lives had meant to their family and friends. Once in the course of the night Mme Dramchini had cried out, "My sons! My sons!" in Arabic. Then she had taken Anne-Marie in her bosom and rocked her like an infant, sobbing.

"He loved you," she moaned in broken French. "You mourn with us. We sad together."

It seemed to Anne-Marie like a healthy, healing experience, the wailing and the questioning, the open display of grief. The women had requested to be left alone in the dining hall, and there they spent the night.

Tomorrow was a new day. The waiting was over. It was time to go forward. The peaceful feeling never left Anne-Marie, and when she lay down on her cot at 3 A.M., she immediately fell asleep.

* * *

When David awoke it was light, and he had no idea where he was. It could have been Rémi's farmhouse or the ferry. It took him a moment to register that he was in Mme Pons' apartment in his own room.

He had no idea how long he had slept as he pulled himself out of bed. It was the first time he had looked in the mirror for days. A grisly, swollen face stared back. It seemed the most natural thing to do was to shower and shave. He was washing away months of fine, Algerian sand that had seeped into his pores. If only he could wash away some of the intense pain.

The wound in his head had not seeped blood in the night, which seemed a positive sign. He found a pair of lightweight pants hanging in the closet where he had left them three-and-a-half months ago, and he put them on. He wrapped his torso with a thick, white bandage. Carefully he pulled on a short-sleeved Oxford shirt. The ribs still hurt when he moved too quickly.

The clay *santon* of the baker smiled at him from his desk. Poor Gabriella. What had he said to her yesterday? Had he said anything? And Anne-Marie? He intended to keep the promise he had spoken to her in the chapel. He did not yet know how, but he would keep it.

He remembered his father in the hospital and phoned to

find out his condition. Stable, resting. Good. His old man needed complete rest, and that suited David fine.

He wanted more than anything to see Ophélie, and he finished dressing quickly. Mme Pons let out a scream when he appeared in her kitchen, then cackled. "*Oh là là!* M. Hoffmann! You're back."

"*Bonjour,* Mme Pons." He kissed her cheek. "Please excuse me for frightening you. Thoughtless of me."

"Let me fix you some breakfast. Poor M. Hoffmann. You are not well. *Oh là là.*" She bustled about her kitchen, whistling happily. "We were so worried, M. Hoffmann. So very worried about you. And now you appear in my kitchen and frighten the wits out of me!" She chuckled. "We are very glad to have you back."

Thirty minutes later, David left the apartment with his belly full. The pure banality of another summer's day with nothing much happening clashed with the memories of crowds of helpless refugees, of guns and knives. He forced Algeria out of his mind and waved at the women at the *marché* as they nodded and blushed.

He let himself into the parsonage, hurrying down the steps into the basement. The children were already in class. It surprised him to see Gabriella teaching. He walked into the classroom, which was crammed with desks and chairs and children, strode to Ophélie's desk and picked her up out of the chair. He hugged her tightly, then turned to Gabriella. "May I borrow my daughter for a little while?"

"Of course, M. Hoffmann," she stammered.

He saw that she did not know what to expect of him. Holding Ophélie's hand, he walked behind the desk, cupped Gabby's face in his other hand and, to the great delight of the whole class, kissed her forcefully on the lips. The children cheered, a few chanted, "*Encore! Encore!*" Little Christophe shouted, "*Oh oh, les amoureux!*" and everyone clapped.

"See you after class," he whispered. She only nodded and

watched them leave, her face bright red.

*   *   *

They sat on the warm grass in the shade of an olive tree in the courtyard and laughed for the longest time about nothing at all. Every few minutes, Ophélie reached out and gently touched the bandage around David's head.

"Does it hurt very much, Papa?"

"No, sweetie, not now."

"You look funny, Papa," she giggled.

"Tell me. Tell me what I look like."

"Well . . . " She furrowed her little brow and thought. Then she exclaimed gleefully. "I know! You look like a palm tree! You know how its trunk is wrapped around and around, and then suddenly at the very top, there are these big wide leaves bursting out and draping down, like your hair, Papa. It is so long and curly on the ends." She touched it with her fingers. David placed his hand over hers.

"I'm so glad to be with you, Ophélie. Papa has missed you so much."

"Will you ever go away again, Papa?"

"Not for a long time, *ma chérie*. Don't you worry."

Ophélie's face clouded. "But you couldn't bring Moustafa back for Mama, could you?"

"No, Ophélie. I tried. Very hard. And Moustafa wanted so much to come."

"But he won't be coming, will he?"

David shook his head and felt the tightness in his throat.

She contemplated this revelation for quite some time, looking very perplexed. "But I know I saw him coming, Papa. I *know* it."

He took her in his arms, and she cuddled in his lap. "There are things we can't understand," he said finally. "I'm sorry, Ophélie. So sorry."

"Oh, Papa. It's not your fault. It's not your fault. It's just that Jesus has another way. That's all."

He stared in wonder at Ophélie. He did not understand her words, but he marveled at her faith. Perhaps healing would come to him through the faith of his small daughter. It made him smile to think so.

Chapter 24

After the day of joy for the Algerians on July the third, the following week in the long summer of 1962 was less than jovial. Three separate Algerian factions were set on gaining power, and between them, the struggles continued—games of cat-and-mouse with bloody aftermaths.

Ali watched the fury and debates among the political leaders with little surprise. He backed Ben Bella, the man who had, after all, been named as the perpetrator of the War for Independence back in 1954. Soon after the beginnings of the war, Ben Bella had been arrested and imprisoned by the French, where he spent five long years in jail. Nonetheless his presence during the war had been keenly felt. Now was his chance, Ali felt sure. Liberated since the Evian accords in March, Ben Bella launched a helter-skelter campaign among his people.

Ali followed his movements with great interest and greed. He deserved a high place in this new government, whatever form it took. He deserved it, but would he have it? Now that independence was here, Ali's confidence wavered. Would the others in the FLN recognize his shrewd leadership abilities?

He had never questioned this before, but now, he thought he read the slightest bit of pity in their eyes when they came to visit him. Surely not! He deserved a place in the new government, and he would have it!

The lack of news from Hussein irritated Ali. Killing the boy's mother was easy enough, but what if Hussein never knew of it? The threat was his strongest card to hold. But how to contact the boy? He considered his granddaughter, Fatima. She was eager to prove her worth. But it was much too dangerous to send her to France.

He paced in his cubicle, his walk now punctuated by a heavy limp from the bullet wound to his calf. It would heal. So would the wound that had come so near his heart. Rest, the doctor pleaded.

It was not the time to rest, when the new republic was being birthed. It was time for fast, cunning action. He thought about the young boy in France again, spit his cigarette on the floor, and crushed it with his toe. There was nothing to do but wait for news. Hussein was a faithful follower. He had been trained well. He would not let Ali down.

* * *

Henri Krugler worked late into the nights, trying to figure out a way to help Mother Griolet. Since independence a week ago, many *harki* families were moving into Lodève. They were pitiful to see, but they were alive. They filled up the streets like a litter of puppies with nowhere to go.

He contemplated bringing some of the children from St. Joseph's to live with him. That would be better than the refugee camps. But he did not have the setup to house children indefinitely. His was not an orphanage.

In the evenings after the *centre aéré* had closed, he called on the newly arrived Arab families. What did they think? The men and women listened and nodded. Possible. Anything was possible. But in three weeks? He shook his white head back and forth. A tall order to fill. He hoped that God would allow him to be part of the plan to fill it.

* * *

When Hussein heard the news about Moustafa from Ophélie, it made him sick. He did not dare go to David Hoffmann and beg for help now. He was responsible for Moustafa's death. He felt a sharp pain, almost like a knife in his stomach, when he saw David striding over to him after class. He could not disappear, so he prepared himself to look indifferent.

"Hello, Hussein." David held out his hand. "Glad to see that you made it safely to St. Joseph's."

Hussein took his hand without meeting his eyes.

"Let's take a little walk. Just the two of us."

With his hand heavy on Hussein's shoulder, David led him out into the streets of Castelnau. He walked him straight to an apartment. "This is my place. I thought we could talk better here."

Hussein felt a chill go down his spine. He half expected David to produce a knife. That had always been Ali's method.

"Tell me about everything, Hussein." David's eyes were intense, penetrating. "I am not going to harm you, but I want the truth. You owe me that much."

Hussein bit his lip. Curse it all. He still had the explosives. Why not blow the whole place up with himself included? He said nothing.

"Hussein, it is not your fault about Moustafa. Ali didn't kill him. It is not your fault."

So the American was trying to soften him up. If only he knew.

"Hussein, listen." Now David took him by the shoulders and shook him forcefully. "I lived there. I saw what young boys were forced to do. It's not your fault."

The strength of David's hands on him somehow brought

comfort. His mother's hands were strong. Before he could stop himself, Hussein was clutching David and crying, "I'm sorry! I'm sorry about Moustafa. I'm sorry about the trunk." He rested his head against David's shoulder and was surprised by the tall American's soothing voice.

"Can you tell me what happened?"

"He trained me for it. For months he trained me to be strong. I was afraid he would kill me. Kill Mama if I didn't. Can't you see? I wanted to hate you. I wanted to hate you both so it wouldn't matter. But it did matter. I prayed every day to Allah that he would not kill you. And now . . . "

"He didn't, Hussein. It wasn't Ali. It was a massacre. Moustafa died in a massacre."

Perspiration formed on Hussein's forehead. He thought of Ophélie, David's daughter. How close he had been to pulling the trigger. He felt nauseated and dizzy.

"I'll do anything, M. Hoffmann. Anything. Only please don't send me back there. Please!"

"Do you have weapons?"

"In my drawer."

"Let's go get them."

"Anything, but please help me. I am afraid."

M. Hoffmann looked very tired and weak. He patted Hussein's head. "We'll work it out, Hussein. It's going to be okay. Now let's go back to your dormitory."

* * *

Whatever Gabriella had expected when David got back, this was not it. She gathered her books for the children's class and spoke politely to Mme Leclerc over a *tartine* and cup of hot chocolate.

"So he has come back for you, Gabriella. I knew he would. *Ooh là là!* I just knew it." Gabriella kissed her lightly on the cheeks, a forced smile on her face.

"I'm off! I'm teaching the children this morning."

Perhaps Mme Leclerc was convinced of David's loyalty, but she wasn't. David seemed to her confused. All she wanted to do was to listen to him, to care and understand, but he was avoiding her. There was no other explanation. After the kiss in front of the children two days ago, he had not come back to talk. Gabriella had the most awful feeling that David was trying to choose between her and Anne-Marie.

She felt sick inside. Sick about Moustafa. Angry that David would not explain his actions. Why had he kissed her in front of the children if he wasn't even sure of his feelings toward her? What was the matter with him? She reprimanded herself. He had witnessed beastly acts, murders, the death of a friend. She must give him time.

She let herself into the classroom and spread the French grammar book out before her. Today she was teaching the children the difference between *et* and *est.* Pronounced the same way, the meaning was completely different. But it was simply a matter of memorizing a rule. Why couldn't life be that simple? The rule said that David had written the words "I love you" in black-and-white. If he had written it, it should not change. That was the rule.

The worst part was that she could not confide in Anne-Marie. A sort of tension hung between them. They smiled at each other politely and talked of the children. But so much was lost. Gabriella had imagined them ecstatic upon the return of Moustafa and David, laughing, dreaming dreams. Two couples in love.

Instead there were two women for one man, and in spite of all that David had promised her in his letters, in spite of the fact that Anne-Marie had assured her that David was right for her, she doubted. She was not making it up in her head. It was happening. What she had hoped would be the happiest time at St. Joseph's had turned into a time when she dreaded running into either of them. The waiting had been terrible, long, full of questions. But now David was back, and she was terrified to know the outcome.

The children meandered into the classroom, teasing one another. Gabriella tapped lightly on her desk. *"Bonjour, les enfants."*

"Bonjour, Maîtresse."

"Today the older students, as I told you yesterday, will have an *auto-dictée.* You may begin now." There were a few groans as they pulled out their notebooks and began to write a series of sentences they had learned by heart. Gabriella found this typically French spelling test challenging for the children. Still, they needed to follow a program similar to that of the public schools.

Turning her attention to the younger children, she wrote the words *et* and *est* on the blackboard. "Who can tell me the difference in these two words?" Several hands shot into the air. A simple rule that even a child could memorize.

* * *

David flashed Gabriella a smile as they waited for the dinner bell. He was sitting in the courtyard talking with a handful of the boys, showing them how to make paper airplanes. She could barely look at him, and when she did, her eyes filled up with tears. Once inside the refectory, the children insisted that they eat at the same table and whispered about the lovers. David regretted a hundred times that impromptu kiss in the classroom.

"How were classes today?" he asked flatly.

Gabriella had a look of disdain on her face. "The classes? They were fine." The conversation ended.

He did not know how to get around the awkwardness between them. Every time he thought of going to Gabby, taking her on a long walk or to a *café*, he was overcome by a sense of guilt. *Anne-Marie.* He had not expected to feel so strongly about her. It was as if Moustafa's fierce loyalty to her had been transferred onto his shoulders. He could not leave her alone. He would not. So it was unfair to Gabby to intimate otherwise.

"M. Hoffmann, *regarde!* Watch how it flies!" Jérémy had folded a sheet of paper into the form of an airplane and let it sail through the air. It landed smoothly in a pile of mashed potatoes on Anne-Sophie's plate. Several children giggled.

David shook his finger playfully. "None of that. Not here." He scratched his head. "I tell you what. Come to my classroom tomorrow afternoon, and we'll make paper airplanes. All kinds." The boys sitting around him narrowed their eyes. "No, I'm serious. I give you permission to come upstairs to my classroom tomorrow after classes."

"*Ouais! Super!*" Christophe and Jérémy shouted as one.

David turned back to Gabriella and shrugged. "It doesn't take much to make them happy."

She only nodded. He could see the hurt and misunderstanding in her eyes. He could read a hundred questions there and a deep desire just to talk with him. But he could not allow it. He loved Gabby with abandon and hope and passion. He loved Anne-Marie because she needed him, because Ophélie belonged to both of them, and it was right to be together.

It was too complicated, and his head began to throb. He stood up and took his tray to the kitchen with seven boys tagging behind. They followed him into the courtyard.

Momentarily forgetting his cracked ribs, David hefted André onto his back and rode him piggyback to the dorms. Immediately six other little boys begged for a ride. The children stared at him in awe, this teacher who used to be so aloof and who had suddenly catapulted into their world. He watched the boys wrestle each other on the dormitory floor, bumping into cots and bunks. Sister Isabelle entered the room and raised her eyebrows disapprovingly, but said nothing.

After the boys were tucked into bed and he had entertained them with stories of dinosaurs and dragons, David tiptoed into the girls' dorm and kissed Ophélie on the forehead. "Goodnight, sweetheart." Again he felt the disapproving eyes of Sister Isabelle. He went outside and stood in the courtyard staring at the sky.

Anne-Marie appeared beside him. "Thank you for telling Ophélie goodnight. It means the world to her to have you here."

"I'm not sure Sister Isabelle feels the same way," he chuckled.

"Oh, no. It's not that. It's just that we try not to get the children too riled up before bed. And . . . and usually men are not allowed in the girls' dorm."

"Ah yes. Rather thoughtless of me. Tomorrow night Ophélie shall have her kisses in the courtyard." He winked at Anne-Marie. "And I will have to postpone any more piggyback rides," he said, holding his side.

"David, could we talk?"

"Of course."

He took her arm and began walking toward the dining hall. At that moment, Gabriella stepped out of the dormitory and practically bumped into them both. Her face went white, then red. She glanced at his hand on Anne-Marie's arm, then looked away.

"*Bonsoir,*" she mumbled and left the courtyard, not looking back.

It hurt David to hurt her. He did not know what to say, so he let her go.

The dining hall was quiet and dark. David did not turn on a light. They sat across from each other, saying nothing at first.

"David. I want to talk about us."

He was glad it was dark, for he could feel his face turning hot with embarrassment. "I meant what I said." He reiterated his words from the other night. "I meant it."

"I know you did." Anne-Marie brushed her hair over her

shoulders nervously as if she was not sure what to say next. "David, you have done everything for me. Why? Why did you come here in the first place to help me? What is it that brought you here?"

"I've already told you that back in Algiers. I cared."

"Yes, you cared. You care for me. But you do not love me." She shut her eyes, concentrating. "You are Gabriella's, and you are killing her with your silence. Can't you see it in her eyes? You don't love me. Not the way you love her. You care, you feel a duty, a desire to do the right thing for me, and for Ophélie." Here she took his hand. "I will not let you do this. You are not obligated to me. You have paid me back a hundred times if you feel that you owed me something. I love you, David. I will love you till the day I die. But I will never be yours. I can't explain it. I just know. It is not right."

He sighed deeply. He felt so terribly confused. "What can I say to you? Nothing is simple, Anne-Marie. I love Gabby, but you're wrong. I'm not the one for her. She wants a husband who is strong and spiritual. Whatever faith I had died with Mou—" He slammed his fist on the table. "God, I'm sorry. Forgive me."

She kissed his hands. "We are all hurting very badly." Her eyes were liquid. It was the first time he had seen her cry since his return. "But listen to me, David. I was in love with Moustafa. Ready to give my life, everything for him. I had thought about it a lot. For all these months. And I will be faithful to him until . . ." A flicker of a smile was on her lips. "Until the heavens show me otherwise."

"What do you mean?"

"I have the strangest peace, David. As if Someone is carrying me. But it all goes away when I think of you giving up Gabriella for me. Please, David, this time listen to your heart. Share with her all you have lived. She deserves it, wants it. If you only knew how she loves you." She took a tissue from her pocket and wiped her eyes. "What do you think we've been doing all these months but talking of the men we love? She is my friend. If I know anything at all, it is that you are meant to be with Gabriella."

So she was freeing him. She had read his heart. "Yes, perhaps. Yes, I will tell her tomorrow. Thank you, Anne-Marie." They stood up, and he held her for a long moment, kissing her forehead. "I love you like my sister. I will always be here for you."

"I know it. Now promise me only one thing."

"What is it?"

"That you will not wait till tomorrow. Don't make her spend another tortured night, David Hoffmann. Go now."

"Yes," he said, laughing. "Yes." He left her standing in the courtyard.

*　*　*

Anne-Marie sank onto the damp ground and cried and cried. She had done it, what she had somehow felt called to do, but it was breaking her heart. She had said it because it had to be said. Because she knew what David was thinking, she understood his reasoning. But how it hurt! It was truth she had spoken, and she had somehow had the strength to speak it.

"I'm alone," she whispered. "Alone with my daughter. What will we do when we have nowhere to go? When David and Gabriella are far away and this orphanage is closed up?"

She was kneeling on the ground, her eyes closed and her hands clutched together. Only a minute later did she realize that she had been praying. The peacefulness invaded her again. Such a friendly invasion! Absolutely nothing was certain, and yet she left the courtyard in peace. She could not explain why.

*　*　*

The light was on in Gabriella's room. David tossed a stone at the window. It missed, falling into the olive tree. The second stone hit the window with a *pat* and bounced off. When the third stone rang true, Gabriella came to the window, peering down at David. He motioned to her. She frowned and shook her head. He motioned again. She hesitated.

"Please, Gabby!" he shouted.

Embarrassed, she put a finger to her lips.

"Come, please!" She left the window, and the light went off in her room. He waited for her below.

She looked irritated when she joined him on the cobblestones. "What do you want?" she snapped.

"You. I just want you."

"Don't give me that, David Hoffmann. I don't believe you anymore." Her eyes were flashing.

"Yes, I know. You're right. I'm a jerk. I've been so confused, so upset."

"I've noticed." Her tone was cutting.

"Can we talk?" he asked.

"How many young women will you make promises to tonight, David? I don't have time for that. I'm very busy." She whipped around and walked away.

"Gabby, wait." He caught her arm, and she shook it free.

"Leave me alone!" she said loudly as he grabbed both of her wrists. "You've done enough harm here. Don't cause a scene!"

"Gabby, please, wait!" His voice was a loud whisper. He spoke quickly. "At least give me a chance to explain. You have every right to be mad and hurt. Please listen."

She pulled her hands away from his, crossed her arms across her chest, and walked in front of him to the little park outside the walls of the church. She sat down on a bench. The moon was full and the air balmy, scented with honeysuckle. "I'm listening."

David stood in front of her, leaning against the stone wall. He chewed his upper lip and ran his hand through his hair. He needed the right words. "This isn't how the homecoming was supposed to be. Gabby, I'm so confused. I have seen the most awful things, and God seemed so silent. I wanted to be the man for you. I wanted to be a man of faith.

"But when Moustafa . . . " He lowered his voice and spoke with difficulty. "When the massacre occurred, rage overtook me. I hated your God. I hated Him so. I blamed Him. I begged Him to leave. And I begged Him to stay." He shook his head. "I'm messed up, Gabby."

Almost unconsciously, he sat down beside her and took her hand. "All I want is to do the right thing. But it isn't as simple as that. I feel, I feel responsible for Anne-Marie. She has no one now. My rational mind says that it is my duty, to her, to Ophélie. I care deeply for her. It isn't love as I feel for you." He squeezed her hand, but she continued sitting rigidly in her place.

"She asked to see me tonight, to talk. Anne-Marie knows my heart. She will not accept my charity. She knows I belong to you. That is what she told me tonight."

Gabriella leaned her head back, and her curly mane brushed the back of the bench. She sighed deeply. "How can you know? I thought I knew. I thought I was sure of you. And now a few miserable days have made me think it is impossible. I can understand your sense of duty to Anne-Marie. I could understand it if you loved her. She is an exquisite woman. She has that depth of character. . . . "

She stood up and walked into the shadows. "I guess what I'm saying, David, is that you need time to make up your mind about a lot of things. It can't be decided in a convincing soliloquy." There was a breeze, but the leaves were quiet, as if they dared not rustle. The moon was stark white with small distant gray patches. "I'm sorry for all you have lived through, David. I have hurt and cried and prayed for you." She ran her fingers through his hair. "You need time to decide about so many things. And so do I. Everything is, as you say, confused."

"What do you want me to do? About us?" He watched the

moon so luminous, sitting high and white beside the steeple of St. Joseph's.

Gabriella sighed. "I don't know. How can I know? I only know this hurts very badly. Can that be right?"

"Love will hurt, Gabby. A lot. The hurting doesn't make it right or wrong. It's just so hard to know."

"Yes, so I guess we should just wait and see. Goodnight, David." She touched his cheek and walked back to Mme Leclerc's apartment.

It was the saddest she had ever sounded.

* * *

Because it was expected of him, David went to see his father in the hospital each day. This morning, Roger Hoffmann looked much better. He flirted with the nurse who took his temperature and cracked a joke with another who checked his pulse. He was clean-shaven. The man looked again like his father, and David felt uncomfortable. He had not seized the opportunity to talk while his father was vulnerable. Perhaps it would not come again.

David did not stay long. After exchanging a few banal words, he returned to St. Joseph's. He had not slept much during the night. Gabby's words haunted him. Maybe they were all crazy. Maybe he just needed to get away from this place, go back to the States, let his mind clear.

The one thing he knew on this morning was that as long as he was still here, he was going to help Mother Griolet. The thought of that practicality helped him put aside the matters of the heart.

He had asked to see her at 11 o'clock, and she was waiting when he knocked on her door. The old nun did not look well to David, but her eyes sparkled as she welcomed him into her office.

"There now, David. You look much better today. What a relief to have you back among us. And how is your father?"

"He is resting well. His condition has stabilized. I went by earlier today."

"You must have been surprised to see him in Algeria."

"To say the least."

"I hope you are able to settle your differences with him, David." The way she spoke made David squirm the slightest bit in his chair.

"Perhaps that will come one day. But I do not wish to talk of my father. I want to know about you. I've heard rumors that this place may close."

"Yes, we've had quite a time. First it was the exchange program. Then the overcrowding at the orphanage." She pointed to several neat stacks of papers on her desk. "Angry parents, angry superiors, angry townspeople. So much anger around here!"

"Dear Mother Griolet. I am sorry I caused you such problems. Perhaps it was foolish for me to return to Algeria. In the end it has only complicated matters for everyone."

She shook her head in reply. "No, David. You're not to blame. Don't second-guess yourself. People just look for opportunities to complain and bicker. That's what is happening here in Castelnau. But we trust that God was leading you. We can't see the whole scheme of things as He does."

"I'm afraid I don't see much the way He does." David grimaced. "What I want to know is, how I can help you."

"What are your plans, David?"

"I don't know." He shrugged. "I guess my real reason for being at St. Joseph's is over. But I'm perfectly willing to help you with the children through the end of the summer. I never realized what fun it could be."

She breathed in deeply, then smiled. "Yes, that would be a great help." She studied a few pieces of paper absentmindedly. Then sitting back in her chair, she said, "You know, after the heart attack, I realized I needed to slow down. Hand over the baton. I was planning to retire, gradually. I was going to ask

343

you to consider taking over the direction of the exchange program." She cleared her throat. "But now, well, it seems that question is settled."

"I'm very sorry to hear it."

Mother Griolet closed her eyes. "I had it all worked out in my mind. You would direct the exchange program and Gabriella the orphanage. Such plans! It seems the Lord has something else in store for us."

David sat forward in his chair. "Mother Griolet, you must get some rest. I'll teach the children as much as you need. It will be a refreshing change from the ladies. There are many things yet to be decided. But don't worry about the children. Between Gabby and Anne-Marie, the Sisters, and me, they will be in good hands. You must rest."

"We have only three weeks left, David. I will be most obliged if you can stay on until then. There will be many details to take care of." She frowned. "It is not the way I wanted it to end, but God knows best."

David thought he saw a lone tear in the nun's eye.

She continued, "So often the things that seem like the worst mistakes in our lives turn out to be the stepping-stones for something much better, something that will bring Him glory. Exceeding abundantly beyond all that we ask or think." She closed her eyes, and David watched her wrinkled eyelids flutter. "That is one of my favorite verses, David, found in the third chapter of St. Paul's Epistle to the Ephesians. God has proven it again and again. Don't give up on Him yet."

David listened intently to the wise woman's words, feeling that he must keep them in mind to help him sometime later. He stood awkwardly. "I will stay until the end. You have nothing to worry about."

She wiped her brow, looking up at him. "Thank you, David."

He helped her stand and led her back to her bedroom. "You must rest, Mother Griolet. Rest. Everything will be fine."

He pulled the door closed and as he did, the old nun whispered, "Don't give up on Gabriella. She needs you more than she will say."

David walked up the flight of steps and let himself into his classroom. From his window he watched the children playing in the courtyard. He counted them. Fifty-eight. Something had to change and quickly. Perhaps it was best for the whole place to shut down. Mother Griolet certainly did not have the strength to continue.

He sat down at his desk, opened a drawer, and took out a thick stack of white paper. Slowly, deliberately, he began folding the paper, relishing the feel of it as he creased it carefully with his fingers. The bell rang for lunch. Satisfied, he left the room, looking back at seven paper airplanes, all different models, that sat neatly on his desk, waiting for eager little hands to give them flight.

Chapter 25

Eliane Cebrian went over and over the phone conversation in her mind. David Hoffmann, the man she had met at the port in Algiers, had called to give her news. Rémi was still in Algiers. Amar and Abdul had helped in rescuing them from the Casbah, and Madira had tended to them as a nursemaid. Rémi would be there soon. But Moustafa was gone.

That was five days ago. Dear, proud Rémi. Staying until the end. She did not let the children see the worry lines on her face, but sometimes at night she would cry into her pillow, terrified that Rémi would wait too long and he too would be lost. She tossed and turned in her bed. It seemed that her prayers were bumping against the ceiling and falling back upon her, hollow, unanswered.

The next morning, as she hastened to nurse José before he awoke Samuel and Rachel, a thought struck her as if she saw it painted on the dull gray wall in front of her. *Weep with those who weep.* Anne-Marie was the one who needed help. Anne-Marie was grieving a real loss. Eliane suddenly knew what to do to lift her own spirits.

It was impossible to get through to the orphanage these

days by telephone, but St. Joseph's was merely thirty minutes away by bus. After breakfast, she dressed the children and pulled them close around her. "Today we are going to bring sunshine."

Samuel wiped his brow. "It's hot enough, Mama, as it is. Why should we bring any more sun?"

Eliane laughed. "You will see. You will see."

* * *

Gabriella opened her backpack and took out the children's grammar book, preparing to greet her class. As she turned it over, a slip of paper fell out on the desk. It said simply *vendredi 13h00 café-bar.* Then there was an added reference: *anthology p. 435 ln. 62–69.* She felt the blood rise in her cheeks. David's handwriting still made her heart beat faster. She frowned at first, then could not suppress the smile that flickered on her lips. So this was how David planned to break her silent treatment. The anthology sat in her bedroom at Mme Leclerc's. She barely got through the morning with the children.

Rushing home, she dropped her pack and grabbed the thick book. Leafing through the pages, she found page 435 and laughed as she read the lines from Lord Byron's satire, *Don Juan:*

> *A long, long kiss of youth and love*
> *And beauty all concentrating like rays*
> *Into one focus kindled from above*
> *Such kisses as belong to early days,*
> *Where heart and soul and sense in concert move,*
> *And the blood's lava, and the pulse a blaze*
> *Each kiss a heart-quake—for a kiss's strength,*
> *I think, it must be reckoned by its length*

She shut the volume, a smile curling on her lips. He made her laugh! She had never liked Byron, especially not *Don Juan.* It was brilliant and rather immoral, she had told David.

But her face was burning with excitement. This man she loved was coming back to her, teasing her with a silly verse on kisses. She knew she would meet him at the *café-bar.* She could hardly wait for 1 o'clock to come.

* * *

David was sitting in the back at "their table." He stood up as she approached, bowed slightly, and pulled out a chair for her.

Gabriella rolled her eyes. "Really," she teased.

"Thank you for coming," David said softly.

"How could I resist when you tempt me with stories of passionate kisses?" She blushed. It felt to Gabriella that the old ease and playfulness they had shared was returning. Perhaps it would be possible to see into his soul again too.

He leaned forward, raised his eyebrows slowly, and said in a smooth, seductive voice, "So, what are you doing for the rest of your life?"

Gabriella laughed. Then pretended to pout. "I have no idea. What about you?"

"Well," he said while narrowing his eyes, "I don't *know,* but I certainly have several ideas."

"Name one," she countered.

"A walk through the gardens of Versailles hand-in-hand with a knockout redhead."

"Hmm . . ."

"And a long passionate kiss in the gazebo leading to Marie Antoinette's hamlet."

"Sounds nice."

"And an evening at the Opera, maybe *La Flute Enchantée,* and then a late night dinner at Maxim's."

"Very intriguing."

"And then . . ." He reached across the table and took her hand. "Standing in the rain in front of Notre Dame, the young man whisks his lady into his arms and dashes down a flight of steps where they find refuge in the galleys of the metro as a lone violinist plays Vivaldi's *Spring*. Wet and shivering, they walk back in the foggy night to their hotel..." As he spoke, he lightly stroked her finger. "... where they spend a night of youthful bliss."

She stared at him, enchanted, out of breath though she had not even moved. "David! You're embarrassing me." She said it too loudly, and several men at the bar turned in their seats.

David took her hands again, then reached over and brushed a strand of her hair. "I was just trying out an idea, if ever... if ever I needed to convince you of anything. What do you think? Pretty good, *n'est-ce pas?*"

She didn't miss a beat. "Pretty good. Although there are many more things in Paris to see, and you didn't describe the hotel at all."

"Good point," he reflected. "I guess that's because the hotel itself was of little significance, as long as there was a room and a bed."

"David! You're sounding like a modern-day Chaucer."

"I beg your pardon. In my tale it's all very moral. After all, they are married."

"Well, you didn't say anything about that part."

"No, I haven't quite imagined how it could happen."

"Oh, I see. Just a small detail."

He closed his eyes, concentrating, then opened them to look directly at her. "Someday, I promise—" He stopped. "Someday I hope I'll have an answer to that." Then quickly, "Let's get out of here." He stood again, waited for Gabriella, and took her hand. "Can we go somewhere to talk, Gabby?"

"Talk?" She raised her eyebrows. "I've heard that line before."

"Silly girl. I have so much to tell you if you want to hear it. A hundred things to share and know before I can plan the future."

"Well . . . if it's talking you want to do, I think I know just the place."

* * *

They sat in the little stone alcove in the tiny street behind St. Joseph's and told each other story after story of the months they were apart. Gabriella wept as David described the horror of the war. He held her close, wiping a tear off her cheek. Gabriella felt that her emotions were raw and exposed, but today she did not care. David was back, and he was going to be okay.

"David. I know you don't want to talk of it, but Moustafa . . . Did he leave anything, say anything for Anne-Marie?"

"There was a letter, but it was in the trunk. The one Hussein came over in."

"That boy! He scares me."

"He's a terrified kid, another casualty of war. There's no reason to worry about him now."

She bit her lip, not wanting to broach the next subject. "What about Anne-Marie? I didn't want to hear anything you said the other night. I was so mad. So hurt and so mad."

"You had every right to be. I'm sorry. I wanted to explain, but I did it all wrong. Please hear me out, Gabby." He rose, massaged his temples, and offered Gabriella his hand. "Can we walk for a while?"

"Sure, if you don't mind the heat." She followed him through the tiny cobblestone street, pointing out the healthy geraniums that tumbled from their window pots.

David only nodded, and she saw that he was preoccupied with other thoughts. "When Moustafa was killed, I felt responsible. I had envisioned myself rescuing the fair lady and her lover, and I failed. Nothing was as I had imagined. It was so much darker, crueler. I was terrified. And I was so angry at God for allowing it. And with that anger came some kind of loyalty to Moustafa. I reasoned, and I know it sounds crazy, but I reasoned that what I should do was care for Anne-Marie and my daughter. To put my emotions for you aside and marry Anne-Marie. I cannot lie to you, Gabby. I care deeply for her. It is more of a sibling love. But she is alone. You are beautiful, loved by many, spunky." He walked on, not looking at her. "You would be okay without me—as long as you didn't marry an old boring preacher." He laughed weakly. "Please understand—this was my reasoning, with my heart set aside.

"But Anne-Marie guessed it and refused. She said I belonged to you. I suppose you have shared stories. I don't know how it will work out, Gabby. I know I will want to be near Anne-Marie, to see my daughter grow up. I know I will always feel a certain responsibility for their well-being." They had come to a small park filled with chestnut trees. He motioned to a bench in the shade of one tree's wide limbs. "And now," he said gently. "It is time to talk of us. What are your plans?"

"My parents are arriving in three days with my sisters. They will be staying with me at Mme Leclerc's while she is away for the month of August. Then, I guess I'll go back to the States with them, to Bible college." She couldn't help saying what she felt. "But I am so afraid that we'll lose touch, you and I. That it will be too hard, that I'll never see you again when I leave this little town."

"I know what you mean."

"Mother Griolet asked me to stay on and be her apprentice. Can you imagine? And I actually considered it, before everything fell apart. I prayed and thought it out and made lists and came to the conclusion that God wanted me to stay here in Castelnau. It was the hardest decision I've ever had to make. And then it didn't matter after all."

"You would have done a terrific job." He shook his head, smiling. "That dear woman had it all worked out. You with the orphans and I with the 'ladies.' I mean, heading up the exchange program."

"Would you have stayed, David?"

"Of course." He took her hand. "I would have stayed right here with you for a long, long time." Her head was bent, and David reached over and tenderly took her chin in his hand. "Look at me, please, Gabby."

Her eyes, bright blue, shining, dared to look.

"You have said we must trust. I have done a miserable job at times. But He won't let me get away. Your God, and mine. I'm not sure I'm the man for you, with my raging and questions. But I catch on pretty quick. It says in the New Testament that Christ is in us and we are in Him. It says it a lot. So it seems we're pretty secure." He stood up, looking at his watch. "Grief! It's past three. I've got a date with some pretty special guys back at the orphanage."

"So did we decide anything, David?"

"Yes," he said softly, and drew her into his arms. "We decided to trust."

* * *

When Eliane appeared at the parsonage door, Sister Isabelle answered her knock, a flustered look on her face. "*Bonjour,* Mme Cebrian. How very nice to see you." She focused on the three children, and Eliane noticed the color draining from her face.

"Don't worry, Sister Isabelle. We aren't staying. We've only come to fetch Anne-Marie and Ophélie."

The sister showed obvious relief. "Well, please come in. I'll go get her. She is expecting you?"

"No, not at all. I guess you could say I'm kidnapping her."

"What a lovely idea!" She reddened. "I mean, well, you know what I mean."

"I know."

It didn't take much convincing to get Anne-Marie and Ophélie to leave St. Joseph's for the afternoon. "I'm treating you to lunch," Eliane stated flatly.

"To lunch? With all the children?"

"Don't worry. It's all arranged."

They rode into Montpellier and got off the bus at Place de la Comedie. Anne-Marie sighed with delight. "It's beautiful."

"You've never been to the Comedie?"

"No." Lazy students sipped drinks in *cafés,* finding refuge from the heat under the brightly striped parasols that adorned every table. "Look at the fountain!" Anne-Marie pointed to the statue of the Three Muses that stood several hundred feet away from the ornate Opera House.

"Mama," Ophélie said, tugging on Anne-Marie's sleeve. "That's where Bribri and I met that awful man, Jean-Claude. Right over there."

"Oh, sweetheart," Anne-Marie said, hugging her close. "What an awful memory. I'm glad that's all over."

"*Ah oui.* Let's not talk of bad things today," Eliane chimed. "Come this way; there's the most lovely park with a pond and ducks and swans and lots of swings and jungle gyms for the children. It's just over there, on the Esplanade."

The long tree-lined promenade with its splashing fountains opened before them. Again, Anne-Marie stopped and stared. "Just being here is like a taste of paradise. A city whose *vieille ville* is intact, where there are fountains and flowers and people enjoying the sunshine." She grabbed Eliane's hand, swinging it playfully to and fro. "Thank you. Thank you for bringing me here!"

As they arrived at the park, a young Arab woman waved and came over to Eliane. "Anne-Marie, this is Sarah. She lives beside our hotel. She's going to watch the children while we have a bite to eat."

Before Anne-Marie could protest, Eliane led her back across the Esplanade where spacious, grassy rectangles were outlined with red and white impatiens that fluffed out into a round, brilliant hedge. On the other side of the Esplanade, they stopped at a little kiosk. The luncheon special for the day was written on a large blackboard that sat on a tripod. They studied it for a moment.

"What do think? A salad, quiche, and *sorbet* for only 40F. With a *pichet* of *rosé* included."

"It looks divine, but can you afford it?"

"Yes, of course. Don't worry about that. This is our luncheon together." They chose a table and sat down.

"Eliane, you are so kind. It is beautiful here. But what about the children, their lunch?"

"I packed sandwiches and *petits suisses* and fruits and cookies and plenty of water. They'll be fine, and the park is in the shade. Sarah is very good with them. She's helped me several times when I thought I might just pull out my hair."

Anne-Marie looked surprised. "You feel that way too?"

"Are you kidding? With three little kids confined to a hotel room?" She chuckled. "I feel that way most of the time."

Anne-Marie laughed, her face lit up, and Eliane thought how lovely she was. For that brief moment she looked like a young, carefree woman, slim and stunning in her simple white silk blouse and floral skirt. Her hair was pulled back into a neat French braid.

"You look beautiful," Eliane remarked.

"Me? *Merci.* It's just the clothes." She blushed. "It was a gift from God—some rich woman donated a pile of clothes just my size to the orphanage."

"A gift from God, you said?"

Anne-Marie's dark eyes blinked, and she nodded slowly, pensive. "Yes. I don't know why I said that." Suddenly she became intense. She lowered her voice to only a whisper, so that Eliane had to lean forward and strain to hear. "Something strange has happened, Eliane. I haven't told anyone. It's been too . . . difficult and confusing at St. Joseph's lately, with David arriving and . . . Moustafa—" She frowned, her eyes filling up with tears. "Can you tell me what it feels like to believe?"

"To believe what?"

"In God, in the Christ. It is just so strange. When I learned about Moustafa, I couldn't cry at first. I was numb, but a sweet sort of numbness, as if Someone were carrying me in His arms. It was like that beautiful psalm, 'The Lord is my Shepherd,' and I am a scared lamb that He is gently leading by the still waters, through the valley of death. Could that be so? Could it be God?"

Eliane wiped her eyes, moved by Anne-Marie's simple explanation. "Yes. I think so." She smiled. "It sounds a lot like Him."

"David talked to me. He . . . he offered to take care of me. Of us."

Eliane nodded, not saying anything.

"I don't know why, but I told him it would be wrong. That he belongs with Gabriella. I don't know why I said it. It would be so nice to have someone to take care of me. But it was like I wasn't saying it." She took a sip of the wine. "He cares for me, but he loves her. So, here I am. The orphanage is closing, and I don't know what we will do. But I am not worried." She gave a short laugh. "I try to worry, but I can't. It's that same feeling. Being carried."

"And how can I help you?"

"You are helping me now. Taking me away for a moment to this beautiful place. I haven't forgotten what you said: we can start over. A new chance." She folded her hands on the table as the waitress brought a salad drenched in vinaigrette. "So what do I do now? While God is holding me?"

Eliane placed a white starched napkin in her lap and said in her brightest voice, "You wait. Jesus calls it abiding. Abide in Me, He says. He will show you what is next." She took a bite of the lettuce, chewing thoughtfully. "And Anne-Marie, I want you to know that we will always help you in any way we can. Anything."

"*Merci.*"

For a few minutes they ate in silence. The sky was a fervent blue without a cloud to be seen. The heat would have been unbearable if it were not for the faintest breeze that rustled the trees on the Esplanade. Eliane sensed that Anne-Marie needed to talk of lighter things. "Ophélie has grown an inch, I'll bet, since I last saw her. She is such an insightful little girl. And compassionate. Did you see how she kept asking Rachel if she wanted to trade seats on the bus so she could see out the window? You must be very proud of her."

It was the perfect subject. "I am. I can hardly believe she is mine. This graceful child who looks at me with big brown eyes and asks the deepest questions. She is a puzzle to me sometimes. And a joy."

Eliane's lilting voice agreed. "Yes, isn't it fun when they get to the age where you can actually reason with them? Samuel is like that too. And did I tell you he's about to lose his first tooth?"

"Ophélie has one that's loose too. And she wrote her first poem, a beautiful thing. Gabriella asked the older children to write, and she wanted to also. The spelling is atrocious, but the words are from her heart." She dabbed her lips with the napkin. "I was so glad to read it. So relieved because, Eliane, it was a happy poem. She wrote it the day after we learned of Moustafa. It was not angry at all. I think it has something to do with a picture she drew for David. All these ponies were running toward the sun, and each pony represented one of the people she loves." She fished in her purse and pulled out a small sheet of lined paper, then she blushed. "I keep it with me. Do you mind if I read it?"

"*Au contraire*, I'd love to hear it."

Anne-Marie cleared her throat, then read the poem:

"*Ponies
Different colors
Different sizes
Some jump jumps*

356

And some win prizes
Ponies run and ponies walk
I even knew of one who could talk
Black and white
gray and tan
Red and brown
On and on they ran
The brown one ran
And won the race
He waits for the others
In a special place"
"It's lovely, Anne-Marie."

Then the children suddenly appeared, dashing across the Esplanade and squealing. It looked like Samuel was catching the girls and playfully pulling their pigtails. José wriggled in Sarah's arms.

"Shall we go for a stroll?" Eliane asked, paying the bill.

"Oh yes, let's. For just a little while. It is *une journée magnifique.* I don't want this day to end."

When the two women said good-bye, kissing lightly on the cheeks and each taking a different bus toward home, Eliane felt happier than she had felt in her two months in France. *Anne-Marie is remarkable,* Eliane thought to herself. *I imagined it would be a day for weeping, and instead, we are rejoicing together. Keep holding her, Lord. She has a long road ahead.*

*   *   *

The 14th of July was a day of celebration throughout France. Bastille Day, they called it, in memory of that summer day in 1789 when French citizens stormed the prison in Paris and liberated the seven prisoners held within. The French Revolution had begun.

Gabriella wondered, on this hot day in July, if in many of the French minds the revolution were not still going on. They seemed to her so rebellious, mocking authority, cynical about certain ethics, so different, so proud. What was it that drew people to love the French? She was not sure, but it had drawn her too.

Fireworks were being displayed down by the Lez River. Hundreds of Montpellieriens had crammed together on the grassy slopes on either side of the river to watch the celebration. At 9:30 all they waited for was dark to touch the sky.

Ophélie snuggled between Gabriella and Anne-Marie, rubbing her eyes, eager for the spectacle to begin. Ten other girls from the orphanage crowded close to the two women. David had found a spot nearby and busily entertained fifteen boys, threatening that they would be forced to memorize all of *La Chanson de Roland* if they so much as strayed an arm's length from him. It amused Gabriella to see the respect these boys had for David. She bet they would've gladly jumped in the river and swum a mile upstream if he had asked it.

Mme Dramchini with Saiyda and Rachida kept watch on another bunch of children, and the Sisters had their hands full as well. M. Vidal was even full of stories tonight, and children huddled close to him, listening intently. Seeing the growing crowds, Gabriella wondered if they had been foolish to bring all fifty-eight children into this mob. But when the first of the fireworks was launched and exploded in brilliant oranges and reds above the children's heads, she knew it had not been a mistake. They oohed and aahed, clapping enthusiastically with each burst of light. They traced the trail of the streaming fireworks down with their fingers, their voices diminishing as the flame finally fizzled, only to pick up into another loud ooh for the next. Many of them had never seen fireworks before.

At least we can give them this, thought Gabriella, *before we send them off to who knows where*. She was enjoying the display, but her thoughts wandered. There were only two weeks left for the orphanage. Mother Griolet had received word from Henri Krugler yesterday that he had found homes for several of the *harki* children in Lodève. That news had brought such a smile of relief to Mother Griolet's pale face that Gabriella almost wished she could fabricate a place for each child, just so the nun wouldn't worry.

And in less than forty-eight hours her parents and sisters would arrive in Castelnau. She had not had a moment to consider it, really. She felt excited when she did think about it, but she also felt afraid. Her family's arrival meant, in a way, the end of this experience. She was not sure she was ready to let go, especially of the young man who sat on the grassy slope, entertaining boys with stories of war and literature as fire from the sky broke into an array of different colors and floated down, shimmering in the waters of the Lez.

* * *

The plane touched down on the runway, and butterflies danced in Gabriella's stomach. Her family was really here. David and M. Vidal had both brought their cars to the airport so there would be plenty of room for everyone. Gabriella suddenly felt terrified for her family to meet David. What would they think?

Jessica and Henrietta were the first through customs, waving and giggling shyly. They looked older, as if this year had matured them indeed beyond the adolescents they were when she had left. They were tanned, with their long, thick hair falling over their shoulders. Henrietta's was blond, Jessica's auburn. "Gabriella!" they both exclaimed at once and rushed to embrace their sister.

"Oh, it's so good to see you," she answered, laughing. "You both look great."

"Well, it sure feels good to be off that plane," Henrietta complained, scooping her hair up into one thick strand and holding it off her neck. "But it's like an oven in here."

"Wait till you go outside! Welcome to the Midi!"

"Ugh! I prefer the climate of Senegal."

Jessica lowered her voice. "Is that him over there?" She glanced in the direction of where David stood a little ways off.

Gabriella could not suppress a smile. "Yes," she whispered. "But please don't stare!"

Jessica laughed, turning her back toward David and mouthing "Wow!" without making a sound. "I would never have expected it of you, Gabe."

Gabriella rolled her eyes. "Thanks a lot."

Then her parents came through the doors, pushing a flat trolley filled with suitcases and duffel bags.

"Mother!" Rebecca Madison looked ever the same, tall, poised, gracious, her long auburn hair pulled back in a thick braid that fell down her back.

"Gabriella," she said softly, her voice cracking the tiniest bit with emotion. She hugged her daughter to her breast. "It's good to see you."

Then Gabriella was in the arms of her father, tall and sturdy with his own shocking curly red hair. He picked Gabriella off the ground with his hug. "Sweetheart! So good to see you!"

They talked about everything and nothing, until Gabriella motioned to David and M. Vidal to come over. "I want you to meet two friends of mine. They teach at the exchange program. This is Jean-Louis Vidal. He teaches European History."

The balding man pushed his glasses up on his nose, reddened, and extended his hand. *"Enchanté."*

"Yes, very good to meet you," Gabriella's father replied in French. "I'm William Madison. This is my wife, Rebecca." They both shook hands.

"And this is David. David Hoffmann. He teaches the Visions of Man course I told you about."

David smiled stiffly and shook hands. "Pleased to meet you," he said in English. "I have greatly enjoyed having your daughter in my class. She has spoken often of you."

Gabriella sighed with relief. At least he was behaving in a charming, civil manner. David then took the hand of Jessica and said, "Let's see, you must be Henri . . . no, Jessica." When he squeezed her hand softly, Gabriella noted with amusement that Jessica's face went quite red. "And Henrietta. Good to meet you both."

Still in perfect control, David stood alongside the trolley. "Shall we get these bags to the cars?"

"I hope they'll all fit. Or perhaps we should call a taxi?" William Madison suggested.

"No, I think we'll be fine. We've brought two cars."

The ride back to Castelnau was a blur to Gabriella. Her father rode in the front seat with David. Jessica and Henrietta were in the back seat, hemmed in by luggage. Gabriella accompanied her mother and M. Vidal in his car. Her eyes never left the pale blue *deux chevaux* in front of them. She wished with all her might that she could be privy to the conversation between her dad and David. Instead she chatted with her mother and felt a sudden peacefulness that she was there.

Chapter 26

Late into the night, Gabriella sat around Mme Leclerc's dining room table talking with her family. Her landlady had served a delicious meal and then discreetly disappeared into the kitchen and later her room. At first, there was so much to be told that the Madisons constantly interrupted each other to give details of life over the past nine months.

Finally Jessica held up her hand and proclaimed, "I suggest we hear one story at a time. Since the four of us know a lot about what's been going on in Senegal, I vote that we let Gabriella tell her whole story, from beginning to end."

Rebecca Madison agreed. "I can hardly keep up with all you've been through."

Gabriella was beaming. There was something so right, so comfortable about being together, the five of them again. With all the events of the past months, she had not realized how much she had missed them. She began with Mother Griolet and the classes and David. She told about the mysterious little child, Ophélie, and the cruel Jean-Claude and the operation David had started up to rescue children from Algeria. Her father's face grew grave, concerned. Her mother only nodded from time to time.

When Gabriella mentioned her flashback about Ericka, her mother reached across the table and gently took her hand. For a moment Gabriella could not continue, and she noticed that everyone's eyes were shining with tears.

She spoke of Anne-Marie's arrival, Mother Griolet's heart attack, and the threat to close the orphanage and exchange program. "Mother Griolet offered me an internship with her, to eventually step into the position of director of the orphanage, and I accepted, before either of us knew it would be closed. I have learned so much from that dear woman. It would have been a privilege to sit under her tutelage. As it is, I don't know where she will go.

"And then when David finally came back, he brought with him the terrible news of Moustafa's death. Anne-Marie has taken it amazingly well. It is just awful. His mother and sisters escaped two and a half weeks ago and are staying here. But Moustafa and his brother didn't make it." She sighed. "It has been the worst and the best of times, as Dickens says."

Rebecca Madison broke in. "And have you made any other plans for what will come next, Gabriella?"

"I suppose I will come with you all and finish my degree in the States, as we had originally planned. There is nothing to keep me here and . . . I'm . . . well, I'm just not sure what will happen between David and me. He needs time." She chuckled mournfully. "Trouble is, time is running out."

"So the two of you have made no definite plans?" her father reaffirmed.

She shook her head.

"Well," he said, and Gabriella thought he sounded relieved. "I do look forward to getting to know this young man while I'm here."

The evening ended with the whole family holding hands, as William Madison bowed his head and prayed for his eldest daughter.

* * *

The reunion between Mother Griolet and Rebecca Madison took place at the nun's bedside on the morning after the Madisons arrived in Castelnau. The tall auburn-haired woman warmly kissed Mother Griolet's cheeks before pulling a chair up beside the bed. "It is so good to see you again, Mother Griolet!"

Mother Griolet chuckled. "Yes, Rebecca, God be praised. You are a bright light to me today. Please forgive me for not receiving you properly. For some silly reason," she reprimanded herself, "this old body does not want to get out of bed today. Quite lazy of me, I'm afraid."

Rebecca's voice was firm and reassuring. "You have enormous pressure on you from every side. For anyone it would be overwhelming, but you are recovering from a heart attack. You must rest. These other women are doing a fine job handling the children. And I thoroughly enjoyed seeing M. Vidal again." She laughed. "He hasn't changed much in fifteen years."

"No, dear Jean-Louis is still the same. Quite a big help to me, he is." Her face clouded. "And I suppose you have met M. Hoffmann?"

"Yes, he was there at the airport to meet us. Very striking and polite. I hope I will get to know him better. I must confess I was relieved when Gabriella told us they had made no immediate plans."

"Yes, I can imagine. But Rebecca, I just want you to know he is a fine young man. I misjudged him for many months. He is finding his way. I believe that he would be a good man for Gabriella." She smiled. "I thought they should stay here and run the show. He"—and she glanced heavenward—"obviously had other plans."

"Well, thank you for telling me, Mother Griolet. It means a lot to have your opinion. I could not find a better one anywhere." She patted the nun's hand. "And now I am going to let you rest. I'm sure there is work that I can help with around here."

"Yes." Mother Griolet caught her hand, an almost furtive look in her green eyes. "Rebecca. Did Gabriella mention about . . . about Ericka?"

Rebecca locked her hands together and bent her head. "Yes. We have talked. All of us talked about it together last night. Thank you, thank you for being here for her, as you were for me all those years ago." She took a long breath. "I'm sorry you had to be the one who got the brunt of Gabriella's anger. I suppose it should have been me."

"No, Rebecca. I am glad I was here, and now I am glad to know that you and your daughter have talked. It is good."

"It never seems to hurt less, losing a child. But God has filled up the emptiness in other ways. For that I am grateful. *Merci.*"

Rebecca bent over and kissed Mother Griolet's forehead, then left the nun sitting in her bed and quietly slipped out the door.

* * *

Mother Griolet could not get out of the bed on the following morning either. She awoke well before six. She felt extremely dizzy and weak and especially irritated at her failing body. She prayed and read Scripture for a long while, knowing that eventually, at breakfast, the Sisters would wonder what had happened and come to her.

She turned often to her favorite passages in Scripture, the promises of God, and more specifically, the promises for the future with Him where there would be no more sorrow or crying or death. She dozed in between her readings, seeing herself in a state of semi-consciousness, bathed in a warm, soothing light. In her lucid moments, her prayers were for the children, for the Sisters and the young women she had grown to love. For David Hoffmann and for Jean-Louis.

She winced as a sharp pain shot through her chest. "Now to Him who is able to do exceeding abundantly above all that we ask or think," she spoke slowly, taking long breaths between each phrase. ". . . according to the power that worketh in us, unto Him be the glory in the church by Christ Jesus throughout all ages, world without end. Amen." It was one of her favorite verses. Reciting it out loud brought serenity again.

"Lord, I am Yours." The pain lessened. She relaxed. "Do with me as You will. You know . . . You know that I am longing to see You, to be with You." She felt so very tired. "If it must be so, please use this too for Your glory. These people are young and full of hope. Guide them on."

She clutched her Bible to her breast and closed her eyes. The warm, soothing light was drawing nearer. A faint smile crossed her lips. *"Mon Sauveur!"* she said out loud. Then, quite peacefully, Mother Griolet fell asleep.

* * *

When Mother Griolet did not show up for breakfast, Sister Rosaline excused herself from kitchen duty and went through the courtyard into the parsonage. She walked in her typically brisk manner, reaching the nun's quarters out of breath. As she opened the door to the apartment, an eerie silence greeted her. She thought of the vivid dream that had awakened her from her sleep three and a half months ago, and how she had rushed to find the nun after her heart attack.

"Yoo-hoo, Mother Griolet?" she called out, trying to sound cheery. No response. The walk down the hall took a few seconds, but to Sister Rosaline it seemed like hours. She came to the nun's bedroom. There she lay, with a peaceful smile on her face and her worn Bible lying in one arm.

She is only asleep, Sister Rosaline told herself as she felt for a pulse, but Mother Griolet's hand felt cool to the touch. Sister Rosaline recoiled, a look of stupefaction on her face. She inadvertently let out a scream. *"Non! Ce n'est pas possible!"*

Then she came to Mother Griolet's side again. Was there no breath, no hope? She looked so serene, lying there with her long silver hair strewn out on the pillow. Sister Rosaline knew immediately that this body no longer housed the nun's soul. She bit her lip, crossed herself, then burst into tears.

"Why, Father? Why did You not warn me today as before? I would have come in a blink. You know it. Why?" She sank to her knees with a low groan, leaned on the bed, and tenderly took Mother Griolet's white hand and kissed it.

"You know I always admired you. Your faith gave me faith in the worst of times. I loved you like my own mother. I would have done anything for you. You were the one who led. We only followed." She sniffed and wiped her round cheeks with the back of her hand.

Sister Rosaline thought for a moment that she had heard a sound. She glanced up. No movement. Outside it was beginning to rain, and the drops hit the window in sharp pellet-like strokes. "Are You weeping, Lord?" she asked. "Not for Yourself, not for *her*, for she is with You now. But for us. Oh, what shall we do now, Lord Jesus? What shall we do?"

The rain fell harder, and Sister Rosaline knelt by the bed and watched it for a long time. "You took her, Father. You took her before she was forced away from here. You took her peacefully. It would have killed her to leave St. Joseph's." The large nun's tears fell down her face and made a dark stain of water on her black robe.

She waited for a while longer, watching from the bedroom window as Gabriella and Sister Isabelle dashed across the courtyard and retrieved a handful of umbrellas from the dorm. Then, in single file, Gabriella led the children into the basement of the parsonage. Soon Sister Rosaline could hear their sweet voices chattering excitedly about the rain in the classroom below.

"Show me how to tell them, Father." She stood up slowly, her joints aching. She stood for another moment staring at the nun, bowed slightly, crossed herself again, and left the room.

* * *

It rained steadily, the sky a dismal gray, the kind that sets in for the whole day. Gabriella, Sister Isabelle, and Sister Rosaline sat in stunned silence and watched the downpour, listening to its drowning repetition. It seemed appropriate for it to rain, particularly this type of driving, persistent rain, as if the storm itself were delivering the final, deliberate blow to the women at St. Joseph's.

David had heard the news from Sister Rosaline first and had immediately come to take Gabriella's place with the children. When he entered the room, Gabriella guessed the truth. He had only given her a sad little smile and said, "May I have the pleasure of teaching these children the conjugations of the verbs *aller, être,* and *avoir?*" And as she had looked at him quizzically, he had whispered, "Sister Rosaline needs to see you for a moment."

Reflecting on that, Gabriella thought David had been right. She had found Sister Rosaline and Sister Isabelle crying in the dining hall where they now sat. Amidst hugs and tears, Sister Rosaline had pronounced the words, "She is gone."

The thirty days would soon be up, and the orphanage closed. It did not seem to matter at all, now that Mother Griolet was gone. Sitting with these two women, Gabriella swallowed, but the lump in her throat would not go away. She thought about Henri Krugler working hard to find more places for the children. She thought about Mother Griolet's files and how she had begun to study them with David and the nun, preparing for the school's closing. She thought about the children who had already found homes in Lodève.

And then she thought about Mother Griolet lying, as Sister Rosaline had described, serene and still on her bed, with her ash-white hands folded over her abdomen.

Gabriella had no desire to fight anymore. Let the

authorities come and pronounce their sentence. Had they no respect for the dead? She watched the windowpane fill up with drops of rain.

Presently Sister Rosaline sighed and stood up. "I'm going to call M. Cohen. He will know what to do next. He'll help us inform people. There are so many who will want to know." She wiped her brow. "And I suppose I shall need to inform her superiors in the church. There's a certain protocol for that." Her voice caught, and she turned quickly and left the room.

"*Alors, moi,*" said Sister Isabelle, wiping her eyes. "I'm going to tell Pierre. He'll see to it that the whole town knows quickly." She tiptoed out of the room without looking back, an umbrella tucked under her arm.

In that short moment, Gabriella saw her future more clearly. Soon she was really going to leave St. Joseph's with her parents and start a new life in the States. Her soul ached. Her mouth went dry. "But, Lord, I don't want to leave," she whispered.

She buried her head in her hands. Even as she did so, she could hear the voice of Mother Griolet chiding her. *Don't give up. If you are convinced that you are right, don't give up until the Lord Himself convinces you otherwise.*

She was doing no good just sitting there. A hundred details needed attending to. It was not the time to give in to the numbing power of the rain. But before she did anything else, Gabriella had an appointment to keep. She left the room and walked outside, letting hundreds of wet drops fall on her face before she found refuge in the parsonage.

* * *

It did indeed look as if the nun were merely asleep, Gabriella thought as she tiptoed into the room. The smile on the old nun's face reassured Gabriella that she had not suffered long. It was as if Mother Griolet had known what was happening, and it brought a faint smile to her lips. "At home with the Lord," Gabriella said softly.

She fiddled with a corner of the comforter, touched the nun's hand, and drew back in surprise. It was cool. "I know you are not here," she said, her voice strained. "Only, I had to come see you again. I had to tell you that you were the godliest woman I have ever known."

She dropped to her knees, resting her head against the bed. "I am not ready for you to be gone. No! I could have stayed beside you, just observing you work, for many years. I wanted that. You saw it, didn't you?" She spoke in little, erratic sobs. "You helped me so much." She covered her face with her hands and cried out, "Oh, God, why? I don't want her to be gone. It was so much easier to trust when she was here."

Gabriella sat back on her feet, blinked several times, and stood up. "You said He turns tragedy to triumph. You said it. But I don't see it. There's only a whole lot of hurt around here right now." She unfastened the gold Huguenot cross from around her neck, cupped it in her hands, then placed it on the Bible that sat securely under Mother Griolet's folded arms.

She studied the gold chain in contrast to the worn black leather. She bent forward and kissed Mother Griolet's cold cheeks. "I haven't forgotten that He is in control. I won't forget." She picked the cross back up and held it dangling from her fingers. It spun slowly around on its chain. The rain continued to fall outside.

* * *

When Joseph Cohen learned of Mother Griolet's death, he felt a great sadness come over him, as if a part of his past had suddenly disappeared. He kept his voice calm as he listened to the stricken Sister Rosaline on the other end of the phone line.

"Do not worry, Sister. I will inform the Jewish families who should know. I have most of the addresses, and what is missing, surely others will provide. And I am sure you will find among her own files the names of the other orphans. Perhaps you yourself know how to contact some of them." He listened as Sister Rosaline assured him that she had already begun taking out the files, finding updated addresses.

"That is good, Sister. I suggest you schedule the funeral on Saturday. That gives us three days to take care of all the details, and people from out of town will have a chance to come." They discussed the necessary arrangements in a very practical manner. Sister Rosaline had always been good for that, he mused.

"And one more thing," he added as she was about to hang up. "I am the executor of her will. You needn't worry about any of those details. I'll take full charge."

She sounded relieved to hear that. He listened, then said, "Yes, well good. I'll be in Castelnau on Friday then with Emeline. *Bon courage, ma Soeur.* I'm very sorry for the news. Yes, *au revoir.*"

He hung up the phone, gnawing on a pencil. Opening the bottom drawer of his desk, Joseph fished through stacks of papers and retrieved a thick manila file. Inside were page after page of information of the Jewish children hidden at St. Joseph's during the Second World War. He sighed heavily, put on a pair of bifocals, and leafed through the papers, dialing the first number.

* * *

David's initial response to the news of Mother Griolet's death was to take charge. It was easier for him to handle his grief this way. It helped him to be busy, because the crazy, angry questions did not come as quickly to mind. He spent the morning with the orphans, working on verbs. When he felt composed enough himself, he gently broke the news about Mother Griolet to the children. They stared at him, speechless. Finally little Christophe blurted out, "Where is she? Is she still up there? In her room?"

When David nodded, several girls squealed and hid their faces. Most of the boys remained silent, their young faces stoic. Ophélie began to cry and ran to the front of the room, hugging her father. "It can't be! It just can't be!"

"Shh." David cuddled his daughter. "It will be all right." He cleared his throat. "I am very, very sorry to have to tell you this. We all loved Mother Griolet very much." He could not think of what else to say. Their sad eyes were pleading for comfort, but he had none to give.

"What will happen to us now?" Anne-Sophie asked. "Will they send us away?" The other children nodded, the sadness in their eyes changing to fear.

"No, children. Do not worry. It will be all right. It is okay to be sad and to cry, but remember, as Mother Griolet has told you . . . " He faltered for a moment. "God is in control." Saying those words, whether he truly believed them or not, somehow helped David regain his composure.

"Shall we pray?" he suggested. The children nodded. He watched them, their heads bowed, eyes closed, small hands folded neatly on top of the desks. It struck him as poignant. They trusted him completely in that moment. No words came to his mind at all. Ophélie, who was sitting on his desk, whispered to him, "Do you want me to pray, Papa?"

He nodded.

"Oh, Lord," she prayed in a strong, sorrowful voice. "Thank You for Mother Griolet. Thank You that she took good care of us. Thank You that she has gone to heaven now, and I'm sure she must be very happy." She began to cry again. "Please take care of us, Jesus. Please, oh please, take care of us. We don't want to leave. Amen."

For several minutes afterward, the children sat in silence. Then one little girl started to sing a simple chorus. Soon the others joined in. "God is watching over me, no matter how small I may be. He is listening to my prayers. How good to know that my God cares. God is watching over me." It seemed to calm them; it also calmed David's heart.

Sister Isabelle came into the classroom, red-eyed and sniffling. "Thank you, M. Hoffmann, for your help. Children, you have thirty minutes of rest time in the dorms before lunch. We'll take you by threes under the umbrellas."

David left the classroom, promising Sister Isabelle that he would take the responsibility for letting M. Vidal know about the news. She smiled gratefully at him as the children lined up three by three at the door.

David had never been to the old history teacher's house, but he knew where it was located, down the hill and back in a tiny side street of the village. The rain was coming with such force that even with an umbrella, by the time he reached the small stone house his shoes and the legs of his pants were sopping wet.

He knocked forcefully on the door. After what seemed an eternity, the older man opened it, blinking behind his glasses. "David! *Quelle surprise!* Look at you. Please, come in."

David felt vulnerable, unprepared, and unworthy to speak to this dear man, as he stood before him dripping on the tile floor.

"What brings you here today?" Jean-Louis asked brightly. Then he saw David's face. "Something is wrong?"

"Yes, I'm afraid so. Could we . . ."

Jean-Louis hurried him into the kitchen, where a single chair sat in front of the small, narrow table. A half-full bottle of red wine was the only thing on the table. Jean-Louis retrieved another chair from the *salon,* and they sat down. He cleared the wine bottle off the table and wiped his bloodshot eyes.

"It's Jeanette, *n'est-ce pas?*" he guessed immediately.

David nodded very slowly. "I'm sorry to be the one to bring you this news." He shivered, although the air was heavy and warm. "Sister Rosaline found her this morning. It appears she died peacefully in her sleep."

"I see." Jean-Louis thoughtfully stroked his chin. "Yes, I

see." He turned away from David, and it made David feel like an intruder in this man's grief. "Would you like me to leave?" he asked finally.

"No," Jean-Louis said quickly, almost desperately. "Could you stay for a moment? I'll get a drink. Yes, would that do?" Jean-Louis went into his *salon* again and returned with a bottle of *pastis*. "Will you have a drink with me, David? I think I need a drink."

"Yes, of course."

For the next hour they sat in strained silence and slowly sipped their tall glasses of *pastis*. Jean-Louis seemed completely lost in thought, perhaps anesthetized by the constant sound of the pouring rain. At length he said, "She was my dearest friend." Then he looked down at his empty glass, his face bright red, and mumbled. "I loved that woman. I swear it. I did."

After another long silence, he asked, "She is still . . . she is still in her room?"

"Yes. I need to call the authorities to report the death, but I thought you might . . ."

"Yes, I shall go and see her. Would you please wait for me to get my coat?"

"Of course." They left the little stone house five minutes later, and walked with their umbrellas pushed in front of them to keep the driving rain away.

* * *

Word of Mother Griolet's death spread quickly throughout the town of Castelnau. In their voices over the phone, Pierre Cabrol could hear it as he announced the news. In the eyes of those who came into the bakery, he could see it. Sorrow and embarrassment. *They wonder*, Pierre thought to himself, *if their obstinate complaining had anything to do with it. Well, let them wonder.* Even his wife, Denise, had shed quite a few tears.

A hundred different scenarios flashed through Pierre's

mind that day as he rolled out his dough and baked it in the large ovens in the back of his shop. He remembered when Mother Griolet had first come to Castelnau, little more than an adolescent. The black habit she had worn had never been able to hide her beauty. He could still recall the way her eyes danced and her laughter rippled throughout the chapel or the park, or his father's store, when he had been a lad of sixteen and enchanted by the young nun.

He remembered Sebastien Vidal, who had stolen her heart while she was still in training. That had been the talk of the town! Would the pretty young novice give up her calling for the fleshly desire of marriage? And then he remembered, with sorrow, the news of Sebastien's death on the battlefield so far away. Pierre had helped Jean-Louis install the stone plaque on a column in the chapel all those years ago, in remembrance of those lost during the First World War.

He thought of the really terrifying times during the Second War when the three of them, Jeanette, Jean-Louis, and he, had taken their part in the Resistance. Terrifying and extremely rewarding. Denise had always watched Mother Griolet jealously when she had business to do with Pierre. More than once, Pierre had felt a pang of guilt. He cared for this nun. It had long ago stopped being the foolish love of his youth. Over the years it mellowed into great respect for this woman who had a wonderful ability to joke and trust in God's surprises.

He brushed his flour-coated hand across his face to wipe a tear, leaving a patch of dough over his right eye. "I'm going to miss you, Jeanette," he stated. "And I'm not the only one. Not by a long shot."

* * *

After the orphans were snuggled on their beds for nap time, Anne-Marie quietly made her way to the parsonage and up to Mother Griolet's apartment, which Sister Isabelle had assured her was unlocked. The rain had stopped, and from

time to time a ray of the sun peeped out from behind thick
gray clouds.

She did not turn on any lights, but made her way to the
bedroom. The corpse looked very white in the room's
shadows. Anne-Marie stood transfixed in the doorway. She did
not feel worthy to go in.

"I came to tell you good-bye," she whispered. "I wish I
could have known you better. But anyway, I thought you would
want to know that . . . that I believe. In spite of Moustafa, in
spite of the war, and this place closing and David going and
now you . . . I still believe. I can't tell you why. I think you must
know that better than I. But wherever you are now"—she
looked upward—"for I know you are with Him if ever anyone
is, well, I just wanted you to know. Thank you." She took her
gold chain with its strange cross in her hands, tracing its
outline with her fingers. She whispered again, "I believe."

Then hesitantly, she walked into the room, bent down,
and kissed the old woman's forehead. "Good-bye," she
murmured. "You will be missed."

Chapter 27

The Place at the port in Philippeville was busy with activity. The Arab woman quickly bought her pears and peaches, a head of lettuce, carrots, potatoes. The mood was happy today, but every time she came into the square, she remembered the massacre that had taken place before her eyes and the eyes of her old father. She remembered the horrifying screams and then the chilling silence.

She shivered to remember as the heat of midday blazed on her shoulders. Algeria was free. A shaky freedom. And oh, the price! A vendor weighed the fruits and vegetables, handing them to her. She placed them carefully in her straw basket and fiddled with her change purse.

"Allah be praised. It's a good day!" the vendor sang out in robust Arabic. The woman merely nodded.

She was neither old nor young, a soft, timid woman who had never married and who spent her days caring for her elderly father. The people of Philippeville called her Selma, which meant "peaceful one," although her real name was Fatiah. She was respected and thought of as wise. Rumor had it that she had once healed a young boy who was deathly ill with hepatitis simply by rubbing grated garlic into his scalp.

At different times of the night and day, hurting people appeared at her door. Without a sound she moved her hands carefully, thoughtfully over their bodies or prepared strange herbal dressings. Those who were healed did not leave money. They left chickens and vegetables and olives.

Selma pulled her white scarf around her neck as she climbed the stairs to her apartment. She knocked four times, pausing in between. It was their code. Her father opened the door, relief in his eyes. "You were not followed?"

"No, Father. All is well. How is he?"

The old man smiled. "Better. You will see. He has opened his eyes."

Selma set down her basket in the tiny kitchen and hurried to the back of the apartment, entering a darkened room. A young man lay perfectly still on the bed, his olive skin glistening with perspiration. She bent over him. His eyes were closed, but he sensed her presence, and they flickered open. They were soft brown in color, kind eyes, fearful.

"It is okay. Do not be afraid," she whispered as she gently brushed his thick black curls away from his face. She held a glass of water to his lips, and he drank. "You are going to be fine."

The young man opened his mouth, trying to speak. His words were garbled. He was frustrated with the effort.

"Do not worry. There is time. You will speak in time. Rest now. You are safe here."

Selma left the room, closing the door behind her. "It is good, Father. He is awake. We will have to move him soon."

But where? It had been their question for these twelve days. Where could they hide a *harki* man? She stood out on the tiny balcony with its wrought-iron railing, staring into the square. Twelve days ago she had stood with tears streaming down her face, watching the bodies and the terrible stillness before the Algerian army men had carried the dead away to nameless graves. Then out by the sea, she had seen it. A movement. A movement amidst the stillness.

With quivering legs, she had walked out into the terrible heat of the afternoon, the stench of death overpowering her. She had covered her entire face with her white veil, stepping over bodies, trying not to look at the faces with their wide eyes filled with their last feeling: terror. There, by the water, a young man lay bleeding, pulling himself slowly to the water.

Now he lay in her bed. She forced herself to think of lunch. Not the struggle, the backbreaking struggle to bring the man, nearly dead, here. Not the agonizing fear that these madmen would come back and kill her as well.

The young man had lived. It was a miracle that even she could not explain. He had lived, and now he had opened his eyes. Allah be praised.

* * *

Later in the afternoon, Selma tiptoed back into the bedroom where the young man lay. His head was turned toward the door, his eyes open, and when he saw her, he smiled. She lowered her eyes and sat down in the chair by his bed. She reached down to retrieve a cool rag that lay in a small bucket by the bed. Day and night she had sponged cool water over his body, trying to bring the fever down.

As Selma touched his forehead with the cool rag, the young man opened his mouth. "Thank you," he said with difficulty. She glanced at him, smiled, then again lowered her eyes. She felt almost embarrassed to be with him, now that he was awake. For days she had cleaned his wounds and sponged his body while he slept. But now he knew what she was doing.

She gave him a drink of water, which he sipped quickly. Before it had been almost impossible to get him to drink liquids, and they had feared he would die of dehydration. At times he had come into a sort of semiconsciousness where he would drink. But always his eyes had remained closed.

He made another sound. She leaned closer. "What is it?"

"Bro . . . brother?"

Selma shook her head. "I do not know. You were the only one."

His eyes were intense. "Tell me."

She had no desire to recount it again. "It was a terrible, terrible thing, but somehow you have survived. I found you by the dock, at the edge of the water, crawling out from under two other slain men. You had been stabbed, twice."

"How long?"

"You have been here over two weeks."

Pain registered on his face. "Where am I?"

"In Philippeville. In my apartment. It looks over the square where it happened. That is how I found you."

"Take me—Algiers," he choked.

"I have no car, nor does my father. Do you have someone in Algiers?" She felt a terrible pity for him. Surely anyone from his family would have long since been killed.

"Friends. *Pied-noirs.* Help me, please." He closed his eyes and seemed exhausted with his effort to speak.

Selma wiped his brow again. "If I find a car, do you know somewhere to go? It is so extremely dangerous for you now."

"Yes," he mumbled with his eyes still closed, and Selma was not sure what he meant.

*   *   *

The last bag was packed, and Rémi Cebrian put it in the old car. He had salvaged every possible item that he could transport from the farmhouse. There were two suitcases, a large duffel bag, a cardboard box, and the trunk. He was determined he wouldn't lose this one. Rémi ran his fingers over the little openings he had installed in the front and back of this trunk, just like the other. But no one would be hiding in this one.

Abdul and Amar followed him back into the farmhouse,

where Madira was preparing their last meal together. The scent of the *couscous* greeted them in the den. The table was set for five.

"El Amin! Quick. Help me get the food on the table!" Madira called to her son, and the young boy went into the kitchen.

They all sat down. Rémi bowed his head; the others did so too. "God our Protector and Provider, thank You for this food. Be with my friends." He paused and sniffed. "Have mercy upon them, protect them. Grant me safe passage. Amen." There was a stinging in his chest at the thought of really leaving. He wanted to get it over with now.

"Remember, Abdul. This house is yours, for your family. You keep it. The fields, the groves, it is yours as we have spoken. You have all the papers."

"Yes, M. Rémi. We will see what happens. We will do our best to keep the house."

"Will you ever come back?" El Amin blurted out. "Will Samuel ever come back to play with me?"

Madira regarded him crossly.

"I cannot say what will happen," Rémi said to the child. "I know he misses you. This I know."

The sound of a car pulling up to the house startled them all. Rémi's eyes darted to Madira, who immediately took the boy to the back of the house. The men stood up, quickly positioning themselves by the windows, where the rifles lay. Rémi shook his head, disgusted. So close, and now was the FLN coming to his door?

They watched as a veiled Arab woman stepped out of the car, and waited. Perhaps it was a trap. She glanced back at the car, then tentatively walked toward the house. When she came to the door, she spoke slowly and distinctly. "M. Rémi Cebrian. I have come from Philippeville to bring you a friend whom you thought dead. A man named Moustafa Dramchini. He is in the car. Please help us bring him to the house."

Rémi's mind whirled. Moustafa! Impossible. Had Ali somehow cooked up another scheme? "Who are you?"

"My name is Fatiah; people call me Selma."

Rémi peered through the window, trying to see the car. An old man sat in the passenger's seat. "Show me Moustafa," Rémi called.

The veiled woman bowed and returned to the car. She opened the door to the back seat and bent over. A few minutes later, with the woman supporting him, a young man sat up. Rémi's eyes grew wide. It *was* Moustafa!

Without hesitation he raced out the door. He stood beside the car, calling softly with amazement, "Moustafa? Moustafa!"

Moustafa laughed weakly. "Rémi. You are still here."

"Yes." He felt his eyes well up with tears as he realized how, in another hour, he would have already left for the docks.

Carefully Abdul, Amar, and Rémi lifted Moustafa from the car and carried him to the worn couch in the den. When Rémi turned around to thank the woman, she was gone. The car was disappearing from sight in a stream of dust.

* * *

Rémi did not leave for France that day. Instead he called the same doctor who had helped him three weeks ago. When the doctor saw Moustafa, he cursed lightly. "You again? My son, what has happened now? Weren't two bullets enough for you?"

Removing the bandages, he examined the wounds. He whistled lowly. "You're mighty lucky, lad. It's a wonder you did not bleed to death. And how they kept the infection out ... amazing."

He went to speak with Rémi. "He was sliced up in the chest and the side. How long has he been here?"

"Just an hour. A woman brought him here. We thought he had been murdered at Philippeville with the rest of the *harkis*."

"*Bon sang*. He's worse than a cat with nine lives. What

will you do with him?"

"I'll take him with me."

"Rémi, are you mad? No one will let him on a boat. You know that. They'll get him for sure, and I guarantee you he won't survive another wound."

"But if I had a way, doctor. If I did, could he travel? Could he sit up?"

"What are you thinking, Rémi?"

He nodded to the car. "There's a trunk in the car. It has already worked once. We smuggled a boy over to France. He would fit. He's already tried."

The doctor rubbed his chin thoughtfully, looking skeptical. "Take him in a trunk to the port and get him on the boat, you say?"

"Yes. Yes. The crowds aren't nearly so large, I hear. If we got on the ferry quickly . . . Once we debark, he could get out."

"I don't know. It's quite a risk. He is so weak. If you could wait a few more days . . . feed him well. Get a little strength into him. Perhaps."

"Thanks, Doc."

"*De rien.* You take care of yourself, Rémi."

"I will. And you? You're still determined to stay?"

"As long as I have work to do, I'm staying right here in Algiers. Good-bye."

Rémi watched the doctor go. Then he called to Amar, and they took the heavy trunk from the car. Setting it in the den, Rémi smiled at Moustafa. "Looks like I'm not through packing after all."

* * *

Gabriella and the Sisters painstakingly went through every drawer and every file in Mother Griolet's office, finding names and addresses, trying to contact those who would want to know about the funeral. It was slow, painful work.

Sister Isabelle stood in front of a bookcase, touching the brittle spines of Mother Griolet's treasured volumes. "Ah, here she is. The *santon*." She carefully picked up the clay figurine, studying the face of the old woman who was hunched over under her bundle of sticks. "I've always loved this little lady," she commented. "Do you remember that day when the children brought her to Mother Griolet?"

Sister Rosaline came to Sister Isabelle's side. "I could never forget that day," she said softly. "Those pitiful children begging to be hidden here, imploring Mother Griolet to take them in. And offering her this old *santon* as their only way of paying." She bit her lip.

"The parents were never found, were they?"

"Their names eventually appeared on the list of those who were lost in the camps."

"Yes, now I remember."

Sister Rosaline cleared her throat. "Now what were those children's names? Have we contacted them yet? They would certainly want to know."

Sister Isabelle replaced the *santon* on the shelf and picked up a manila folder, stuffed with papers. "I think I saw it yesterday. Christine and Yves Millot. I believe M. Cohen said he had contacted them."

"Good."

"I just love the *santons*," Gabriella stated, now standing in front of the old clay woman. She was thinking of the clay baker she had given David for Christmas.

Sister Isabelle nodded. "The first *crèche* dates back to the thirteenth century and Saint Francis of Assisi. But it wasn't until the eighteenth century that the characters from the villages in Provence were created. It's all the people you would have seen in the road, selling their wares, from the last two centuries. Very picturesque. Bringing their treasures, humble though they be, to lay at the feet of the Christ Child. *Santon . . . petit saint.*"

"Little saint!" said Gabriella. "That makes sense. The New Testament calls believers 'saints.'"

"Precisely."

"I've always loved the *santons*. They are the epitome of Provence," Sister Isabelle said softly.

Gabriella touched the fine pieces of real wood on the old woman's back. "You are bringing your burden to the Christ Child. He will carry it for you now." When she looked around, the two nuns' faces were shining with tears.

* * *

It took quite a few phone calls to Washington for Roger Hoffmann to update his colleagues on the extraordinary circumstances he had encountered in Algeria and to reassure them that he was now safe in France. It took only one more call to convince them that he needed an extended vacation there. So he moved into Monique Pons' apartment at the widow's insistence.

"Of course he must stay with you, M. Hoffmann!" she told David. "It is no trouble. You may have the place to yourselves. I will be leaving on vacation with Yvette Leclerc immediately following the funeral." She lowered her voice, shook her head, and blew her nose loudly into a plaid handkerchief. "It is too sad. Too terribly sad."

That evening, Mme Pons prepared them a *taboulé* salad and put a plate of cold cuts on the table beside it. "Eat whenever you want. I'm afraid I must go out for a while."

David found himself facing his father at the oblong dining room table. "You look much better, Father."

"Feel much better too, Son. I am certainly glad to be out of that hospital."

"Yes." He loaded his plate with *taboulé*, then passed it to his father.

"Looks good. Very nice woman, this Mme Pons. You say you've been here two years?"

"Two years this month."

Roger Hoffmann put down his fork. "Can you tell me what brought you over here, David? What was it that really motivated you to come?"

"I've told you before." His voice was crisp. "I came to help Anne-Marie."

Roger picked up a glass of wine and took a sip. "You haven't told me everything, David. I learned quite a bit from the wild man, Ali. A most fascinating story. 'Operation Hugo,' I believe he called it."

"Yes, well, I'm sorry you had to be involved in this. The guy is a lunatic. Dragging you into something that had nothing to do with you."

"I'm proud of you, David." He said it stiffly, formally, a stern expression on his face.

David did not want to talk, did not want his father's accolades. He started to say something sharp. Instead, he simply replied, "Thank you."

"I've been a wretched father to you, David," Roger said at length. "I don't blame you for whatever you feel toward me." He dabbed the white cloth napkin over his mouth. "Could we perhaps. . . ? I would like to catch up with you, David. Before I go back to Washington. Could we try?"

"Maybe," he said unenthusiastically. Then something pierced him, like a sharp knife. This was his chance. He had missed it on the boat. "Sure, Father. Would you like to go for a drive?"

* * *

In the evening the air was cooler, and they drove out into the country as the sun left the sky. Roger Hoffmann seemed to want to talk, and David forced himself to listen, driving the anger away for this one night.

"I have always thought this part of France to be one of the loveliest spots on earth. It brought back hope all those years

386

ago. When I got out of the camp, I searched for you and your mother and sister for a long, long time. Eventually I learned of the fate of Annette and Greta, but I still had a tiny hope for you. St. Joseph's was the twenty-fifth institution I visited, looking for you."

"Mother Griolet said you cried when you found me."

"Yes, I did."

"Why? Why did I not see it?"

"No one saw it except that dear woman (may she rest in peace). Can you forgive me, Son? You realize I am not very good at saying I'm sorry. But I want you to know I mean it. I have had a lot of time lately to think."

Roger stared out into the dark, at the vineyards where the vines grew, barely visible, looking in the night like twisted dwarves. He coughed lightly. "I have thought about how much time I have wasted." He scratched his nose nervously, and David could see the strain on his father's face. Every word was an effort to pronounce, an admission of his failure. "Do you think we could start over, Son?"

David shrugged and kept his eyes on the road. "I suppose anything is possible." He took a long breath and thought about his father's question. The silence between them pounded in his ears. It was his chance and his choice. He could cut the proud man down with one simple word. Or he could find his father after all these years. It was agony to decide. To ignore his feelings of anger and hate, to push past them. In another minute, the opportunity would be gone. David blinked his eyes and heard himself say quietly, "I forgive you, Father."

He said it without emotion, but as soon as the words were out of his mouth, he felt a lifting of a weight from his shoulders. A smile flickered on his lips. With one hand on the steering wheel, he held the other out to his father, who took it warmly in his. "I forgive you."

* * *

It felt very strange to have his father back. They sat up late that night, sipping a *liqueur* and recalling their days at Princeton, sharing stories of their antics in the eating clubs there. David was amazed that they had so much to talk about, amazed that he could appreciate his father's dry sense of humor, used without its typical biting tone.

Eventually Roger turned the conversation to the present. "And this girl, Gabriella? What is she like?"

David smiled. "Dad, she's like no one I've ever met before in my life. She is an innocent angel, a witty intellectual, and a devout Christian. I can't get over her." He wrinkled his brow. "She has been very good for me, Dad. She has helped me understand so many things—things in my soul."

"She sounds delightful. Did you say her parents are here also? Perhaps I could invite them all for a meal in a restaurant."

"Perhaps, after the funeral. It has been very hard on Gabby. And her mother. They were both extremely close to Mother Griolet."

"It appears that many people felt that way about the saintly woman. Is there anything I can do to help with the arrangements for the funeral?"

David stared at his father in shock. "To help?"

His father shook with laughter. "Yes, David. Strange as it may seem, I'd like to help."

* * *

Bedtime was the hardest for the children. They plagued Gabriella, Anne-Marie, and the Sisters with questions about the future. The orphans who had been at St. Joseph's for a good while cried into their pillows, calling out for Mother Griolet.

The Arab children simply cried out in fear, feeling the tension and the overwhelming sadness all around them. Mme Dramchini held each crying child close to her bosom and sang to them softly in Arabic. She spent her tears with the children, and they fell asleep in her arms.

Ophélie clung to Anne-Marie, begging to sleep in her bed with her. "And why hasn't Papa come to tell me good night? Where is he?"

"He is with his father, sweetheart. He will see you in the morning, but tonight he had to be with his father. Tomorrow you will meet your grandfather."

"I don't want another grandfather. I want my own granddaddy Duchemin."

Anne-Marie's face clouded. "Oh, honey. You know that isn't possible. You must calm down tonight."

"No, I won't! I won't." She sat up in bed, clutching her mother. "Mother Griolet is dead, and Moustafa is dead. Are you going to die too, Mama?"

Anne-Marie sighed. So this was what was bothering her daughter. "No, Ophélie. We are together. We are safe. Mama will never leave you again. I promise."

Ophélie would not be comforted. She sniffled and wiped her nose and then burst into tears again. Finally, Anne-Marie led her out of the dormitory. She knelt down beside her daughter in the bathroom, wiping the child's eyes with a tissue. "Darling, I am so sorry about Mother Griolet and Moustafa." She could not stop Ophélie's tears.

"But it is going to be all right. I just know it is because, because I believe. I believe in this strange, kind Savior, and He has given me His peace." She took Ophélie in her arms and held her tightly.

"Oh, Mama," the child sobbed. "You believe! I knew you would someday. And you have told me on the day I needed it most."

Anne-Marie cupped Ophélie's face in her hands. "You see so much, my child. Sometimes I think this God has given you a different type of eyes, eyes that see the heart." She kissed Ophélie on the forehead. "Shall I pray?"

The little girl nodded.

"Dear God," Anne-Marie's voice was shaky. "We are very

sad, God." She bit her lips and brushed her hand across her face. "We miss Moustafa and Mother Griolet very much. I think You must understand, because You lost someone very dear to You once. Please help us, as we are sad. And please, God, don't stop holding us in Your arms. We need You. Amen."

She carried her daughter back to her bed, pulled the sheet over her, and kissed her cheek. "I love you, Ophélie, very much." The child was already asleep.

*　*　*

Gabriella waited for Anne-Marie in the hallway. With her family in Castelnau and then Mother Griolet's death, she had not had any time to talk with Anne-Marie alone. There was so much she needed to say. She only hoped her friend wanted to hear it.

It surprised Anne-Marie to see Gabriella waiting there. "Hello," she said shyly. "I thought you would be with your family by now."

"They are doing fine with Mme Leclerc. I, I really wanted to talk with you, Anne-Marie. So much has happened so quickly. I've hardly seen you. I want to know how you are, really."

The young women locked arms and walked into the courtyard, strolling over to the stone wall that overlooked the small park below. They leaned on it and peered over.

"David told me what you said," Gabriella began, feeling awkward. "Thank you."

"He is a good man, Gabriella. He wants to do what is right. He has changed so much. He cares. He cares for the right reasons. But he does not belong to me. I love him. I have always loved him. For the longest time he represented freedom to me, a way of escape from all I didn't like in Algeria. And when I needed him, after so many years of my silence, he came back. In a strange way, I thought I held a power over him. He was my rescuer, but I held him.

"And then I met you, and your love for him was so pure and innocent and good. It was a needing, sharing, trusting love. As I had for Moustafa. The right kind of love.

"Moustafa is gone, but I cannot take David back. Somehow, in the deepest part of me, I know it is wrong. So I have released him. Only it wasn't really me." She flashed Gabriella a timid smile. "You will think it crazy when I say this, but I think it was your God. Your God who helped me release him. I have done it, Gabriella. I have believed. And now I am going to do what you said. I am going to wait and trust."

The two women hugged, and when they bade each other good night, Gabriella realized that she had hardly spoken a word.

* * *

A heavy depression took hold of Hussein when he heard of Mother Griolet's death. His thoughts became morbid, and hopeless and fear gripped him in his inner being. If Allah had permitted that Moustafa and the good nun should die, why, why should he allow Hussein to live?

David Hoffmann had tried to help him, but the words had fallen flat. Staring at the top of the bed above him, Hussein frowned. Yes, the American had taken all the explosives, but he didn't know that Hussein also had a gun. Hussein had kept it hidden under his mattress, the pistol that had almost been used on Ophélie. He did not plan to use it on any of these people at St. Joseph's. There was already enough grief for them. But he would use it. He had already composed the letter to Ali.

Master Ali,

Allah be praised. Algeria is free and my work here is accomplished. Rest assured that these children and nuns pose you no longer any threat. Nor do the Duchemins or the Hoffmanns or the redheaded woman. I have done my job, completely and thoroughly. There is no more St.

Joseph's, no more orphanage. The old nun is dead, and everyone is gone. Moustafa never made it from Algeria, slaughtered at the docks.

I have completed my task, and you may celebrate. By the time you read of this note, I will be no more. My final task will be accomplished. A death with honor for Allah.

Farewell, Ali.

Your humble servant, Hussein

It pleased Hussein in a twisted sort of way that he had not lied to Ali in the letter. Everything he had written was perfectly true. The orphanage would soon be closed, and everyone gone. Somehow he felt inspired to write the truth in a way that Ali would not understand.

He would wait until after the funeral tomorrow, then he would simply disappear. He turned the cold revolver over in his hands. With one bullet from this pistol, he could end his misery. When someone finally discovered his body, for he intended to make that hard, there would be no one left at St. Joseph's to remember him anyway.

Chapter 28

When Saturday arrived, bright and sunny, there was almost a feeling of joy in the air that neither the Sisters nor Gabriella could explain as they busied themselves in the dining hall, preparing food to be offered after the funeral. Sister Rosaline took pride in creating the centerpiece, a hollowed-out watermelon filled with Mother Griolet's favorite summer fruits.

Pierre Cabrol appeared at the parsonage door early in the morning, carrying an elaborate *pièce montée*, layers of pastry puffs that had been stuffed with cream and stacked up to form a tall pyramid. Denise Cabrol followed, carrying every imaginable type of bread. The smell was enticing. Jean-Louis came next, with two large trays full of pizza.

"Pierre, you've prepared a feast!" Sister Isabelle gasped.

Pierre's eyes twinkled. "It is the least I could do for Mother Griolet. A farewell party for a dear friend."

Gabriella noted that Denise Cabrol's expression had softened, and she nodded in agreement with her husband.

Mme Leclerc and Mme Pons came to St. Joseph's together, slipping into the dining hall and placing large platters of sliced pork garnished with red potatoes, parsley, and tomatoes, in the kitchen. "We expect there will be a big crowd," Mme Leclerc whispered to Sister Rosaline. "Is there anything else we can do to help?"

As they were speaking, Roger Hoffmann, looking stronger and refreshed, carried in a wooden carton filled with bottles of wine. "It is a small contribution. I hope it will help." He flashed Monique Pons a smile, and she reddened. In spite of themselves, the women giggled happily when the debonair man left the room.

"Oh, forgive me," said Sister Isabelle repentantly. "I'm not showing proper respect for Mother Griolet."

"Don't be silly," chirped Sister Rosaline, pulling the wine bottles out of the carton and setting one on each table. "Can't you just see Mother Griolet laughing, smiling, approving of our merriment? The last thing she would want is a bunch of long, distraught faces at her funeral."

Mme Dramchini and her daughters brought in three large bowls full of steaming *tagine*. "If you please," Mme Dramchini said awkwardly. "You can use this?" She motioned to Saiyda and Rachida, who presented the bowls to Sister Rosaline. Mme Pons, Mme Cabrol, and Mme Leclerc eyed the Arab women suspiciously. Immediately Sister Rosaline took the bowls of food. "It looks delicious. How thoughtful of you." She kissed the Arab women on the cheeks, and the tension in the room seemed to melt. Soon the French women were gathered around the Arab women, inspecting the bowls of thick stew and asking for the recipe.

"I'm sure my girls would love this dish," Mme Leclerc clucked. She reflected for a moment, then added under her breath, "If I have any more girls."

Mme Pons heard her friend's comment and brushed it away. "Oh yes, I've always heard that this Algerian stew is superb." Mme Dramchini beamed.

Gabriella left the dining hall, shaking her head in amazement. French and Arab women laughing together as they prepared for a funeral! She went through the parsonage to the chapel. Rebecca Madison was setting up bouquet after bouquet of flowers at the front of the chapel, and the sweet scent permeated the whole interior. Gabriella gasped to see the display of bright colors in the normally somber room. "They are gorgeous."

"And they just keep coming. Why, I know we've received at least two dozen arrangements from people all over France. Listen to this." She carefully removed a card from a large bouquet of bright pink roses, softer pink gerber daisies, purple irises, and baby's breath.

" 'It is with great sadness that we learned of the passing of Mother Griolet. All we have become today we owe to that dear woman, who took us in during the war and taught us how to love, forgive, and get on with life.' It's from a brother and sister who live in Normandy."

She picked up a smaller arrangement and, bending close, read, " 'I lost everything in the war, my family, my possessions, my will to live. Until by God's grace, I came to St. Joseph's and found shelter and hope. God be praised. Mother Griolet will be greatly missed.' "

"Oh, and Mother, look at these! Aren't they beautiful?" Gabriella bent over and inhaled the sweet aroma from a bunch of bright white daisies. " 'I stayed at St. Joseph's for many years in the days when the orphanage first opened. Mother Griolet taught me to read, no small feat, for I was dyslexic. She gave me dignity and let me help with the younger children. I learned to have pride in who I am and to trust the Almighty for the rest. Today I run a center for mistreated children. I have a family like Mother Griolet's. My debt to her is immense.' "

Sitting up, Gabriella reflected, "It is such a touching testimony of her life, Mother. There's a stack of letters on her desk that we haven't even had time to open." She sat down in a pew and closed her eyes. "I can't explain it, but it's as if my heart were lighter today. Isn't that strange, Mother?"

Kneeling beside her daughter, Rebecca Madison smiled. "Not so strange, my dear. After all, this is a celebration."

Gabriella looked up, surprised.

"Mother Griolet is with the Lord. She is exquisitely happy."

"Yes, I see what you mean. Perhaps it is that. It is not nearly so sad as with Ericka." Her eyes met her mother's and held them in a steady gaze.

Then Rebecca gently brushed her daughter's cheek. "No, it is quite different. Mother Griolet lived a full, productive life. She served God and touched lives. But one thing is the same for Ericka and Mother Griolet. They are both happy now. We cannot understand the mind of God. Someday we will, just as they do now."

"Yes, Mother."

A celebration. Perhaps her mother was right. Whatever the reason, Gabriella found herself humming a hymn later that morning as she checked on the children, helping to tie a bow or straighten a sock. She had instructed them to wear their darkest clothes as proper etiquette for a funeral.

As she left the dormitories, David came to her and held her hands. "How are you doing, Gabby?"

"I'm doing well. I can't explain it exactly. It warms me deep inside to see what one life can mean to so many. I want to be like her, David. Oh, how I want to be like her."

He held her in his arms and stroked her hair. "Yes, quite an awe-inspiring woman." Reaching in his pants pocket, he pulled out a folded sheet of paper. "I've written something . . . a eulogy of sorts. I wondered if you'd take a look at it and tell me if you think it would be appropriate to read at the funeral."

"Why, David," Gabriella said as her eyes went down the page. "It's beautiful. Yes, you must read it."

"You don't think it would be too radical, for someone to just get up and read something at a funeral? I don't want to horrify anyone."

"I think it would be in perfect keeping with Mother Griolet's life. I don't know of anyone who was more radical than she. Can't you hear her chuckling up there?" She squeezed his hand.

"Could you read it for me?" David asked.

"Me? Why me? You wrote it."

"Yes, but I'd like for you to read it."

Gabriella did not argue. David always had a reason. "Okay. And you will help me if I find it too hard?"

"Yes, I promise." He handed her the piece of paper, softly squeezing her hand.

*   *   *

In the late morning, Joseph and Emeline Cohen drove to St. Joseph's from their hotel in Montpellier. They had arrived from Switzerland the day before. After offering their condolences, they immediately began helping the Sisters in planning for the funeral. Now M. Cohen spoke in hushed tones to Sister Rosaline, who lifted her eyebrows in surprise and nodded. A moment later, Henri Krugler came into the dining hall.

"Pleased to meet you, M. Krugler," Sister Rosaline bowed slightly. "M. Cohen says that you wish to say a few words during the funeral service?"

"If I may, yes."

"Well, I suppose that would be fine. M. Madison will be speaking as well. And the curé, Père Thomas, will officiate. He should be here any minute now." She shrugged. "It will not be a typical funeral, but"—and she glanced heavenward—"somehow I am sure she would approve."

"Yes," Joseph said, squinting as he presented Sister Rosaline with a letter. "She left these instructions with me when we reworked her will. She has specified several things about the funeral, as you can see. She wants no pomp and circumstance. There are quite a few Bible verses she would like to have read. She even mentioned that the children could repeat them by heart." He adjusted his tie, wiping his glistening forehead with a white handkerchief.

Sister Rosaline chuckled as she read the letter, "Yes, it will certainly be different. She wants rejoicing at the funeral. Rejoicing in the Lord and her presence with Him. Short and simple, she says. And pointing to the Lord."

* * *

The funeral was scheduled for 2 o'clock, but by 1:30 rows and rows of cars were parked up and down the side streets of Castelnau. People were standing outside the chapel, peering in. Inside, the air was heavy. Every inch of space was filling up. At the front of the nave, just before the altar rail, sat the casket.

Gabriella waited near the doors, helping the Sisters find empty seats for those who were arriving. David and his father, along with several of the older boys from the orphanage, had gone into the parsonage to bring in extra chairs from the dining hall, should the need arise. The other children sat fidgeting on the first three rows of pews. Anne-Marie, Mme Dramchini, and her daughters were dispersed among them, intent on keeping them quiet.

Eliane Cebrian came down the aisle with her three children. Anne-Marie scooted closer to the orphans, making room for Eliane with baby José, who stared wide-eyed at the crowds and clutched his mother's arm. Samuel and Rachel squeezed in beside Ophélie. M. Krugler took a seat directly behind the children on the same row as the Madison family.

Pierre and Denise Cabrol found an empty pew and were immediately joined by Yvette Leclerc and Monique Pons, both of whom wore hats with veils and dabbed their eyes now and then with handkerchiefs. Jean-Louis Vidal shuffled into the chapel, dressed in a neatly pressed dark brown suit with a white carnation in the lapel. He looked around the chapel, walked to the front, crossed himself, and sat down. The chapel was full, and still the townspeople poured in, nodding to one another in solemn silence, wiping the perspiration from their faces, closing their eyes to say a silent prayer.

Joseph Cohen stood near the back of the chapel, shaking hands with many young people who were not from the village. Sister Rosaline greeted them warmly as well. "Some of the Jewish children who were here during the war," Sister Isabelle whispered to Gabriella. "M. Cohen contacted them. They've come quite a ways to pay their respects to Mother Griolet."

Gabriella thought for sure that the crowds would thin out, but when she peeped out the side door to the chapel, she saw that there was still a long line waiting to come in. Inside, some of the younger attendants were moving to the left where there were no pews, and standing tightly together. Meanwhile, David and Roger Hoffmann placed folding chairs on either side of the pews, so that the center aisle became a narrow path.

Gabriella greeted the goldsmith from Montpellier, Edouard Auguste, at the door, then kissed Madeleine de Saléon from Aix-en-Provence lightly on the cheeks as she slipped into a chair that David had just installed. Lucie Lachat hurried inside, her head bent, and sat at the back of the chapel, followed by a handful of other villagers, who looked somewhat ashamed. A group of nuns who evidently knew the Sisters patted their hands warmly, offering their sympathy, and walked into the packed room.

Three men, staunch and solemn in their black robes, came piously into the chapel, lifting their eyebrows in surprise when they saw the crowded conditions. "Père Thomas and two of Mother Griolet's superiors from the church," Sister Isabelle whispered to Gabriella when the men were out of earshot. "Oh dear, oh dear. What are we going to do? There are no more seats."

"Don't worry. I've got an idea." Gabriella made her way to the front three pews where the children sat. "This is our last chance to help Mother Griolet. Will you?"

They nodded, surprised.

"So many people have come to the funeral that there is no more room to sit. Would you mind too much moving to the side and sitting on the stones?"

The children's faces lit up with glee as if to say "No, no, of course not, *Maîtresse.*"

"But you must behave. Sit absolutely still until it is your turn. Understand?" Again they nodded. Quietly they left the pews and took seats on the cool stone floor.

The three priests immediately took a place in one of the vacated pews. They looked down their long noses at the children seated on the floor beside them and furrowed their brows. Little Christophe lifted his shoulders and peeped up at them with an angelic smile on his face. One of the men, gray-haired with a wrinkled face, smiled back and reached over and patted Christophe on the head. The little boy put his hand over his mouth and giggled.

Gabriella, sitting on the stone floor beside the children, counted silently to herself. Over 350 people were crowded into the chapel. The air was muggy and pungent with the smell of flowers.

Père Thomas watched, perplexed, as the line of people continued to file into the chapel. He mopped his brow and caught Joseph Cohen's eye. Joseph shook his head as if to say that the funeral could not yet start.

It was stuffy and hot, but no one spoke. Gabriella felt it again. A velvety softness, a hushed anticipation. At long last, Père Thomas stood and walked to the simple wooden pulpit.

"*Messieurs, dames,* we are here today to honor the life of Jeanette Griolet, a faithful servant of our Lord Jesus for well over fifty years." His voice droned in monotone, and it struck Gabriella as completely inappropriate to have this man who barely knew Mother Griolet preside at her funeral. But he spoke for no more than five minutes before leaving his place to Henri Krugler.

Henri smiled down and out at the people of Castelnau. "You do not know me," he greeted them in his booming voice, "and I do not know you. But for years I have heard of a feisty little nun in Castelnau who ran an orphanage. Recently I had the privilege of meeting this rare woman. You, like me, have been blessed by this woman's life. You, like me, have come to pay your respects to her.

"Some of you have only walked through the town to be here today. Others have traveled from the farthest parts of France. There are people from Switzerland, Senegal, America, Algeria. We represent many different countries, we are Catholic and Protestant, Jew and Muslim, French and Algerian. But we are gathered together to honor a woman who honored her God."

The chapel was silent, adult and child alike mesmerized by the presence and strong, soothing voice of Henri Krugler. People sniffed and dabbed their eyes. Henri continued, "And although we are sad, let us not grieve for Jeanette Griolet, but rejoice that she is at last in the presence of the One she loved so dearly. We will miss her terribly. Her desire would simply be that we imitate her example and carry on." Henri spoke for a few more minutes, then took his seat.

William Madison then went to the pulpit. "You do not know me either, but some of you have come to know my daughter, Gabriella Madison. Fifteen years ago, when the war had just ended, my wife, with Gabriella and her two sisters, spent three months in Montpellier where they met Mother Griolet. The circumstances of those months drew my wife, a Protestant missionary, and Mother Griolet, a Catholic nun, close. Mother Griolet had a remarkable impact on our family during the hardest time in our lives. Now, all these years later, God has seen fit to let our daughter benefit from this godly woman's example. We stand here today in thanks to a woman who lived her faith and reached out to others."

Gabriella listened to her father's words. The woman had brought people together. The funeral was the testimony. People coming together. It was hot, and beads of perspiration dripped down her back. The letter David had given her grew moist in her sweaty palms. She was terrified to stand, but some unseen force pushed her to do so.

"With all due respect and with great reverence," she began, trembling, "I would like to read something that a friend of mine wrote about Mother Griolet."

She cleared her throat. Her legs felt wobbly, her head was spinning in the heat. " 'Rarely in this life do we meet such a woman as Mother Griolet. A woman of goodness and humility. A woman who refuses to judge and embraces love. A woman with courage enough to stand up to prejudice and hatred, and yet humility to trust a Higher Power for direction.

"She knew how to listen, to find something good in each person, and to offer hope . . . " Gabriella's voice cracked. She paused and wiped her eyes. Others in the chapel did the same. She started again. "She had the gift of knowing how to make God real . . . " Gabriella could not go on.

From somewhere in the crowded chapel, a low, strong voice rang out. "She had the gift of knowing how to make God real to the most common of us. She was not religious. She lived her faith."

Gabriella turned around and watched David. From the side of the church, he was talking, reciting his requiem by heart. He imparted the same confidence as if he were standing in front of his class, and yet, by his words, he drew attention not to himself, but to the woman whom they had come to honor. And ultimately, he called the congregation to consider the God whom the courageous nun had served.

David's eyes met Gabriella's as he spoke. She was crying steadily now. ". . . It has been my privilege to know this woman. And to inherit her faith. A faith that says in the midst of the worst in life . . . " Here his voice caught. He spoke in broken tones, with the pain resounding in his voice. "... In the midst of the worst in life, there is a hope for tomorrow. Because there is a God who sees past our differences and calls us to Himself."

David stepped across those seated in his pew and walked down the aisle to the front of the church, where he placed a simple rose on the casket. Then he turned back around, and with tears running down his cheeks, walked back to his seat.

* * *

The people in the chapel had never seen anything like it. One by one, townspeople from Castelnau as well as guests who had come from far away stood and gave brief testimony to what Mother Griolet meant to them.

When Mme Leclerc began to speak, she sniffed through her words. "She gave me something to do as an aging widow. The college girls who have stayed with me throughout these years have been a delight, as well as a great help to my widow's pension. Mother Griolet was innovative. She thought of ways to give income to those who needed it without simply handing out charity. This town will miss her. She was a woman of great wisdom."

Then Joseph Cohen rose and spoke of the role Mother Griolet had played in saving the Jews. "Seventeen years ago, my wife and I made our way to this town as broken people. Survivors of the death camps. We came to St. Joseph's and stood before Mother Griolet in rags, weeping for our children. And we found them here. Happy, healthy, full of faith. We have rebuilt our lives, by Jehovah's hand. But it would never have been possible without that dear woman. She dared to do what was forbidden by law because she took orders from the Lord.

"And now this place will be closed because she has once again overstepped the boundaries of what is considered safe and reached out to the poorest, neediest of people. As a final gesture to this selfless woman, can we not look inside ourselves and find compassion for these children who sit before us?" His eyes filled up with tears and haltingly he added, "They could have been my children, needing a home...."

As Joseph sat down, several young Jewish men and women took turns telling of their time at the orphanage and how Mother Griolet had helped them get a new start in life.

Then Anne-Marie rose stiffly. "I know Mother Griolet's decision to keep the *pied-noir* and *harki* children here has not been a popular one. But I bless her for it. Here my daughter's life was spared, and many others as well. Here I was reunited with Ophélie. It used to bother me that everyone at St. Joseph's quoted Mother Griolet, but now I see why. It was because she received her words from the Master. I have finally understood. I beg you, let us choose life together. Choose life."

Mme Dramchini nodded, and holding tightly to Anne-Marie, told her story in broken French. Immediately afterward, Hakim got up, and in a shaking voice, spoke his heart. Then Sister Rosaline came over to where the children sat, squeezing her buxom body in between the people, and motioned to the children.

Six-year-old André rose, staring down at his shoes with a stern, terrified expression. He cast a furtive glance at Gabriella, who urged him on with her smile. In a beautiful voice, full of emotion, he recited the Twenty-Third Psalm. "*L'Eternel est mon berger; je ne manquerai de rien....*" As he recited, all fear and timidity left his voice. When he finished and sat down, the audience seemed stunned.

Ophélie then stood, speaking softly, "Now to Him who is able to do exceeding abundantly beyond all that we ask or think, according to the power that works within us, to Him be the glory."

"I will lead the blind by a way they do not know." The soft voice of Anne-Sophie was barely audible. One after another the orphans recited Scripture, pronouncing the words with conviction, as if they truly believed. And the congregation listened attentively. It was as if the children were preaching their own sermon on God's faithfulness.

Then, at a cue from Gabriella, all the orphans stood where they were and broke forth into song.

My Jesus I love Thee, I know Thou art mine,
To Thee all the follies of sin, I resign.
My gracious Redeemer, my Savior art Thou
If ever I loved Thee, my Jesus 'tis now.

I'll love Thee in life, I will love Thee in death
And praise Thee as long as Thou lendest me breath
And say when the death dew lies cold on my brow
If ever I loved Thee, my Jesus 'tis now.

Then almost joyfully, they lifted their voices louder, higher, and sang the last verse:

In mansions of glory and endless delight
I'll ever adore Thee in heaven so bright.
I'll sing with the glittering crown on my brow,
If ever I loved Thee, my Jesus 'tis now.

They sang the simple hymn, and it echoed in the church and out into the streets of Castelnau, and there was a radiance and a knowing in the sweet voices of the children.

Quite unexpectedly, Denise Cabrol rose with difficulty and stared about the room. "I ... I was perhaps wrong in my judgment of the orphanage," she choked out. "I have never seen sweeter, more well-behaved children in my life. Mother Griolet has worked her magic on them." She pursed her lips and looked toward the front of the chapel. "Forgive me. Can you ever forgive me?"

She covered her face with her hands and began to sob. Pierre wrapped his arms around her and comforted his wife. Then she too walked to the front of the chapel, stepping between the people, and placed a small bunch of lilies on the casket. Before she made her way back to her seat, Denise Cabrol stooped down beside the children, and cradling

Hussein's face in her palm, said "God bless you all."

Roger Hoffmann's six-foot-four frame commanded the audience's attention when he rose to speak. He looked around the chapel for several moments, until his eyes met David's. He licked his lips slowly, fumbled with his tie, and wiped his wet brow. His words were spoken with warmth and clarity. "Thanks to this orphanage and to that dear woman"—he gestured toward the casket—"I have found my son twice." He spoke briefly of his experience during the Second World War; then he told of his present situation. "On both occasions, I thought he was lost forever. I have been doubly blessed to find him this time." David nodded to his father, a soft expression on his face.

Jean-Louis Vidal coughed dryly two or three times. He removed his wire-rimmed glasses, rubbed his eyes and nose. "It has been said that to love another person is to see the face of God. I have seen His face in my dear Jeanette." He removed the white carnation from his lapel, and trembling the slightest bit, he walked to the casket and tenderly placed his flower with the others. As he turned away from the casket, David came to his side and helped him back to his seat. The only sound in the chapel was of soft sniffling.

When Sister Isabelle rose to speak, Gabriella doubted she could get a word out. However, the shy nun surprised her. "I have served under Mother Griolet for twenty-seven years. And the longer I have been here and the harder the circumstances, the more I have seen the good come out of this woman. She did not simply talk of faith. She lived it, in the midst of all of life's questions and hurts.

"She called life a tapestry that we see from the wrong side, full of knots and tangled threads. But God is weaving it, each life, each circumstance, to make something beautiful for Him. The tapestry of Mother Griolet's life is represented here today by you. Can't you see it? A magnificent work. There are faults, but even so, remember what she used to say?" Before the nun had voiced the words, many in the chapel were nodding. " 'God specializes in turning tragedy into triumph.' Perhaps, by her death, He has done that again for us today." She bit her lip, blinked twice and sat down.

* * *

Henri Krugler saw his dream give birth to reality that day. The French, the Jews, the Arabs, the *pied-noirs*, the young and old, the Protestants and Catholics for one brief hour forgot their prejudices and were joined together in homage to a woman whose faith had at last broken down the last barrier. He was there. God Himself was there, and every person in the chapel felt His presence.

And so in his mind, and the minds of many others that day, Mother Griolet became a symbol. No one could have perhaps explained it with words, but in Henri's mind it was quite clear. By this good woman's death, many had been called together from all over the globe. In a small way, she represented the Christ who had died and, by His death, reconciled many to Himself. God had used this godly woman's last act on earth, that of dying, to bring a glimpse of the future hope. Henri's soul swelled within him. Only God Himself could predict the outcome of such a day.

It was only as the chapel was emptying of people that Henri got a good look at the lovely young woman who had spoken earlier. He stared at her as she took her daughter's hand and led the child toward the casket. He rubbed his eyes, a dozen questions racing through his head. The young woman caught him staring at her and turned away shyly.

The eight pallbearers came and carefully lifted the casket from the stone floor and stoically carried it into the town square where the hearse waited. The long black car crawled over the cobblestones, and the people walked behind it in a solemn procession, through the town to the small cemetery that was enclosed by a low stone wall in the fields beyond Castelnau.

Henri Krugler drew Joseph Cohen aside. "Who is that woman there? Do you know her?" He pointed to the black-haired young woman walking in front of them.

"No, I don't. Mother Griolet mentioned a young woman who had just come to St. Joseph's when she visited us in Switzerland. I gather it is she."

"But you do not know her name?"

"No, I can't recall it now."

Later, in the dining hall, as the mourners consumed the food and talked in soft, respectful tones, Henri drew Gabriella aside. "Miss Madison," he said. "I am happy to see you again, even under these circumstances."

Gabriella smiled sympathetically. "It has been a remarkable day, hasn't it, M. Krugler?"

"Yes, indeed. The Lord has met us here." He coughed uncomfortably. "Could I ask you, could you tell me the name of the young woman who said she had found her daughter at St. Joseph's?"

"You mean Anne-Marie?"

He lifted his eyebrows. "Yes, is that her name? Anne-Marie? And her last name? Do you know it?"

"Why, of course. She's Anne-Marie Duchemin."

For a moment the color drained from Henri Krugler's face.

"Is something the matter, M. Krugler?"

"The matter? No, no, not at all. Thank you, Miss Madison. Thank you very much."

It was not the time for further questions. Henri mingled among the people and silently thanked God for this day. "A day of miracles," he said to himself. His work with the orphanage at St. Joseph's was far from over.

Chapter 29

In the marshlands outside of the city of Arles, an hour's drive from Montpellier, mile after mile of flat farmland stretched out until eventually, at the back door of the immense Rhône River, there sat a tiny community called Mas Thibert. The village had been there for centuries, housing a handful of families who had tried to tame the swampy plains, making them bear fruit.

Now, the *bachaga* Boualem, a wealthy Muslim landowner in western Algeria who had sided with the French throughout the war, had another idea for Mas Thibert. With his own money, he had decided to make Mas Thibert into a village for his people, the *harki* refugees. And so some *harki* families came to live there, among the already existing French population. Here, there was hope of integration.

But in other parts of France, the housing that was offered to the refugees looked surprisingly like the barracks in the death camps of another war. These refugee camps were set up away from the French people. The leaders of the country reasoned that more camps should be fabricated. In this way, these people could live together, secluded and safe with their own traditions.

The French government boasted of this humanitarian step to provide for their loyal brothers. But it seemed that the whole country breathed a sigh of relief that these Arabs, these strange misfits, were hidden away from the rest of the nation. France had its hands more than full with the *pied-noirs*.

In other pockets of France, and especially the southern part, groups of *harkis* gathered in the low-rent housing they found available within the cities and hid themselves from the angry glances of the French. There was no way to tell, after all, if these Arabs were the enemy that had claimed so many young French lives or those who had fought for France. Most French did not give it a thought. Even more than the bothersome *pied-noirs*, the *harkis* were completely unwanted.

* * *

In the middle of the humid Algerian night, as the stars twinkled in the black sky, Rémi Cebrian shook Moustafa Dramchini awake. The curly-haired Arab managed a smile and blinked a few times. There was a gleam of excitement in his brown eyes.

"So this is it. This time we will make it, Moustafa. By God's grace, we will make it."

Moustafa regarded the strong farmer. "You are a good man, Rémi. A good man." He stood, resting his arm on Rémi's shoulders. In the midst of the heat, he felt a chill run through him. Another chance to leave. Another chance to find Anne-Marie, his mother, his sisters, Ophélie. A letter had arrived from Eliane just yesterday confirming that all was well at the orphanage. David and his father had arrived safely a few days earlier. Eliane expressed her extreme sorrow over Moustafa. *They are mourning for me,* he realized. It made him long to be there even more quickly, to end their pain.

The car was packed, except for the rounded-top wooden trunk.

"I'll wake Amar," Rémi said.

410

Moustafa placed his hand on Rémi's shoulder, holding him back. "Could we pray, first, Rémi?" It was an urgent request that Moustafa made without really knowing why.

"Of course."

Moustafa sat on the dust-covered couch and bent over, resting his elbows on his knees. "You know the first time I prayed?" he chuckled with a slight grimace. "I mean really prayed, my own prayer?"

"When?"

"When I woke up in this very same house after we escaped from the Casbah. It seems like a hundred years ago. I have died a hundred deaths since then."

"You have lived, Moustafa. God has His hand on you."

Moustafa shrugged, his long curls almost touching his shoulders. "I hope so, Rémi. I hope so."

Silently they bent their heads, and Rémi spoke quietly. "Holy God. You have brought us this far. Protect us now. We are afraid. Give Moustafa strength. Take us to France. Our lives are in Your hands."

The men whispered "Amen" together, then Rémi opened the lid of the trunk. "Are you ready?"

In answer, Moustafa climbed into the trunk and sat down, his knees hugged tightly against him. Rémi placed two canteens filled with water in Moustafa's lap. Then he shut the lid. "Can you manage a drink?"

Cramped inside the trunk, with his head touching his knees, Moustafa fumbled with the top of the canteen, unscrewed it, and brought the bottle to his mouth. "Yes, it's okay." His voice was calm, but he felt himself shaking. Perhaps he would panic and cry out at the port, begging to be released. He had not realized how tightly he fit in the trunk. Hussein was much smaller. His clothes were drenched with sweat even before Abdul, Amar, and Rémi carried him to the car.

He heard the catch in Rémi's voice as he hugged his Arab friend good-bye.

"God be with you, Abdul. Tell Madira and El Amin one more good-bye from me." The trunk was placed on the back seat, and Rémi took off for the port with Amar. Inside the stuffy compartment, Moustafa repeated over and over to himself something he had read in David's New Testament, the comforting words of the Christ, "For lo I am with you even unto the very ends of the earth." It was the verse that had swum through his mind as he lay in a coma in the Arab woman's apartment in Philippeville. Somehow it had brought him peace. And tonight, when again he felt he had no more strength, he said it again and again to himself. In the end he fell asleep.

* * *

Moustafa awoke with a start as the trunk tilted and was lifted from the car. The horn of a ferry sounded loudly beside them. Another chill ran through Moustafa's body.

"We've been waiting in the car for the ferry. It's here now," Rémi whispered through the small opening in the trunk. "There are no crowds. We'll be getting on very soon."

Peering through the small hole, Moustafa could make out a few suitcases in the predawn light. There were shouts and commands. Fear struck him like a cold knife. He could almost feel it slicing through him as the soldier's knife had done in Philippeville. Blood pumped in his ears. His body rebelled, every joint tingling with sleep. Now he was swaying slightly, now the trunk bumped against a railing, now it was lifted at a steep angle. The gangplank! Would he make it?

A French officer cursed Amar. "Who is he?"

Moustafa listened for Rémi's calm reply. "A worker. Helping me with my things. He is not leaving on the ferry."

At long last the trunk was placed on the ground. The odor of gas made Moustafa's head swim. *Take me home,* he thought to himself. *Oh please, someone, take me home.*

Sometime later, Rémi spoke again. "I can't get you out

just yet. You'd be spotted. Can you hold on?"

Moustafa groaned back his response. Sharp, terrible pain from his wounds and his cramped position shot through him. He longed to sit up straight for only a minute. He struggled to take a drink of the water. The fumes from the boat rushed upon him again. His head felt so light, so very dizzy. Moustafa fainted.

* * *

Several times during the ferry ride over, Rémi came and lifted the lid of the trunk and helped Moustafa to step out and stretch his limbs. He walked him cautiously to the bathroom, which was nearby. But Moustafa saw that Rémi was afraid of trouble, even in the middle of the sea. He did not stay out for long.

Each time Moustafa climbed back into his cage, he dreaded the claustrophobic feeling when the lid was shut. He rested his head against his knees and thought of what was on the other side of the sea. His stomach churned with every rise and swell of the waves. He longed to escape, to cry out. Instead he repeated that same verse in his mind. Eventually he dozed off.

Hours later, he felt a wet splash on his face and opened his eyes to see Rémi's concerned face peering down at him.

"Moustafa! Moustafa!" Rémi shouted, and tears came into his eyes. "We made it. You are alive, and we are here! France. Marseilles!"

Rémi put both hands under Moustafa's armpits, slowly lifting him to his feet. Again Moustafa was overcome with dizziness. He fell against Rémi's shoulder.

"Hold on," Rémi said. "Sit down a sec." He lowered him back into the trunk. Rémi placed the canteen to Moustafa's lips, and he drank in several long gulps. He rubbed his temples.

"Ready to try again?"

"Ready."

This time he was able to stand and, leaning heavily on

Rémi, he stepped with one leg, then the other, out of the trunk. Immediately his legs buckled, and he collapsed in Rémi's arms.

They sat down together with a bump and burst into laughter. Every joint in his body burned with pain, but still Moustafa laughed, an uncontrollable laugh, until tears ran down the faces of the two men, and they held each other in their arms.

"We made it! Is it true? We made it!" Moustafa grabbed Rémi's shirt collar and shook his friend.

Rémi was almost giddy with joy. "It's true!"

In between breaths, Moustafa gasped, "People will think we're drunk."

"But we are," said Rémi. "Drunk with life. Drunk with life!"

Moustafa took in his surroundings for the first time. They were in a secluded area of the port, just off the docks. The ferry floated peacefully 500 yards in front of them. "How did you manage to get me over here?"

"A few friendly sailors. And listen, I've got us a hotel room. I'm taking you there. I'll get you something to eat, wash you up. You can rest while I look for the other trunk. Do you mind terribly? I promised Eliane."

"No, of course not. Will you call her? Will you tell them we are here?"

"Don't worry, Moustafa. I'll take care of everything. Just relax. We are here."

They laughed again, until their sides ached and their faces were stained with tears. It felt incredibly good.

* * *

It took a while for Rémi to get Moustafa to the hotel, although it was only a block away. It was located in a seamy, foul-smelling part of town, and the room backed up on a putrid alley. But there was a bed and a sink in the corner of the room. After changing Moustafa's bandages and coaxing him to eat a small quiche purchased at the *boulangerie* around the corner, Rémi left Moustafa to sleep.

He looked at his watch. He had only an hour to get to the warehouse where the lost baggage was stored before it closed for the day. He called a taxi and directed the driver to the side street the sailors had indicated. He paid the cabbie with his newly changed French francs, leaving a sizable tip. "I'll make it worth it to you if you can be back here in an hour to pick me up."

The cabbie nodded, grinned, and mumbled, *"Bonne chance."*

The warehouse was immense and, on first glance, completely disorganized. The soldier in charge was a young man, barely more than a boy. He slid the heavy wooden doors open and gestured for Rémi to go inside.

"A bunch of junk, I tell you," the soldier muttered. "What are you looking for anyway? And when was it lost? We arrange things by month."

Rémi lifted his eyebrows. It didn't look as though they "arranged" things at all. "A big wooden trunk with black metal casing." He thought for a moment, counting backward in his head. "It would've gotten here around the twentieth of May or thereabouts. Yes, a good two months ago."

The young soldier scratched the stubble on his beard, eyeing Rémi with distrust. "An old trunk, you say?"

"Yes, about this high. It had little openings built in the front and the back. If you'll just show me where to start looking, I won't bother you anymore."

The boy frowned, kicked the floor, and pointed in a vague direction. "Over there, I think. This isn't my normal job. I'm just here filling in." He followed Rémi, peering over his shoulder.

Rémi shuffled through the stacks of lost items: two torn duffel bags, with clothes strewn on the floor, a yellow leather suitcase, tied around the middle with a piece of string, several children's toys. He spent twenty minutes sifting through the paraphernalia in this part of the warehouse. Nothing.

"You're sure this is all you have from the month of May? Is it possible it could've been put elsewhere?"

The soldier shrugged. "Have a look if you like." He let his arm circle the whole room, a slight smirk on his face.

Rémi felt irritated. He sighed heavily. "Surely it's still here. I must find it."

"What kinda stuff have you got inside?"

"Nothing of much interest to anyone else. Photo albums, china, a few books. Family papers."

The soldier scratched his head. "And the trunk, is it valuable?"

"No, it's not the trunk I want. It's the contents."

The boy narrowed his eyes. "I'll make you a deal. You leave me the trunk, if we find it, and you can have all the stuff inside."

Rémi's head was throbbing. In frustration, he grabbed the boy by the shirt collar. "Look here, do you know where that trunk is?"

Grudgingly, the soldier led him to the other end of the warehouse. He disappeared behind row upon row of suitcases; eventually he revealed the trunk. Several smaller boxes had been stacked on top, wedged in place by other containers.

A smile broke out on Rémi's face. He hugged the soldier, who recoiled and cursed. Rémi paid no attention. "You found it!"

The boy reddened. "Yeah, I saw it here a month ago. I was planning to take the trunk for my mom's birthday. You know, to store quilts in."

"You can have the trunk, my boy. Take it! But first help me get it out of here and find me something else to put my things in."

They heaved and rearranged suitcases and finally managed

to dislodge the trunk. Rémi was surprised with how light it felt after handling the other trunk with Moustafa inside. For a moment he dared not open the top. What if everything was gone?

The lid fell open, and Rémi laughed again. Quickly he shuffled through the contents. Papers strewn inside. One broken teacup. But it was all there! The family Bible, the pictures of the children. He found himself brushing away the tears that stung his eyes. The young soldier came back with several cardboard boxes.

"Will these do?"

"Absolutely." Carefully, delicately, Rémi placed his wife's treasures in the boxes, and for the first time in many weeks, he let himself imagine what it would be like to hold her again. To kiss her soft lips while the children grabbed onto his legs, squealing, "Papa!"

At the bottom of the trunk in the open center space where the boy had sat, a letter marked "Anne-Marie" lay amidst the fallen papers. He recognized Moustafa's handwriting. The documents for the Duchemin will were there too, with the sealed letter from Anne-Marie's father.

By the time the taxi drove up to the old warehouse, Rémi had carried three full cardboard boxes out to the curb. He placed the boxes in the taxi, a simple smile answering the puzzled expression on the cabbie's face. As they drove off, Rémi waved to the young soldier, who was sitting contentedly on top of his empty treasure chest.

* * *

It was with trembling fingers that Rémi dialed the number and let it ring. The receptionist answered and explained that Mme Cebrian had left for the afternoon.

"Do you have any idea where she went?"

The man on the other end of the line explained she had gone to an orphanage just out of town.

Rémi woke Moustafa. "Do you feel up to a train ride to Montpellier?"

Moustafa grinned. "I've been waiting for this day for a long time."

"And I found this." Rémi handed Moustafa the letter. "Thought you might know what to do with it."

"Do I ever." He made a feeble effort to comb his hair, staring in the cracked mirror above the sink. "I wonder if she'll know me. I look like some wild man escaped from the jungle."

"Escaped. That's the important word."

A taxi took them to the train station where a porter helped Rémi with the trunk, duffel bags, and boxes. Moustafa waited on a bench, and it struck Rémi as odd and sad that Moustafa had nothing to bring with him. No clothes, no bags. He had escaped with his life. That was all. As Rémi helped him onto the train, the Arab grinned a very tired grin, clutching the letter for Anne-Marie in his hands. "It's all I've got for her. All I have in the world." He collapsed into the seat on the train. "Somehow I think it will be enough."

* * *

It was fortunate that there was so much work to be done at St. Joseph's that Anne-Marie could not let herself analyze her thoughts. After the inexplicable beauty and peace of the last two weeks, reality had suddenly hit her full in the face. The orphanage was closing, and she had nowhere to go. No one to go to. She felt the hollowness as she entered the cool chapel. It was solemn and still once again, empty of the throngs of people who had come on Saturday. On this Monday afternoon, only the scent of the flowers rising to greet her bore testimony to the moving funeral forty-eight hours ago. Sister Rosaline had asked her to bring a few of the bouquets downstairs to the dining hall, to add a little color. Anne-Marie chose a bouquet of roses and gerber daisies and another with blue, pink, and white carnations. She found herself praying in her head.

Strength for today, God. Just for today. Immediately a verse came into her mind. *"Chaque jour suffit sa peine."*

It had been the verse Mother Griolet had showed her only a few days before her death. She had patted Anne-Marie's hands and said with quiet confidence, "This is what I have held onto in the times of deep pain, my child. He will get us through one day at a time. It is enough. He says so."

Anne-Marie had memorized that verse, and now she said it to herself. "But seek first the kingdom of God and His righteousness, and all these things shall be added unto you. Take therefore no thought of the morrow; for the morrow shall take thought for the things of itself. Sufficient unto the day is the evil thereof."

A soft rap on the chapel door surprised Anne-Marie. She got up off her knees and walked to the back of the chapel.

"Yes?" she said, squinting into the bright sun. A stocky, ruggedly handsome young man in his thirties stood there with his hands in his pockets, looking quite lost.

"May I help you?" she asked. Then before he could answer, she narrowed her eyes. "Rémi? Rémi Cebrian, is it you?"

"Anne-Marie?" They shook hands forcefully, then embraced, laughing.

"Thank God you're here! You've made it to us! Did you know that Eliane is here? Let me go fetch her." Rémi caught her hand. He had the strangest look on his face.

"No, don't bother, Anne-Marie. I'll go find her. But over there, in the taxi. I've brought our things and—"

"Of course, let me help you. But don't you want to take them to your hotel room?"

She followed him across the square as he explained, "I wasn't quite sure where to find the orphanage, so I just asked the taxi driver to wait over there."

"Yes, of course. Oh, how wonderful to see you again. It is just what we needed today. We've had quite a time lately." She wondered why Rémi didn't hurry to his wife.

"There is something here for you, Anne-Marie," he said.

"For me?" She looked perplexed. Then she said, "Oh, you must have found the trunk."

"Yes, I did. Go ahead." He pushed her along to the taxi, then turned back to the orphanage. She looked back over her shoulder with a question in her eyes.

"Go on," Rémi said. There was an urgency in his voice that made her feel funny inside. She broke into a run, crossing the cobblestone road to where the taxi sat in the shade. The cabbie stood on the other side of the car, leaning against the driver's door. She saw that someone was sitting in the back seat, a man with his head resting on the back of the seat. A young man with long curly hair.

She was beside the car now, peering in the window. It couldn't be! Anne-Marie gave a cry and grabbed the handle. Pulling the door open, she burst into tears.

"Moustafa?" she could barely get out the word.

He laughed and weakly held out both hands toward her. Anne-Marie climbed into the car, ignoring the thick, suffocating heat. "Moustafa . . . how can it be?"

She reached out to touch his face, run her fingers through his hair. "You are real. You are alive! But how?"

"Shh," he cooed softly. He put his arms around her and held her there in the unbearable heat. She could hear his heart beating rapidly in his chest.

"I love you, Anne-Marie," he mumbled.

She kissed him softly on the lips, afraid that even a gentle kiss might harm him.

The cabbie poked his head into the car, a broad smile on his face. "M. Cebrian said I was to take him to the hospital in Montpellier just as soon as a lovely young woman came."

"Yes, yes, of course. Only let me tell his mother."

Moustafa squeezed her hand. "Rémi is taking care of all of that. Come with me, now, Anne-Marie. Just you and me right now."

* * *

It was a miracle. When David had announced that Moustafa had been killed in Philippeville, Anne-Marie had never thought to question it. So she could not really believe that she was actually riding through the streets of Montpellier with him now.

It was that strange peace that welled up inside of her. They did not talk. She only leaned very lightly on his shoulder, touching his face and hair every so often to be sure that it really was Moustafa. He looked so thin and weak. "Are you hurt very badly?"

"I will be all right now, my love."

"I thought, I was so sure, you were—"

"Shh. It is inexplicable. I am back." He was fighting to remain conscious. She took the canteen lying on the seat and gently dabbed water onto his face. "Rest, Moustafa. It will be okay."

"I brought you this," he said, handing her a sealed envelope. "You should have had it months ago."

She carefully unsealed the envelope and took out two folded pages. The letter was dated May 20th.

Ma chère Anne-Marie,

Surely I will be with you soon, if we can only wait just a little longer. Surely there is something bigger than the terror that surrounds us here. Please do not grow weary of waiting for me. Knowing that you are there spurs me on. Remember that you are beautiful to me, that all I have ever wanted from the first days of our childhood is to spend every day with you. To grow old together.

And even if it be in another country, far away from all we have known, I am sure we will be happy together. With little Ophélie. You will see.

I think of you constantly. I try to imagine your life at this orphanage, try to see you with all the different people that David has told me about. And I think they must be so very happy to have you there.

To pass the time, David and I are looking at the Koran and the New Testament. It is quite fascinating. I have been convinced of neither so far. David says there is a God, although he questions His silence amidst the atrocities of this war. I like this man. He is very real.

We speak often of the women we love, and I dream of you at night. Do not worry. Someday very soon, we will be together.

Hug Ophélie for me very tight. Tell her that Moustafa will be coming very soon.

With all my love, je t'embrasse avec tout mon coeur.

Moustafa

* * *

Rémi Cebrian went back into the chapel, gathered up an armful of flowers, and found his way to the parsonage door. It occurred to him that there had been a funeral, and he had not even asked anything of Anne-Marie. He rapped on the door loudly, and it opened a few moments later. Roger Hoffmann stood in the doorway, tall, distinguished, healthy.

"Rémi! Rémi Cebrian! You've made it, my boy. Come in. Come in. Your wife is just down in the courtyard."

The older man, looking like a complete gentleman and very strong, led Rémi down the steps and through the basement.

"It is nothing like I imagined," Rémi confided. "And who has died?"

"Mother Griolet, the head nun. It's been a most exhausting weekend. I'm afraid this place is a bit in chaos, but we are trying to set things in order."

Children were running everywhere in the courtyard, so that it took Rémi a moment to spot his own. When he did, he dropped the flowers on the ground and yelled out, "Samuel! Rachel!"

The children wheeled around, and seeing their father,

squealed with delight, tackling him in a bear hug.

Eliane came out of the dining hall, with José on her hip. Her face was shining. "Rémi! Rémi, you've come." She came into his arms and gave him a sweet kiss while the children hugged his legs. "How did you find me here?"

"The receptionist knew where you were. I called from Marseilles. We got in around noon, and I was looking for the trunk."

"We? Who do you mean? Did you bring others with you?"

"Yes! Yes, Eliane. Come, we must tell the others. David, the Dramchini women."

There was a bustling from the dining hall, and soon Roger Hoffmann emerged with David, two nuns, and a striking redhead.

David embraced Rémi. "It is so good to see you! Have you seen Anne-Marie?"

"Yes," he said, beaming. "She's gone to the hospital with all of our things."

The small group stared at him, puzzled. Rémi spoke slowly, a broad smile on his face. "She's gone to take Moustafa to the hospital."

David's face drained of color. "Moustafa?"

"I know it is impossible, but it is true. He survived, and an Arab woman nursed him back from the grave. She brought him to my door four days ago."

There was a loud "Whoop" as David hugged Gabriella, then ran to tell the Dramchini women who were changing sheets in the dormitories.

"Moustafa!" he yelled. "Moustafa is here. He's alive."

The Arab women came rushing from the dormitories, shaking their heads, flustered. Then, recognizing Rémi, they rushed upon him.

"What is it? What is David saying?"

"He is saying that Moustafa is alive. I have brought him to France."

Within the next few minutes, David had loaded Mme Dramchini and her daughters and Ophélie into his *deux chevaux*. Rémi and Eliane waved to them. "Send the cabbie back here. He's got all our things!"

Eliane was crying and giggling, the children suffocating Rémi with kisses. The orphans looked on, confused by all the commotion. Sister Rosaline called them to dinner.

"We'll be going now. Can you handle it?" Eliane asked Sister Isabelle.

"Yes, we'll be fine. The Madisons are coming to help."

Hand in hand, with baby José riding on Rémi's shoulders, they walked out into the streets of Castelnau. True to his word, the cabbie was waiting for them there. They crowded into the taxi, holding suitcases and bags on their laps.

Eliane gave directions to the hotel. She rested her head against Rémi's shoulder. "I thought you'd never come."

"I'm sorry I waited so long. I tried everything I could, but in the end I saw it was hopeless to think we might be able to return. For now Abdul and Madira have the place. I pray they can keep it."

"You are here. That is all that matters. You are here, and you brought Moustafa back."

He sighed. "After all, there was a reason for my waiting, Eliane. Something I had no idea would happen. Moustafa appeared at the door an hour before I was planning to leave Algeria. Can you see? The incredible timing of the thing? I didn't know what I was waiting for, but God did."

Eliane kissed his lips very softly. "Who can explain it? All I know is that He is in control. Every moment of our lives is in His hands."

"Yes, everything. And I even found the trunk. We are going to be okay now. Everything will be fine, my little *orangier*." Rémi held Eliane close to him, breathed in her fresh fragrance and kissed her hair. "Everything will be okay now."

* * *

The scene at the hospital was almost comic. Moustafa lay in the steel bed with several needles poked in his arms, hooking him to intravenous liquids, while Mme Dramchini, Saiyda, Rachida, and Anne-Marie hovered over him, crying, kissing, exclaiming. Ophélie perched herself on his bed and made sure the white sheets were smooth, covering his legs. David grasped Moustafa's hand tightly and shook his head back and forth in wonder.

For Moustafa, it was as though a fog was lifting slowly so that the true scenery was revealed. The people he loved, those around whom his world revolved, were crowded around him with expressions of delight in their eyes. Could it be real? The sharp, intense pain in his side became duller until he forgot it altogether. He had never thought he could enjoy a hospital room so much. Several times a nurse poked her head in the door, raised her eyebrows, and said, "He needs rest." But the gaggle of women ignored her warning, fairly smothering him in affection.

At length David explained that he had to get back to St. Joseph's where he, his father, and the Madison family were meeting to go out for dinner. The women nodded and sighed and cried and hugged. Anne-Marie took Mme Dramchini by the hand and stated softly, "I am going to stay with him tonight. You will take care of Ophélie, make sure she gets in bed all right?"

The Arab woman smiled and nodded under her veil, her large frame swaying as she stroked Ophélie's hair. "Yes. It is good. You stay with my son. It is good."

* * *

Anne-Marie could not get close enough to him or hold his hands tightly enough. "I don't ever want to let go of you again, now that you are here." She played with his curls, and the feel of her hand brushing his head pleased him immensely. "Your hair is so long," she giggled. "You look like a wild, rugged, handsome prince."

"And you must be a mirage before my eyes. You have never looked more beautiful. You are glowing."

Her cheeks grew red. "Moustafa, how can I explain it? I thought you were dead. I had given up hope, and then hope came and took me by surprise. Can anything be more wonderful than that?"

"Nothing. It makes the waiting worth it, *n'est-ce pas?*"

"*Oh, oui.* And I learned so much while I was waiting for you," she confided. "I thought that waiting was a horrid, stagnant place to be until I came to St. Joseph's and saw what these women did while they waited. It wasn't idle, Moustafa. Nor was it simply filling up their days with activity so they could not consider the problems. In their waiting, there was a trust and assurance that very important things were happening not only around them, but inside of them. It was the most remarkable thing."

"You have learned what I am beginning to understand." His words came slowly now, as if thick cotton were in his mouth. He wanted to say more, but fatigue pulled at him. "There is a sense to the suffering—it changes us, doesn't it, Anne-Marie?"

She squeezed his hand and nodded.

"I thought it would make me angry and bitter, but somehow it made me thankful for life, for the smallest shred of hope. I am so glad that our time apart was not wasted."

"Mother Griolet said that God never wastes our pain. He always uses it and transforms us by it for the good."

Moustafa heard her words, soft and velvety, peaceful and calm. He smiled at her, his eyes heavy, transforming the room into a hazy glow so that she resembled an angel beside him. Then he closed his eyes. He remembered the feeling of her lips on his forehead and the incredible peace that filled him. He was in a safe place at last.

Chapter 30

When the dorm lights were turned out and the other boys were quiet, Hussein took the pistol from under his mattress, tucked it into his pajamas, and went to the restroom. He stepped onto the toilet, climbed up to the window, and peered down into the courtyard. Dusk had fallen, but it was not yet completely dark. He could hear voices coming from the girls' dorm, but the courtyard was empty. Quickly he slid through the window and ran into the shadows. He climbed onto the stone wall and let himself over it, holding on to the jagged stones as he let himself down fifteen feet into the small park below.

He did not know where to go, but he had all night to get there and complete his task before anyone at St. Joseph's noticed he was gone. There was only one thing left to do. He held the letter he had written for Ali in his hand; it was addressed and even the stamp was in place. No one had questioned his need for a stamp amidst the activities of the last few days.

Tonight there had been much excitement, with people coming and going. But Hussein had stayed to himself. He did not want to let anything deter him from his task. He kept repeating to himself "There is no God but Allah and Mohammed is his prophet," but the words sounded empty and dull. He came to the little square with the fountain and cursed. There were too many people milling about for him to post the letter unnoticed. He should have done it earlier in the day.

He went back to the deserted park and waited in the shadows. He had all night. Nothing would spoil his plan.

* * *

Ophélie could not settle down. She chattered excitedly with Mme Dramchini and insisted on seeing Hussein. He must know the news! Moustafa was alive.

"No news tonight," Mme Dramchini scolded her playfully, tucking the covers around her.

She pouted. "Please!" she begged. For some reason, it seemed urgent to see Hussein, now that she had seen Moustafa. She thought of another tactic. "I didn't get to tell Papa good-night," she complained. "Please let me see him."

Mme Dramchini pursed her lips and frowned, shaking her finger at the child. "You tease me." But she left the dorm room and came back a moment later.

"Papa leaves. You must hurry."

Ophélie sprang from bed and fell into David's arms in the hallway. He looked at her with a hint of disapproval in his eyes. "Ophélie, I have already told you good-night."

She grabbed his shirt and pulled him close to her. "Papa, does Hussein know about Moustafa? He has to know!"

"If he hasn't heard tonight, he'll hear in the morning."

"But that will be too late," she blurted out, without knowing why.

"Too late?" He sounded irritated. "What do you mean?"

Ophélie started crying, real, worried tears. "I don't know, Papa. I don't know. Please tell him tonight. Please."

David sighed. "All right. You win. Now run back to bed. I'll tell him, even if it does make us late to dinner."

She watched him carefully, until she was sure he had gone into the boys' dormitory, then turned on her heels and dashed to her bed. She snuggled under the covers, feeling content. Everyone had made it home safely. Even Mother Griolet. And now Hussein would know that everything was okay.

* * *

It struck David as strange that Ophélie would insist so. In the past months he had learned not to question his daughter's intuition, though she was only a child. So he peeked into the boys' dorm. Hussein's bed was empty.

"Have you seen Hussein?" he questioned Sister Isabelle, coming back into the hallway. "He's not in his bed."

"Well, I'm sure he was there fifteen minutes ago, when we turned the lights out. Perhaps he got up to use the bathroom."

David checked the bathroom. Then he stepped into the courtyard where Gabriella met him.

"What's up? We're going to be late."

"Ophélie wanted me to tell Hussein about Moustafa. She was quite insistent. But I can't find the boy. He's not in his bed or the bathroom."

"Oh, great. Do we have to go looking for *him?*" Gabriella said crossly. "He's a strange kid. Maybe he wanted a little night air."

"Gabby. Look." He grabbed her arm. "I know this evening is important to you. It is to me too. But I think there's something the matter. I think Hussein has run away."

Gabriella sighed, exasperated. "Well, if he has, he can't have gone too far. I know I saw him a little while ago."

"Will you help me look? It won't take long."

"Oh, all right. But Mme Leclerc and Mme Pons are waiting to tell us all good-bye. They're leaving early tomorrow morning, you know. And the dinner reservations were for 8:30."

He took her by the hand and kissed it. "I promise I'll make it up to you, Gabby. This will be a night you won't forget."

She rolled her eyes and laughed. "Right."

It took only five minutes to inspect the dining hall and the parsonage. No Hussein.

"Now what?" Gabriella asked. "We could just shout out for him."

"Good idea." David cupped his hands around his mouth and called out loudly, "Hussein. Hey, Hussein. Wherever you're hiding, come here. I've got some great news to tell you." He paused. Nothing. "Hey, Hussein. Moustafa is alive! He's here in Montpellier. I saw him tonight. He wants to see you too." They waited a few more minutes. Then they looked at each other and shrugged.

* * *

Crouching in the shadows of the little park below the courtyard, Hussein was startled to hear David's voice. He kicked a rock and cursed again. They knew he was gone. What rotten luck. *Just go away and leave me alone.* He said nothing. Whatever great news he had, Hussein didn't want to hear it.

Then David's voice called out again. Something about Moustafa. Moustafa! Alive? Here in Montpellier. What in the heck was he making up a story like that for? A little chill ran through him. A stupid lie. That was all. A ploy to get him to come back. For what reason, he could not imagine. No one cared about him anyway.

David said nothing more. Hussein sat in the dark and thought about the voice from above telling him that Moustafa was all right. He remembered again the excitement of the afternoon and how the Dramchini women had left in a rush. And Ophélie too. Maybe it was true.

Naw. And even if it was true, what did it matter? He had made up his mind.

* * *

Ophélie still could not sleep. She heard her father's faint

voice calling out to Hussein. She stared at the top of the bunk bed, chewed on her hair, and wondered what to do. Tiptoeing into the hall, she went into the bathroom. She could never make it up into the window without Hussein's help. She came back into the hallway. Sister Isabelle poked her head out of her room. "Ophélie! What are you doing?"

"Didn't you hear Papa calling out? Hussein is missing."

Sister Isabelle looked very tired. "Sweetheart, he'll come back. You go on to bed."

"Please, let me just check. If he's sad, he might listen to me."

"Oh, all right."

Ophélie ran out into the courtyard. Her father was no longer there. "Hussein!" she whispered. "Hussein, where are you? I know you are around here. You can't have gotten out! Please, come back." She looked around and tried the doors. The dining room and parsonage were both locked. She went over to the stone wall and stood on her tiptoes. "Hussein! Are you down there? Please come back. Moustafa is alive. I saw him. I promise."

Sister Isabelle patted her head. "I'm afraid it will have to wait until tomorrow, dear."

Ophélie swung around. "Do you hate him? Is that it? You would be worried if another child had escaped. Don't you care about Hussein?"

Sister Isabelle was taken aback. She knelt down beside Ophélie. "Of course I care about Hussein, dear. I love all of the children. Every one of you. It is just that I am so tired tonight. So much has happened. But you are right; we must find him. Wait for me here. I'll get my robe."

A stone hit the wall. Then another came over the wall from the park below and landed near Ophélie's feet. She peered over. "Hussein? Is it you?"

A voice called up to her. "Shh. Yes. Is it true? About Moustafa?"

"Yes! Yes! Mama's staying with him at the hospital tonight. Isn't it wonderful? Now come back here. Whatever is the matter anyway?" She made a face. "You know it wasn't very nice of you. If you were going to run away, you could have at least told me. I thought we were friends."

She leaned far over the wall, trying to see him. Hussein walked out into the middle of the park.

"Hey, what are you doing, Ophélie? You're going to fall!"

She laughed. "I'm staying right here until you come back up, that's what I'm doing."

"You little brat," he muttered, but she could tell he was smiling. "You promise he's alive?"

"Yes, you big bully. I promise. And if you get up here and go to bed, we can both go see him in the morning."

"All right, but I don't know if I can climb back up."

"Well, don't then. Go all the way around. I'll fetch Sister Isabelle and we'll meet you at the front door to the parsonage."

"D'accord."

"You're coming, aren't you? You promise?"

"I'm coming."

*   *   *

It was the second time in his life that he had felt this way. As if something outside of himself was controlling his destiny. The first time had been when he had not shot the little girl. And now here she was begging him to come back. It was very, very strange.

He walked around the exterior of the church, and as he came into the street, he almost bumped into David and Gabriella.

"Hussein! There you are! Whatever are you doing?"

He regarded David sullenly.

"You go on, Gabby. I'll be there in a minute."

David put his arm around Hussein's shoulder and walked him back toward the parsonage. "What's the matter? Did you

432

hear the good news?"

"Yeah, I heard you."

David stopped him and ran his hands down Hussein's torso. He touched the gun and brought it out. "What's this for?"

"What do you think? Anyway, it's none of your business."

David shook him hard. "What do you mean? Look kid, people here care about you. What good will it do you to blow your brains out?"

"What do you know? I've screwed it all up. Everything." He began to cry, and he hated himself for it.

"You're only a child, Hussein. A child caught up in a terrible grown-up war. It's going to be okay, Hussein. Somehow, I promise, it's going to be okay."

Hussein sobbed into David's shirt. "You can say that. Your mother isn't weeping for you. You aren't worried that any day, Ali will go into her house and shoot her because he hasn't heard from me. I'm a murderer."

He handed David the envelope. "Will you mail this for me?" A thin smile crossed his lips. "I think it's all right. You can read it if you want."

"Yes, Hussein. We'll take care of this tomorrow. I'll help you. Now go back to bed." They were at the parsonage door where Ophélie and Sister Isabelle waited.

"You don't have any more little toys like this, do you?" David asked, turning the gun over in his hands. Hussein shook his head. "Go on then. We'll work it out tomorrow." Hussein suddenly felt a great wave of relief. Impulsively, he gave David a hug.

As Hussein walked into the parsonage, Ophélie took his hand. He heard David whisper to Sister Isabelle. "Keep an eye on him tonight, will you? He's having a rough time. When I get back, I'll sleep in the dorm . We won't be too late."

Maybe they do care, Hussein thought. *Maybe they do care after all.*

* * *

There were several tears shed as Gabriella said good-bye to Mme Leclerc that night. "I'm afraid we'll be leaving quite early tomorrow morn," the landlady apologized to the Madison family. "I hope I won't bother you." She bade everyone good-night, then paused before Gabriella. "My dear, you've been such a delight. I will certainly miss you." Then in a whisper, "You must write and tell me how everything turns out with M. Hoffmann."

Gabriella kissed her wrinkled cheeks. "Don't worry. I'll keep in touch."

"Now let's see. You know to give the keys to the apartment to Sister Rosaline when you leave." She looked around. "Have a wonderful time in America, my child. *Au revoir.*"

Gabriella saw that David had come up the stairs and was now bidding Mme Pons farewell. "It has been a pleasure to know you," the widow said, addressing Roger Hoffmann. "You have a most remarkable son. We've so enjoyed following his adventures." She laughed heartily, then rolled her eyes when David's father kissed her on the cheeks.

David took her hand in his and said, "You are a very patient woman to put up with me for two years. I appreciate everything you've done." He too kissed her lightly on the cheeks, which flustered her enormously.

"G . . . go on with you all now. Have a good time!"

David had chosen a restaurant overlooking the Lez River, which ran between Montpellier and Castelnau. It took two trips in his *deux chevaux* to get all seven of them to the restaurant. The *maître d'* frowned a bit, explaining that it had been impossible to hold their reservation for an hour, but eventually they were seated at a round table outside under the parasols. The river reflected the images of the buildings around it through a light on the sidewalk. A large fountain spewed water high into the sky, and some of the sprinkles drifted in the slight breeze to their table, refreshing them.

Gabriella, excited and nervous, made recommendations for her family. David cracked a joke with his father, remembering a particular incident years ago when his father had ordered snails. At the time he had been pleased to see his father make a face as he had swallowed the slimy mollusk. A point of weakness. Tonight it was merely a funny memory.

The conversation flowed smoothly between William Madison and Roger Hoffmann, with David interjecting ideas here and there. Gabriella babbled happily with her sisters and her mother. Jessica and Henrietta raved over the food, laughing at the way the waiter brought the delicate and delicious appetizers before each course.

"This must be a really expensive place," Jessica whispered.

"Shh," Gabriella warned. "David's dad is paying."

When the main course arrived, each plate was covered with a silver dome. Three waiters surrounded the table and, all at once, lifted the domes to reveal the artistically arranged food on the plates. "Well, if it tastes as good as it looks, we're in for a treat," Roger Hoffmann noted, thanking the waiters and picking up his fork to taste his *tournedos au poivre.*

Rebecca Madison addressed David politely. "Do you have any plans for the future now that the exchange program has been discontinued?"

David dabbed his mouth, a tiny grin playing there as he watched Gabriella squirm. "Actually, I have several possibilities, but nothing definite. I'm afraid I haven't had the time to think of much beyond the moment."

"Of course not. Do you think you will stay in France?"

"I know I want to be close to my daughter, to see her as often as possible." He felt a little tension at the table. "But of course, I plan to keep in close touch with your daughter also." He touched Gabriella's hand, and she blushed. "That is, if you don't mind."

This he said to William Madison who scratched his brow nervously, chewed for a moment, then said, "Well, no. I'm sure that's a good idea, however it can be arranged. If nothing else, letters are a great way to get to know each other better."

"I for one have had quite enough of letters for a while," David stated, winking at Gabriella. There was a moment of awkwardness and David pressed on, feeling the beads of sweat forming on his brow. "What I mean is ..." He looked around the table, then turned to Gabriella and took her hands in his. Staring only at her, he started again, "What I mean is that I would like to keep her very close to me for a while. For a long, long while."

No one spoke. Gabriella looked at him, horrified, as if to say *You are ruining the evening. Please don't shock them.* Rebecca cleared her throat, and Jessica giggled.

"What I'm trying to say, Mr. and Mrs. Madison, is that I would like to marry your daughter." Then he added, almost sheepishly, "If, if that is all right with you."

Gabriella burst into tears, a waiter rushed to the table looking terribly flustered, and Rebecca stood up and hugged her daughter. Roger Hoffmann looked at his son sternly with a hint of amusement in his eyes. Henrietta kicked Jessica under the table. And William Madison, speechless, held his fork in midair, sauce dripping from it onto the plate.

Regaining his composure, William set down his fork and looked at his daughter. "I think you had better ask her first." Then he added, "And if she says yes, well, I have nothing to say to the contrary."

Roger stood up, wine glass in hand. "Dear Gabriella, what do you say?"

Eyes shining, she stuttered, "I ... I ... I say yes. Yes, of course, yes." She glanced at David, her eyes filled with questions.

"Very good, then," Roger continued. "I propose a toast to the newly engaged couple, Gabriella and David." Wine glasses and water goblets clinked together; everyone began talking at once. There was cheek kissing and handshaking and laughter.

The waiters raised their eyebrows and shrugged and left the happy party alone.

"This is just right," Roger Hoffmann continued. "In France, when a young couple becomes engaged, the two families plan a meal together to discuss the happy event. It's called the *fiançailles*. Bravo, David."

* * *

When the meal was over, David gave his father the keys to the car to drive the Madisons home. "We'll be back later," he said. "It's a pleasant walk down by the river." The others nodded and smiled and waved them good-night.

When the *deux chevaux* was out of sight, David cocked his head and motioned for Gabriella to follow. She obeyed, saying nothing. "Are you angry with me?" he asked.

She shook her head.

"Are you terribly disappointed?"

She shrugged.

"I know it was a shock. It was unplanned. I wanted to ask you first, when the moon was full, and we were alone by the smooth flowing river with the smell of hyacinth and honeysuckle in the air." He took her in his arms, and she grinned slightly, but did not look up at him.

"But all of a sudden it seemed like it was my chance. My best chance to show them, to let them know that even though I don't know what is next, I do know I want you to share it with me."

She did not reply.

"Talk to me, Gabby. Please say something. Did you mean it when you said yes?"

She looked up at him coyly. "Did you mean it when you asked?"

"Yes, a thousand times, yes."

"Are you sure?" She narrowed her eyes, teasing. "It wasn't the most convincing proposal in the world, you know. I think you could've done better."

A hurt expression registered on his face, like a rebuked puppy, as he watched her and the outline of the river behind her. "Yes, I know. I had it all planned. Honest, I did."

"Really?"

"Yes, I was going to take you on a walk tonight, by this very river. And just when we were out of sight of everyone, with only those splendid tall plane trees looking down on us, I was going to fall to my knees, like this, and kiss your hands, like this, and say, with Romeo, 'It is my lady; O! it is my love. O! that she knew she were.'

"Then I would swear by my life, my love unto no other, as I do now. And then I would borrow Mrs. Browning's words for a moment: 'How do I love thee? Let me count the ways. I love thee to the depth and breadth and height, my soul can reach.' And I would name your beauty, Gabby, your bright blue eyes that light up your whole face when you smile. I would say that your hair is like Rapunzel's, if you would only let it down for me to admire its thick texture and bountiful red curls.

"Then I would speak as the Lover speaks in the Song of Songs, 'How fair is thy love, my sister, my spouse! How much better is thy love than wine and smell of thine ointments than all spices!' All this, Gabby, is but the beginning, because if I were to describe your soul, if I were to try..." and his voice grew soft, tender, "...I would only say that I have never met a soul mate like you, and I am quite sure that if I travel for a hundred years and launch a thousand ships, I will come back again and again to you."

She was on her knees beside him, holding him, unable to speak or move. He watched her soak in the magic of the moment, letting his words wash over her like a gentle refreshing stream on the hottest of nights. She opened her mouth to speak, but he placed his finger over her mouth and she kissed it softly.

In a whisper David continued, "That is what I was going to

tell you, Gabby. I was then going to beg you to say yes, to marry me, to come with me wherever this strange God leads us together, reminding you of Solomon's words that 'two are better than one, for if they fall, the one will lift up his fellow... and again if two lie together, then they have heat.' And then, I would lay you gently on your back, like this, and kiss you softly on your lips, like this, and stare into those eyes and say, what is your answer, my precious Gabby?"

He heard her heart beating quickly. He kissed her again. Holding his face in her hands, she looked deep into his black eyes. "I would say, 'That's more like it! Of course I'll marry you!' "

They broke into a gentle, delicate laughter, almost afraid to realize what was happening. Gabriella's face was shining with embarrassment and understanding and anticipation.

"And if you say yes, Gabby, then this is for you." David handed her a small envelope with a single sheet inside. It was a poem penned in his hand.

"Read it for me, David. Read it to me."

"Gladly," he consented, kissing her cheek, her forehead, her neck.

"*Sonnet for the wife of my youth*

I asked one balmy night to take your hand
And make it mine, your lips, your love, your soul.
Then tied your heartstrings with one strong, smooth,
*   strand*
Unending love, you, better half, my whole.
Bestowed a golden band to hold my heart
Forever in the sweetness of your charm,
To braid together what was once apart
And promise peace from anger and alarm.

And springing from our 'yes' of equal love,
Unequaled by desire to give and serve,

To want to please and, pleased, to want above
To plan, protect, provide for and preserve,
A three strand cord, entwined to wait and trust
One will divine, eternity with us
I love you, Gabby. Will you marry me?"

She looked up quickly, with a soft little gasp. "You really were planning to ask me tonight." He nodded. "You really did write this for me." He nodded again.

"It is beautiful. Read it again, David." And he did. She leaned over and kissed him. "Is this real?"

"Oui, Mademoiselle."

Then her eyes gleamed, she furrowed her brow playfully and asked, "There's just one thing I don't quite understand. It's in the first verse here where it says 'Bestowed a golden band to hold my heart.' I suppose that is merely symbolic?"

"Well, now that you ask, I seem to remember something having to do with that line. Yes," he fished in the pocket of his suit coat. "Ah, yes. Here it is." With a confident smile, he handed her a tiny, square box.

"For me?" she asked meekly.

He nodded once again.

Gabriella opened the box, and there inside was a simple gold band, embedded with tiny diamonds and sapphires. She started crying, sniffed, wiped her nose, and cried again. "However did you have time to find this? It's absolutely gorgeous. How did you know I wanted sapphires? I never even thought . . ."

He slipped the ring on her finger. "I have connections, my dear. A fellow has to find a way to surprise a girl, doesn't he? It would be a pity for her to refuse to marry him simply because he bungled the proposal."

Gabriella tilted her head. "When did you know?"

"Know what?"

"That you wanted to marry me?"

"I think it must have been that first day in class when you

knew Pope's poem, or maybe it was when you reminded me of that field of poppies, or when you took in my daughter. Ah, no, now I remember. It was when you were hanging off the cliff in les Baux, holding to my hand for dear life, that it hit me. I didn't ever want to let you go."

"Quit teasing, David. I mean it. You've never even said the word before tonight."

They stood up and continued walking. "It was when your God convinced me that even if I could never be good enough for you, I was still the right one."

"I'm so glad He did. It makes all the waiting worth it."

"I love you, Gabby." There was the faintest breeze, the leaves rustled slightly, as if the limbs of the trees were waving their approval. "I love you with every part of me." He grinned down at her, with his dimpled cheek. "And I look forward to learning to love you even more, day by day."

* * *

They reached St. Joseph's when the clock in the bell tower was striking one. It was so comfortable to be together in the stark stillness of the night, when the rest of the town and all its ensuing problems lay dormant around them. They walked interlaced, arm in arm, never quite close enough and yet as naturally as if they had been walking like this for years. Gabriella was surprised by the sudden, easy intimacy. Now they were walking toward a point of time when they would be one, and it was right to hold each other closer as they neared that moment.

They were standing in front of Mme Leclerc's apartment. "I must leave you for a few hours, my love," David sighed, their arms locked around each other's neck, their foreheads touching. He brushed her lips with his. "Did you really say yes?"

"Yes, and I will say it a hundred more times, if you wish."

"I'm going to spend the night on the dorm floor. Poor

Sister Isabelle. I hope she hasn't waited up."

"Why would she?"

"Hussein. I was afraid . . . " He did not finish his thought. "I didn't want him to try to escape again." He gradually released her, unfolding little by little. "Good night, Gabby. *Je t'aime.*"

He was before her a vulnerable boy, held now completely in her hands. It thrilled and frightened her to realize her freedom and her constraints. She never wanted to hurt him, always wished she could keep him as he was there, tender, trusting, with every bit of cynicism washed away in a look of love.

She let herself into the apartment, where one lamp from the *salon* was lit. She slid into a thick chair and breathed deeply, turning the ring around on her finger. It was a simple ring, and she loved it for its simplicity.

Was she really engaged? It had all been so surprising. She felt as if the script from someone else's life had somehow gotten mixed in with hers by accident, and she was suddenly repeating someone else's lines.

"Lord, let it be true," she prayed. "It petrifies me to believe it." She had not even let herself imagine a proposal from David, certain that it was years away. And now his ring was on her finger, with the inscription *je t'aime, Gabby* inside the band.

They had decided absolutely nothing at the meal that night. No one had pressed, only celebrated, and she loved her family all the more for accepting David and the news. Perhaps they would all settle in the States and have the wedding in a white church with a tall steeple. That was months away. It didn't matter at all. She had the ring on her finger and the sonnet in her mind. She could wait because the hope was certain.

Jessica and Henrietta were asleep on her bed, with the covers thrown off to escape the stifling heat. She silently undressed and lay down on the cot Mme Leclerc had provided. She listened to every sound in the night and turned over every memory of the past year again and again in her mind. In the early hours of the morning, she heard Mme Leclerc in the kitchen. Unable to sleep, Gabriella went through the apartment in her night robe.

"Child! Why are you awake?" her landlady greeted her, obviously pleased.

"I couldn't sleep. I wanted you to know, before you left." She held out her left hand.

"A ring? *Oh là là!* A ring! From M. Hoffmann?"

Gabriella nodded.

The aging woman took Gabriella's face in her hand and squeezed her as if she were a toddler. "I knew it! I knew he would come back for you, Gabriella." With a hearty laugh, she kissed Gabriella's cheeks. *"Félicitations, ma fille!* Congratulations. This will give Monique and me something to talk about on our trip!"

They embraced, then Gabriella went quietly back to her bedroom, lay down, and fell asleep.

Chapter 31

On the afternoon of July 26, the air in the dining hall was stuffy. Sister Rosaline fanned herself, perspiring profusely in her black robes. Gabriella lifted her hair off her neck and glanced around at the other people seated at one of the long tables in the room. Joseph Cohen had convened them for the reading of Mother Griolet's will, but she could tell that no one's mind was on it.

Instead they talked among themselves about the end of the thirty-day period when St. Joseph's would be closed. Only four days left. The deed was as good as done. The end of the thirty days and the end of an era. It caused a large knot to form in her throat when Gabriella thought of it. She turned her attention to Anne-Marie, who sat in between Sister Rosaline and Sister Isabelle, telling them about Moustafa, who was still in the hospital but recovering quickly.

"He has a lot of motivation to get well now," Sister Rosaline broke in. "His family is waiting for him and a beautiful woman as well."

Anne-Marie self-consciously ran her fingers through her black hair, pushing it away from her face, which glistened with perspiration. "I believe summer in the Midi is worse even than in Algiers. But it doesn't matter one bit. What matters is that we are all here together."

David, Roger, Jean-Louis, and Pierre the *boulanger* talked in low tones with Rémi and Eliane. Joseph and Emeline Cohen made polite conversation with William and Rebecca Madison. Henri Krugler came through the door, breathing heavily, his white hair wet with sweat. "Excuse me for being late. At the last moment we had a problem with one of the kids." Joseph welcomed him warmly, introducing him to those who had not already met him at the funeral.

When Anne-Marie was introduced to him, he smiled faintly and held her hand for a long, awkward moment. "I'm very glad to meet you, Mademoiselle Duchemin," he said finally. "A real pleasure."

After a few more moments, Père Thomas, the curé from the church, arrived. "Please forgive me for being late," the priest apologized. "I hope I haven't inconvenienced anyone." The thin, stooped man straightened his white collar, shook hands with the men, and nodded politely to the women. The door to the dining hall opened once again and Edouard Auguste, the goldsmith from Montpellier, came in, equally apologetic.

Joseph invited Père Thomas and M. Auguste to sit on either side of him. Then Joseph Cohen wiped his brow and shuffled through a pile of official-looking documents. He glanced at Sister Rosaline. "Everyone is present now. May we begin? The children are cared for?"

"Heavens, yes!" the rotund nun assured him. "Between Saiyda and Rachida and the Madison girls, the orphans are being thoroughly entertained." She addressed Anne-Marie. "Mme Dramchini is not here?"

"No, she is with Moustafa."

"Well then, M. Cohen, everyone is accounted for. You may begin."

Joseph Cohen looked at his watch and rubbed his chin. "We are here today, as all of you know, to read the last will and testament of Jeanette Griolet. I have summoned each of you here for a purpose, and I appreciate your willingness to attend. Mother Griolet was a woman of few earthly possessions, but she was very specific about which of you was to receive what.

"I must add, as we are all aware, that St. Joseph's faces closure in the imminent future. Père Thomas is here as a representative of the church, and he will explain the procedures after the will has been read." Several heads nodded, their expressions grim.

"A few months ago, Mother Griolet spent two weeks with Emeline and me at our chalet in Switzerland. At that time, she asked me to help her update her will. As you will see, the good woman guessed that death was near. As executor of her will, I have tried as far as possible to accord her her wishes. In the course of the past week, there have been a few, shall we say, complications that have taken me several days to work through."

He paused and mopped his brow. There was a slight hesitation. Then he said, "I shall now read the will. 'I, Jeanette Griolet, on this the 3rd day of May, 1962, do hereby write my last will and testament.

" 'To Jean-Louis Vidal, I leave my personal possessions included in this *dossier.*" Joseph smiled and handed Jean-Louis a thick folder. The red-cheeked professor took it, startled, shaking his head and saying, "*Merci.*"

" 'You have been my oldest and most faithful friend, and it is my desire that you continue to be employed by the school as Professor of European History for as long as the school shall run!' "

Jean-Louis tried to concentrate on Joseph's words, but as he rummaged through the folder, his eyes were blinking back tears.

" 'To Sister Rosaline I leave all of the items in my personal kitchen with prayers that you can use them to bring glory to our Lord as you prepare meals for the children. This includes my recipe books, my old rolling pin, and the apron you gave me for Christmas one year.' "

Joseph looked up. "Sister Rosaline, I will leave it to your discretion to arrange these utensils as you see fit."

"*Oui*, M. Cohen. *Bien sûr et merci.*" She wiped her eyes and blew her nose loudly.

"This is also for you." Joseph gave her a small envelope.

" 'To Sister Isabelle, I leave you my family Bible. My dear friend and student of God's Word, may it bless you as it has me. I know you will care for it as a daughter would.' "

Sister Isabelle stood, shaking her head and murmuring, "It is too much, too much." She thanked Joseph profusely as she took the large, black Bible with its crumbling leather and held it to her breast.

" 'To both of the Sisters I leave my many photographs that line the walls of the office. Keep those that please you, distribute the other pictures to those with whom you may have kept in contact.' "

" 'To Pierre Cabrol, who has worked with me in many a dangerous mission, I leave all the documents of those days gone by, some long past and others more recent, when we worked clandestinely to provide for children in hiding. It is my wish that you, Pierre, shall continue to provide bread for St. Joseph's as long as you are able to do so!' " This Joseph said adamantly, and the small group of people laughed.

" 'To Rebecca Madison, I leave my silver comb and brush as a token of our friendship. I have included a small folder of pictures that I have kept near to me all these years.' " Joseph Cohen handed Rebecca an uncovered shoe box. A yellowed photograph of the Madison girls with Mother Griolet and Rebecca lay on top.

" 'To David Hoffmann, I leave my worn volumes of French and English literature, with prayers that you will find great pleasure in perusing them from time to time. I ask that you make sure that any other books that perhaps do not interest you find a proper home.

" 'I also wish to state that, should my death precede the opening of a new school year at St. Joseph's, it is my wish to name M. David Hoffmann as the future director of the Franco-American exchange program, and hereby entrust to him the school's records of all the past years as well as the lists of benefactors to the program.' " Joseph looked up at David, who nodded solemnly.

" 'To Gabriella Madison, I leave my old *santon*, knowing how she has admired it. And with this, should I not be around, I symbolically pass on to her the directorship of the orphanage of St. Joseph's. It is my hope that she will have already completed an apprenticeship with me. I am confident in her complete capability, seconded by Sister Rosaline and Sister Isabelle, to continue the work.' "

Gabriella jumped up, bumping her leg against the chair, and went forward to retrieve the *santon* of the old woman, dressed in floral Provençal print, with a bundle of twigs on her back. "How did she know? Oh, it is the perfect gift!"

Joseph wiped his brow and looked up. "We all realize, of course, that Mother Griolet was merely expressing her desire for the continuation of the programs at St. Joseph's. Since the time of the writing of the will, many things have transpired, as you are all aware. This we will discuss momentarily.

" 'To Joseph and Emeline Cohen, friends from far back, I leave these documents of the days when the Jewish children were among us. May they always remind you of the power of our God.' " Joseph Cohen, obviously moved, set the papers down in front of him, pushed his glasses up on his nose, and picked up a piece of white stationery.

"Mother Griolet added a simple letter to be read to all of you here. Sister Rosaline, I think it might be more appropriate for you to read this."

"Why, of course," she said, taking the letter. She skimmed

it and began reading: " 'You have been my true friends, whether I have known you for months or years. Always remember that our service for the Lord, no matter how challenging and filled with suffering, is never in vain. Carry on and may the Lord Jesus, our gentle Shepherd, be with you always.' "

Joseph rose, looking slightly embarrassed. "Thank you for your patience. This concludes the reading of the will. But I would like to share with you some most surprising news. Following the funeral of Mother Griolet, we have received an abundance of donations for St. Joseph's."

He picked up a letter. "From the Jewish children hidden during the war, we have received a check for 50,000F. The enclosed note reads, 'It is our deep desire that this money be used in any way necessary to provide for the orphanage of St. Joseph so that it may remain open and ready to welcome children like us and so many others, who found shelter and hope there.' " There was a soft murmur as the men and women turned their heads and raised their eyebrows.

"How did they know about the problems at St. Joseph's?" Sister Isabelle asked naively.

Joseph pursed his lips, repressing a grin. "I felt it was my duty to inform those who asked about the orphanage of its particular plight. But I was not responsible for the rest. Several of the young people organized everything."

He chose another letter. "From the townspeople of Castelnau, 60,000F."

Sister Rosaline gasped, and Sister Isabelle exclaimed "Oh my!" and fanned herself rapidly.

"This letter specifies, and I quote, 'We the people of said Castelnau, in appreciation for the faithful work of Mother Jeanette Griolet and in desire to see St. Joseph's continue in its important service to children and to its community, do hereby give the said amount and revoke our previously given petition.' "

"It's unbelievable! It's a miracle," Sister Isabelle exclaimed.

"Well, I'll be," whistled Jean-Louis.

Gabriella embraced David, and he kissed her on the lips. Eliane reached across the table and squeezed Anne-Marie's hand.

But Joseph Cohen had not finished. "We have received many more donations as well, from orphans who were housed at St. Joseph's over the years and from others who appreciate what this place has done. To put it simply . . . " Joseph grinned, unable to hide his extreme pleasure. "By my calculations, based on the records from previous years, the money St. Joseph's has received in memory of Mother Griolet will allow the orphanage to function, on its own with no aid from anyone, for two and a half years."

The small group stared at each other, mouths opened, then burst into laughter, hugging and kissing and back slapping and handshaking.

"It truly is a miracle," Gabriella whispered to David.

Joseph spoke again. "Before I invite Père Thomas to give us his opinion on this matter, I have one other story to recount to you.

"At Mother Griolet's funeral were a brother and sister, Yves and Christine Millot. Seventeen years ago they arrived at St. Joseph's half starved and in rags, Jewish orphans. They presented Mother Griolet with the aforementioned *santon.*" He pointed to the clay statue of the bent-over old woman, which Gabriella was holding.

"While at the funeral this weekend, the young woman, Christine, spotted the *santon.* She was surprised to see it among Mother Griolet's possessions, and asked me why no one had broken it. I looked at her quite stupidly and assured her I had no idea why anyone would want to do such a thing.

"She replied that when they had given the *santon* to Mother Griolet, she had repeated the words her mother had told her to say to whoever agreed to take care of her children. The words were these: 'Break this old woman whenever you find yourself in desperate need.'"

Joseph Cohen motioned to Gabriella. "Since this *santon* is yours now, I will ask you to do the honors."

Gabriella looked baffled. "But I don't want to break her. I will treasure her forever!"

Joseph called Edouard Auguste to come to his aid. M. Auguste produced a small tool, like a delicate, finely sharpened knife. "I believe this will do the trick."

Worried, Gabriella approached the two men. "Why in the world would you want to break her?"

"If you will allow me to show you, Gabriella, I believe this will be of great importance to all of us." Carefully the goldsmith removed the floral material of the old woman's skirts as if he were undressing a doll. With tiny scissors he snipped away at the underclothes until a plain, red clay figurine was exposed, completely devoid of warmth.

"Just as I thought," he said, pointing to the center of the clay woman. "She has been broken before, just here. See?" Gabriella leaned forward to inspect an uneven crack that ran around the *santon's* middle.

"I'm afraid I will need to break her again," M. Auguste said, almost apologetically. He inserted a small knife in the crack and tapped it with a tiny hammer. The *santon* broke in two.

Gabriella had hardly heard his words, for as the *santon* broke, she saw concealed inside the lower torso a piece of wrinkled newsprint. She touched it, pulling it carefully out with two fingers. It was bunched together, and the withered paper practically disintegrated as she held it. Carefully opening the newsprint, she saw that wrapped inside were what appeared to be a cluster of diamonds, rubies, emeralds, pearls, and sapphires.

"Jewels!" Gabriella shrieked. The others crowded around for a look.

Joseph was shaking his head in wonder. "So Christine

Millot was right. On Saturday, she related this story to me.

"The Millot family, living in Lyons, feared the worst for their children. As more and more Jews were deported to concentration camps, the family, well-known jewelers, began hiding their possessions. Christine remembers watching her father break this *santon,* hollow out the interior, and stuff it with the most precious of his stones. She even helped him glue the statue back together and put back on the clothes. 'This will adequately provide for those who care for you,' her father told her.

"Obviously Mother Griolet never broke the *santon,* although she surely had been told to do so. When Christine revealed to me what was inside, she had no idea of its real worth, but she felt it was extremely valuable. I offered the *santon* to her, at least what was inside, but she refused, stating vehemently that whatever was inside belonged to Mother Griolet alone." He took a deep breath. "Christine Millot begged me to make sure that whatever was found in this *santon* would go toward helping with the upkeep of the orphanage.

"And so, I have invited M. Auguste here, assuming that there would indeed be jewels for him to inspect."

The handsome, silver-haired gentleman with the silver mustache set down the broken *santon.* He seated himself, brought out an eyepiece, and looked through it as he picked up the first diamond. He turned it over in his fingers, inspecting every detail. One by one, he studied each stone without comment, until he had seen the whole lot.

He looked up at Joseph Cohen, wrinkled his brow and said, "I must admit to you that I find this hard to believe. These jewels are worth a small fortune." He broke into a smile. "If you sold these stones today, I would say you could keep this place running for a long, long time."

There was a moment of shocked silence, then all eyes turned to Joseph. "Yes, you see there have been quite a few surprises this week. After hearing Christine's story and counting all the other contributions, I took it upon myself to call Père Thomas and discuss matters with him."

The aged priest now spoke. "St. Joseph's has always been for us in the church a bit of an enigma. With such little funding from the church it managed to stay open and thrive. Mother Griolet was a genius with stretching the *centimes*. And she believed in a God of miracles. I would say that He has granted her, by her death, the miracle St. Joseph's needed. I have come to report that St. Joseph's will remain open—"

Before he could continue, Sister Rosaline and Sister Isabelle gave out a loud *"Ouais!"* and hugged each other.

"There will be several revisions that the church will wish to make. Precisely, in accordance with Mother Griolet's wishes, I am ready to name M. Hoffmann as the new director of St. Joseph's exchange program." He grinned in spite of himself. "And the church is willing to allow Mlle Madison to assume the role as director of the orphanage with a few stipulations."

He addressed Gabriella. "If you agree, the church wishes for you to take classes at the Faculté des Lettres in Montpellier to complete your teaching degree. The church will send someone, probably myself, every three to six months to inspect the orphanage and its school program." He turned to David. "M. Hoffmann will have ultimate control over the whole functioning of the orphanage until Mlle Madison has completed her degree."

Gabriella turned to David. Her face went white, then red, then little pools of tears formed in her eyes.

After a long pause, Sister Rosaline asked, "Well, what do you say?"

"Oh, isn't it just perfect?" cooed Sister Isabelle. "They got engaged two days ago, and today they get their marching orders. How wonderful."

Gabriella looked at David, who grinned back at her. He took Gabriella's hand and spoke, "I am thrilled with the happy turn of events here today. It seems events have been turning and turning for a good while now, so that I'm not sure any of us know which end is up anymore. So please give us a few days to reflect and pray on this together. We, at least I, am deeply flattered. And in keeping with my desire to start our life together on the right foot, I will let Gabriella speak for herself."

Gabriella stood, still holding the bottom half of the broken *santon*, and stuttered, "David is right. Too much has happened at once. I don't know what to say. Only that I am very, very happy, and I only wish Mother Griolet could be here to see us now."

"Don't you worry about that, Gabriella," piped in Sister Rosaline. "I'm sure she knows."

Joseph spoke. "I know we have had quite enough surprises for today. Sister Isabelle has provided some drinks, if you would like to take a pause. There is, however, another matter of business to be discussed, which is why we have asked M. et Mme Cebrian, Mlle Duchemin, and M. Krugler to join us." He addressed them personally, "If you would meet back here in ten minutes, please. The rest of you are welcome to stay, if you wish."

The small group stretched and rose. David squeezed Gabriella around the waist. "We have so much to talk about, you and I."

"I can't believe it. It is like a dream." She picked up the other piece of the *santon*, walked out into the courtyard, and stared down at the statue. She thought of what Mother Griolet had said a few months back, "We must be broken before we are useful to the Lord. Broken of our selfishness, broken of ourselves. And in that brokenness, we have so much more to offer Him." Gabriella hugged the statue to herself and cried.

* * *

Anne-Marie did not like the way the man called Henri Krugler looked at her. She had not completely understood why this big, white-haired man from Lodève had shown up at

Mother Griolet's funeral. She understood even less why he was here today.

Joseph Cohen motioned to the group to once again take their seats. A butterfly danced in Anne-Marie's stomach as she anticipated the letter from her father. She was almost afraid to read it. She had set her hopes on a few simple words—as important to her as a fistful of jewels.

"As you all know," Joseph began, "Rémi has recovered the contents of his lost trunk in a warehouse in Marseilles. Within the trunk was the will of Captain Maxime Duchemin. Eliane, I will let you explain the rest."

"Thank you, M. Cohen. I was the executor of this testament." She held up a thick envelope. "But when I studied the will four years ago now, I realized that there was nothing left. The Duchemin home neighboring ours in Algiers was looted." Eliane turned to Anne-Marie. "As I have told you before, there is nothing to be done, nothing to be recovered from the house or the banks in Algiers." She handed the thick envelope to Anne-Marie. "I'm sorry.

"However, there was also this letter for Anne-Marie to be given to you in case of his death." Eliane produced a folded piece of parchment sealed with a gold medallion that had not been broken. "I'm very happy for you to have it at long last."

Anne-Marie took the letter, stared at it, and ran her fingers over the seal. Then she looked up questioningly. "Am I supposed to open it now?"

"I think that would be best, if you don't mind. You will understand, I believe, afterward," Joseph said softly.

She tore the gold seal with her fingernail. Inside was a one-page letter written in her father's hand. Anne-Marie's deep brown eyes soaked in the words, and suddenly she was transported back to Algiers, in the large farmhouse, with her father singing lullabies to Ophélie.

November 15, 1957

My dearest Anne-Marie,

If you are reading this letter, it is because my fears have become a reality. I will not see you again on this earth, but one of my fears will be put aside. You must know how much I love you, how much I have always loved you, even though my proud, disciplined manner might have at times suggested otherwise. Go forward, my precious child, with Ophélie. That is my wish and your mother's as well.

Anne-Marie, all that we had in Algeria is worthless now, as you have doubtless understood from the will. You must leave Algeria at once. Flee to France. I know it will be hard, but I have provided for you there. This past summer, when I went to France for talks, I took some of our money and put it in an account in Switzerland. And I bought a house in a small town in the Cevennes mountains called Lodève. It is not too far from the city of Montpellier. My good friend, Henri Krugler, has the property rights for the house. It has been paid for in full, and he has agreed on the upkeep until you have need of it.

Henri is a Swiss pastor, a Huguenot descendant, a great man of faith. You would not remember him, but he was in Algeria years ago, and it was through his preaching that I began to see things differently. He is a man of God. He will help you, Anne-Marie, should anything befall me. Please contact him. In this way, I have made provision for you and Ophélie.

It is my fervent wish that we all be reunited at this little place in Lodève, in the foothills of the Cevennes mountains. But if you hold this letter, I fear that this wish shall not be granted. Therefore, I pray night and day that we will be reunited in another place where the God of the Bible promises no more crying or death.

Until then, remember always that I have loved you—

never have I stopped and never will I. You have brought me great delight and now, with Ophélie, I am overwhelmed.

With love. Je t'embrasse avec tout mon coeur,
Papa

He had written in an address in Lodève with Henri Krugler's name above it and a phone number.

Anne-Marie let the letter drop onto the table. She bit her lip, sniffed, and brushed her hand across her eyes, which were filling with tears. It seemed too incredibly impossible, and she was afraid to meet Henri Krugler's eyes for confirmation.

Eventually she did glance up at the robust man. "I see now," she said simply. "That is why you have been looking at me so intently. Papa says that he bought a house in the city of Lodève and that you, M. Krugler, have been keeping it up for me. Can it possibly be true?"

The white-haired man's face broke into a gentle smile. "Yes, it's true, Anne-Marie. I had given up hope, but you see, our God is full of surprises. When I saw you at the funeral, I was almost certain." He produced a small photo of Anne-Marie holding Ophélie when she was an infant. "I went home and found this picture that your father had given me, and then I contacted Joseph. He suggested that I come this afternoon because, well, because my story is a bit wrapped up in St. Joseph's as well."

He stroked his goatee. "I'm afraid that the house is being used as a *centre aéré* at the present time. It is a rather complicated story. But don't worry." He flashed another smile. "The house is yours, all yours. I have the deed here in your name." He handed her an envelope. "You'll find also the number of your Swiss account. Everything is quite in order. I'm delighted that this has worked out so well for you, Mademoiselle Duchemin."

"And what about the *centre aéré*?" Gabriella blurted out. She addressed Anne-Marie. "It's a beautiful place. I've been there with Mother Griolet. It's all been redone. There is land, and the mountains for a backyard."

"Don't worry about the *centre aéré*," Henri Krugler stated. "The Lord has always provided just what I needed. If I could have a little time to warn the parents that the center will be closing. . . ."

"But you've only just opened!" Gabriella protested.

Anne-Marie repressed a chuckle at her friend's obvious distress. Gabriella turned to her. "I'm sorry, Anne-Marie. You know I'm thrilled for you, but it is only that I know of M. Krugler's story. He came to reach out to the Arabs, the *harkis*, and he has only recently opened the center. It is most fascinating. Didn't you say, M. Krugler, that you had looked for other buildings?"

"Dear Mlle Madison. Thank you for your vote of confidence, but the house is by no means mine. As I said, I had given up hope and decided to put the place to good use."

"Is it a large house?" Anne-Marie asked.

"Yes, actually it is. Very spacious. What they call an old *mas.* We have fixed it up a bit from when your father bought it. Paid cash he did," Henri chuckled. "And he said he'd spend all of his years in retirement trying to get it suitable for your mother." He paused awkwardly.

Anne-Marie felt sorry for this gentle man with the rich, soothing voice and the blazing eyes. "Oh, M. Krugler. I'm sure something can be worked out. Ophélie and I are quite used to living with other people, you see." She smiled at Gabriella and the Sisters. "Don't close the center."

Henri shook his head. "The house is yours, Mlle Duchemin. You must come see it. Then you can decide."

"Yes, yes. That is right. Of course." She felt suddenly so light-headed, the room was spinning around her. "I don't know what to say. It is like a dream that I never even thought to dream."

"*Oh là,* my child! Look how pale you are!" Sister Rosaline

rushed to the kitchen and fetched a glass of water. "Drink this up now. Such a shock for you, and in this terrible heat."

Anne-Marie closed her eyes and rested her head in her hands. She thought for a moment she saw Ophélie running in an open field with the mountains as a backdrop, and behind her daughter, Moustafa coming in from the fields, smiling and covered in sweat. It was a delicious vision. Today, she had come to know another facet of her God. She had met the Christ first as a Comforter; now she saw Him as a Provider. She was sure that it would take her whole life, if she lived a very long time, to be fully introduced to this Person. It baffled her to think of it.

She cried softly into her hands and did not apologize. One after another, these acquaintances, these newfound friends, came to touch her shoulder as if they understood perfectly. There was a feeling that surpassed surprise or joy. It overwhelmed her and seeped into every part of her. She had a home, a place to come to. She cried on.

* * *

Later in the afternoon, Henri Krugler laid out his plan to the people at St. Joseph's. "There is a good possibility of some of these *pied-noir* and *harki* refugees throughout France taking in the children at St. Joseph's, perhaps not through adoptions, but at least as foster children. It may take a little while to get the word out, but I have hope. I have heard nothing mentioned of the problem of overcrowding at St. Joseph's?"

Père Thomas nodded. "This is certainly a problem and a health hazard. However, in view of the extraordinary circumstances of the aftermath of the war, the church is willing to allow St. Joseph's to continue functioning, with the stipulation that the number of children be reduced to a maximum of thirty-five by year's end."

Joseph broke in. "I motion that we close this meeting for today. Much has been revealed. We must digest it now. We will, of course, be waiting for your answer, M. Hoffmann and

Mlle Madison. Not to rush you, but you do understand the importance."

"Of course," murmured Gabriella.

"Very well then. *A bientôt.*"

* * *

Gabriella felt chilled, and she could not imagine why. Perhaps she was coming down with the flu. Why else would she be shivering when the hot summer sun was setting records in the Midi? "The world is too much with us, late and soon," she said out loud, remembering one of David's favorite lines from Wordsworth. She felt terribly confused.

She hoped David had understood that she had to be alone. Completely alone for one hour. She tried to think back on the past few days and weeks, but they were a blur. Everything in her ached. She felt as though for months someone had been tossing her emotions to and fro until she was sore and exhausted. It was all good. Good? Wonderful, extravagantly wonderful. The climax to her year abroad was turning out better and more exciting than anything she could have possibly dreamed up. Then why did she feel so completely drained?

She twirled the engagement ring on her finger. She needed time to think. Think! But there was no time. They needed an answer soon. If St. Joseph's was to remain open, the answer must be given. The thirty days were almost up.

Only yesterday she had dreamed of a final year in school in the States with weekend trips to visit David and months to plan every detail of their wedding with her mother. And only days before that she had been sure there would never be a wedding at all. And if she thought further back, she had been wrestling through the same question that was before her now. To take on a job that was nothing by the world's standards, yet which would require every ounce of her energy.

She thought of Mother Griolet. She saw her in her mind's eye—the serene smile, the lively green eyes, the tiny frame that

Mother Griolet held erect as she walked through the halls of St. Joseph's. "Why did you have to leave when I need you most?"

The question tumbled back toward her. It was by her death that all of this had come to pass. It was the strangest answer to the old nun's prayer. Gabriella sat down in a field of dried grass. A few yellow dandelions offered the only color to the countryside. She lay down on her back, shading her eyes from the sun with one hand. She rolled over on her stomach, picked a dandelion, and twirled a strand of her red hair around the wildflower's stem. "I need to know, and I need to know now."

She thought of Mother Griolet on that day in May when she had offered Gabriella the job. Her words came back to her now. *My child, do not be afraid. God will provide. He has always provided in the past. Ask the Lord what He wants of you. But before you answer at all, I simply ask that you talk to Him about it. Trust, Gabriella. God does not change. Neither does His Word. Through all the changes in our lives, He does not change. He is truth. Seek Him. He is perfectly trustworthy.*

Yes, of course. That same little word. Trust. She had made her decision two months ago. Now it was coming back to welcome her. The only thing that was left for her to do was to walk into it with outstretched arms and a heart ready to serve.

Chapter 32

When Anne-Marie walked into the restored farmhouse in Lodève, she had the sudden feeling that she had been there before. The couch in the spacious living room was the same tan leather one that had been in her parents' home in Algiers for years. Two mahogany chairs, which her father had refinished, sat on the other side of a large, stuccoed fireplace. Several paintings, her mother's favorites, hung on the walls.

Anne-Marie vaguely remembered the furniture disappearing from their house in Algiers and being replaced by other, less valuable items. "How did these get here?" she asked Henri.

"Your father brought them over when he purchased the house. He knew trouble was coming."

Yes. Father had hinted at it, but she had been too preoccupied with baby Ophélie and her own concerns to let it register. And now, these furnishings reached out to surprise and welcome her to her new home. She could barely take it in.

Opening behind the living room was an eating room that expanded the whole length of the house. It was crowded with five long metal tables, much like the ones in the refectory at

St. Joseph's. This room adjoined a well-equipped kitchen, clean, orderly, the appliances new.

"We had to enlarge a bit to meet the regulations for the center," Henri explained as Anne-Marie stared wide-eyed into the shining facility. She touched the counters, the cabinets, the white gas stove. Then Henri led her through a long hallway that smelled of fresh paint and was lined with photographs. There was even one of M. Krugler with her father in his army uniform. She touched it in a daze.

The staircase leading to the second floor was an old, tiled, winding one that emptied into a vast hall with doorways running off it in every direction. "How many rooms are there up here?" she questioned, stunned.

"You've got seven, Mlle Duchemin, not counting the bathrooms. There are two of them."

"Seven bedrooms? Why, it's practically a castle!"

Henri chuckled. "It's big, all right."

Anne-Marie felt distressed. "I can't take this place from you. You've spent your own money fixing it up. It wouldn't be right." She began opening doors and peering into the rooms, each one expansive and recently redecorated. At the end of the hall, one door led into an apartment.

"It was the servants' quarters long ago, and was later joined to the house," Henri explained.

"Is this where you live?"

Henri shook his head. "No, I have a little place in town. It's quite nearby."

Anne-Marie pushed open the doors. "Servants' quarters! Why, it's a perfect place for us! And look! There's even a fireplace and bathroom." She turned her radiant face to Henri. "May I go in?"

"Of course," he said kindly, and she thought there was a strange catch in his voice.

Anne-Marie gasped. In the corner of the room sat an old oak rocking chair with a crocheted baby quilt hanging over one arm. She ran to it, fell on her knees, and buried her face in the pink and green needlework. She looked around at Henri Krugler as if he were her closest friend. "The quilt Mama crocheted for Ophélie when she was born . . . The chair I rocked her in."

She clutched the quilt, pulling it close to her, and then squealed with pleasure. "And look! Ophélie's baby book!" A narrow bookshelf stood on the opposite wall, filled with scrapbooks and worn volumes. "It is all from home. All of it!" Anne-Marie sat down in the rocker and began to rock back and forth, back and forth. It was as if someone had come ahead to prepare this place for her, a home just to her liking. Someone who knew all about her.

"It's like this room has been just waiting for me," she said in wonder.

"Indeed it has, Mlle Duchemin. For the longest time."

Overwhelmed, Anne-Marie reached out and clasped Henri's big, rough hand. "M. Krugler, keep your center open. We will help you run it. Ophélie and I will live here, in these rooms. Where we belong." For just a brief second, she looked longingly at the sturdy double bed and thought of Moustafa.

"Mlle Duchemin, give yourself time. We will talk of details later. If you desire it, I'm sure something can be arranged. I cannot tell you how much it means to me."

Anne-Marie, still holding his hand, rocked back and forth gently. "Nor I. Thank you, M. Krugler. You are a very good man."

* * *

On July 31, the official end of the church's thirty-day period, Gabriella and David met with Père Thomas at his office in the old part of Montpellier to sign the papers concerning St. Joseph's. To Gabriella, it seemed she was signing away her life. Her hand trembled, and her simple ring caught the rays of the sun and glittered. What might have been was swallowed up in what was actually happening. She signed her name.

"Excuse me for asking, Père Thomas," she said after penning her signature. "But I am so curious. What made the church change its mind? Just the money? Even with the funds, you could have decided to send another nun to take over the place. Why did you choose us?"

Père Thomas chuckled, scratching his white head. He sighed heavily. "My child, do you know the verse in the Holy Scriptures that says, 'His ways are far above ours?' "

"Yes, Père."

"Then that is my answer. He made hard hearts soft. How else can you explain a French Catholic priest listening to a Swiss Jewish businessman who wanted him to hire two American Protestant young people to run an orphanage filled with French, *pied-noir*, and Arab children?"

Gabriella laughed out loud. "Yes, I see what you mean. Are you telling me not to try to understand?"

The old priest smiled, and the wrinkles by his eyes spread across his temples. "I am merely saying that I myself am confounded. Confounded and delighted. As for your question about the church's backing, you must also realize that Mother Griolet did not come to us very often for help."

Gabriella blushed. "Yes, I am not surprised."

"And by this new contract, we will keep St. Joseph's under the church's standing, with minimal aid," David clarified.

"Yes. As M. Cohen has told you, the donations given at the time of the funeral will assure that the orphanage functions smoothly for several years. In that time, the church will decide upon its funding. And of course you have the jewels. I suppose M. Cohen is working on that end with the goldsmith?"

"Yes," David replied. "And then there is the question of the exchange program. It will have to borrow funds from the orphanage at first, until we can find other benefactors. But I am not worried. My father has several ideas." He grinned at Gabriella. "Old friends from Princeton whose kids are college-age now and just itching for a year abroad."

"Oh, yes, very good of you to mention that, M. Hoffmann," Père Thomas added. "This letter came a few days ago. I opened it only to realize that it would be best for you now, considering the circumstances." Père Thomas shuffled through a stack of papers, retrieved a letter, and handed it to David. Then the priest stood up, shaking hands with Gabriella and David. "God be with you, children. You are taking on quite a task. I must say, I believe Mother Griolet knew what she was doing when she picked you. *Au revoir.* Don't hesitate to call if you need anything." He smiled warmly.

As they left his office, David skimmed the letter he had just received. "Hey, listen to this, Gabby. It's from Caroline Harland's father, sending his condolences for Mother Griolet's death. He says that he has contacted his friends and that, under the circumstances, they are willing to continue their support if the right director is found."

"And you think they'll approve of you, after all the heartache you've caused Caroline?" Gabriella teased.

"Of course! All is forgiven," David countered quickly. "He even says Caroline will be coming back for another year."

Gabriella's face went white. "No . . . "

David picked her up in his arms and kissed her hard on the mouth. "Just kidding!"

She flashed her eyes. "Honestly, David. You are always looking for a reaction! And you usually get one!"

He took her hands and led her beside the fountain of the Three Graces on the Place de la Comedie. "Gabby," he said, "Now that the question of our jobs is settled, is there any reason we shouldn't get married soon? Right in Castelnau, while our families and friends are here with us?"

"Are you serious? We couldn't possibly be ready!"

To which he raised his eyebrows, pulled her close to him, and murmured, "I've been ready for a long time."

* * *

They were still discussing the idea of an impromptu wedding two hours later, as they stepped off the bus in Castelnau. "All emotions aside, my dear Gabby, it only makes sense. If we're married, we can share Mother Griolet's apartment. We'll both be right there at St. Joseph's should any emergency arise in the night."

Gabriella pursed her lips and pouted. "Purely for practical reasons, you say."

"Oh, come on, Gab. Of course not. But think about it. It would work."

"David, I feel like my head will explode with decisions. How can I know? It seems that for the year I've known you we've only jumped from one crisis to the next, one wild adventure to another. I wish I had some time just to get to know you, the way normal people do. You know, I think it's called dating."

"You're right, dear girl. But as long as we're doing everything else backward, couldn't we start being normal after we're married? We'll be legal and can do whatever we jolly well please. I'll even take you on a two-week honeymoon to Paris and Switzerland."

"You will? How? We've got our jobs to do."

He flashed her a smile. "Leave it to me. There are many willing souls around here right now. I'll bet the Madison family could be persuaded to stick around a few more weeks to help out while we go away. And my dad is having a blast here. He keeps prolonging his leave of absence. And Moustafa's mom and sisters. Hey, it'll work. Piece of cake."

"It sounds so nice," she sighed. "David, I'm so very, very tired. Let me rest for a while. You do what you want, just let me rest for a few days."

"Good idea!" he said and scooped her up in his arms. He carried her across the cobblestones, as she settled comfortably against him. She handed him her keys, and he let them into Mme Leclerc's apartment, where he laid her gently on her bed.

Bending down, he kissed her softly. "To bed with you, my dear. Sweet dreams. I'll work it out. And I don't want to see you until breakfast tomorrow, understand?"

She smiled up at him dreamily as she kicked off her shoes and snuggled beneath the sheets. She hardly remembered him leaving the room. She was already dreaming of a long white dress.

*   *   *

It was not the first time David had seen Moustafa, but it was the first time they had been alone since their planned escape had failed in Algiers. The two friends regarded each other with a mixture of compassion and awe.

"I never expected to see you again."

"No," Moustafa smiled wryly. "I imagine not."

"How did it happen? Rémi mentioned a woman in Philippeville who cared for you. But how?"

"There were perhaps what you call angels around me. I do not know. I only remember that I was lying by the dock, waiting for Hacène, when the massacre began. It was too gruesome to describe."

David nodded. "I saw it."

"I saw Hacène pushed off the boat, and . . . " He bent his head down, as if feeling the agony again. " . . . Slain. I was transfixed with terror—I couldn't move. There was no escape. An Arab soldier found me lying there, and with hate and satisfaction gleaming in his eyes, he stabbed me, twice. He would have slit my throat, only, right then, from out in the harbor, floating up to me in the midst of the bedlam, I heard it. My name. Shouted, fervent.

"The FLN soldier heard it too. It distracted him. He called over a comrade and went to the water's edge, firing into the water. In that brief time, I managed to pull myself under the corpses of two other *harkis,* and that was my shelter from the butchery. It was a blessing that my wounds were cruel and deep, for I fainted from loss of blood. I guess the soldiers thought I was dead." Moustafa paused and rubbed his chin.

"I expected to die there. But much later I woke up to a terrible silence. Bodies everywhere. My compatriots, my brother." Moustafa closed his eyes and wiped his hand over his face. "I began crawling out from under those dead bodies. They had concealed me. They saved my life. Ironic, isn't it? Why me? I crawled back to the water, petrified that the soldiers were watching. But as it turns out, only a poor Arab woman with kind eyes saw me. And she came into the bloody square. Can you imagine the courage it took? The courage and iron will to walk past the slaughter and drag me to the safety of her apartment?

"I must have lain there for two weeks, coming in and out of consciousness. Until one day I opened my eyes and asked her to take me to Rémi's house."

David whistled softly. "What a remarkable story."

"I still wonder about the voice calling my name, distracting the soldier. It was like a messenger from heaven."

"It was I," David said simply. Moustafa's eyes grew wide, and David shrugged. "We swam, Rémi and I, toward the dock, the boat. I couldn't see you, but I screamed your name, twice. Then when the soldiers came to the water's edge, we knew we had to leave."

"You?" Moustafa shook his head and grinned. "I should have known. You promised you would get me out, and you did. You're a pretty rough-looking angel, I might add."

They clasped hands and held the grip, neither saying a word. Finally Moustafa asked, "Why? Why did I survive? What do you call it? Luck?"

"I call it an answer to prayer."

Moustafa leaned back in the bed, his eyes closed. "An answer to prayer. Yes, I believe you are right."

* * *

Later, as David saw Moustafa's strength waning, he asked, "When are they going to let you out of here anyway?"

"In a week, they say."

"Good. Then you'll be able to make it to my wedding."

Moustafa's surprise was complete. "Your wedding? So soon?"

"I figured we might as well do it while we have all the family and friends in one spot. Who knows when that will happen again."

"And your girl, Gabriella? What does she think?"

David laughed. "Poor Gabby. Completely overwhelmed. She panicked at first, declaring that we weren't ready, that it couldn't be done. But I promised her a two-week honeymoon, complete with Paris and Switzerland. She has reconsidered."

Moustafa laughed heartily. "You are a strange man, David Hoffmann. I must meet this Gabriella, you know. Imagine! A wedding! So soon. Well, just tell me the date, and I will be there."

"And what about you? And Anne-Marie?"

"At first I thought it perhaps too soon. I didn't want to impose." He made a tight fist. "I think I'm afraid that, now that she has the farmhouse, she won't want me. You know, in Algeria, the bridegroom presents his bride with a lot of gold jewelry. Many men work for years to be able to have this dowry. I have nothing to give her."

David thumped his friend's head playfully. "You're crazy! Anne-Marie would do anything to be with you. And she is *pied-noir*. She's not bound to Algerian customs. She is a very loyal woman. And she loves you. She loves you with the right kind of love."

"Yes, I know. I know."

"I'll be going now." David turned in the doorway. "Don't wait too long, Moustafa. She needs to know."

* * *

He had said the phrase almost glibly to Moustafa. *An answer to prayer.* But as David walked out of the hospital toward his car, he did not feel glib. He felt, instead, tears stinging his eyes. How did this God work? It was too far above and beyond him to be understood. In his rage and folly and helplessness, he had jumped into a polluted harbor and screamed out foolishly for Moustafa. It had been a weak and desperate attempt. Yet God had used it, supported it with His own divine design, to save his friend's life.

"Forgive me for hating You," David prayed silently as the *deux chevaux* bumped its way back to Castelnau. It wasn't simply that Moustafa had survived that awed him. It was the way he had survived. David had played a part in the end, and now the knowledge of that strengthened his faith. It was that complex weaving of lives, that tapestry that Mother Griolet had talked about.

He doubted he would ever understand. But it was one more thread, this one bright red in his memory, that he would hold onto for the rest of his life. He breathed deeply, thought of the thread running through so many lives: Moustafa's, Anne-Marie's, Ophélie's, even his father's. That made him shake his head and lift his eyebrows, perplexed. And of course, Gabriella's. With a picture of her face in his mind, he thought of the red thread being tied into a simple knot as Gabby became his wife. This too was past comprehension.

He parked his car on the cobblestones and walked to the church, a humbled man. It moved him to think of it all. It hurt, a deep, piercing hurt that healed with its intensity. He entered the chapel, walked between the empty pews, and knelt in front of the stained-glass window and the stone altar. "You really are in control, aren't You?" The same piercing hurt again. He laughed; he cried; he sobbed. "Thank You."

* * *

When Anne-Marie saw Moustafa at the hospital that day,

she bubbled over with enthusiasm about the farmhouse in Lodève. "The *harkis* are moving to the city. M. Krugler is already working among them. Can you imagine, Moustafa? We can all move there, to Lodève. You and your family, Ophélie and me. We can help him with his work."

Moustafa, who was sitting up in bed and laughing, pulled Anne-Marie close to him. "I don't want you to think I am taking advantage of a good situation," he joked, "but Anne-Marie . . . " His voice became serious. "I want you to marry me. I want us to be together forever. Will you?"

She let him hold her in his arms and said softly, "I thought you would never ask."

"Is that a yes?"

"It is a yes, my love." She pushed the curls from his face and kissed him softly.

"I didn't believe this moment would actually arrive. I am so very thankful." He furrowed his brow. "But I have nothing to give you."

"Hush, now, Moustafa. You have given me yourself, forever. It is far better than I had hoped. It is a miracle." She kissed his lips, his forehead, his hands. "Rest, my love. Get well. I will be waiting for you. Now we have a place to call our own."

* * *

Gabriella slept straight through the night and late into the next morning. It was an exhausted, deep sleep without dream or movement. When she awoke, her mother was sitting in a chair by her bedside, reading to herself from Gabriella's anthology of English literature.

"Sleeping Beauty awakes." Rebecca Madison laid down the book and brushed a few hairs from Gabriella's face. "How do you feel, sweetheart?"

"Groggy." Gabriella sat up in bed, stretched and yawned. "But better. Much better. And I'm starving." She hopped out of bed, her feet touching the cool tiles, and went to the large oak armoire. Opening the heavy doors, she turned back around to her mother. "What have I missed, Mama, while I've been sleeping?"

She heard her mother laugh and, at the same moment, she gave a gasp. Hanging in the armoire was an exquisite white wedding dress. Gabriella felt the smooth, cool silk material. "What is this?"

"Well, my dear, it seems that while you have slept, your charming fiancé has planned a wedding."

"He has?"

"Yes, would you like to know the date?"

Gabriella gulped. "I don't know. What do you think?"

Rebecca smiled, hugging her daughter. "It's planned for August 25th. Everyone insisted we must wait for Mme Pons and Mme Leclerc to return from their *vacances*. And that will give you two time after the wedding for a honeymoon before David needs to be back for the week of orientation in the exchange program."

As she spoke, Rebecca took the white dress from the armoire and draped it across the bed. "It will coincide nicely with our plans too. We can be here to help with the children while you and David are away, and still get back to America by September 15th when Jessica and Henrietta's school begins."

As if in a trance, Gabriella had undressed and now lifted her arms as Rebecca slipped the dress over her head. "Oh, my, there are a hundred buttons in the back," her mother commented. She led her daughter to the mirror over the porcelain sink. "But at least you can get an idea." She took a few straight pins from her pocket and pulled the dress closed in the back, pinning it in place. Then she quickly braided Gabriella's thick hair in a French braid and let it fall over one shoulder.

"Mama," Gabriella gasped again. "It is the most gorgeous dress I've ever seen." She turned to the side, admiring the snug bodice and the modestly sloping neckline that gave her a slight cleavage.

"French silk. You can't get any better than that."

"But where did it come from?" She wheeled around and grabbed her mother's hands. "Am I dreaming? You tell me my wedding has been planned while I slept, and now my dress has appeared magically in my armoire."

"Yes, that's right," said Rebecca matter-of-factly, with a hint of humor in her voice. She pulled at the sides of the dress. "And with minimal alterations, it will fit you just fine."

"Mother! Tell me!"

"It came from St. Joseph's. You should have seen Sister Isabelle's face last night when David announced that the wedding would be taking place in Castelnau. I thought the dear nun might pop with excitement. She raced out of the room and when she reappeared, she was holding this dress and explaining, out of breath, that it had been given to St. Joseph's years ago by a wealthy woman in Castelnau.

"Even though the Sisters saw no need for it, they could not bear to give it away. It's been waiting all these years for you." She examined Gabriella, walking around her. "You look radiant." Then she caught her daughter in her arms and hugged her fiercely.

"Oh, Gabriella. I know this is all so wild and new. And of course, we are only half serious. David is waiting to know what you think. My child, you are beautiful." Rebecca's voice faltered for a moment.

"Mama, can it be true? Do you think me a light-headed dreamer? Am I crazy to marry him so soon?"

"Gabriella, when I was twenty-one, I had been married two years and you were on the way. We moved to Africa only weeks after our wedding. It was so hard to be far away from everyone. We struggled. But God drew us close because we only had each other and Him."

"Thank you, Mama." Gabriella twirled around again, sneaking another peek in the mirror. Then she put her hand to her mouth. "There's no time to waste. I've got to find David! We have so many plans to make!"

* * *

It was Mme Dramchini who brought Ophélie and Hussein to the hospital later that afternoon. Hussein stayed with the Arab woman in the hall while Ophélie timidly knocked on the door. It reminded her of visiting her father when he had been at this same hospital a few months ago.

She stepped into the room and studied Moustafa. He was asleep. He looked very peaceful. She did not want to wake him. She tiptoed to the side of the bed, bent over, and kissed his tangled hair. Its smooth, tight texture had always fascinated her, and now she touched it with her hand.

Moustafa's eyes flickered open. She had always liked his eyes too. They were a delicious looking chocolate brown, warm, inviting.

"Ophélie," he murmured. "Dear child, how good it is to see you."

She sat lightly on the bed and grasped his hands. "Oh, Moustafa! I knew you would come back! I knew you were not dead. You were the very last pony to come, but you made it."

He wrinkled his brow. "Pony?"

Ophélie produced her colored picture. "See," she said, pointing to the brown pony, running behind a group of others. "See, that's you. You caught up after all."

"I remember now, Ophélie. You drew it for your papa. Yes, he showed it to me in Algeria."

Ophélie threw her arms around Moustafa's neck, burying her head in his curls. "I knew you would come back. I prayed to God every day. And now everyone is here. No one is lost. Even Mother Griolet, see here?" She pointed to the gray pony. "She has just gone ahead of us, to Jesus. I wish you could have known her."

"Me too, little one."

She touched his cheek. It was wet. "Did I make you cry?"

Moustafa shook his head and swallowed. "Happy tears, Ophélie. Do you know what I mean?"

"Oh, yes! I know what happy tears are!"

Moustafa scooted up in bed, took Ophélie's hands, and asked, "Has your mama told you the good news?"

"About the farmhouse?" she said eagerly.

"Yes, the farmhouse, but also . . . has she told you that we are all going to live there together? You and Mama and me."

She furrowed her brow. "No, she didn't say it."

"I'm going to marry your mama, Ophélie. Is that all right with you?"

The child's eyes grew wide; she clapped her hands together. "Oh yes. Oh yes! Now I see. It will all work out. Papa will marry Bribri, and you will marry Mama. Then it will be like I have two mamas and two papas." She laughed, then grew serious. "I guess it wouldn't work for you to marry Gabriella and Papa to marry Mama?"

Moustafa laughed. "No, dear, I don't think so."

She contemplated the idea. "Then this will be fine. I am a very lucky girl."

Then, "There is someone who wants to see you, Moustafa," Ophélie confided. Then she whispered into his ear, "Please don't be mad at him. He's been so very worried."

Ophélie left the room. Moustafa guessed whom Ophélie meant and closed his eyes, exhausted from his visits. He heard the door open again, but did not look up immediately. He had no desire to see the boy.

Someone cleared his throat, "Hunhmm."

"Hello, Hussein," Moustafa said without looking up.

"Hello, Moustafa," the boy answered.

In sharp contrast to the ethereal feeling from his time with Ophélie, quite suddenly Moustafa felt the room draw round him, close and confining. Almost suffocating. He felt a stab of hatred, remembered helping the boy, remembered learning of his betrayal. He could not bear to look at him.

The boy did not move and at length, Moustafa opened his eyes. Hussein stood in the middle of the room, shoulders slumped, looking very small and very vulnerable, like a frightened puppy.

"Come sit down, Hussein," he said, but the words were dry in his mouth, like cotton.

Mechanically the boy obeyed. He stared blankly around the room, a hollowness in his eyes. He sniffed twice.

"How are you, Hussein?"

The boy fumbled with his hands, staring down at them. "Fine."

"Doing okay in France?"

He nodded.

"I'm glad you got out of Algeria."

Suddenly the boy burst into tears, leaned forward, and grabbed Moustafa by the shoulders. "I'm so sorry. It was all my fault. I don't know how you got here, Moustafa, but seeing you here means that maybe, maybe I can go on." He sobbed for a moment, out of control, then composed himself. "I know what I did was wrong, but I didn't know what else to do. I was so afraid. Can you forgive me?"

Moustafa closed his hand softly around the boy's neck. These words were not rehearsed. They rang true, coming up from the deepest part of his soul. "It's okay, Hussein. Everything is okay."

Pronouncing the words, Moustafa looked away, out the window. At fourteen, he had run through the orange groves with Anne-Marie. He had dreamed of an impossibility and followed it all his life. And today, his stubborn hope had paid off. He had a feeling it was not at all his hope so much as that little phrase that both David and Ophélie had said. An answer to prayer.

Compassion welled up within Moustafa and warmed him, like a gulp of hot mint tea going down his throat. Maybe this boy deserved a chance too. He had hardly had time to dream in his short lifetime. "I forgive you, Hussein."

* * *

The letter from Hussein could not have arrived at a better time, according to Ali Boudani. On this the fourth of August, Ben Bella took his position as Head of State in Algeria. He immediately began in his charismatic way to put into place the socialist government he had planned for the newly independent state. Ali's hopes for his own future seemed secure with this appointment. And today, he also had news from Hussein.

Ali ripped open the envelope and perused the letter, nodding with satisfaction. "Ha, it is no more, this orphanage! No more." He frowned to read of Hussein's planned suicide. Why would the boy choose that? He had other plans for him. A moment of doubt registered on Ali's face. Where were the newspaper articles attesting to the explosions, the deaths? Why had Hussein neglected to send the proof?

It frustrated him that his satisfaction could not be certain and therefore complete. The urge to power and the need for revenge were in conflict now, and Ali had to choose. To push forward or to remain in the past. To trust the letter of an adolescent boy and put it out of his mind, or to find someone else to carry out his anger and revenge. He wondered why he could never find the blessed peace that came from being totally satisfied. Why did he crave the power?

It gnawed at him, as if he were ravenously hungry. But the pain inside could not be abated with food. Perhaps if he climbed high enough, became truly important to the new Algeria, perhaps then he would fill the shoes that his father had left empty so abruptly.

Nothing could be sure in this life, he reasoned. He tore the letter into fine, small pieces. "Father, you are avenged. Quiet now my soul." He held the torn pieces in his clutched fists as tears ran down his cheeks. "You are avenged, Father!" He spoke loudly now, almost shouting. "Avenged!"

He stood, limped pitifully to a trash can, deposited the letter, and threw in a match. "Good-bye, Father. Good-bye, Hussein." He watched the paper curl and turn red and then black. Still the pain gnawed at him. Still he cried. He fell back into his chair, grasping his head in his hands, agony written on his face.

"Is there no peace?" he cried out. "Is there no peace?" Ali Boudani did not have the answer to that question. Algeria was free, but he felt no peace inside. He swore to himself that he would spend the rest of his life trying to find it.

Chapter 33

It seemed perfectly appropriate that the wedding of Gabriella Madison and David Hoffmann have a mixture of European and American flair. The simple ceremony was to take place in the chapel of St. Joseph at 4 o'clock on August 25; later that evening, in true French fashion, the reception was scheduled to be a seven-course meal in the refectory that lasted all night long. Gabriella insisted on bridesmaids, an American tradition, choosing her sisters and Anne-Marie, with Ophélie as a flower girl. But she also insisted that David's *deux chevaux* be covered, not with tin cans and toilet paper, but rather with carnations as she had seen so often in wedding processions in France.

"You're a bundle of nerves, Gab," Jessica laughed, as she helped her sister with the buttons on the back of her wedding gown.

Gabriella bit her lip nervously. "I know it. I can't believe it. I'm marrying David today!"

Mme Leclerc's apartment had been transformed into a bride's parlor with Henrietta, Jessica, Anne-Marie, and Ophélie busily putting on the pastel Provençal print dresses that Rebecca Madison had made for them. They crowded around the one small mirror over the sink in Gabriella's room until Mme Leclerc came in and saw them pinching their cheeks and trying to apply makeup.

"For goodness' sakes, girls! Come back to my room. I have a proper mirror, the whole length of the armoire."

They followed after her, giggling and primping, so that Gabriella and her mother were left in the room alone. As Rebecca plaited a small strand of Gabriella's hair, she interlaced it with baby's breath. Then she observed the wedding gown, which, after minimal alterations, now fit Gabriella like a glove.

"You're glowing!" her mother attested.

Gabriella hugged Rebecca tightly.

"Oh, Mother! Do I really look all right?"

"Perfect, sweetheart. Perfect."

Gabriella took a deep breath. "Well then, I guess I'm ready!"

* * *

Mme Leclerc watched the women leave for the chapel. *"Ooh là là! Ma fille!"* she exclaimed, kissing Gabriella's cheek. "There's never been a prettier bride." When the apartment was empty, Mme Leclerc scurried around, putting on her fanciest dress and pinning her hat with the lace veil in place. She grabbed her purse and hurried into the street toward Monique Pons' apartment.

They were both delighted with the change of events that had transpired during their vacation. They had returned three days ago to find the town abuzz with news. The orphanage was staying open, the exchange program would continue also, the Madisons were still in Castelnau, and best of all, Gabriella and David were getting married. Imagine! Two Americans getting married at St. Joseph's, right here in Castelnau. And she and Mme Pons were invited to the meal after the ceremony. She hummed to herself. Such excitement!

"Do you think they'll want to stay here with me?" Mme

Leclerc asked Mme Pons. "I mean, they will have to have a place to live, the young couple."

"With you, Yvette! Nonsense. M. Hoffmann has already arranged everything. While they're gone on their honeymoon, the fathers of the young couple are going to give Mother Griolet's apartment a fresh coat of paint. Mrs. Madison will make curtains and the like. Oh, they're turning it into a little love nest. No, don't you worry! At least they'll have a little bit of privacy." The old woman rolled her eyes, then continued.

"And M. Hoffmann assures me that enrollment for the new year is not down. We'll both have new boarders. He says, that sly M. Hoffmann, that he expects the enrollment to double once the young ladies hear that a wedding took place after a couple met at St. Joseph's!"

They laughed merrily, then took turns pinning a corsage on each other's dress. "For the groom's beloved landlady," Mme Leclerc giggled.

"And for the bride's adoring *proprietaire*," Mme Pons cooed. "Just as we predicted. Now we really are practically related!"

* * *

The bride was indeed radiant, her flaming hair swept delicately back with a short lace veil covering her face and baby's breath sprinkled in her hair. Everything was jumping inside of Gabriella, and she was sure she must look delirious with joy. That was how she felt as she walked down the aisle beside her father. She nodded to the small group of family and friends gathered in the chapel as she slowly walked past them: Pierre and Denise Cabrol, Madeleine de Saléon, Henri Krugler, Edouard Auguste, Joseph and Emeline Cohen, Moustafa's mother and sisters, Mme Leclerc and Mme Pons, Eliane and Rémi with their three children, Sister Rosaline and Sister Isabelle and all the orphans. Gabriella's mother sat in the front row.

At the altar stood her bridesmaids, Jessica, Henrietta, and Anne-Marie, beaming back at her. Ophélie clutched a small woven basket filled with real rose petals from the bushes in the courtyard of the orphanage. From Mme Pons' old phonograph played Purcell's Trumpet Tune. The scene before Gabriella seemed enveloped in a kind of hazy cloud.

And mostly, there was David, tall and erect, smiling at her with that vulnerable look on his face, a look of awe and fascination and love. He wore a black pin-striped suit that matched his eyes. Beside him stood his father, Jean-Louis, and Moustafa.

William Madison presided over the ceremony. Having walked his daughter down the aisle, he then placed Gabriella's hand in David's and turned to face the congregation. Gabriella watched her father with pride, holding on to his every word. "Marriage is a solemn ceremony and a joyful celebration. It is the first sacrament prescribed by God in the Bible. 'Therefore a man shall leave his father and mother and cleave to his wife and the two shall become one flesh.'" He paused several times to clear his throat.

Gabriella looked up at David. He seemed so serious, stiff, staring intently at William Madison. She squeezed his hand, and his eyes met hers. She raised one eyebrow to remind him that it was she he should be focusing on. He squeezed her hand back and throughout the rest of the ceremony, his black, shining eyes never left hers.

* * *

Sister Isabelle and Sister Rosaline sat behind Rebecca Madison, giggling together and intermittently shooting warning glances at the children, some of whom were making paper airplanes to throw at the happy couple when they left on their honeymoon.

"A novel idea," Sister Rosaline had chuckled when Sister Isabelle had threatened to take the paper away. "Let them have fun."

Now the children rose and from their place in the pews, began to sing "Joyful, Joyful We Adore Thee." Several of the smallest children waved to Gabriella and David as they sang.

Mme Pons and Mme Leclerc sat side by side, wiping their eyes and whispering throughout the whole ceremony, "Now didn't we just know it! I told you that M. Hoffmann would come through." And while the bride and groom repeated their vows, Mme Pons stole a glance at the groom's father, who looked quite sophisticated himself this morning.

William Madison concluded the ceremony with a few final reflections. "God has brought you two together through the most remarkable of circumstances. He has called you to Himself. May you remember that as long as He is the focal part of your marriage, whatever difficulties you may encounter, He will bring you through. Trust Him, my dear young friends."

When at last William Madison pronounced the happy couple husband and wife, David lifted Gabriella's veil and kissed her for a long moment. The children grew restless, giggling among themselves. Christophe whispered "Yuck" and then, in spite of themselves, the whole audience broke into applause as the couple walked down the aisle and out into the bright August sun.

* * *

Each course in the meal was followed by a dance or some type of light entertainment. David and Gabriella were amazed at the silly skits and poems their friends and family came up with during the evening. The refectory had been transformed into a celebration hall, all the tables adorned with flower arrangements and candles.

Halfway through the meal, at 10 o'clock, the Dramchini women hurried the children off to bed to dream of the beautiful bride and her dashing groom. As they left, the boys sent a vast array of paper airplanes floating toward David's plate. The girls came and sprinkled rose petals onto Gabriella's white dress. Then Ophélie sat in David's lap.

"I'm so happy for you, Papa. And you too, Bribri." She hugged them tightly and whispered, "This is even better than I imagined!"

David held his daughter closely. He looked to Gabriella so tender and mature, a kindness written on his face. The cocky allure, the arrogance was no longer evident. He had changed so much in this short year. She ached inside watching him with Ophélie. Could it truly be that he was her husband? It took her breath away.

It was 4 A.M. when the meal was finished and the good-byes said. Rebecca caught Gabriella in a long embrace. "God be with you, my dear. And have a wonderful time!"

She wondered in that moment if her mother had been afraid when she had married her father. It was not exactly fear. It was anticipation.

Roger Hoffmann drove the young couple to a secluded inn amidst the vineyards in a small village outside of Montpellier. David shook his father's hand and met his eyes. "Have a delightful honeymoon, Son. Congratulations! You have made an excellent choice, if I do say so myself!" He kissed Gabriella on the cheek, got back in the car, and drove off.

Gabriella's eyes were shining as David registered with the night clerk who led them to a gracious suite overlooking the swimming pool. The door was barely closed when they fell into one another's arms, laughing and giggling. "Mrs. Hoffmann," David whistled. "My, but you look exquisite!" He twirled her around him, admiring his bride. Then he added, "But don't you want to get into something a little more comfortable?"

"Yes," she agreed, blushing. "But you'll have to help me." She lifted her hair off her neck, her back turned to David. For one moment he looked perplexed, studying the long row of silk-covered buttons. "This will take me all night to get undone."

Gabriella laughed, her soft, lilting voice charming him.

"No need to hurry, my love. We have all the time in the world now."

* * *

Henri liked the wiry young Arab the first time he laid eyes on him. The young man made no apologies for his pained movements or slowness, but worked beside Henri without complaint, painting, hammering, fixing up. Moustafa was a good man for Anne-Marie, Henri concluded. This old *mas* was going to suit them well. There were bedrooms enough for Mme Dramchini and Saiyda and Rachida each to have her own. The little apartment at the end of the hall would give Moustafa and Anne-Marie their privacy, with a small, adjoining room for Ophélie.

As they worked up on the roof in the blazing heat of the end of August, Moustafa asked Henri questions, and the gentle pastor delighted in answering. "You see what I mean," he concluded on that day. "One God, three distinct personalities. Father, Son, and Holy Spirit. It is a relationship with God."

Henri Krugler breathed heavily in the sun and patted Moustafa on the back. "Keep up your questions. God is not afraid of them."

"M. Krugler. Pastor. I have wanted to ask you. I know this will seem odd. Perhaps you will not agree. But Anne-Marie and I would consider it a great privilege if you would marry us, right here in your church in Lodève." He spoke quickly, as if he were afraid to be reprimanded. "We have spoken of our love for so long. It seems impossible, the cultures that separate us. But we are in love. And we have been through so much. We are not afraid. Will you help us, M. Krugler?"

Henri was too touched to speak. *Would he help them! It was his dream.*

Moustafa frowned as Henri remained silent. "If it is too awkward, we do not have to be married in a church."

"Too awkward. No, my son! There is nothing I would enjoy

more. Nothing." They shook hands on the top of the roof. *An impossible love,* Henri thought. But nothing was impossible with God. Nothing.

* * *

Roger Hoffmann and William Madison worked side by side, not only repainting Mother Griolet's apartment, but also fixing the many items in disrepair throughout the orphanage. "Oh, to have men at St. Joseph's who have the time to do handywork!" Sister Rosaline had enthused. "It is a gift from our Father."

At first they worked in silence, but gradually William Madison's patient questions gave Roger the desire to speak. He found, to his great surprise, that this missionary man was not so odd as he had thought. He was intelligent, well-traveled, thoroughly up to date on the events in the world. That surprised Roger the most. How could a man living in the bush country of Africa among tribespeople with no modern conveniences understand so well the world situation? By the end of the week, Roger Hoffmann had a budding respect for the father of his new daughter-in-law.

He also began to appreciate Rebecca Madison, who spent the week sewing curtains for the newlyweds while her daughters helped with the hemming. These women were ingenious. On a shoestring budget, they were turning the old apartment into a warm haven of colors and creativity. It gave Roger a lot to think about. He found himself looking forward to getting to know this family better, and surprised himself by inviting them to visit him in Washington in the spring.

The orphans were often underfoot, scrubbing and cleaning throughout the parsonage. This too pleased Roger. It had been so long since he had been around children. He spent one afternoon in town with his granddaughter, Ophélie, and found real pleasure being with her. He thought for a fleeting moment about other grandchildren, then shook his head and chuckled. He was growing sentimental. It was high time to get back to Washington.

On the first of September, he accompanied the whole troop of children to the beach with the Madisons. Even the Sisters put on casual clothes and headed to the sea, only fifteen minutes away. Most of the vacationers had already left so that the children had a long stretch of beach to themselves. He liked watching the little ones diving under waves while Sister Rosaline stood at the water's edge, giggling as the foamy water touched her pudgy toes. Every once in a while she yelled, "Oh Jérémy! Christophe! *Non!* You're too far out in the water. Come back. For heaven's sake. Come back!"

Roger laughed and laughed until his sides ached. It felt so good. Was he getting used to this Mediterranean lifestyle? Grief! It was time to go home.

* * *

After numerous phone calls between Joseph Cohen in Geneva and Henri Krugler in Lodève, they were most pleased with the progress they had made. Many *pied-noirs* and *harkis* throughout France had heard through word of mouth about the rescued children at St. Joseph's. Some adoptions were pending. Other families gladly agreed to take in foster children. Amazingly, a few Algerian parents escaped from Algeria and found their children in Castelnau.

And throughout France, those who had come to Mother Griolet's funeral or had heard the news of her death began to respond to the overcrowded situation. A number of orphans who years ago had found a home at St. Joseph's and then had been adopted, wrote to say that they themselves were interested in adopting a child. In a whirlwind of activity, Joseph Cohen and Henri Krugler secured homes for many of the children at St. Joseph's. Before the end of the year of 1962, by their calculations, the orphanage would once again house under thirty children.

Henri Krugler was truly worried for only one child: Hussein. No *harki* family wanted to take in an Arab child. They looked the same, these *harkis* and Arabs, but the war had made them enemies. The boy did not really fit in anywhere. He would probably end up staying at St. Joseph's with the French children, Henri reflected. At least the boy was safe. Things could be much worse.

* * *

"Mmm, this is heaven," Gabriella murmured, stretching and staring at the Swiss mountains outside the picture window. She cuddled up against David, and was surprised again with how natural, how right, that simple movement felt. Husband and wife.

She reflected that the week at Joseph and Emeline Cohen's chalet in Switzerland had been the ideal way to start their married life. There had been long walks through the mountains past the cows jiggling their lazy heads, time to taste the strong Swiss cheeses and eat *fondue* as the nights cooled ever so slightly. And mostly, there had just been time. Time to know each other and begin to learn how to love.

On their last afternoon there, Gabriella insisted on leaving the chalet, as she had at least once every day. "Otherwise, people will ask us what we did all the time, and what will we say?"

David picked her up, squeezing her hard. "I love you, Gabby. My angel! What will we say?" He grabbed her, and they toppled on the bed together, laughing. "We'll say, 'What do you think a young couple would do on their honeymoon! I bet you can't even guess.'"

Gabriella's face turned red as David smothered her with kisses. "Just guess . . ."

* * *

Anne-Marie grew impatient during the two weeks Gabriella

and David were gone on their honeymoon. She had such wonderful news! Moustafa wanted for them to get married as soon as the *mas* was ready. Day after day he worked alongside Henri Krugler, making the place into their home. Henri talked of hiring Moustafa as his assistant at the *centre aéré*. This plus the funds from her father would be adequate money to start with. It seemed to both of them a small fortune. They had lived so long on nothing.

Anne-Marie and Ophélie spent the afternoons at the farmhouse in Lodève rearranging furniture, cleaning spots where paint had been spilt, giving the place a feminine touch. Often Anne-Marie found herself standing beside the couch, caressing it lovingly with her fingers, remembering the time gone by, when it sat in the farmhouse in Algiers. She could almost hear her father's stern voice becoming soft as he held baby Ophélie.

When Anne-Marie shook herself back to the present, she was smiling. Her father had loved her, cared immensely for Ophélie. He had provided for them. She had been loved by him, and now she was loved by Moustafa. They had a lifetime in front of them, and nothing, not the prejudice or difficulties, could change that. They had survived. God be praised. Yes, this God really did seem to be in control, not only of the universe, but also of her life. He was trustworthy, and He was in charge.

Anne-Marie wondered at all the people who had showed up in her life in the past year. It was like Mother Griolet's image of a tapestry, the many-colored threads inching themselves through her life, weaving their pattern of hope and faith. She told herself then that the waiting, the impossible months of waiting and wondering, had been worth it. She too had discovered something, Someone, during that time. Perhaps if things had gone more smoothly, she would have never taken the time to seek and to understand.

She did not know. All she knew was that when Eliane came that afternoon to take her shopping for a wedding suit, she was going to buy white. She felt clean, pure, and what was it? Ah yes, forgiven. She was no longer condemned. This God accepted her as she was. And so did Moustafa. She had gotten her new chance after all.

* * *

Eliane and Anne-Marie came back from shopping, their faces glowing. "We've found the perfect suit for the wedding," Eliane confided to Rémi and Moustafa. "But that's all we'll tell you for now."

The two couples sipped *tisane* in the den of the farmhouse, talking excitedly. "I want to hear about you," Anne-Marie insisted. "I've been talking on and on, and we haven't even heard. What have you found?"

"An apartment on the west side of Montpellier. Many *pied-noirs* are moving into the complex."

"Oh, so you won't have a yard?"

"No, not yet, but after three months in a hotel room, this apartment looks pretty good." She sounded, as always, cheery and optimistic. "And Rémi has several leads for work. It will all be fine." She leaned back against Rémi. They seemed so happy just to be together. They shared a cozy familiarity, an easy intimacy that came, Anne-Marie suspected, from years of living together, sharing dreams, hurts, practicalities. She hoped she and Moustafa would grow into that same kind of love.

"Oh, I almost forgot! We brought your wedding gift," Eliane exclaimed. She motioned to Rémi, who slipped outside and came back a few minutes later carrying the old trunk which had brought Moustafa to France.

"You can't give this away!" Anne-Marie cried. "It's an heirloom."

Eliane shook her head. "No. It held my heirlooms. But this trunk is for you two." She suddenly looked at Rémi, unsure. "If you want it, that is."

"Of course we do. What a lovely idea." Anne-Marie kissed

Eliane softly on the cheeks. "You do like it, don't you, Moustafa?"

The young man grinned. "Let's just say I'm glad I can be observing it from the outside."

"Well then, open it up!" Rémi said.

Moustafa lifted the lid and laughed. Anne-Marie came alongside and peered in the trunk. It was filled with towels and sheets.

"A young couple's got to have something to start out with," Rémi explained.

"Oh, Eliane, Rémi. You shouldn't have. You're having to start over yourselves. It's too much." Anne-Marie was genuinely concerned.

"Our pleasure," Eliane reassured her. "Don't forget, these two trunks did eventually bring me my things from Algeria." She reached inside the trunk. "Oh, and there's something else." Lifting the towels and sheets, Eliane brought out a thick black leather Bible with *Moustafa and Anne-Marie* engraved on the front in gold.

The young couple took the book and reverently leafed through its gold-lined pages. "It's beautiful. Really."

"We thought you might as well start out with one together."

Anne-Marie touched Moustafa's hand. "Yes, we have so much to learn . . . together."

* * *

In the end, David did indeed get to introduce Gabriella to Paris. He made his promise good. After Switzerland, they spent a week in the City of Lights. Gabby and Paris. Sisters in love. He only had to make brief introductions, since they had met once before, and the deed was as good as done. Gabby soaked it all up like a sponge and squeezed her enthusiasm back out for David to enjoy.

Late on their last night in Paris, David showed Gabriella where he had found Ophélie by the Pont Neuf. They sat down and leaned against the same lamp post. The air was thick and still, the screams and shouts and treacheries of that October night a mere memory to David. It hardly seemed real. "Do you suppose my finding Ophélie was from God too?"

Gabriella thought for a long time. "I think so. He is in control, completely in control. He uses the good and the bad, every circumstance. He is not limited at all, is He, David?"

They moved to the ancient bridge, staring into the Seine.

"I think not. I think He teaches us through it all." He pulled her in front of him, encircling her waist with his long arms, holding her tightly against him. He breathed in deeply. He was sharing Paris with Gabby.

The Seine floated along, steadily, smoothly below them. But there was something deeper than the river, more detailed than the intricate sculptured faces on the facade of Notre Dame. The human soul. It was a vast museum, filled with treasures worth infinitely more than those locked inside the Louvre.

He thought it would take them a very long time to plumb the depths of Paris. It would take him much longer, a whole lifetime, to soak up all the passion and intensity and exuberance that Gabby held in her soul. That was the beauty of it, of sharing a whole life together. Of going ever deeper in the knowing, until they might one day touch the very soul of God.

He did not speak out loud, but with Gabriella cuddled beside him on the bridge, he prayed as he stared at the sky. "Make me worthy of her. Help us to grow together and to grow old together with You. That is all I ask."

* * *

When the young couple returned from their honeymoon, at everyone's insistence, David carried Gabriella over the threshold into their new apartment. Gabriella gasped. It looked new. The walls were lighter, encouraging the sun, the windows outlined by curtains in bright, bold prints. The worn furniture in the den had been replaced with more modern pieces, and there was a double bed in the bedroom.

Gabriella had wondered how it would feel to live in Mother Griolet's apartment. But it was so transformed that it seemed to have taken on a life of its own.

"Thank you! Thank you, everyone. I, I don't know what else to say." She walked into their bedroom. The bed was covered with a thick yellow comforter and half a dozen pillows. "Mother! It looks like something from a designer's magazine! It's beautiful!"

David muttered to her, "Beautiful, sure, but don't expect it to stay like that for long." He politely shooed the happy group of spectators out of the apartment, caught Gabriella in his arms, and whispered, "Welcome home."

* * *

The Madisons and Roger Hoffmann left on the same train for Paris. David was surprised by the funny feeling in the pit of his stomach when his father shook his hand and looked him in the eyes. "You're a good man, Son." His voice cracked slightly. "I hope to see more of you and Gabriella."

It surprised him even more how easily his own words came. "Yes, Dad. We'd like that. We'd like that a lot." His father seemed almost reluctant to let go, his icy blue eyes clouded with tears. One escaped down his cheek. He didn't bother to brush it away.

"Good-bye, David." Roger bit his lip. "I love you." With that he turned, mounted the steps to the train, and disappeared.

* * *

Gabriella's good-bye to her family was filled with hugs and tears, kisses and promises of letters.

"Remember, dear, hold on to the Lord. He will be with you both. You will do a grand job." Rebecca Madison sounded strong and sure, but Gabriella knew she was holding back tears.

"Come on, everyone," her father said, his voice catching.

"The train will be pulling out any minute now."

Gabriella wrapped her arm around David's waist and raised her hand, waving to her family, who pressed their faces against the window and waved back. The whistle blew, the wheels screeched, and the train slowly moved away from the *quai*.

A stabbing pain, a quick fear ran through her. David squeezed her closely to himself. "It's going to be fine, Gabby. We've got each other." She was glad he didn't seem to mind her tears.

Chapter 34

During the fall of 1962, routine murders took place throughout Algeria in the FLN's attempt to rid the country of every last *harki* and his family. For the most part, they were totally successful. For this reason, Selma and her father never talked about the *harki* they had housed in their apartment. It was a badge they wore on their hearts, along with many other secrets.

They prayed to Allah for the new Algeria. The country was in ruins, and many cities resembled deserted battlegrounds. Selma could not look out in the square without remembering the day of bloodshed. From the carnage, one life had been spared. She wondered about the young Arab man. Had he reached France? Had he indeed been saved?

She wondered too what the future held for the *pied-noirs* whose empty stores testified, like sealed tombs, to their flight from this world. Their world. Algeria. Had they found peace in France, among their own? The questions had no answers. Selma's young independent country was struggling, struggling. The birth had been so long and painful. Would the new child survive? She did not know. She only knew that she loved this land. She prayed five times a day to Allah that their costly freedom would bring to them peace at last.

* * *

Throughout France, in pockets of cities, the *pied-noirs* settled among themselves. Perhaps it was their pride in their origins, perhaps it was the distrust of the French, more likely their complete indifference, but early on the lines seemed drawn. The *pied-noirs* were not truly French.

Many struggled to find jobs and rebuild their lives. They appreciated the government loans. Still a bitterness settled in their souls against all that came from President de Gaulle. That traitor. They would never be able to make the French understand how he had betrayed them. The war was over, and that was all that seemed to matter to the French.

Eliane and Rémi saw that the rift was inevitable. But at least their one small family would try to go forward, to forgive and be forgiven. As Eliane put on her fanciest dress, she called out to Rémi, "The excitement of the weddings has certainly brought a bright spot to the situation, *n'est-ce pas?*"

"Quite remarkable the way it has all turned out, Eliane." Rémi came and wrapped his arms around her. "Remarkable, like you."

There was no news from Algeria, but at night, Rémi and Eliane prayed together for their Arab friends, for Abdul and Madira and El Amin and Amar and many others. For their safety and courage to continue, to build back a country.

Eliane was so thankful for the apartment, even if the neighbors seemed a bit cold. There were other *pied-noir* families scattered throughout the building. With them she felt a quick bond. She hoped it would happen with the French. She hoped that the years would not solidify the distance, but rather melt it, bringing them closer. She fiddled with the zipper on her dress, sucking in her tummy as she forced it along.

"How do I look?"

"Lovely. Divine. You'd better hurry me out of here before

I change my mind about the wedding and just decide to stay here and celebrate on our own!"

She pushed him playfully out of the room, retrieved her hat and purse, and picked up baby José who was chewing on a soggy cookie. "Oh dear. Look at you, child. Ah well. *Tant pis.* I don't have time to change you now. We've got to go. We can't be late for Anne-Marie and Moustafa's wedding!"

* * *

One week after Gabriella and David returned from their honeymoon, Anne-Marie and Moustafa were married in the chapel of *le Temple Protestant* in Lodève. They wanted the simplest of ceremonies. No reception. Only let them be married, legally. Anne-Marie tried to rush the time along. Finally. Finally!

She was blushing under the lace veil of her cream-colored hat. She glanced out at Gabriella, who winked back. Eliane was smiling from ear to ear. David and Rémi held their wives close as they watched the bride and groom. Ophélie sat beside David with Mme Dramchini on the other side. The little girl bounced in the pew, whispering, "My mama is sooo beautiful!" loud enough for everyone to hear. Saiyda and Rachida covered their mouths and giggled. Anne-Marie thought she had never been happier. She felt she would burst with emotion. She had friends, she had a family, and now, God be praised, she had a husband. It was impossible, and yet it was true.

She gazed at Moustafa, and a lifetime of memories ran through her mind. He had pursued her, loved her, waited for her without thought of another. A strong, yet tender fidelity. A faithfulness that would not let her go. And now, at last, she was his bride.

She felt radiant, and gazing at Moustafa, he seemed to her the most handsome man, the most perfect husband. His curls had been cut and he had gained several pounds. He was not completely recovered, but she thought she loved him all the more for his scars.

Henri Krugler read a passage of Scripture, and Moustafa was listening intently to every word. "Husbands, love your wives even as Christ also loved the church and gave Himself for it."

They had agreed on a Christian ceremony. This thought brought tears into Anne-Marie's eyes. Apart for all these months, they had each come to believe in the Christ. She was overcome with thankfulness as she considered it.

Near the end of the brief ceremony, several Arab children peeped in the door, whispering and pointing. One stern look from M. Krugler, and they were gone. He pronounced them husband and wife.

Moustafa lifted the net veil and kissed Anne-Marie softly. Then he took her in an embrace, lifted her off the floor, and cried, "At last! You are mine! You are my wife."

He set her down, their eyes met, and they embraced again. Henri Krugler put a hand on Moustafa's shoulder.

"Please remember, my children. I am here for you. Whenever. I am here."

He was a mixture of father and guardian angel, Anne-Marie speculated. Why did he care so for her, for them? How did he find the love in him for two people so different from himself? Amazingly, she believed him. He was here to help and protect a *pied-noir* bride with her *harki* husband. She wondered if it had been planned long ago that M. Krugler's life would be woven into theirs. Perhaps it was back when he had preached in Algeria and her father had believed. She thought that it must go even further back than that, to the heart of a perfect God who had chosen to die for His people. She was thankful.

There were a few angry stares from townspeople milling in the square as the couple left the church, but they did not register with Anne-Marie. She saw only the love in Moustafa's eyes. That same peace came back to carry her along as she received hugs and kisses from David and Gabriella, Eliane and

Rémi. Mme Dramchini smothered her in her big bosom for a moment, saying something in Arabic. The Arab sisters were smiling. It touched Anne-Marie deeply that they had come into this church to watch their brother marry with Christian vows.

Leaving Ophélie for a week was the hardest to bear. She scooped her daughter up in her arms. "*Ma chérie,* you will be fine? You don't mind too much if Mama and Moustafa go away?"

Ophélie squeezed her mother tightly. "Oh, Mama! I'll be okay with Papa and Gabriella. Don't you worry. Only have a really good time." She seemed reluctant to let go. "You will be back soon?"

"One week. I promise. And if you need anything, your papa knows how to reach us."

"She'll be fine," Gabriella assured her. "Now go on!"

* * *

All that Moustafa wanted was a little room hidden from the rest of the world to share with his bride. That had not been hard to arrange. A stone's throw from Lodève, in a tiny village that dated centuries back, they found a room in one of the ancient apartments that now belonged to the village's only hotel. It was cozy and intimate, with low-vaulted ceilings and smooth-worn stones and a double bed. Loving her came so naturally. It was young love, but its roots were already deep and sure. It seemed to Moustafa that the years of waiting only made the gift so much more precious and pleasurable. He could not get over it. He could not get over her.

They spent their days walking on well-trodden paths and eating under vine-covered trellises. They walked hand in hand through the vineyards that stretched out around them like a chessboard. Moustafa closed his eyes. It was almost like Algeria, if he just imagined hard enough, when he had taken the hand of his beautiful, teenage neighbor. And now, after the longest of times, she was his, forever. When he held Anne-

Marie close, it could have been only a moment that had passed between that time and now. The suffering was erased, and all he knew was the fierce, strong love.

* * *

When Anne-Marie and Moustafa returned from their honeymoon, the Dramchini women were waiting for them, grinning from ear to ear. They bustled about the farmhouse, showing the young couple the changes they had made, cooing over the fancy kitchen and the beautiful bedrooms. Then they shooed the couple into their little apartment. The bed was filled with wrapped gifts. Moustafa and Anne-Marie exchanged baffled glances.

"Wherever did they come from? Do you suppose they are really for us?" Inspecting the tags, they found gifts from the Sisters, the Cohens, Gabriella and David, Ophélie, and Henri Krugler. Without unwrapping them, they placed the gifts on the floor and fell onto the bed.

"Welcome home, Mme Dramchini. Welcome home."

There was plenty of work to keep both Henri and Moustafa busy all day and often well into the evenings. For Moustafa, it was like another exquisitely wrapped gift that was being offered to him: the ability to work and work hard. Then at night, he sat at one of the long tables, surrounded by women. *His women,* he thought often to himself, playfully. Sometimes he stared so long and intently at Anne-Marie that the others started teasing and whistling. But he could not help it. She still seemed like a mirage and yet, he was holding her hand.

The farmhouse suited them well. It was big enough to give Moustafa and his bride the privacy they needed, and yet still give his mother and sisters a feeling of belonging there. He appreciated how quickly and fully they accepted Anne-Marie into the family with kindness, letting her fill some of the void left by his father and Hacène.

Impossible love. He considered the words and then smiled.

At least for them, for Anne-Marie and himself, it had worked. They had gotten their impossible love.

Every other week, on Saturday afternoons, Moustafa joined Henri Krugler with a group of Arab teenagers. Each week the number grew as they played sports and board games and talked of their fears and frustrations. These *harki* teens liked the white-haired pastor, and they immediately trusted Moustafa. It was as if his wounds, his struggle, represented a part of each of their lives. When Moustafa spoke of his life, timidly at first, he was surprised that the youths listened intently.

Henri called this informal meeting *Oasis*. That had made Moustafa smile, with a stinging in his eyes. Of course. An oasis. The kids weren't the only ones searching. He too had looked and longed for something strong and intangible. He had not understood at first. But now he knew. He had stumbled onto it, like a famished traveler in the desert. It swept over him, cool and refreshing, full of hope. An oasis for his soul.

* * *

Henri Krugler looked out at his small congregation, smiling at the elderly French who wrinkled their brows and strained to hear his booming voice announce the first hymn. On the other side of the chapel, much farther back, sat a row of Arab kids, huddled together, casting suspicious glances around them.

Moustafa and Anne-Marie entered the chapel with Ophélie. They hesitated, looked at Henri, who waved them in. It was the young couple's first time at the Sunday service. Moustafa rumpled the hair of one of the Arab youths as he walked by, then motioned for the whole group to follow him to the front of the chapel.

Slowly, one by one, the Arabs got out of their seats and moved forward, trailing behind the young couple and the little girl. One elderly French man rose and extended his hand, first to Moustafa and Anne-Marie, then to one of the teenagers. *"Bienvenue,"* he said softly. "Welcome."

It was a humble beginning, Henri mused. But it was a beginning. The first Arabs to attend a service! He stared out at the strange little flock. He swallowed twice, but the lump in his throat did not dislodge itself. "May we all rise," he managed to say. There was a whining as the organ warmed up and the dear old woman pressed her fingers onto the keys to form the first chord. It resounded in the chapel. Blended. Harmony.

Their faces buried in the hymnbooks, the small congregation began to sing, very softly at first. By the third verse, Henri raised his voice to sing more loudly, and they followed. He even saw them smiling at one another. He felt very close to God.

Later, as Henri preached about a woman at a well that Jesus had visited, he pointed out that this woman had no right to Jesus. She was not Jewish, His chosen race, she was from a despised minority, she was only a woman, and she was an adulteress. But Jesus offered her living water. He wondered if they would understand. He thought that maybe, with time, they would. He concluded the service and walked briskly to the back of the church, standing at the door to greet his people as they left. He thought to himself, "I wish you could be here to see it, Maxime Duchemin. You would be mighty surprised at what God has done."

* * *

David awoke and glanced quickly at the clock by the bed. Six forty-five. He turned to Gabriella, who still slept peacefully, and gently shook her awake. "Sweetheart, it's time to get up."

She stretched and yawned as she always did, looking to David like a beautiful red Persian cat. It fascinated him to watch her wake up. She rubbed her eyes, yawned, and fell against David, laughing.

"Do we have to get up yet?"

"Honey, yes," he said with a tinge of impatience in his voice. He climbed out of bed. "Classes start today, remember."

"You're nervous," Gabriella teased.

"Yes, I think I am."

"You will be wonderful. Only . . . " She pouted a bit. "Only don't charm them too much, please. Remember, you're taken now."

He grabbed her and laughed. "Am I ever!" Then, "Gabby? Could you come to the chapel with me this morning? I want the girls to meet you."

"Well, I wish you would have asked earlier. I could have gotten Sister Isabelle to take the class for me."

"Could you ask at breakfast? No, never mind. I'll ask her. She won't dare tell me no."

"David!"

He kissed her forehead. "Don't worry. She likes me more than you think!"

They dressed quietly and then, as had become their habit in the first weeks of marriage, they sat cuddled together in the den and read from the Bible. Then David, quite naturally, took Gabriella's hands and offered up a prayer for those they loved, for the orphanage, and for this day. "Dear God," he concluded. "You see how much has happened since last year at this time. When I think that . . . that only a year ago I first laid eyes on Gabby. Well, You understand the emotion." He held her tightly. "Give us Your grace for today. Amen."

* * *

Yvette Leclerc watched her three young boarders hurrying along the cobblestones to their first day of class. She tried to imagine David presiding over the morning, and smiled to herself. What a darling young couple they made. So blissfully happy. And responsible! That they were. The orphanage was functioning like a dream, she had the word straight from the Sisters.

And to think it had all started right here on this very morn one year ago. Goodness! Ah, well, such was life. Such changes!

She reached for a pen and scribbled a few purchases she needed from the *marché* for the girls' noonday meal. She'd better get ready. Monique would be waiting for their cup of coffee. She was all jitters and emotion. Yvette couldn't wait to see her friend. Yesterday Monique had received a letter from M. Roger Hoffmann! Imagine that! Maybe there was another romance blooming on the horizon. She hurried to get her basket. One could never tell. *Oh là là, non!* One could never tell.

* * *

"Of course I'll keep the children, Gabriella," Sister Isabelle told the young bride at breakfast. "Go help your dear husband. Goodness knows all those women must be quite intimidating for the poor man! Go ahead."

Sister Isabelle crossed her arms, satisfied, as Gabriella took off through the hallway. *"Allez les enfants!"* she sang out happily. "Miss Madison has asked me to take over for a little while this morning. I believe you're conjugating verbs today. Is that right?"

The older children nodded. "Who can tell me the present tense of the verb *aller?"*

The children stared back at her.

"André, give it a try."

The shy young boy stood up and smiled. *"Je vais, tu vas, il, elle, on va, nous allons, vous allez, ils, elles vont."*

"Very good, André."

Christophe's small hand shot into the air. *"Soeur Isabelle?"*

"Yes, Christophe?"

"Can I tell you a poem I learned?"

"Well . . . " Before she could argue, the children had turned her attention from verbs and began reciting the childish verses they had learned from Sister Rosaline. Well, it doesn't really matter. Not for today, thought Sister Isabelle. She laughed to herself contentedly.

* * *

It was the first day of classes for the young women enrolled in the Franco-American exchange program. David watched them enter the chapel in little groups of twos and threes, seating themselves in the pews. He stood at the front, nibbling his lip, and glanced at the professors seated on the front row. Jean-Louis nodded back at him with a smile. The history professor looked to be in fine shape for the first day of class, his cheeks lined with red, as he turned his hands over nervously in his lap. Dear Jean-Louis. With a feeling of relief, David saw Gabriella come in the chapel door and take a seat near the back.

At precisely 8:30, David stood and faced the girls. "Welcome to the Franco-American exchange program. I am David Hoffmann, the director of the program. As you have already discovered during your week of orientation, this church is where you will meet each morning for announcements, after which you will go to your classes."

He addressed them almost casually, a hint of a smile on his lips. It was all so familiar. "As you may know, this program has been going on for fifteen years now. Unfortunately, the founder and director of the program, Mother Griolet, passed away this summer. I have been asked to take her place."

He paused, reflecting, then smiled. "In matters of business concerning your classes or other practicalities, I will be most glad to help. But in matters of the heart . . . " He cleared his throat, and the young women giggled. ". . . I will be delighted to refer you to my beautiful bride of four weeks, Gabriella." He motioned for her to stand. "She has infinitely more wisdom than I, and quite a few stories of her own to tell."

She rolled her eyes at him, then stood and waved slightly.

He finished the introductions and headed to his classroom, catching Gabriella's eye as he left the chapel. She hurried to

506

needs a family. I think we are the ones he needs."

* * *

Hussein stood in the doorway of the farmhouse in Lodève and looked around with wide eyes. It seemed impossible. He was going to live with Anne-Marie and Moustafa, as their ward. Ophélie's brother. He could only shake his head. He didn't know if he could ever get used to this new land. He thought of his mother, alone in Algeria with all her questions. If only he could know she was safe. If only he could bring her to France.

But that was not possible right now. Moustafa had promised that Hussein could write his mother later, when things were calmer in Algeria. Perhaps someday, he would be with her again. For now, he was taking a very big step. It scared him to death.

Why would Anne-Marie and Moustafa want him? He was so different from them. And they were already very different from one another. He thought about it for a long, long time. What was it that broke through walls of hatred and prejudice? Maybe it was the love that pastor, M. Krugler, talked about in his meetings with the young people. Maybe Hussein would be able to fit in there. He didn't know. They were *harki* kids, and he was just plain Arab. The enemy.

He wondered again if he were making a big mistake. What would he become, tied to these people? There were no bloodlines. The hatred that had brewed and exploded in Algeria was not swept away with the end of the war. What could he do?

Start over. Trust.

"Come on in, Hussein," Ophélie encouraged him. He stepped through the doorway and let Anne-Marie and Moustafa take him in their arms. It felt good.

That night he lounged in the den with his new family, watching the embers of the fire change from blue to orange to red. The old trunk with its black casing sat in front of the couch. It intrigued him more than ever. He could not look at it without thinking of it first as a prison and then as a way of escape. Freedom, confining freedom. Maybe that was how life was supposed to be.

*   *   *

When mid-October came to Castelnau, the first pansies went on sale. Gabriella bought three trays from the florist in the village. She planted some in the courtyard, one tray by the dormitory, and another by the dining room. Then on a windy afternoon, with the Mistral beginning to blow and the leaves on the vines a bright red, she walked alone through the town of Castelnau, past the fountain in the square and the olive tree outside Mme Leclerc's apartment.

She came to the old cemetery where Mother Griolet was buried. It was filled with thick, massive tombstones that stood high and wide, engraved with names and dates. Occasionally a photo of a loved one had been placed on the tomb. A little further out, she knelt by the grave of Mother Griolet. In sharp contrast to the larger tombstones, her simple tombstone read, "For to me, to live is Christ and to die is gain." Gabriella removed a small trowel from her pocket and dug in the soft earth. She planted a row of bright yellow pansies in front of the tombstone.

Satisfied, she stood, brushed the dirt from her dress, and watched the flowers bob their heads. She peered at them closely. She thought indeed that she saw a face in each flower. The faces of those she loved: her family, Ophélie and Anne-Marie and Moustafa, the two Sisters, Jean-Louis, Mme Leclerc and Mme Pons, the children. And David. And then the twinkling eyes of Mother Griolet came into her mind. "Now unto Him that is able to do exceeding abundantly above all that we ask or think . . . ." She could almost hear the old nun's voice, floating out to her, full of hope and faith, carried in the wind.

Historical Note

In France, the integration of *pied-noirs* into French society has been slow and painful, and many to this day do not feel welcome, harboring bitter memories of all they left in Algeria in 1962. Most of these families have never returned to Algeria, even for a visit. Among those who have, some have found in their homes, now inhabited by Algerians, the exact same furniture and other household goods that they had left in their flight to France.

The *harkis,* with their children and grandchildren, remain an enigma and embarrassment for France. Many years after the war when the truth came out about the mass murders of the *harkis* who were abandoned in Algeria, France felt great sorrow and great shame. Many *harkis* living in France still feel like outcasts, neither comfortable with the millions of Algerians in France nor with the French, although the children and grandchildren are French citizens.

With the end of the Algerian War for Independence in July, 1962, different factions within Algeria struggled to gain control of the new republic. Finally, it was Ben Bella who triumphed and began a revolutionary socialist government. Three years later, Houari Boumediène took over as chief of state through a *coup d'état*. For fifteen years Algeria prospered under his leadership, as profits from its natural resource of oil allowed Boumediène to move the country forward in agriculture and industrialization, becoming an example for the whole Third World. However, Boumediène enforced a single party, military-backed socialist government, with which many were dissatisfied. This ended in 1988 when a new constitution was voted in by referendum, separating the socialist party from the state and allowing a multiparty system to emerge.

It was in this context that a political movement of fundamentalist Islam swept across the nation. In 1984, a law was passed which severely restricted women's rights. Mosques in every village and hamlet became the forum from which the ideology of fanatical Islam was spread to an unwary populace. The government was trapped within the religious and cultural aspects of Algeria which undermined its economic progress.

In 1992, civil war broke out in Algeria. An extremist militant Muslim faction (FIS) was on the brink of winning national elections when the vote was canceled and the military installed a president. In the past five years, over 50,000 people have lost their lives in Algeria, many civilians murdered by the FIS who wishes to make Algeria an Islamic state. Missionaries have left the country, and Algerian Christians have been forced into hiding, worshiping in secret, often traveling long distances to find other believers.

How these events affected the lives of the Hoffmanns, the Dramchinis, the Madisons, the Duchemins, the Cebrians, and many other characters is another story that is waiting to be told. . . .